# *THE HOSHIYAN CHRONICLES*

## Book I

# SEEKING

## THE

# LIGHT OF JUSTICE

### BY

### BARRY NADEL

Published by Agrosearch

ISBN 13:9781505314427

**Dedication**:

I dedicate this book to the loving memory of

my late wife,

Hadassah Nadel (1962-2004).

She taught me the true meaning of a deep mutual spiritual love.

Rabbi Shimon said,

"There are three crowns: the crown of Torah

The crown of the priesthood and the crown of kingship.

And the crown of a good name is surpasses them all."

Perkie Avot 4:17

Request of the Author

This book has many references from holy sources. Please do not read it in the restroom.

.

# Contents

# PROLOGUE

Ilo Sungila felt he could see vast expanses of war-torn Mozambique from the hilltop of his new agricultural supply store. The store beamed light into his rural Bantu village, which had been stagnant and depressed for the past forty years.

"It will not be easy, but farmers' yields will be better and life in the entire village will improve," said Olumide."

The Sungilas worked hard. The shop, which doubled as their home, became the focal point of the village. Villagers sat on Ilo's stoop in the late afternoon, drinking and telling stories.

Only Huso, the mason, worried Ilo from all the village members. Huso had been out of work a long time, drank too much, and often spoke enviously regarding Ilo and Olumide's success. One night, Ilo heard glass breaking in the store. His uncle got up first and went to investigate. As Ilo rose, he heard sounds of a struggle, and then something falling to the floor. When Ilo entered the store, he found Huso, drunk, armed with a club, clutching the small cigar box filled with their money. Ilo's anger took over him, and he ran at Huso, who struck him three times. Ilo heard his bone crack. He watched powerless as Huso pocketed the money and fled.

Cautiously, Ilo attempted to probe the damage to his arm. The slightest touch sparked a burst of pain that made him woozy. Holding his injured arm still, Ilo rolled onto his knees, stood up shakily, and limped to the rusty tap in the backyard. He tried to lift a bucket with both hands and winced in pain. He turned on the tap and filled the bucket, using one arm. The world spun around him as he lugged the bucket to the house.

With no doctor within thirty kilometers, Ilo had no choice but to treat his uncle's injuries. With his good hand, he washed the blood from his uncle's face and shoulder.

"Wake up, Uncle! We worked so hard to bring agricultural technology to our village. At last, we're seeing results; don't let everything fall to pieces." Olumide didn't move or make a sound. Finding a gash on Olumide's head, Ilo wrapped it with a piece of cloth torn from his sleeve.

"Please, venerable ancestors, save my Uncle Olumide, the son of Folami, the son of Chinedu, the son of Dumisa," Ilo prayed. He paused, feeling confused and foolish, and tried again.

"Most honored ancestors, whoever is the true God, ask him to save uncle's life!" Ilo listened for an answer. The crickets chirped, the night birds chattered, and the jackals growled. Ilo shivered, bore his pain, and remained next to his uncle throughout the night, dozing off here and there.

At dawn, his uncle moaned. As the rising sun appeared through the slats in the window, Olumide's eyes flickered. Ilo brought him a cup of water. Uncle smiled, sipped the water, and patted on the mat for Ilo to sit. "There are stories I must tell you. They are a treasure, a tradition, passed from father to son that will end with me," Olumide related. He glanced at his nephew. "But you are like a son to me."

"What is this treasure?"

"Stories," said Olumide, "of a great king who ruled with justice, righteousness, and faith. People called him the Light of Justice. Any person, great or small, could speak his mind to the king."

By now, opening time had passed, and people crowded around outside the store, banging on the door, rattling the shutters, and shouting.

"Open up!"

Ilo limped to the window and raised the shutter three centimeters.

"My friends, Olumide is ailing. I promise to open the store as soon as possible!" he whispered He let the shutter drop.

Ilo listened as Olumide taught him the art of storytelling: how to touch people's hearts, the dissimilarity between true and false humility, how to address a crowd with one utterance and yet give each man the words he needed. Ilo learned to control his face, body, and tone of voice.

After five days, Olumide succumbed to the beating. Ilo embraced his uncle's words and began his career as a storyteller. For the next twenty years, he ran his shop and told stories about the Light of Justice.

People came from near and far; walking up to twenty kilometers across the parched savanna to listen to the superb storyteller, Ilo Sungila. People arrived alone, others in groups—by foot, bicycle, bus, and car. Throughout the day, people gathered from surrounding villages and towns to learn about the fabled king, the Light of Justice.

One particular night, Ilo gazed at the gathering of child-soldiers, looters, rapists, and murderers, their way of life cultivated by false leaders.

"As a young man," Ilo began, hushing the crowd, "the king served as a junior judge in court. Two men claimed the same girl as a bride. The first man presented a document signed by the girl's father, and the second showed one signed by the mother. Reputable witnesses made their marks on both documents. Each parent promised money to the groom."

Ilo stroked his beard, playing a judge deep in thought. He slid to one side of his chair and acted the part of the haughty father. He slid to the other side and played the mischievous mother.

"The king and his fellow judges questioned each groom's motivation to marry. Both men cited good looks, money, and social standing. The judges examined the grooms' and parents' intentions. The senior judge called for a recess in another hut. 'If we consider only legal documents,' he said, 'the father's words have more legal weight."

"Let us question the intended bride," the young king pronounced. The judges questioned the girl, and then the king made a pronouncement.

"On the surface, what do we have here: two parents who seek a husband for their daughter," the king summarized.

Ilo paused as the people moved closer to catch every word.

"But to let either of these men marry this girl is a travesty of justice." The plaintiffs burst out shouting, and the senior judge hammered for silence.

"Parents spoke separately to two men and made two separate contracts on the same night! They intended to sow discord. In fact, they didn't consider their daughter's desires! I wouldn't want either of these men as sons or brothers-in-law. Why, you ask? They want a wife for the wrong intentions! It's evident the young woman is well-intentioned and respectable. These two don't want her virtues; rather, they want cattle and social esteem. My opinion is the parents wrote both engagement documents in bad faith toward the bride and are void!" the Light of Justice declared. Everyone in the audience remained seated; each person deep in thought, absorbing Ilo's words.

Wherever people strive to live a more moral and just life, you find stories of the Light of Justice. The Mayans, Chinese, Incas, Malaysians, and Fijians tell stories of ships lost at sea in terrible storms that reach the land of the legendary Light of Justice. In the far North, the saga is told of Andvett the Terrible. Shipwrecked with his crew after a storm, the murderous company encountered the king, and returned home as changed men.

*****

Father Leonardo Franconi was researching a book on the history of the Church during the fifteenth century. In the Vatican's archives, Father Franconi came across to seven unusual references. They referred to accounts of troubadours who sang of a mysterious king called the Light of Justice. Intrigued, Father Franconi sought the identity of this fabled king. He searched the library for the originals, but found none.

After consulting with the librarian, Father Franconi found out why the originals weren't available.

Pope Alexander sealed the originals in an underground vault beneath the Vatican. Inside the vault laid dangerous secrets of the Catholic Church. Among those secrets were many references to the Light of Justice and lengths the church went to bury those stories.

In cities across the world, secret communities wait for a sign, a secret name, and a day to come, to fulfill a long awaited prophecy.

\*\*\*\*\*

For twenty-five years, Yoshua Rosenberg, Hebrew University Professor of Archaeology, stalked the legendary Light of Justice from the lowlands of East Africa to Scandinavian Vikings to Mayan adventurers. He struggled to explain how this king's fame transverse so many far-flung ancient cultures. People who met this king lived hundreds of years and thousands of kilometers apart, as if he existed in spherical rather than linear time.

Yoshua's search continued until his work centered on these legends.

# ENCOUNTER IN ITALY

Fabio Mancini stood behind the counter of his news kiosk on a cloudless, hot September day in the town of Benevento, east of Naples. Fabio wiped his brow and sipped ice water as he scanned the plaza, stunned to see someone walking around in the midday heat. The man, dressed in hiking boots and multi-pocketed khaki pants, was obviously a foreigner. Fabio watched him wander into the dusty town square. He noticed the stranger carried a standard synthetic, faded blue backpack used by schoolchildren. A washed-out olive drab floppy cap crowned the stranger's head. His face was symmetrical, with the wide cheekbones and blue eyes typical of eastern Europeans. Fabio noted he walked confidently, his eyes darting from side to side, aware of his surroundings. The stranger approached the kiosk and Fabio, in broken English, said, "Hello, I no speak Anglese."

"*Espanola?*" The stranger asked.

"*Capisco Spagnolo come è simile an Italiano,*" (I understand Spanish because of it is similarity to Italian) Fabio replied.

"Good afternoon. Please direct me to the synagogue of the Jews," the stranger replied in fluent Spanish with a slight Andalusian accent.

Fabio looked at the stranger. How could he know of the old synagogue that stood vacant for centuries?

"The building you're looking for is on the northeast end of town, an eight-minute walk from here." Fabio pointed to a cobblestone street that entered the square from the west.

"Follow this winding road until it ends at a T-junction. Turn left and then take the first right about one hundred meters up the road. The synagogue is another two hundred meters. You'll see a parking lot and an art gallery nearby." Fabio couldn't control his curiosity. "Why are you interested in an old disused synagogue?"

"I'm an archaeologist. The building may hold important information for my research."

"Ah, I see."

"Thank you for your help. Have a pleasant day," the stranger said and turned to leave.

Curious, Fabio thought; *this stranger spoke almost like a native Spaniard.*

"Excuse me, where are you from?"

"From Israel, the Holy Land," the man said, smiling.

Fabio never met an Israeli or a Jew. What he thought a Jew was, looked nothing like the man who stood before him. He watched the Israeli disappear down the street.

\*\*\*\*\*

Yoshua found his Italian colleague, the provincial archaeologist Angelo De Luca, waiting for him outside the entrance to the synagogue's courtyard. After greeting each other, De Luca led Yoshua through a corridor to a second courtyard. There was a small, well-kept garden with a fountain that trickled water into an oval fishpond. A lemon tree stood next to the pond. Its flowers gave off a pleasant citrus scent. The ancient synagogue occupied the northeast corner.

"As I mentioned in my email," Yoshua said, removing a letter from his jacket pocket, "a colleague of mine found this letter, mentioning a certain Joseph Lopez, connected to the Light of Justice."

De Luca read the letter and smiled. Yoshua, feeling encouraged, returned the smile.

"Today," the Italian told him, "the synagogue is an official museum. It's only open to academics, and one needs an appointment to visit. The property belongs to state, but county funds maintain it as a museum. There aren't enough funds to support it. Most of the books in the small library are disintegrating. To prevent further damage, the museum is closed."

"I'm sorry to hear that such an old library isn't being preserved," Yoshua said.

"However," the Italian said, "A donation could alleviate the scenario."

Instinctively, Yoshua's hand reached to his back, but his 9 mm wasn't there. *He was in Italy for academic reasons, not counter-terrorism. Yoshua pieced the scenario together. This was southern Italy, where the Mafia wielded more power than the government. De Luca had lured him from Israel to Italy, so he would have no choice but to pay. Confident that I won't want to fly home empty-handed, De Luca was sure I would pay him a bribe.* Yoshua knew there was etiquette to this procedure, but he wasn't in the mood. He had five hundred euros in his wallet, his entire budget for the trip. Now his only choice was to dip into his emergency fund. He pulled out his wallet and opened it in front of De Luca.

"Yoshua, where are your manners?"

Yoshua laughed.

"Angelo, be a man! You're robbing me and want me to be polite also?" Yoshua felt stressed. His stomach cramped, and his hands trembled. He knew he had to act swiftly to relieve the familiar symptoms caused by this Italian. Yoshua removed a pen from his shirt pocket and hefted it for a second.

"Do you see this pen," Yoshua said.

"What are you doing with your pen?" Deluca asked.

With every once his strength, Yoshua threw the pen at the lemon tree in the garden. It hit the tree; penetrating about three centimeters.

DeLuca's pupils dilated and droplets of sweat burst from his forehead. Yoshua's cramps subsided, and the shaking stopped.

"Angelo," Yoshua whispered, making DeLuca strain to hear him, "next time you shake someone down, do a little research first. You would've found out I'm a very dangerous man." Yoshua removed two hundred euros from his wallet, stuffed them into DeLuca's pocket and took the key from his unsteady hand.

"I'll call you when I'm finished here and you can come and get the key."

DeLuca left, shaken up, but two hundred euros richer.

Yoshua opened the door, and the smell of mildew accosted his nostrils. He flipped open his cell phone and called his wife, Ruthie.

"Honey, it's me." He listened as she updated him about their four children and her work.

After three days of sifting through the little library, Yoshua called his wife.

"Any luck?" Ruth asked.

"I spent two days sifting through the decaying little library, but found nothing about Joseph Lopez. Yesterday, I hit pay dirt. I found the booklet written by Lopez. It contained four stories of the Light of Justice."

"Anything new?" Ruth asked.

"Sorry babe, they are stories we have found elsewhere. However, this book predates the other books we have found so far. That makes it much closer to the source," Yoshua said.

"I found a wooden box found a wooden box containing disintegrated books. The only parts that still maintained a shape are the bindings."

"Are you going to ask DeLuca for the material? Maybe the bindings concealed pages from unknown books," Ruth suggested.

"My exact sentiments."

When DeLuca returned for the key, Yoshua asked, "Angelo, what are these in the box?"

"I keep forgetting to throw them out. The pages are so faded that no one can read them."

"May I have them?"

"Sure, but why?"

"Sentimental value," Yoshua lied. He didn't want to remind De Luca of the importance of old bindings. They used to make book bindings from older books. They discovered several previously unknown books by dismantling the bindings of old books.

"Take them. It'll save me the problem of disposal."

# IN THE LAB

Tzion Vardi, Yoshua's lab assistant, dropped off his youngest daughter at the day care center. He drove to the Israel Archaeological Institute on Mount Scopus in Jerusalem, arriving at 7:40 am every day. A gregarious man, he greeted everyone he met on the way to his lab.

Tzion entered the empty building. He swept the hall and the lab for security risks. These included booby traps and surveillance equipment. Tzion's actual job was security, but he didn't work for the university. His orders, to protect Yoshua, came straight from the leaders of the Hoshiyan community. As a well-known officer in the Israeli army's elite anti-terrorist unit, Hezbollah had a bounty on Yoshua's head for the past fifteen years.

Unknown to Yoshua, his ancestors and Tzion's had known each other for over ten generations. They served together in the Aluzian Royal Guards, but Yoshua was unaware of his heritage. His lack of knowledge allowed him freedom of choice. Only by accepting the existence of Hoshiya, its people and culture would he fulfill the prophecy of Elisha Arieli. Yoshua was the eldest son of the previous crown prince of Aluz. This made him the only one who could fulfill the hope, the prophecy, and the dream to integrate the Hoshiyans with the rest of humanity.

Tzion glanced through the window behind Yoshua's desk. He said a silent prayer as he peeked at the shrubs he planted outside Yoshua's window. Last week, he had secretly buried two terrorists and their bomb there. With nothing pressing to do, he sat at Yoshua's computer and entered data from a joint study with the Literature

Department. They were searching for common elements in various versions of stories about the Light of Justice.

Yoshua entered his lab and headed to his office. When he saw Tzion, he called out.

"Tzion, *Baruch nimtza* (bless those present)."

"*Baruch ha'ba*, boss (bless those who come)!" Tzion looked up, startled.

"I brought you a present from Benevento," Yoshua said, opening the package he was carrying and removing the bubble wrap. He handed over the crumbling bindings.

"One second, I'll need gloves for this." Like a surgeon, Tzion snapped on latex gloves.

"I'll setup the equipment to dissolve the glue holding the bindings together. Tzion laid the three bindings into separate ten liter rectangular plastic tank. He added a chemical reagent to dissolve the glue a little at a time. The solvent had a low boiling point and evaporated at low temperatures. So Tzion conducted the procedure in a chemical fume hood that pulled the fumes through an activated charcoal filter. He graciously endured the tedious work.

The first binding came apart with ease after three hours.

"Hey, boss, you want to come here. There is a document written in Hebrew," Tzion said.

Together, they scanned the document. "This will be a small find for a historian, it's the account record of a Jewish a lumber merchant in fourteenth century Italy. Tzion contact Prof. Yigal Goldstein in the history department."

"What's in the second binding?" Yoshua asked.

"These are also old, as they are handwritten and not printed," Tzion observed.

Yoshua, with his total recalled at once identified the source of the first page.

"This is from *Megillat Esther* (book of Esther) the third chapter."

"Boss, I'll call the Rare Book Collection at the National Library and have them pick these up. Are there any discrepancies between this version and what we are familiar with today?" Tzion asked.

Yoshua read through the three sheets in the time it took him to glance at each sheet.

"Of what is legible, it is identical to the accepted version of *Megillat Esther* that we use today," Yoshua commented.

"Maybe the third binding will yield something more interesting," Tzion said.

"That would be nice," Yoshua agreed. The process was slow, but soon Tzion could already tell that the binding comprised eight separate sheets of parchment.

"The binding has been soaking for several hours. Why don't we try to separate them, boss?

"Good idea, Tzion."

Yoshua and Tzion tried to separate the eight sheets. The backside of the top sheet came apart.

"Look boss, even though the parchment is in terrible shape and faded, it's the first page of the book of Yechezkel."

"Whoever glued these next two, must have spilled glue over them. They are resisting our efforts to separate them. Tzion put those two back in the solvent tank," Yoshua suggested.

"Boss, it's almost four o'clock. I have to pick up my kids," Tzion said. Since Tzion's wife had died, there were no more extra hours in the lab.

"Those other four sheets are coming apart easily. We'll leave it for tomorrow. You go and I'll clean up," Yoshua said.

The next morning, Tzion arrived early and rushed to the solvent tank. The sheets have only partially come apart. Tzion selected a wide Teflon-coated tongs and a pair of forceps, removed the sheets, and laid them on a large pane of clean glass. Little by little, with great patience, he teased the two sheets apart.

"Good morning Tzion, have the pages come apart?" Yoshua asked.

"Boss, grab two more forceps with sponge tips to prevent damage to the parchment and give me a hand."

"I'll anchor the sheets while you slip that long thin spatula between the sheets," Yoshua told his assistant. Neither man spoke. The sheets resisted Tzion's gentle attempts.

"There is too much resistance still. We'll tear the parchment if we continue," Tzion said. Yoshua lifted the sheets and placed them back in the solvent. "Let's give them another twenty minutes," he suggested, and retreated to his office.

Tzion leaned over the other five pages of the book of Yechezkel and spent the next twenty minutes comparing them word for word with the modern printing of Tanach (the Bible).

"Tzion, how's the comparison going?"

"So far it's one hundred percent compatibility, boss."

"Are you available? I want to separate the last two sheets before my 10:00 am lecture."

"Another ten minutes. Can you take them out of the solvent meanwhile?"

When the two men returned to the vat, they eased the glued sheets onto the slab of glass, and with the slightest pressure, Yoshua coaxed the sheets of parchment apart.

"My God, what have we found," Tzion blurted out. The two men were unprepared for what it exposed. They stared at a hand-paint parchment in bright red, grass green, cobalt blue, and gold leaf. The excess glue makes most of the designs and letters blurred. The intricate geometric design had an almost three-dimensional feeling, like a hologram.

The two men couldn't take their eyes off the magnificently illustrated document.

"Tzion, do you know if Sasha is around this morning?"

Tzion checked his watch.

"His last lecture finished ten minutes ago."

Three minutes later, Alexander (Sasha) Chrominsky sauntered into the lab, grinning like a Cheshire cat. The handsome Russian grinned and waved.

"Hey boss, Tzion; how you doing today?"

Tzion winked at Sasha.

"Good morning, Sasha. We found an interesting document inside the binding I brought back from Italy," Yoshua said.

When Sasha saw the document, he asked his professor.

"Do you want me to take a few photos even though it's still blurry?"

"Yes, let's transfer this beauty to a separate container," Yoshua said. With trembling hands, he and Tzion moved the illustrated sheet to a clean glass dish.

During this time, Sasha photographed the two men working.

Yoshua's hands shook as he fumbled with his cell phone. He called Dr. Aviva Berger, his wife's best friend and an expert at art restoration.

"Aviva, drop what you are doing and come to the lab. We have found something unique." Yoshua then called his wife.

"Ruthie, come to the lab. See what we found in a binding of Maimonides Mishne Torah," Yoshua told her, with his excitement coming through his tone of voice.

"I'm busy, babe, but I'll come as soon as I can."

"I called Aviva and asked her to meet us at the lab for a consultation."

"Why?"

"Drop what you're doing and get over here."

\*\*\*\*\*

Dr. Ruth Rosenberg and Dr. Aviva Berger walked into the lab, chatting. No one greeted them. Whatever the men stared at, it had them glued to the document in the glass dish in front of them. Even Sasha didn't stop taking photos to say a quick hello. Not until Ruth and Aviva were right behind the men did they respond by moving to the side. This allowed the two women to get a good look at what was in the dish. Tzion watched the women's faces as the shock of the discovery sank into their brains. The first time he saw the document, it had shocked him to his core. He was sure Ruth understood its significance to an even greater extent. Tzion prayed in silence.

*"Holy One, thank you for allowing me to reach this point in time. For the first time in history, we have the opportunity to fulfill the prophecy."*

"Babe," Yoshua said, "what do you think?"

"I've seen nothing like it," Ruth responded, not able to control the shock on her face.

Aviva shooed the men aside and took command.

"I have a better solvent for removing the remaining glue so the print will become readable." She couldn't take her eyes off the parchment as she poked around for her cell phone and called the Israel Museum.

"Boss, there's an unusual development at the university. Can you cover for me until I get there?"

Aviva enlisted Yoshua's and Tzion's help in treating and identifying the illustrated parchment. She scraped small samples of parchment and ink into sterile vials. She sent them to the organic chemistry lab for gas chromatograph and mass spectrometer analysis. At 10:00 am Yoshua left, already late for his lecture.

Ruth called Professor Emeritus Gavriel Yaroni, Yoshua's mentor in the Archaeology Department, but he was out of his office. "Professor Yaroni, please call me when you hear this message. You must call me. The matter is imperative." Next, she called the campus security chief.

"Dr. Ruth Rosenberg speaking. We have found a precious illustration hidden in a binding of a book. Do you have a mobile strong box with temperature control?"

"The national library has one," came the replied.

"Please rush the mobile strongbox over to my lab in the Archaeology Institute," Ruth requested.

"How valuable, Dr. Rosenberg?" the chief of campus security asked.

"The document is one of a kind over five hundred years old."

"I'll send a team to pick up the unit from the library and bring it to you at once."

"Thank you for your cooperation."

Sasha left and returned with two more cameras. In fifteen minutes, he snapped over one hundred photos. He sifted through the photos on his laptop, selecting which to print.

At 3:30 pm, Gavriel arrived at the lab. "

"Professor, you have seen" Yoshua said as he grabbed him by the sleeve and led him to the bench.

"Hello Dr. Berger, what are you doing?" Prof. Yaroni asked.

"Nice to see you, professor. Tzion and I are treating the parchment with an ink fixative to prevent any further fading," Aviva replied.

Aviva and Tzion stepped away to allow Gavriel an unobstructed view of the document. As they observed the parchment, the solvent continued to dissolve the glue, revealing, in large bold print, the words *The Hoshiyan Chronicles.*

"What are the *Hoshiyan Chronicles*?" Yoshua asked.

Gavriel's reaction caught Tzion unprepared. The elderly professor's eyes opened wide and his jaw dropped. He raised his right hand to his heart, turned red, and swayed. Tzion grabbed one arm and Ruth the other and helped him to a chair. He whispered to Ruth, "My God, General Dori's book exists."

Yoshua hurried to his mentor's side.

"Professor, are you all right?"

"I'm fine." Gavriel shook his head, as if to clear his thoughts.

"A little wobbly from rushing over here." Gavriel shot a look into Tzion's eyes. Tzion, standing behind his boss, smiled a tight, brief smile. Yoshua walked back to reexamine the document. Gavriel leaned closer to Tzion and Ruth.

"No one in the world can lend credibility to this project but Yoshua. No one else can fulfill our destiny." Gavriel whispered. Tzion and Ruth nodded.

"The two of you need to be strong. No matter what, you can't let on that you know anything." They nodded again.

Aviva decanted the solution Tzion had used and replaced it with her solvent of citrus oil and propane. She then placed the document in the security box for the night.

Tzion and Ruth left the lab to go pick up their children. Once outside, Tzion felt free to unleash his frustration on his second boss.

"I wanted to scream at your husband, 'What are the *Hoshiyan Chronicles*? They're your heritage!' but the code of silence forced me to keep quiet."

"I understand how maddening this maintaining of silence around Yoshua is to everyone. Tzion, but no matter how much we want Yoshua to accept Hoshiya, we can't intercede even with incontestable proof. According to the prophecy, a prince of Aluz (the tribe of Asher), raised without knowledge of his people or inheritance—Yoshua in this case—must accept the existence of Hoshiya by his own free choice, without outside influence."

"Ruth, everyone understands you're in a difficult position that you must keep silent no matter what. Everyone is behind you." Tzion paused.

"When I saw the words '*Hoshiyan Chronicles*' on the cover page, I thought my head will explode!"

"You're not the only one; Professor Yaroni almost had a heart attack."

# GEFEN NIMRODI

Later in the afternoon, Aviva walked home, changed clothes, and took off for a run in central Jerusalem. When she got to *Kikar* Paris, she turned right onto *Keren Hayesod* Street. She jogged to the traffic light at the northern end of Liberty Bell Park, where she crossed the street to *Mishkanot Sha'ananim* and jogged into the park. The route took her to Bloomfield Garden and the *Yemin Moshe* neighborhood.

At a small observation point overlooking Jerusalem's Old City stood a teenager, her long brunette hair pulled back from her face. She stood opposite an easel with paintbrushes in her right hand and a palette in her left. Aviva slowed to a walk and glanced at the canvas. She had seen such paintings before, a beam of light radiating from the Temple Mount. She looked closer and saw that the light comprised a long series of numbers and Hebrew letters. Aviva squinted at the written words: "*Or chadash al Tzion ta'ir*" (a new light will shine from Tzion). She watched as the girl studied the sky and intermittently dabbed her sketch with white paint, trying to capture the wispy clouds from the sky to the canvas. Her hand worked little by little, using a brush with only a few fine camel hairs. Aviva steadied herself on a nearby utility pole, did several stretches, and tilted her head up toward the sky, following the girl's line of sight. Soon there wouldn't be enough daylight.

Satisfied with the clouds, the girl sketched the Old City walls. She now reached for her paintbrush. Aviva watched as she tried four different combinations of white and brown.

"Honey, you won't get the color you want that way. White and brown aren't enough; Jerusalem stone has a reddish tinge. Add a little red." The girl looked at Aviva, probing her face.

"Try it on your palette." Aviva saw her hesitation and laughed.

"Try it!"

The girl picked up a tube of red paint and added a small dab to her glob of white and brown. She laid down the red tube, took a spatula, and mixed the three colors.

"Wow! Thanks," she said. With a sure hand, the walls came alive on her canvas.

Aviva walked up to the girl.

"What are these numbers?" she asked.

"I encrypted a story."

"Which story?" Aviva noticed a paperback on the ground at the foot of the easel, Yoshua's latest book of legends surrounding the Light of Justice.

"That's the mystery. Decipher the code and figure out the mystery."

"How is anyone supposed to know what's written here?" Aviva studied the canvas.

"I have a program."

"That's a unique approach to art: combining math and painting," Aviva said and reached out her hand. "I'm Aviva Berger."

"Gefen Nimrodi."

"It's very nice to meet you, Gefen Nimrodi!" After a few moments of silence, Aviva asked,

"Do you live around here?"

"A few blocks away in Talbiya."

"It's on my way home would you like a hand with your things?"

"No thanks," Gefen said, gathering her paints and brushes. "I'm used to walking home from here. It's not far."

"If you ever have a problem with colors or textures, come to the Archaeological Institute lab at Hebrew U on Mt. Scopus. I am working there at the moment," Aviva called after the girl.

Gefen, balancing her art equipment bags on her shoulders, nodded and continued walking toward Talbiya.

# THE ARIELIS

Gavriel left the university at 6:30 pm. Instead of driving home, he detoured to Dr. Arieli Arieli's clinic. He walked straight through the waiting room to a private entrance and pressed the buzzer. A familiar voice answered.

"Yes."

"It's Gavriel." He heard a clack as the door unlocked, and he entered.

*Rebbetzin* Rivka looked up from her work in the kitchen and greeted him. Gavriel saluted her in the Hoshiyan manner. He extended his right hand from his heart, palm open, facing upward toward the *Rebbetzin* he knew for over sixty-five years. "I see you, beloved, humble matriarch of the House of Arieli. May you come and go in peace."

The *Rebbetzin* nodded toward her husband's office. Gavriel hoped the soothing atmosphere of his friend's book-lined office would help him contain his excitement. He settled into the familiar chair in the nook where he and Dr. Arieli spent many hours studying together. With reverence, Gavriel opened a volume of the Hoshiyan prophet's commentaries on *Pirkei Avot* (*Ethics of the Fathers*) and learned aloud.

"Rabbi Shimon said, 'there are three crowns: the crown of Torah, the crown of priesthood—'"

Dr. Arieli entered the study; Gavriel stood up, losing his place in the book. Dr. Arieli picked up the book, motioned for Gavriel to sit, and found the page.

"Finish," he said.

"—and the crown of royalty." Gavriel marveled at Dr. Arieli's arrival before he read the words referring to the crown that Dr. Arieli still refused.

Dr. Arieli frowned. "Gavriel, you haven't finished the *mishne* (passage). There's something greater than these three crowns."

"But the crown of a good name excels them all," Gavriel read.

"There are things more important than the crown of royalty. That's the lesson of the king. The man is more important than the title. Gavriel, do you remember the story regarding the king during the early days when Bet Yani became the capital of Free Hoshiya? The king faced a dilemma: on one side, he worried about the honor of the crown, and on the other side, about honoring one's elders. Avshalom Chorev, the king's fiancée's grandfather, was a refugee like everyone else, lacking even a blanket. The king gave his blanket to the old man, saying, 'I would rather the world know me as a pauper than a man who refused to help an elderly man stay warm.' You see Gavriel, like the *mishne* says, 'The crown of a good name is greater than the crown of royalty.' Now let's get to business. You're here concerning Yoshua. Don't look so shocked, Tzion called me."

"Yoshua brought book bindings from southern Italy and exposed every page in his lab. One of those pages was the cover page of Aluf Aharon Dori's book, *The Hoshiyan Chronicles*. Yoshua found a clue to the existence of Hoshiya." Gavriel paused.

"For the first time in hundreds of years, there's a possibility for someone to fulfill the prophecy." Dr. Arieli closed his eyes and his lips moved in silent prayer.

Gavriel's eyes filled with tears. So many years had passed that he had doubted the prophet's words. Now, everything changed in the blink of an eye.

# DISCOVERY

The next morning, when Yoshua and Ruth arrived at the lab at 8:15, the place already buzzed with activity. Aviva had removed the document from the controlled environment security box. Like a parent checking on his child after putting him to bed, Yoshua wanted to take another look at the document. He smiled to himself. Even though he had doubts about the facts written on the cover page, they did, for the first time, provide a significant lead in solving the mystery of the Light of Justice.

Sasha sauntered in a short while later, smiling. "Where were you, Sasha?" Yoshua asked.

"I attended a seminar on creative photography."

"Why're you smiling like the cat that ate the canary?"

"Boss, I have a hot date tonight."

Yoshua turned to Tzion.

"How come you're not dating?"

Tzion laughed.

"The difference between me and Sasha is that he's looking for a good time while I'm looking for a soul mate. Besides, you know I found her and lost her.

"Yocheved?" Yoshua asked.

"Yes."

"I'm likewise looking for a soul mate, but she's impossible to find."

"Sasha, pubs aren't the places to find a soul mate. The easiest way is to find a reputable website and search for someone that has similar interests to yours," Aviva said.

She helped Tzion transfer the cover page from the glass dish to a slab of clean glass, which sat on top of a piece of black velvet.

"Are you going to get that camera?" Tzion and Sasha hurried to set up the camera for another full set of photos. Yoshua admired the way Sasha worked the camera. He had several of Sasha's black and white prints hanging in his office.

The lab phone rang, and Yoshua picked up the receiver.

"Aviva, it's the chemistry lab. They uploaded the results of the analysis of the parchment and ink into your account." Aviva stopped cleaning the parchment, jogged into Ruth's office, logged into her analysis account, and read:

"The ink's composition matched samples on file from the late fifteenth century and early sixteenth century Iberian Peninsula. The parchment matched other samples from the mid-fifteenth to early sixteenth century period. Test results verify the samples are authentic for that period."

Yoshua sat on his lab stool and enjoyed watching his team work together. They meshed like a fine Swiss watch. Sasha mounted the camera on a tripod and attached it to the computer monitor. He took a set of photos, uploaded them, opened the image processing software, and examined them.

Yoshua joined Aviva and Sasha in front of the computer monitor.

"Look at each corner. There are identical elaborate small two by three centimeter seven-branched menorah in gold leaf," Aviva pointed out.

"Look at the bottom right-hand corner. There are three rows of tiny black block letters in a dark blackish ink," Yoshua commented.

Sasha shifted the camera and increased the zoom with the joystick. The script zoomed into focus, and it was Hebrew. Aviva read,

"Nachemia Toledano, *Sofer Stam.* Written in the seventh year of His Majesty the Emir Abu Abdullah Muhammad XII of Granada."

Shifting the camera's position, Yoshua scanned the rest of the page. He drifted, savoring the artist's choice of color, harmony, and three-dimensional effect. In the middle of the page, in gold leaf surrounded by geometric figures in blue, were the words:

The *Hoshiyan Chronicles: History of My People* by Aharon ben Ephraim ben Eliezer Dori, Commander of the Guards Division

Including the Stories of Aharon Dori as Told by Shmuel ibn Musa ibn Aharon

Dedicated to the KING: The Light of Justice, of Blessed Memory,

Yoshua fell off his stool, knocking over an Erlenmeyer flask with his flailing arm. It exploded, shooting shards in every direction.

"Shuki, are you okay? What made you fall?" Ruth asked, rushing over to help her husband.

"I fell from the shock of seeing the line linking the King of Hoshiya to the Light of Justice."

Tzion put down the light he held and gave Yoshua a hand.

"Boss, what happened?"

"Do you know what this means? Now, we can link the Light of Justice with a country called Hoshiya!" Yoshua smiled and asked Ruth to finish reading the last line while he brushed slivers of glass from his clothes. Ruth read the next line in the document:

Compiled at *Bet Midrash Ohel Rivka* in the year 5248 (Hebrew Calendar)

Yoshua looked up from brushing off his clothes to notice Tzion's facial muscles relax in the same way as one, forcing oneself to become calm after being angry. He wondered, *"Could Tzion be angry because he didn't prevent me from falling, or angry about something to do with the cover page?" Yoshua thought for a moment, "It couldn't be the cover page because it's a new discovery to every one of us."*

"Tzion, correct me if I'm wrong," Yoshua said, taking the broom and sweeping the broken glass. His face clouded over.

"As far as I know, there's no place called 'Hoshiya' outside the modern boundaries of the Land of Israel." Again, Yoshua observed Tzion's facial muscles contract and relax.

"Is something bothering you?"

They looked each other in the eye and Tzion replied, "Everything is as it should be."

"Tzion, that's not an answer. You have always been free to express your opinions here."

"Despite how well-read you are and having an eidetic memory, there's a possibility that what's written here is true."

"Do you think I don't believe the document is authentic?"

"Boss, there's no doubt that the document is authentic from the late fifteenth century. The question is whether you think its fact or fiction. From the line of questioning you're taking, you've already decided this document is the title page of a fiction book."

"We both know," Yoshua countered.

"There's a town in Israel's Western Galilee called Hoshiya." Yoshua formed his hypothesis.

"If Shmuel ibn Musa Dori hired Nehemiah Toledano during the reign of Emir Mohammed XII of Granada, then the story in this book must have happened before 1487, which is the Gregorian equivalent of the Hebrew date 5248." Yoshua looked at his assistant.

"Tzion, are you feeling okay? You look like someone ran over your cat."

"It's nothing boss, I'm great." Tzion forced a big smile.

"Does anyone else have an opinion, about this document being fact or fiction?" Yoshua asked.

"Yoshua, the age of novels, had not yet reached Europe. Why would we even consider that this document would not be true?" Ruth answered.

"Ruthie, my dear, no one has ever heard of this book. There are many books no one has knowledge of existing. If the church had considered it seditious or even Jewish, there exists an excellent chance the Church had it burned." Yoshua continued to speculate on what the cover page might reveal.

"We can't pin a definite date on the book. Maybe Toledano copied an older book, and no connection existed between the author and the scribe. The names of the author's descendants indicate they lived in Spain under Moorish rule. In conclusion, Aharon could have lived in the early to mid-fifteenth century."

Tzion tried to hide his emotions, which alarmed Yoshua.

"Tzion, we have known each other for a long time. Something isn't right. You are aware that I comprehend that something is wrong."

The tension was thick, and the lab suddenly got quiet. Yoshua continued sweeping the glass, but he could see that everyone was looking at the two of them. Ruth gave Yoshua a nod toward Tzion. She wanted him to fix the scenario.

"Ben Azzai used to say, 'Despise no man, and deem nothing unworthy of consideration, for there is no man that does not have his hour and no thing that does not have its place (*Pirkei Avot* 4:3)," Tzion quoted.

"What are you trying to say, Tzion? Are you sure you're feeling okay?" Yoshua looked at his lab assistant as if he had lost his senses.

"Dear," Ruth butted in, "Tzion is saying you're seeking reasons to discount the discovery's reality and closing your mind to other plausible explanations."

"Ruthie, I'm only working with what I have. The name Hoshiya outside the borders of *Eretz Yisrael* (Land of Israel) is suspect in my eyes. This Aharon Dori claimed he was a military commander to the Light of Justice, but no record exists of a Jewish army. According to Aharon Dori, though, he led a unit that guarded the king. Bar Kochba led the last Jewish army before 1948 in a revolt against Rome, seventeen hundred years earlier."

"For hundreds of years, researchers considered the Kuzari as mythical people, until archaeological evidence proved their existence," said Ruth.

"Babe, you know I have an eidetic memory. In the thousands of books, manuscripts, and parchments I have read, I never came across a city or town named Ramat Tzion or a country named Hoshiya."

"Yoshua Rosenberg," Ruth said in a tone of voice one shouldn't challenge, "Are you telling me you've read everything in the world? This cover page doesn't fit your pre-conceived opinion, so it has to be fiction?"

Over the years Tzion had worked with them, Yoshua always felt there was something going on between Ruth and Tzion. Not sexual, but shared knowledge to which he wasn't privy. They swore they hadn't known each other before Tzion came to work for him, yet he had seen that same look pass between them, like a secret communication he wasn't privy to understand. There was something about this document that caused the two of them to conspire together. Tzion took the broom from his boss and finished cleaning up the broken glass.

"Maybe Aharon Dori made up stories around the legendary figure about whom he had heard." Yoshua's logic carried him on further.

"If this book is a work of fiction, it would be the first novel ever written in Europe. That would make this project worthwhile."

Ruth smiled at Yoshua. Tzion kept his head down, eyes to the floor, but from the way he was holding the broom, Yoshua wondered whether Tzion would be happier smashing it over his head.

"Perhaps, the opposite is true and we haven't yet found the evidence," Ruth suggested. Yoshua couldn't take it any longer.

"We have fought side by side, eaten, slept, and risked our lives for one another." He turned to face Tzion, closed the distance between them to twenty centimeters, breathed in his face, and lowered his voice.

"Tzion, what's bothering you so much about this document? We've been through far too much to not be one hundred percent honest with each other."

"Boss, I've worked with you for a long time. I have never seen you conclude about the validity of our work so fast without checking every fact. It's as if you want this book to be fiction." Tzion paused for a second and added,

"We know several versions of the Babylonian Talmud exist. People studied those versions for generations without people knowing that the other interpretations can be found. Did that invalidate the entire Talmud? No. As you mentioned before, this would be the first novel, over two hundred years before the next European work of fiction. That, boss, is grabbing at straws. Maybe we don't have all the facts yet. We should reserve our opinions until we have scrutinized the document more. I don't understand your mindset that this cover page represents a book of fiction."

Yoshua nodded and stared into space.

"The only way to authenticate the document is to find this *bet midrash* (house of study) called *Ohel Rivka*, somewhere in what had been Moorish southern Spain, and see if we can find evidence to prove the theory."

*****

The next morning, Yoshua said, "Sasha, please upload photos of the cover page to my website. Make a request that anyone with more information about the document should contact us."

The first responses came from the Yoshua's loyal readers. People commented on the beautiful illustrations. No one responded about knowing Hoshiya or Aharon Dori.

# DEFIANCE

Two minutes after Gavriel arrived, Dr. Arieli walked in from his clinic. Seeing a guest, Dr. Arieli nodded but approached his wife first.

"The Holy One, Blessed be He, gave man *zuggiut* (couplehood), the relationship between husband and wife. Giving more than one receives, without thought of compensation, increases both love and holiness. If this concept is true, you, my wife, are one of the holiest people to have walked this earth," Dr. Arieli praised his wife. He turned to his grandchildren seated around the dinner table and pointed at them.

"These extraordinary children are examples of your selfless giving: each one a prince or princess among men because they learned to be conscientious giving, selfless people at your feet."

The children knew it was time to come to their grandfather. From eldest to youngest, they came to his side, one at a time. Dr. Arieli hugged them, kissed them on the forehead, and exchanged a few whispered words with them. The blessings took several minutes because eleven of their grandchildren were at the table.

After Dr. Arieli finished with the children, the two grandfathers came together in a warm embrace. In private, Dr. Arieli still called Gavriel "my prince." He was the only one to keep his title because it was biblical as the prince of the tribe of Naphtali and unconnected to Hoshiya. He was the hereditary prince of the biblical tribe of Naftali. Dr. Arieli figured that if Gavriel was here at this time of day, it had to be something important.

"Let's eat, and then we'll talk."

Dr. Arieli came to the table and sat next to his eldest grandson, Yona. When Yona passed a bowl of potatoes to Gavriel, the epaulet on Yona's shoulder moved, exposing something on its underside. Dr. Arieli lifted the coat of arms badge attached to his grandson's Israeli army uniform. On the topside was the winged serpent, symbol of the Paratrooper Regiment, the same unit Dr. Arieli had served for decades. On the underside, he found to his astonishment, another emblem: the upper third of a sword with the pommel in the shape of a lion's head. The enormity of the symbolism flashed through his brain in an instant.

"Gavriel, as head of the house of Yaroni, do you know anything about this?" Gavriel froze, speechless, as he stared at the emblem of the King's Guard. Dr. Arieli and Gavriel were young boys when Dr. Arieli's father, the last king of Hoshiya, disbanded his armed forces and asked the guards' division to lie down its arms. Dr. Arieli struggled to control his voice. He turned to Yona. "How widespread is this?"

"*Saba* (Grandfather), we didn't do this on a whim."

"Lieutenant, what do you mean? Explain!"

"Not here,"

"Boys, to my office!" Dr. Arieli marched three grandsons, in their Israeli army uniforms, along a narrow hallway. He pushed past them, sat behind his desk, and left the young men standing. Dr. Arieli's iron stare fixed on each grandson. His worst fears shook his world. Such ill-conceived actions could explode into a major crisis, especially now that Yoshua was on Aharon Dori's trail.

"*Saba*," Yona said, standing at attention on the opposite side of the desk, "we knew you wouldn't approve, so we didn't speak to you about it. This was a unanimous decision by us and our parents. You know we love you, and we would do nothing intentionally to hurt you."

Dr. Arieli felt the weight of his responsibility on his shoulders. No matter how much he loved his grandsons, he couldn't let this continue. His responsibility to every Hoshiyans far outweighed his feelings toward his family. He realized they had caught him in a trap and had to regain control of the scenario.

"Boys, the emblem of the King's Guard is only for those who swear loyalty to the king. A thing you can't do because we have no king." He paused for effect. He could forbid Hoshiyan community members from wearing the badges, but only by exerting the authority he evaded secular chief and de facto king. Now he understood the subtlety of his grandson's actions, but they didn't know what he knew about Yoshua.

"*Saba*," Yona explained, "for generations our people served in the Israeli army, in every branch of service. Often our people were alone, with no other Hoshiyans. There were plenty who died in silence to protect our secrets. Requests for transfers to units primarily made of of Hoshiyans have increased over the years. Four years ago, thirty men approached General Har Zahav to put together a Hoshiyan battalion. Our uncle, Yeshayahu Drori, volunteered to handle the logistics. Three years ago the Army promoted him and made him a commander of a reserve paratroop battalion."

Realizing these maneuvers had gone on behind his back saddened Dr. Arieli, and when he thought the betrayal couldn't get worse, it did.

"Between Uncle Yeshayahu and General Har Zahav, they transferred three hundred Hoshiyan officers and enlisted men into Uncle Yeshayahu's unit. They wear the emblem of the Queen's Guard!"

Dr. Arieli put his head down on his desk. After a few moments, he whispered to his grandsons. "

"It's a moot point now whether we agree or disagree. How I'll deal with this mutiny is likewise moot. I've only one objective: to fulfill the prophecy of Elisha Arieli." The young men remained standing. Dr. Arieli knew every one of them had grown up with stories of Elisha Arieli's final prophecy. They were intelligent boys; he would let them come to their own conclusion. After a few moments, Dr. Arieli dropped the explosive news on them.

"Yoshua found the cover page of the fabled book by General Aharon Dori."

Yona opened his epaulet and removed the badge. The others followed suit. "*Todah rabah* (Thank you very much) boys," Dr. Arieli said, relieved that the contest of wills between generations would, for now, not disturb the common goal. Their grandfather rose from his chair and opened his arms.

"Come give me a kiss and go finish your dinner."

Dr. Arieli had spent seventy years building a flexible system to allow Hoshiyans to exist anywhere in the world. He understood it was a house of cards. Dr. Arieli wanted to believe that Hoshiyans followed his advice because he was their spiritual leader and not the king of Hoshiya. He had done everything possible to prove his loyalty to the State of Israel. His eldest sons have graves on Mt. Herzl, the national military cemetery. One grave had the bones of his son Benyamin, and Chaim's coffin had been empty. Now everything he thought he had built was unraveling. A nation's fate laid in the hands of a single man that didn't even understand that not only was he a Hoshiyan, Crown Prince of Aluz, but the prince of the tribe of Asher.

# RIVKA AND MICKI

Dr. Arieli left the dining room and walked along the hallway to his bedroom. He knew Rivka's body paid a high price for her hours at the archery range, and she wouldn't be in the kitchen washing dishes.

He admired how she kept teaching and shooting a bow. Pulling those high-tension bows caused extreme strain on her shoulder muscles and tendons. At age eighty-four, maybe it was time to give up archery. But he didn't suggest it because he understood how much she loved the sport. Dr. Arieli found his wife sitting in a chair. He checked the heating pad on her shoulder, and Rivka slipped her hand into his. Dr. Arieli kissed her on the cheek, lifted the heating pad off her shoulder, dabbed a small amount of Arnica cream with his fingers, and massaged the injured shoulder.

"Softly, Micki," Rivka whispered. He could see the pain etched in her face. She never complains. After several minutes of massage, he helped her move the shoulder. They were so attuned to each other—her pain was his pain.

Rivka trained three generations of archers. Hoshiyans came from across the globe to study with her. Since the days of the first Hoshiyan kings, despite the existence of modern weaponry, Hoshiyans upheld the archer's tradition of their forefathers as a symbol of their heritage. Dr. Arieli massaged Rivka's legs. He opened his mouth, but Rivka put a finger on his lips.

"Micki, my love, I should quit, but when I see those youngsters holding a bow for the first time, every ache and pain disappears. I sense the immense love we've poured into this silly sport. It's only a symbol, but it's the only symbol of our heritage that we can express in public."

He flexed her leg, touching her knee to her chest, and helped her extend her leg outward. After five repetitions, the blood was circulating.

"How does it feel now?"

"Pins and needles, but it hurts much less."

She opened her arms. Dr. Arieli sat next to Rivka, wrapped her in his arms, her head on his shoulder, and enjoyed the closeness and feel of his wife. He prayed, *"King of Heaven and Earth, I can never praise you enough for giving me Rivka, as my wife. I am satisfied to stay like this for the rest of my life."*

"This is nice," Rivka said.

"No, it's great, stupendous, and momentous!"

"Whoa, Dr. Arieli, momentous might be an exaggeration."

"More than momentous, he found it."

"Who found what?"

"Huh?"

"Who found what?"

"Yoshua found the cover page of General Dori's book."

Rivka met his eye.

"I pray every day for a sign, some proof, and now, a slip of the tongue could ruin everything," Dr. Arieli reminded her. He checked his watch.

"I called a family meeting downstairs in the basement in ten minutes."

# CLASH OF GENERATIONS

The Arieli's children and their spouses stood with their backs to a wall covered with archery awards. Dr. Arieli pulled out a chair for Rivka. After his wife was seated, he took a seat. He signaled for his children to remain standing. Dr. Arieli had done everything possible to avoid this moment for several reasons. He didn't like the conflict between the generations, and he hoped he'd never have to take up the mantle of power his family had held for generations. He hated to argue with his children and thanks to the Holy One, Blessed be He; it happened infrequently. Dr. Arieli wanted to keep the meeting short and to the point.

"You employed a clever strategy," he said. "Either I do nothing and you get what you want, or I take on the title of the King of Hoshiya and order you to stop these actions. In either case, it's a win-win scenario for you. However, every one of these arguments are pointless. This evening, Gavriel told me that Yoshua discovered the cover page of General Aharon Dori's *Hoshiyan Chronicles*."

Dr. Arieli looked at the faces of his children and their spouses. They understood the enormity of his revelation.

"I've no choice but to invoke the powers I avoided my entire life and command every one of you to stop any action that might influence Yoshua. It's only by freedom of choice that he can fulfill the prophecy." He paused and added.

"There will be no Hoshiyan army within the Israeli army. I won't allow you to re-create Hoshiyan units. The Kingdom of Hoshiya no longer exists. God's purpose for

Hoshiya is over. We must do everything possible to increase the unity of the House of Israel and not create factions, but I'm not opposed to our men serving together. I'll encourage General Har Zahav to arrange for Hoshiyans to serve in units that are one hundred percent Hoshiyan." He registered the smiles of his family.

"Father, I am responsible for what has occurred," Shimon Tzurel, his son-in-law, confessed.

"Father, don't pay attention to my husband. I pushed him and the boys," Herut said, attempting to take the blame.

Dr. Arieli turned to his remaining son.

"Father, how blessed am I to have an elder sister- and brother-in-law who would take the blame for my actions," Elisha praised his sibling and her husband. The other girls tried to protect Elisha, but their father cut them off.

"Enough. Your ploy has worked. You are aware how much I prize brotherly love. Every Hoshiyan must stand shoulder to shoulder to avoid influencing the Prince of the Tribe of Asher's opinions. He must accept us by his own free will," Dr. Arieli remaindered them.

Micki and Rivka stood, and each child and grandchildren came to them for a hug and kiss.

Inwardly, Micki smiled. His children have shown shrewd political insight in this encounter. They achieved every one of their goals and allowed him to save face. He looked at his sole surviving son and wondered, would his late sons, Benyamin and Chaim, have stepped aside to allow Elisha to rule?

# RED FLAGGED

The phone rang in the president's office of the Pontifical Commission, Cardinal Antonio Rossini, the administrative head of the Vatican City State.

"Cardinal Rossini, the superior general speaking."

"Superior General, it's nice of you to call. How are you?"

"To my regret, Cardinal, my call isn't a social one," the superior general of the Jesuits informed him, "but an important matter of church security."

"Please, Superior General, tell me what you've found."

"Cardinal, you know we run a special unit that scans the internet for information damaging to the church. Our program will flagged an article if it has a dangerous keyword. Once flagged as suspect, an agent investigates to see if the article could harm the church. The Jesuits use small red X's: one for a minor problem, five for a major problem. We found a recent post with the words 'Hoshiya' and 'Aharon Dori.' Each set off five red X's. An agent called and told me. Excellency, we've come across an article containing two references, tagged with five red X's each. Protocol requires I call you. I told him, 'you've done well, my son.' I'm contacting your office to find out what to do next."

"You've done well; I'll get back to you soon." Cardinal Rossini hung up. He reviewed the website and realized he had to get more information. He called Monsignor Jean-Louis Beliveau, the apostolic nuncio in Israel.

"Monsignor Beliveau, do you know the professor of archaeology, Yoshua Rosenberg?"

"Yes, Excellency, I've known him for many years. Professor Rosenberg has always been helpful in every interaction with me."

"Please contact him for me and arrange a date and time for me to call him as soon as possible."

The cardinal sat at his computer and sent the Pope a formal email.

Your Holiness, May the Lord grant you a long life.

The Superior general has brought to my attention a recently published an article on a website. Our program flagged it twice as having five red Xs. An Israeli professor, Yoshua Rosenberg, published a cover page of an unknown book called the Hoshiyan Chronicles by a General Aharon Dori. I am investigating this scenario and will speak with the professor as soon as possible. I will inform you of what I learn following my phone call with him.

May the Lord Bless you

Cardinal Antonio Rossini.

# CARDINAL ROSSINI

Twenty-four hours after posting the cover page, Yoshua received a call from the apostolic nuncio in Israel After asking about each other's health, the monsignor got down to business.

"Professor, I would like to arrange a conversation between you and the president of the Pontifical Commission for the Vatican City State, Cardinal Rossini." The caller and the request astounded Yoshua. He had met the apostolic nuncio at university, museum, and government functions. Their relationship was proper and cordial.

"Professor, are you still there?"

"Yes, Monsignor, I'm here. I don't understand what the Vatican government could want from me."

"His Holiness the Cardinal has read your books and would like to discuss the cover page published on your website."

"Monsignor, tell Cardinal Rossini I'll be in my office at five pm after my last lecture." Yoshua sensed something wasn't right; but he went along with the request.

"Thank you, Professor," the Monsignor said. The two men wished each other a pleasant day and hung up. The conversation shook Yoshua, and he left a message on Gavriel's voicemail about the call. It was difficult for him to concentrate on his lecture, and he let his class out early.

Ten minutes after returning to his office, the phone rang; a voice with a heavy Italian accent.

"Is this Professor Rosenberg?"

"Yes."

"I'm calling for the president of the Pontifical Commission, Cardinal Rossini. He would like to speak with you now if possible."

"No problem, I am delighted to speak with the cardinal."

They exchanged pleasantries, and the cardinal got to the point.

"I have enjoyed reading your books, especially your theory on the evolution of legends."

"Thank you, your Grace." Yoshua chatted with the Cardinal for an additional five minutes until the cardinal got around to asking about the cover page.

"A magnificent piece of art; is there more? Or, is there a book after this cover page?" It puzzled Yoshua. The caption under the photo on his website stated he found the cover page in the binding of another book.

"What is your opinion of this cover page from a literary viewpoint?"

Yoshua understood heads of state don't call to shoot the breeze about literature. Despite his suspicions about the interest of the Vatican in something so esoteric, he gave the cardinal his opinion.

"Hoshiya as a country and Ramat Tzion as a city don't exist on any ancient or modern map. These facts cause me to think what we're talking about is possibly the first, or one of the first, novels ever written in Europe. So, I conclude from the available data that the names are fictional. It could be a matter of translation, but I doubt it. The Hebrew is clear, with no room for ambiguity. If a copy of this book still exists, it will prove to be a work a fiction."

"Yes, a work of fiction," the cardinal agreed.

"However, Cardinal, if this book is a work of fiction, it makes it the oldest novel in Europe. *The Tale of Genji,* written by Murasaki Shikibu in eleventh century Japan, is world's oldest novel. Every modern literary authority recognized his book as the first novel.

The men spoke for another five minutes until the cardinal summed up.

"Professor Rosenberg, your ideas are most enlightening. Please keep me in the loop concerning this novel about a place called Hoshiya." The hairs on Yoshua's arms stood up. His body had rarely failed him to warn him of danger.

"If you sign up on my website, you will get all the newsletters."

"Thank you. I will."

Yoshua hung up, grabbed his laptop and searched for 'Aharon Dori.' The only references were to living people. When he typed in 'Hoshiya' he got 'Hoshi Ya' sushi bars, and several variations on a Japanese surname.

Yoshua pondered this conundrum. "*Something smelled fishy. Why was the Vatican interested in this subject? Could it be that this Aharon Dori was an oradical and the church knew his book existed? It's possible that Dori used the book as a tool to ridicule the church, or something worse.*"

Too agitated to wait for Gavriel to return his call, Yoshua sent him a detailed text message. A few seconds later, the reply came.

"Why would the Vatican care?"

# ALARMED

Gavriel was sitting in his office when the phone rang.

"Hello, Professor Yaroni speaking."

"Gavriel, its Yoshua. I am concerned about the strange phone call I got. I texted you about it. Why would the Vatican's highest official call me about the cover page we discovered? Why should the Vatican care about a book published over five hundred years ago? As far as anyone knows, no copies exist? People's interest gets aroused for two reasons: either the issue is to their benefit or their detriment."

Alarms went off in Gavriel's head. *The last thing he needed was the church's interference with the prophecy. He wondered if the church suspected Hoshiya no longer existed. Could they know the Hoshiyans had returned to Almiyah (Aramaic for 'this world')? He weighed his words, taking care not to share his thoughts with Yoshua, who had to discover these secrets himself. Gavriel, instead, continued Yoshua's theorem.*

"If the book had a positive outlook on the church, they'd make plenty of copies available. That only leaves the possibility that something in the book is harmful to the church."

"Gavriel, don't let your anxiety over the church spoil your joy in this discovery."

"You're right." Gavriel laughed to himself as he hung up the phone; Gavriel sat for a few moments, thinking about what he would write in an email to Dr. Arieli. He detailed the disturbing conversation with Yoshua.

# THREAT TO THE COMMUNITY

On the top floor of Dr. Arieli's Jerusalem apartment building (Bet Arieli) stood the International Hoshiyan Communications Center. General Seth Har Zahav, retired paratrooper, sipped his black coffee, and read Dr. Arieli's emails. Among his other jobs, he decided which emails went to Dr. Arieli and which a secretary should answer. When he opened and read the most recent one from Gavriel Yaroni, internal alarm bells shouted. Seth yelled to the eighteen technicians seated in cubicles around the room.

"Meeting!" Seth called out. Everyone gathered in the center of office and Seth informed them of the situation.

"Ya'acov, call Professor Yaroni and ask him to come to the office. I'll have Dr. Arieli and his son here. This email needs to direct, in person, evaluation. Uri, send a warning that the Vatican has expressed too much interested in the subject of Hoshiya. It should go out by email to our standard community list of two hundred and fifty-seven thousand. Make sure the text is in the Lomarian to avoid international listeners," Seth ordered.

"Alert everyone on the secure communication list to use only their burner phones. Miriam, tell our intelligence community connections to gather information on the church's interest in every detail concerning Hoshiyan. Please warn the heads of every Hoshiyan educational institution."

Against Dr. Arieli's wishes, the Hoshiyan people maintained their own educational, welfare, and charitable organizations. The Hoshiyans didn't accept the standard Israeli curriculum. They rejected the Israeli government's education funds. Hoshiyan schools emphasized a program of ethics and spiritual development that the Israeli curriculum didn't. Truth to their beliefs, the Hoshiyan supported their educational system.

\*\*\*\*\*

It took another twenty minutes for everyone to assemble in Dr. Arieli's office at the Communication Center.

"The head of the Vatican government called Yoshua directly. The Catholic Church's interest in General Dori's cover page is a very serious problem," Seth stated. He waited to see what Dr. Arieli would say next. He waited a while longer and filled in the silence.

"I've been of the opinion for some time that we need our own intelligence unit, not our own people in Israeli intelligence communities," Elisha Arieli commented.

"Dr. Arieli, I understand you are struggling. Everyone must unify against Israel's internal and external enemies. But the Hoshiyan people will face the Vatican threat alone. They could expose Hoshiya before Prof. Rosenberg comes to the same conclusion. That will delay the fulfillment of the prophecy another two generations," General Har Zahav pointed out.

"You're right. The real danger is interference with Yoshua's free will. Now that Yoshua found evidence of General Dori's book, an opportunity has arisen to fulfill the prophecy. These are the hopes and prayers of more than half a million people."

"*Aba*, general," Elisha said, "an enemy like the Catholic Church is not something we've faced here in

*Almiyah*. This is serious, sir. The recent developments have given us great hope for our future. Now, with the interference of the Church, everyone is anxious. What are we willing to do to bring the prophecy to fruition?" Elisha inquired of his father.

"Elisha, that's for the Hoshiyan high court to decide," Dr. Arieli said.

"That's only because there's no King to make these decisions," Seth said.

"Besides stopping the prophecy, what can the church do?" Dr. Arieli asked.

"It can incite foreign governments to work against us," Seth replied.

"General Dori must've created problems for the church," Elisha said.

"From General Dori, the church would have learned of Hoshiya's massive technological advantage over Medieval Catholic Europe. Hoshiyan philosophies must have appeared foreign and dangerous to the people of Europe hundreds of years ago," Prof. Yaroni added.

"Let's not belittle the fear of a Jewish Hoshiyan army marching on a Jew-hating fifteenth century Europe," Seth added.

"The question is, does the church know of our current status in this world?"

"It's a hard enemy to deal with, especially because there's been no reason for our people to infiltrate their society of priests until now," Dr. Arieli said.

"I agree," Seth said, "even Amatzia Cohen (famous Hoshiyan spy who infiltrated the highest levels of power in the Lomarian Empire) couldn't infiltrate the Vatican." Seth thought for a second and proposed an idea.

"We need to find out the church's position on Hoshiya."

"Seth," you're correct. However, unlike the Catholic Church, we don't have resources to build an intelligence organization. Yet, we need a means of collecting real-time data needed." Elisha said.

"Michal Ben Yosef and Shira Yavetz retired from the Mossad two months ago. They are in contact with sixty-Hoshiyan Mossad and Shin Bet retirees. They are willing to resurrect the Hoshiyan National Intelligence Agency (NIA). We need to know if the church is searching for Hoshiyans," Seth said.

"Doctor, I know you share my feelings on the quandary before us. On one side, Hoshiya no longer exists. Every great institution our people built there no longer exists. The titles and positions we would have held in Hoshiya mean nothing in this world. I also agree with your point of view to integrate with mainstream Israeli society."

"*Aba*, I understand your fear of rebuilding our ancestors' world here. There is a danger it would separate Hoshiyans from the rest of Israel, but on the other side, we can't ignore the threat of a powerful organization like the Vatican. The church can interfere with the prophecy's realization. This scenario could disintegrate into *pikuach nefesh* (a matter of life and death). Since the center of attention is Yoshua, he needs more protection; perhaps not with a bodyguard, but with intelligence to preserve his free will to believe or not believe."

"Seth," Dr. Arieli said cautiously, "To rebuild the Hoshiyan National Intelligence Agency would support those who want to remain separate from the rest of the

Jewish people. However, I have no say in the matter. Here in *Almiyah*, I'm only a doctor."

"Dr. Arieli, you might consider yourself that way. Worldwide, over six hundred thousand Hoshiyans consider you their spiritual leader." Seth weighed his next words; was it necessary to bring up a question that might cause the man pain? This was a question that needed asking.

"What would the KING do in this scenario?" Seth knew Dr. Arieli could hide behind some excuse, or at last take control.

"The KING would call a meeting of the Quartet and draft a policy to glorify the Name of the Lord in this world," Dr. Arieli said. Seth trembled. Dr. Arieli's call for the community leaders to gather would see this as a royal summons. No matter which way he turned, his people's history created a road block that stood in his way. They could not approach the Israeli government for help. Explaining the danger to them would expose the Hoshiyan people's existence. Yoshua might learn the truth from an outside source and thus could not fulfill his destiny.

Seth watched the change wash over his leader's face.

"Call the heads of the houses of Yaroni, Tzurel, Zioni, Drori and Yavetz to a conference; we need to reestablish the NIA. See if you can get Shira Yavetz to accept the directorship." Elisha smiled to himself. There was no going back now. Seth followed his orders.

Elisha walked over to his father and hugged him.

"Father, we all agree that Hoshiya no longer exists in a physical sense. Does that mean the *Brit Shalom* no longer exists?" Elisha inquired.

"The *Brit Shalom* goes beyond national boundaries," his father replied.

"If Hoshiya doesn't exist, why do we care about the Crown Prince Elisha's prophecy?"

Dr. Arieli comprehended where his son tried to lead him.

"Elisha, I understand your point. Hoshiya is something in our hearts. It represents a way of life, not dependent on physical boundaries," Dr. Arieli said, realizing where his son led him.

"Father, you are the leader of a people who, despite every tragedy, choose by their own free will to follow our ancestor's way of life. Faith, righteousness, and justice aren't ephemeral concepts. The people follow you, because you are the best example of what our people have stood for hundreds of years."

Dr. Arieli took his son in his arms and kissed him on the cheeks and forehead.

"If we followed our forefathers and had a vote today, no one would stand against you. You have always been the king, for you led by example. Now, in this time of need, we need a firm hand on the rudder of our people's destiny. You are that hand on the rudder."

# GEFEN AND AVIVA

Ever since meeting her in the park, Gefen hoped she might convince Aviva to give her a job on the team seeking the identity of the Light of Justice. Gefen did a search, found Aviva's email address, and composed a letter.

Dear Dr. A. Berger,

I don't know if you remember me; I was the artist painting in Bloomfield Park, *Mishkanot Sha'ananim*. You helped me mix the beige color. I'd like to know if we could meet. I have questions about color and texture.

Regards,

Gefen Nimrodi

Gefen sat back in her chair, gazed at the ceiling, and thought.
*"If I can get Aviva interested in my artwork, I'd have an opening to the Rosenberg's."* Her computer beeped fifteen minutes later with an incoming email from Aviva.

Dear Gefen,

Yes, I definitely remember you and the unusual combination of themes in your painting. I'd love to meet you. I'm currently working on a project for the Archaeological Institute, restoring several items found on a dig in the City of David. Let's meet during my lunch break (12:00 to 12:30) at Dr. Ruth Rosenberg's office. I'm there Mondays through Thursdays. Let me know which day is convenient.

Regards,

Dr. Aviva Berger

Gefen typed a quick reply.
Dear Dr. Berger,
Would tomorrow be convenient for you?
Regards,
Gefen
The reply came within a few minutes.
Dear Gefen,
No problem. See you tomorrow.
Aviva
Gefen did a search and brought up a map of Jerusalem. She focused in on Hebrew University's Mount Scopus Campus. Gefen found the Archaeology Institute. She clicked 'University Staff' and found the number of Dr. Rosenberg's office. Gefen's next search was the Egged Bus Company to find the most efficient route to the university.

*****

Gefen walked into the Archaeology Institute the next day, a few minutes before noon. The guard at the front desk looked up.

"Good morning, may I help you?"

"I have an appointment with Dr. Berger in Dr. Rosenberg's office, for lunch."

The man raised an eyebrow and pointed.

"That's Professor and Dr. Rosenberg's building. When you enter, go straight and it's the third door on the right.

Gefen followed the guard's instructions and entered through the open door of the lab. A man in a lab coat turned towards her as she entered.

"May I help you, young lady?" Tzion asked.

"I have a lunch meeting with Dr. Berger," Gefen replied.

"Dr. Berger isn't here yet, but you can wait in the office."

Gefen followed the directions, walked into the office, and recognized Dr. Rosenberg from her photo on the back of the book of legends. She plopped her bag on a chair.

"Hi, I'm Gefen Nimrodi. I have a lunch meeting with Dr. Berger."

Ruth took off her reading glasses and smiled.

"Oh, Aviva told me she was meeting a young artist. Hi, I'm Ruth Rosenberg. Please have a seat. I'd love to hear how the Light of Justice inspires your work."

Gefen explained, and Ruth nodded, brows knitted in concentration. Three minutes later, Gefen felt a presence behind her, but she continued to tell how she combined the spirituality of Jerusalem, the legends of the Light of Justice, and her love of cryptography. She reached for her cell phone and showed Ruth photos of her work. When she was ready, Aviva stepped out from behind Gefen to look at the photos. Ruth and Aviva commented.

"Your canvases are impressive, especially the desert sandstorm." Instead of a twister of sand, Gefen painted a whirlwind of coded numbers swirling around a lone acacia tree whose branches bent in the wind.

Gefen took a chance.

"Dr. Berger, Dr. Rosenberg, I already finished high school. I have a full year free before my army service, and I would like to work with you on your current project." Gefen watched Ruth's face. Seconds passed in silence.

"Do you have a CV or resumé?"

Gefen reached into her bag and pulled it out, along with three letters of recommendation. Ruth read the papers and handed them to Aviva.

Gefen had prepared for indecision.

"I'd like an apprenticeship with Dr. Berger so I can use my artistic ability to master the art of conservation and restoration."

"Gefen, dear, Aviva doesn't teach art or art restoration. If you want to learn restoration, you need to study proper subjects at the university," Ruth said.

"I've studied every one of Dr. Berger's projects. Many of them are works of art themselves. I could learn more working with her for one year than I could in four years at the university."

Gefen observed Aviva's eyes; she had liked what Gefen said. Gefen struck while the iron was hot.

"Every artist wants to pass her style and method to the next generation. Maybe it's time you acquire a disciple."

"I have to give you credit, Gefen. When you want something, you go straight to the essence." Aviva paused, picked up Gefen's cell phone, and scrolled through the photos.

"Okay, if you want to work with me, you need to learn several basic disciplines. Those are chemistry—inorganic and organic, structural integrity of materials, art history, and the history of compounds used in art." Gefen nodded, taking care not to flinch.

"I see your email address on your CV. I'll send you a list of books you need to read." Aviva reached out her hand to Gefen and they sealed the deal with a handshake. That evening Gefen received a list of books and a message to meet in a week at 8:00 am at the little sandwich shop on Ibn Gvirol Street, opposite the post office.

\*\*\*\*\*

At the appointed time, Gefen waited at a sidewalk table, her backpack stuffed with reference books.

"*Boker Tov*," Aviva said. She sat, ordered for both of them, and pulled a book from her huge bag; *Art Restoration: a Guide to the Care and Preservation of Works of Art* by Francis Kelly.

Gefen unloaded eight books on the table. "I already studied these chemistry books last year, and I read about forty percent of the rest of them. I made a list of questions on the material." Gefen pretended not to notice Aviva's slight hint of a smile.

Aviva opened her book to the restoration of Rembrandt's famous "Night Watch." She pointed to the badly preserved painting and what it looked like after the restorer did her work.

"See here, Gefen, when they cleaned Rembrandt's canvas properly, it turned out not to be a night scene, only a badly preserved canvas!" Gefen studied the before and after pictures of the famous misnamed painting.

The breakfast meetings became a ritual twice a week. Aviva arrived early, order food, and prepare materials for Gefen. They ate a different omelet each morning. In addition, they had a vegetable salad, cottage cheese, and fresh whole grain rolls. Afterward, while they discussed various aspects of restoration, they enjoyed different herbal teas—today, it was chamomile and honey. Aviva said, "A restorer needs excellent knowledge of art styles and materials. Do you believe in God?"

"What? I don't know."

"To create true art, not the commercial junk, but art that speaks to people, you must achieve harmony with yourself, your surroundings, and God."

Gefen tried to mask the wave of mistrust that washed over her by looking at her omelet.

# OHEL RIVKA

A month after posting the *Hoshiyan Chronicles'* cover page, found Yoshua researching any mention of Ohel Rivka. Yoshua sat in the reading room of the National Library of Israel's rare book collection. He thought about leaving, but it was pleasant to sit in the climate controlled room where they maintained the temperature at twenty-two degrees centigrade and the humidity at forty percent.

Yoshua doubted he could ever find *Ohel Rivka*; the *bet midrash* mentioned on the cover page. As he finished that thought, a colleague from Tel Aviv University sat next to him, preparing to speak. Yoshua nodded toward the exit, indicating they should converse in the hallway.

Yoshua shook the man's hand.

"What brings you to our neck of the woods?"

"You do. I heard you need information on a place in southern Spain; *Bet Midrash Ohel Rivka*?" Yoshua nodded.

"Well, you're in luck. I found a reference to *Ohel Rivka* in a letter of *Responsa* from Rabbi Saadia ben Zacharia. He was a well-known religious leader during the second half of the fifteenth century. In the letter, he mentioned the house of study as being 'a two-day journey southwest of Cordoba, in the region of Andalusia, in the mountains south of Granada.'"

"Thank you from the bottom of my heart. I was almost losing hope."

Yoshua hurried to his office and phoned the provincial archaeologist for Granada, who insisted he never heard of an *Ohel Rivka* in the Granada area.

\*\*\*\*\*

After the revelation in the National Library, Yoshua's eldest son David spoke up at dinner.

"*Aba*, instead of looking for the *bet midrash* by its name, why not locate every building still standing from before 1480 in the area of interest?"

"That's a superb idea. We'll get on it tomorrow."

An exhaustive internet search in Yoshua's laboratory turned up one hundred twenty-two unique buildings. The vast majority of them were churches and farmhouses that fit the search parameters. Emails flew between Israel and Spain. With each new clue, Yoshua erased another candidate for *Ohel Rivka*. Hour by hour, the list shrank. By the second day, Sasha and Tzion joined in, and there was a spirit of competition in the office. At the end of the day, everyone gathered in Yoshua's office.

"I've reduced my list of thirty-five possibilities to only five," Tzion said.

"Of my thirty potential sites, I've reduced the candidates to three," Yoshua said.

"I have only one possibility from my thirty possibilities," Sasha said.

"My list has narrowed from twenty-seven to eight possibilities," Ruth said.

"I'm proud of you. You're making remarkable progress. I hope by tomorrow we'll have narrowed the list more," Yoshua said. Pep talk noted. The team members smiled back at him and dispersed. Yoshua slumped in his chair and turned toward Ruth.

"Babe, we need more information. If we could get into the Bishop of Granada's archives, I'm sure we will find *Ohel Rivka*."

"Shuki, do you want to ask a Catholic bishop for help?"

"Remember, the bishop owes me in a big way. Besides, we've always had a good relationship."

"Isn't there some other way?"

"I can't think of any other source of information. The Bishop's archives contain extensive records not available to the public."

# BISHOP OF GRANADA

The Bishop of Granada, Jose Carlos Garcia-Ortega, dictated a letter to his assistant who typed it on the computer. The assistant scowled when the phone rang and the assistant answered the phone.

"Your Excellency, Its Yoshua Rosenberg calling from Israel."

The bishop's heart skipped a beat and took the phone.

"Shuki, my good man, how are you?" His love was archaeology, and ten years ago he worked with Yoshua as a volunteer on a dig in Israel. They became friends and kept in contact over the years at international conferences.

"I'm well, thank you. I'd like to ask a favor."

"How can I be of assistance?"

"I need access to your archives."

"Why?"

"I'm looking for a structure built during the fifteenth century in the area between Cordoba and Granada."

The bishop considered what his friend could want.

"Why are you looking for it?"

"It's connected to my research into the identity of the Light of Justice."

"*Mi casa es tu casa* (My house is your house)" the bishop replied.

"Thank you, Bishop. I will inform you of my travel plans. I'll try to come between semesters," Yoshua replied.

While they spoke, the assistant tidied the bishop's desk and made a sour face. When the conversation ended, he blurted out,

"Excellency, why are you helping the Jews?"

Jose Carlos gained notoriety for assisting a family accused of being Jewish in secret. He researched the family's background. He learned how the Inquisition confiscated the family's home and belongings. In short, the actions of the Spanish monarchy had done in the name of God horrified him. Jose Carlos, ever patient, turned to his assistant with a story.

"I owe Professor Rosenberg my life. I was in a tunnel digging in the Galilee. It collapsed on me. I gave myself the last sacraments and blacked out. Yoshua dug me out, despite of the danger of another collapse. He gave me CPR and saved my life." The assistant persisted in shaking his head.

"Men of honor return favors, especially one of this magnitude," the Bishop continued, peeved that he needed to explain such things to his assistant.

## ARCHIVES

The archivist of the Diocese of Granada, was a young priest, boasted he had single-handedly computerized the files in the library back to 1750. When Yoshua arrived, he met with the librarian.

"I am looking for a structure built before 1480," Yoshua informed him. The librarian's heart sank.

"I have digitalized none of those files yet. They are in the old wing of the library. The search required looking everything up in the old, handwritten card catalog," the librarian explained.

For four days, the librarian helped Yoshua, Ruth, and the bishop's assistant eliminate seven of the ten possible locations. They established a method of operation. Ruth and the librarian searched the card catalog and went together to find the files in the stacks. The librarian lugged file after file back to the reading room for Yoshua to study. It amazed the librarian the amount of material Yoshua could read in a short time. While the mystery drove up the librarian's adrenaline, the lugging of files and books ran him ragged. He wasn't used to working fifteen-hour days, he complained to the bishop.

"Bishop, your Israeli friends have me working long hours every day. Please assigned an additional priest to help us?"

On the fifth day, they struck pay dirt. Ten minutes after opening the first file, Yoshua shouted, "Another one down!" That left only two structures; a building in Durcal, south of Granada, and a chapel in Nido de Aguila, called Santa Maria del a Compo de Sud.

It took the four of them three hours to find the file on the building in Durcal. Remarkably, right next to it was the file on Santa Maria Del a Compo de Sud! Yoshua opened and read it. Within two minutes he determined that the building was a bodega, a structure for aging sherry. Built in 1485, it was still owned by the original family. With a straight face, he handed the file to the librarian.

"That wasn't it." He turned to Ruth, grinned, grabbed her around the waist, and danced her around the reading room.

"So it has to be the little chapel in Nido de Aguila!"

After the celebration, they opened the file and Yoshua shook his head.

"Every piece of the information before 1520 is in code."

The librarian leaned in to see for himself.

"I don't believe this! I've never seen a coded file in the entire library, especially here in the archives."

"It's a puzzle we will have to investigate. However, I can't solve this puzzle now. Thanks a million for your help," Yoshua told the librarian.

Ruth took out the camera with the macro lens and photographed everything in the file. After she transferred the photos to Yoshua's laptop, she took a second set of pictures with her cell phone as a backup. She closed the file and looked at her watch.

"Shuki, we only have four hours for our flight. We need to be at the airport two hours ahead of time. It takes an hour to get there, so we better order a cab now and go pack."

The librarian respected the foreign professor, who read Spanish as fast as his eyes passed over the page.

"Don't worry about getting a cab. I'll drive you to the airport in an official car of the diocese. We'll get there much faster."

Yoshua and Ruth rushed to their room, packed, and left a letter of thanks for the bishop, who was at a conference in Madrid.

# CODEBREAKER

It wasn't until they were on the plane that Ruth mentioned her suspicion regarding the coded file.

"Shuki, the church is trying to hide something. When the Vatican discovers the bishop helped us, they will reprimand him. If these are the records of *Ohel Rivka*, the information in this file is secret, because of what the Inquisition did there."

With that thought, Yoshua opened his laptop and looked over the file. He gleaned information from the non-coded parts of the file.

"The building had once been a small parish church, but when they built a larger church nearby. They converted it into classrooms. Fifteen years ago, the town built a new school and abandoned the old classrooms. When we get home, I'll reach out to my contacts in the intelligence community and find someone who can help us decipher these documents." Yoshua took Ruth's hand; the two reclined their seats and fell asleep for the rest of the flight.

*****

Although Yoshua was past the age for army reserve duty. He continued to volunteer in the anti-terrorist unit. The unit was his second home for thirty-two years. To those who served with Major Yoshua Rosenberg, he was held in high regard. Yoshua was highly trained, dangerous operative, who completed many difficult and complicated missions. Yoshua's military background gave him access to valuable contacts within the intelligence community.

\*\*\*\*\*

After landing at Ben Gurion Airport, Yoshua and Ruth passed customs and walked through the exit doors to the arrivals hall where their family waited—waving helium balloons and floral bouquets. When Ruth saw her father open his arms, she left Yoshua's side and ran to him. Meanwhile, the children ran to Yoshua. Elimelech and Ruth watched as Yoshua hugged and kissed each of the children. Elimelech whispered in his daughter's ear, "He is such a prince."

At home, more family and the team members gathered to welcome Ruth and Yoshua. Ruth told the story. She finished with, "Yoshua figured out which building was the *bet midrash*. We finally found the file for the structure. When I turned to the pertinent pages surrounding the time in which we're interested, I stood their astounded. They had written every page of interest in a secret code. Tomorrow morning Yoshua will contact friends in the intelligence community to find someone who can decode the files."

"Yoshua! Don't rush to your friends so fast. Do you remember Gefen Nimrodi?" Aviva asked.

"Sure, she's the young artist who wants to work with us."

"Her hobby is codes. I bet she can break this code before you can even find the right contact. Email the file to me. I'll go to her home right now and see if she can do it."

"I don't know about that."

"Yoshua, what do you have to lose?" Aviva shrugged.

Ruth emailed the file to Aviva, who kissed her on the cheek and left for Talbiya.

After the company left, Ruth wiped the kitchen counters and considered how to broach the subject of kosher food for their next trip to Spain. She didn't want to nag Yoshua, but he was washing the dishes in an excellent mood.

"Regarding kosher food, he should be a better example to the children," she thought.

"Shuki, I can't tell you how happy I'm to be home so we can eat a decent meal. I was tiring of instant noodles, soup, and tuna with crackers. Maybe you should contact the Chief Rabbi in Madrid and find out what kosher food is available in Spain?"

*****

Gefen's mother answered the door.

"Dr. Berger, how nice of you to come visit. Gefen is in the kitchen." Mrs. Nimrodi led the way. Mentor and student greeted each other with affection.

"Please excuse me, but I have to go to choir practice. Enjoy yourselves. Your father is meeting me there. We will be back at 10:00. Gefen gave her mother a kiss on the cheek and escorted her to the door. Meanwhile, Aviva dug her cell phone out of her bag and forwarded Yoshua's email to Gefen's phone.

"Yoshua brought these encrypted files back from Granada. Do you think you can break the encryption?"

Gefen's cell phone beeped. She opened the email and took a quick look at the pages.

"How old are these documents?"

"They're from the fifteenth or sixteenth century."

"Awesome! It's the Alberti Cipher described by Leon Battista Alberti, who embodied the first example of poly alphabetic substitution with mixed alphabets and variable period," Gefen said with a smile on her face.

"If you say so," Aviva replied in awe of Gefen.

"They base the system on a device called a *Formula*. The device comprises two concentric disks, attached by a common pin which could rotate one with respect to the other. When I began with cryptographs, I collected replicas of machines used over the centuries to create ciphers. I have a replica of Alberti's original cipher disks I made from drawings. They're in my closet."

"Are you up to deciphering the code right now?"

"Sure!"

Aviva watched as Gefen opened her closet and rummaged around for a few minutes, opening and closing boxes. A smile grew across Gefen's face. She lifted a medium-sized carton and brought it to her desk. "Eureka!" she said, pulling out a machine.

"Here's how machine works. The larger disk is stationary. The smaller one is movable. Alberti divided the circumference of each disk into twenty-four equal cells. The outer ring contains one upper case alphabet for plain text and the inner ring has a lower case mixed alphabet for cipher text. The outer ring also includes the numbers one to four for the super-decipherment of a codebook containing three hundred thirty-six phrases with assigned numerical values. This is a very effective method of concealing the code-numbers, since you can't distinguish their equivalents from the other garbled letters. Key letters control the sliding of the alphabets, which are included in the cyptogram's body."

Aviva found the explanation hard to follow. Her head was swimming from the large number of details. "Can you break the code?"

"I am positive I can break this code," Gefen replied.

Gefen opened her laptop. She worked on permutations of the cipher to see if any made sense. Aviva and Gefen agreed on the assumption that the official language of the church at the time was Latin. Every word Gefen deciphered with the machine, Aviva keyed into an online translator website to see if it made sense.

Gefen and Aviva didn't register that Asher and Ora Nimrodi had come home at 10:30. An hour later, Ora said goodnight and got a wave from her daughter.

It was slow, grinding, painstaking work, but on the fifteenth try Gefen hit the jackpot. It didn't take her more than a few more minutes to set a special program she had previously written. She keyed in the numbers as Aviva read them to her aloud. It took three hours to enter every number from the six pages of encrypted text. Gefen hit the Enter key, and the program deciphered the numbers and printed out copies in Latin and Hebrew.

It was 6:00 am when they finished. Aviva and Gefen were so wired they couldn't sleep.

"Aviva, let's photograph the results and send them to the Rosenbergs by Whats App," Gefen suggested.

"Sure. Ah, I see where you're going with this. Let's send them the translations. Afterwards we will call them on video chat so we can see how shocked they are that you did the job before Yoshua could even call his friends."

They sent the message, and fifteen minutes later Aviva called Yoshua's cell phone on the fifth ring. Ruth answered his phone.

"What do you think of Gefen's work?" Aviva said.

"Aviva, its 6:20 in the morning."

"So, what do you think?"

"I can't get Yoshua to do anything. He's glued to those pages you sent; he waved me away." Ruth turned the phone around so Aviva and Gefen could see Yoshua concentrating on the pages scattered around on the table.

# FINDING THE CHAPEL

When the children woke up, Yoshua was still at the kitchen table, hunched over the pages. He ignored everyone until Ruth interrupted.

"Yoshua Rosenberg!" He glanced at her and turned on his million-dollar smile. Ruth wagged her finger. "You will not get out of this one by charming me. This is your home, and right now you have a family to take care of."

"Babe."

"Professor Rosenberg, go get dressed, *daven* (pray), and eat your breakfast. We'll drop David and Chaim at the *yeshiva* (religious high school) on the way to work. When we get to work, you can spend the entire day reading." Yoshua put on his sad face, and his children laughed. Ruth shook her head. When they left the house, Ruth handed Yoshua the keys. He had hoped Ruth drove so he could read.

At 9:00 am, Yoshua had a lecture, and at 10:00 Sasha had to attend a seminar. From 11:00 until 12:00, Ruth held office hours for undergraduates. They agreed, so, that Tzion will write the overall summary and they would meet at 1:30 pm after lunch.

*****

At the Nimrodi's apartment, Gefen and Aviva slept until noon. When they woke up, Aviva found a voice message from Ruth.

"Meeting at 1:30 to summarize what Gefen deciphered." Still groggy, they showered, dressed, filled two travel mugs with instant coffee, and ran to the car. They got to the lab at 1:35 to find Yoshua and Ruth sitting with the rest of the team and Professor Yaroni.

Ruth patted the chair next to her; Gefen and Aviva took their seats.

Tzion had transferred the information to a power point file. He had set up his laptop computer with a mobile projected and used the wall as the background.

"The first page states, anyone that can read this file, has a copy of the Alberti cipher machine. Under the direct order of Torquemada, the Inquisition Commission for Granada, encrypted these files. Everyone sat there, shocked.

"What insane depravity did Torquemada order upon the Jewish residents of Nido de Aguila?" Professor Yaroni asked.

"The crown confiscated the entire community's property. They burned every copy of Aharon Dori's Hoshiyan Chronicles on the orders of Pope Alexander the VI. The local commissioner of the Inquisition wrote what they stole."

"The next two pages are lists of goods and real estate confiscated by the crown. The fourth page jumps ten years forward. A local magistrate named Sanchez confiscated the local Jewish community building in 1492. This happened after the Jews refused to convert to Christianity. Page five states that drunken soldiers destroyed the mikveh. On pages six and seven summarize the court case against the community members. It describes how the Inquisition tortured seven people, Tzion told them.

"The name, Musa, the son of Aharon Dori, stood out in the report. Musa Dori had refused to answer any of the commission's questions. Even under extreme torture, he revealed nothing. The Inquisition's tribunal convicted and sentenced him to death among the remaining forty-six members of the community. Four died of torture. The local Commission of Inquisition ordered that the entire community eradicated, along with most of the remaining community structures: the cemetery, Mikve (ritual bath), and hall. To teach the Jews a lesson, the commission converted the house of study into a church named Santa Maria del la Compo de Sud. The ninth page reveals a bill of sale of the Jews community building to the Ophosi family, a reward for converting to Catholicism.

Tzion allowed everyone to digest what he had read up till now.

"The next document, from 1493, records the sale of the building from Alfonso Sanchez to Alberto Ophosi. The following document, dated 1580, clarifies the status of the building. Emmanuel Ophosi, head of the family, donated the lease to the property, free, to the church. Once the building fell out of use by the church for over five years, it would default to the Ophosi family. The last page is the donation of the building by the Ophosi family to the church. They identified it as 'the building once known as *Ohel Rivka*.' Once again further along the page, it states that the building will be a chapel and known as the Chapel of Santa Maria del la Campo de Sud."

First to react was Sasha, who got up, went to his desk, opened the bottom drawer, and pulled out a bottle of vodka and six plastic cups. He poured five small shots and a double for himself. He handed them around, including to Gefen. Yoshua raised his eyebrows, but

Sasha gave him the Russian evil eye. Yoshua nodded. Everyone raised their cups to Gefen.

"To Gefen, the wonder woman who solved the mystery of *Ohel Rivka!*" Yoshua toasted her.

Sasha followed with, "*Na zda-ró-vye!*" and downed the double shot of vodka in one gulp. The other four looked at each other, shrugged their shoulders, and followed suit.

Only Gefen took a small sip.

"*Not too bad,*" she thought, and took a bigger sip that burned the entire way to her stomach. The face she made caused everyone to laugh until they had tears in their eyes.

# FUNDING

Gavriel sat at the conference table, replayed Tzion's summary of the file in his head, and mulled over how he should proceed. He turned to Yoshua and struggled to keep his voice steady.

"Did you notice the last document in the file? The Bishop of Granada answered a petition from Juan Martin Ophosi of Nido de Aguila. Juan Martin requested the church uphold the ancient agreement and revert the property back to his family. The structure had lost its usefulness, and over five years had passed," Gavriel reiterated, smiling.

"Yes, I read the decision of the bishop."

"The bishop granted the request five years ago. Yoshua, I need to leave now. I have to give a lecture in fifteen minutes. Will you do me a favor and email the Bishop of Granada in my name—"

"—to ask for his help in finding Juan Ophosi's address."

"You got it." Gavriel handed his laptop to Yoshua and headed for the door.

Yoshua wrote:

Your Excellency, Bishop of Granada,

I respectively request the address of Juan Ophosi of Nido de Aguila, whose family owns the chapel of Santa Maria del la Compo de Sud. I request permission to examine the building, as our research has concluded it was once a Jewish house of study.

Regards,
Professor Gavriel Yaroni,
Archaeology Department, Hebrew University
The bishop replied the next day.
Dear Professor Yaroni,

My communications are with the owner's attorney, Francisco Rodriguez. Please find his contact information attached.
Regards,
JCG

Switching to his own laptop, Yoshua fired off an email to the attorney.

The next day, while sipping coffee at his desk, Gavriel received an email from Yoshua; subject line: "the letter!"
Gavriel,
Here's the reply from the attorney:

> Dear Professor Rosenberg,
>
> My client's intention is to sell the structure as soon as possible. If you are interested, I suggest you come here and negotiate with my client for the purchase of the building.
>
> Respectfully,
>
> F. Rodriguez, Esq.

*****

A moment later, Yoshua appeared in Gavriel's office. "What do you think about the offer?" Gavriel said, still struggling to keep his voice calm.

"How are we going to compete without funds?" Yoshua sat, stared at the desk, and shook his head.

"Tell the attorney we're interested in purchasing the chapel. The economic scenario in Spain isn't positive. There's over twenty-five percent unemployment. Remember, they've owned the building for five years and still haven't sold it. We have to act fast. If the Vatican figures out we know too much, they'll try to stop the sale."

"I agree, but where are we going to find funds?"

"Let me worry about the money. Yoshua, your Spanish is excellent. You need to write to the Spanish Antiquities Authority for permission to excavate the site. If they give conditional approval, I'll find the money to buy the structure."

"Excuse me for laughing, but since when has the department had that kind of money?"

"Not from the department; from private funding. A few people approached me after the press release about the cover page. They said they will put up serious money. One investor is negotiating with the University for Rights to sell the cover page as a lithograph." Gavriel had the urge to wipe his forehead, but he didn't want to show they agitated him.

"Hold on, what's going on here?"

"What do you mean?" He smiled innocently, but his heart rate accelerated, and he feared he appeared overzealous.

"There's something fishy about this entire story. First, the head of the Vatican calls me, and now you tell me we can raise money to buy a building?"

Gavriel's blood pressure sky-rocketed.

"How am I going to get him off this line of questioning?" he thought. An idea came to him.

"Yoshua, as far as the Vatican goes, it's obvious that, over five hundred years ago, the *Hoshiyan Chronicles* must have upset the church. According to your theory, the work is a novel; such things didn't exist in Europe, so the church saw it as disturbing. Today, however, they have nothing to fear from a novel! As far as the money goes, it's a straight-up business deal. There are people who think there's a market for these kinds of things." Gavriel saw his explanation didn't convince Yoshua.

"Are you going to look a gift horse in the mouth?"

Yoshua tilted his head slightly, shrugged, and sat at Gavriel's laptop to search for the Spanish Antiquities Authority's website. Using their Contact Us form, he sent a preliminary message of inquiry. While he was at it, he wrote to the Chief Rabbi in Madrid to ask about the availability of kosher food in Spain.

As Yoshua finished his email to the rabbi in Madrid, Ruth walked in and looked over his shoulder. "What's this document in Spanish?

"I requested forms to ask for permission to conduct an excavation at the chapel in Nido de Aguila. This is the form they sent us," Yoshua replied.

"How many bureaucratic hoops do we have to jump through," Ruth asked.

"It says they want us on site when a surveyor makes a map of the area for excavation. After they approve the excavation site, we will have to pay the registration fee.

Only then can you submit the full proposal," Yoshua informed his wife.

The next day, Yoshua stopped by Gavriel's office during their lunch break. "Did you see the email I forwarded to you from Attorney Rodriguez?"

"No, I forgot to check my email this morning," Gavriel said. He scrolled through his inbox, found the email, and tilted his laptop so Yoshua could see the screen.

Dear Professor Rosenberg,

Because of the extensive interest in the property, we will hold an auction. There is a two thousand euro nonrefundable registration fee. Everyone interested in participating has until March 28th to transfer the funds. Attached is a PDF file with wire transfer instructions, including bank account information and Swift code.

Respectfully,

F. Rodriguez, Esq.

Gavriel surprised Yoshua when he called the bank and ordered a transfer of funds as fast as possible.

"Since when does this department have such sizeable sums of money lying in the bank?" Yoshua asked.

"I won't miss out on the Light of Justice because a weasel of an attorney is conning us. For five years they haven't been able to sell the building, so they can't get away with asking for an outrageous amount now. The building will be more expensive than other properties in the town, but we need to control their enthusiasm over how much they think they will earn from the sale."

"I couldn't agree more," Yoshua said.

"Yoshua, the spring break starts in another two weeks. You'd better get over to Spain and apply for excavation in person and get a receipt so they won't be able to say it got lost in someone's spam filter."

"That doesn't leave me much time before *erev Pesach* (Passover starts)."

"You must hire a surveyor in Nido de Aguila."

"I'll look on the Internet for a surveyor in Granada and ask him to prepare the preliminary work. I can ask him to send a PDF file of the maps."

"We should think about what happens after we buy the building; maybe dismantle it for transfer to Israel."

"I never saw you in such a state," said Yoshua.

"Are you feeling okay? What could be so important concerning finding this *bet midrash*, unless it leads to the Light of Justice? But what if the book is fiction? Why is the Light of Justice so important to you, anyway? It can't be a question of more publications. You have over eighty scientific publications to your credit; you're already a professor emeritus so you won't get any more honor, status, recognition or money. So, what's driving you?"

Gavriel answered Yoshua with the best lie: ninety-nine percent truth.

"The legends of the Light of Justice are close to my heart. I inherited this curiosity from seven generations before me, for good reasons. First, the stories instill pride in our people. Second, the stories teach ethics, justice, righteousness, and faith. Third, they tell of another place and time, when Jews lived free under their own rule and their own armed forces."

Yoshua lowered his head, humbled by Gavriel's explanation. He had the world's single largest collection of stories about the Light of Justice. He knew why he was pursuing the subject, but couldn't figure out Gavriel's interest.

"I understand," he said, "but you have access to stories I haven't heard; we should talk about that soon."

"Yes, let's, but for now, I need to talk to those private investors."

"I still can't wrap my head around this. Most of the time, we get barely enough money together for a short excavation here in Israel. Now you want to raise many times that amount of money."

"Yoshua, you take care of your side of this deal, and I'll take care of mine; like I've taught you over the years—an efficient division of labor!" He looked at Yoshua and thought, "He looks so much like his father. How unfortunate he never knew the man."

# CLASH WITH JESUITS

The rest of the day, Yoshua sat in his office and ruminated over the newly arrived documents from Spain and Gavriel's unusual behavior. At 4:00 pm, he received an email from the Chief Rabbi of Spain:

Dear Professor Rosenberg,

Thank you for your inquiry. There are three kosher restaurants in Madrid. In addition, there are several brands of chocolates imported from England that are kosher. Only one kind of bread is permissible: the 'old style rustic Spanish bread.' They make it from only flour, water, yeast, and salt; and is kosher if baked in a traditional clay oven used solely for that purpose.

At the end of the day, Yoshua stopped by Gavriel's office to say good night. Seeing he was on the phone and not wanting to interrupt, he waved goodbye. "Yoshua, wait a minute, this concerns you." It took another couple of minutes for Gavriel to finish the call. "That was a friend of mine in Amsterdam. After I explained to him what we found and what we intend to do, he said he would set up a fund for the project, and contact several others he knew who would contribute. These people who preserve and transfer Jewish arts, books, religious writings, and artifacts to Israel."

In the evening, Yoshua told Ruth what happened.

"I've never seen Gavriel in such a mood. Something is not right," Yoshua commented. Ruth understood why her husband found Gavriel's explanations unacceptable.

He needs distraction. She wrapped her arms around his neck and kissed him with all the passion she could muster. After sixty long seconds, the tension in his muscles went away and his mind was only on his wife.

"Congratulations Professor Rosenberg; looks like we have a major excavation in front of us." Ruth winked at him. Took his hand and led him to their bedroom.

Elana heard her father lock their bedroom door. She glanced at her siblings.

"That was close," David whispered.

"We are out of here. I'll treat the three of you to an ice cream." Elana went to her elder sister.

"Won't *Aba* be suspicious afterward?" she asked.

"We should go over to Aunt Aviva's after the ice cream. *Ima* will need time to make *Aba* forgot," Elana added.

"We're blessed that *Aba* and *Ima* love each other so much," David said, smiling.

"I thought I would have a heart attack," Chaim commented.

"I don't understand how Ima stands up to the pressure day in and day out," Elana said.

David got his younger siblings out of the house and wrapped his arms around his little sister.

"An entire group of Hoshiyans work with *Ima* to help her cope with the constant strain," David said.

Every one of us knows we can go to the Arielis day or night for help to cope with *Aba*.

Once outside on the street, Chaim pulled out his phone and called Aviva.

"Aunt Aviva, we are invading your house. We are bringing ice cream."

"When you say we. How many?" Aviva inquired.

"The four of us."

"I'll make popcorn and we'll have a party."

"Love you, Auntie.

"Not as much as I love the four of you." Tears of joy filled her eyes. Aviva loved those four children as if they were her biological children.

*****

Seth sent out an email explaining why they needed to raise funds. Emails zoomed back and forth across the globe. They opened five central accounts: In New York, Rio de Janeiro, London, Sydney and Singapore. Thousands of donations came in from every corner of the globe. Eighty percent were between ten and twenty dollars. Emails of praise and hope inundated Bet Arieli. Most people replied to the request.

"If you need more money to fulfill the prophecy, don't hesitate to ask again.

The entire Arieli, Tzurel, Aluz and Yaroni families responded to each email with a personal note.

.

*****

Later that week, Gavriel informed Yoshua concerning the sale of the chapel.

"This minute, I got back from the bank. What a bureaucratic mess," Gavriel complained.

"What happened," Yoshua inquired.

"Part of the funding came from the US. Our regular branch refused to deal with the US Internal Revenue forms. We had to go to the main branch on King George St. Three hours it took to convince them we weren't laundering money. Our silly government allows the US government to get into accounts of duel citizens and funds coming from the US. I must have aged ten years this morning," Gavriel grumbled.

"How much money did you raise?" Yoshua inquired.

"The initial sum is four hundred fifty thousand euros," Gavriel replied.

"I can hardly believe this. I never heard of so much money being raised in so short a time. We have so little information for an unknown archaeological site that might produce nothing," Yoshua stated, taken aback by the amount of funds Prof. Yaroni raised. But, after a moment, he got caught up in the excitement and gave Gavriel a big hug. Thoughts of what he could do with the money buried any lingering doubts.

\*\*\*\*\*

On the first day of the Passover holiday break, Yoshua flew from Tel Aviv to Madrid. He planned to spend only four days in Madrid. Yoshua needed to deal with the Spanish bureaucracy. He would get nowhere near the *bet midrash* or a surveyor in the little town in the Sierra Nevada Mountains.

The second morning, Yoshua left his room and walked down the stairs to the lobby of the Grand Velazquez Hotel. The hotel was two blocks east of the Ministry for the Interior. The desk clerk said, "Professor

Rosenberg, there's a special delivery letter for you from an attorney by the name of Rodriguez."

Yoshua thanked the clerk and opened the letter.

Dear Professor Rosenberg,

The Bishop of Granada's decision to release the building to its original owners is being challenged by the Jesuits. The appeal will take place in Madrid tomorrow at seven in the evening at the cardinal's residence. Please be there.

Best Regards

F. Rodriguez, Esq.

Yoshua called the bishop.

"Excellency, is there any chance you'll be in Madrid tomorrow night?"

"I'll be there. The Jesuits brought this complaint against me!"

"Excellency, the Ophosi family's attorney has asked me to attend the meeting. But I have no standing with the church. Could I impose on you to represent me?"

"It would be my pleasure. I'm curious why the Jesuits would want to reverse my decision. I keep reminding myself that the Lord wants me to be slow to anger."

Yoshua met the bishop at Madrid's Barajas Airport. In the taxi, on the way to the cardinal's residence, they discussed the situation.

"What could be the Jesuits' objection to returning the disused chapel to its rightful owners?" the bishop asked. Yoshua suspected the church, especially after Cardinal Rossini's phone call. He decided not to tell the bishop about the call; better to see if he would mention it. "Its internal church politics," said the bishop, "the plaintiffs being Jesuits and I'm a Dominican." Yoshua nodded, but wondered if the bishop realized how lame that sounded to an outsider.

They arrived a few minutes early. The cardinal's assistant met them at the door. He escorted them to a waiting room where twenty-five members of the Jesuit delegation sat.

"Bishop, your Jesuit friends are out in numbers. They hope to intimidate you," Yoshua whispered to his friend. He watched as several agitated Jesuit hotheads approached the bishop. They disrespected the bishop and berated him. They continued, unaware that Yoshua understood what was being said. Yoshua lashed out at them in Spanish.

"You call yourselves men of the cloth, but you don't even know how to address a bishop. No matter what your opinions, you still must respect the position of the bishop. He's the same rank as an apostle. The proper greeting is 'your Excellency,' and the proper way to greet him is to kiss his ring as a sign of respect."

Amid the Yoshua's tirade, no one paid attention to the cardinal who had opened his office door and stood in the doorway listening to the entire monologue. The cardinal coughed into his hand, and when the Jesuits turned around.

"The professor is correct. Every one of you has sworn loyalty to the Mother Church. There's a hierarchy in this church. The bishop ranks higher than the rest of you. In my diocese, my priests will act properly to all their superiors. Now, those of you who addressed the bishop improperly will bend the knee, kiss his ring, and ask forgiveness for your rudeness and disloyalty to the church and the bishop."

The five priests' faces turned bright red.

"You have little choice but to obey my command," the cardinal said. The five priests still didn't move.

"To ignore me here in front of witnesses would be grounds for dismissal and excommunication from the church," the Cardinal added in a harsh tone. One at a time, the priests bent the knee, kneeled before the bishop, and kissed his ring. Once they finished their penance, the cardinal told the head of the Jesuit delegation.

"My office isn't large enough for so many people. You may enter and bring two others with you." The Jesuits hoped to win the day by sheer numbers, but now the cardinal had upset their strategy. They needed to change tactics if their ploy would succeed.

Once seated, the head of the Jesuit delegation opened the debate.

"Your Eminence, why is this man, who is not a member of the church, here at this meeting?" he inquired.

*"There are many ways to ask a question,"* Yoshua thought, *"The best, in this case, was to do it humbly. However, this Jesuit took the opposite approach and asked arrogantly, which bordered on insubordination."*

"You never assume that tone with me again. You will leave my office immediately, go to your confessor, and accept any punishment he lays upon you," the cardinal replied. Lifting his right arm, the cardinal pointed to the door. The Jesuit rose to his feet, shaking, and left the office. The cardinal possessed substantial power; it wasn't worthwhile to take him on head-to-head without the superior general at his side. For the next ten minutes, the cardinal tried to obtain a clear and concise reason to why he should overturn the Bishop of Granada's decision. The Jesuits failed to convince him.

Yoshua thought, "*It's lucky both the bishop and the cardinal are Dominicans. The cardinal probably rejected the Jesuit's appeal out of spite more than church policy.*"

On the spot, the cardinal had papers drawn up supporting the bishop's decision. Armed with these documents, Yoshua thanked the bishop and the cardinal.

"On behalf of myself, the Hebrew University and the State of Israel, I thank you for their help," Yoshua praised the Cardinal of Madrid and the Bishop of Granada. The cardinal provided the two men with a car and driver to take them back to the airport, where the bishop would fly to Granada and Yoshua to Tel Aviv. During the ride, they discussed what transpired.

"Bishop, do you have any explanation for the Jesuits' strange behavior?" Yoshua asked.

"To tell you the truth, their actions struck me as bizarre, as well. Even though we come from different orders, their behavior was far too aggressive. Church politics can't explain this away. To behave so in front of a cardinal is strange. We need to monitor this priest's activities," the bishop concluded.

The two men said goodbye at the airport and promised to stay in touch. Yoshua had only a sixty-minute wait until his flight. During the long flight home, he reviewed the previous days' events in his head. "*The scenario surrounding this little chapel is getting stranger all the time.*"

When Yoshua returned to Jerusalem, he emailed the documents upholding the Bishop of Granada's decision to Attorney Rodriguez and Gavriel. Gavriel and Juan Martin Alphonso Ophosi, the present head of the Ophosi family, exchange emails about the sale of the building.

This resulted in Ophosi agreeing to meet with Yoshua after final exams in July.

*****

Yoshua's schedule included so many things that the spring semester passed by quickly. Now he sat on a bus from Granada to Nido de Aguila on a hot July morning. The bus passed through the rolling hills of chaparral landscape. Most of the land was agricultural; covered with groves of olive trees, vineyards, greenhouses, and short, yellow wheat stubble harvested six weeks previously. As the bus approached Nido de Aguila, Yoshua watched the locals plow fields, spray grapes with a bluish-copper spray against fungal diseases, hoe weeds, and harvest vegetables. The town maintained its unique, classic architecture. Every home had yellow or orange tile roofs. One and a half-meter high whitewashed plastered walls surrounded the homes. People favored mimosa, carob, or stone pine trees in their gardens. The oldest buildings in the town were over six hundred years ago. The most prominent was the Catholic Church. Yoshua got off the bus and stood in the blazing midmorning heat. After a few deep breaths of the good country air, he opened his phone's GPS app and took off toward the northeast corner of town. After a seven-minute walk through the cobblestone streets, he stood in front of the small parish chapel of Santa Maria de la Compo de Sud.

Even at its height, it must have been a poor parish. The chapel, built of fired brick, was unadorned on the outside. The only indications that it had once been a place of worship were the wooden crosses over the door and on the roof. As Yoshua stood outside the building, a swarm of gnats and flies surrounded him. The gnats and flies were the most recent conquers of the town. The constant buzzing couldn't dampen his enthusiasm.

As he approached the diminished, pathetic ex-church, Yoshua thought about all the months of searching for the place. They had gone through ancient sources in Arabic and Spanish to identify this building as the church converted from the *bet midrash* of the Jewish community. Gefen's deciphered documents indicated that the community's only claim to fame was this *bet midrash*. Near the end of the Moorish rule, there was the legend that a wealthy, wandering merchant-storyteller settled in the village before the end of his life. He provided most of the money to build the *bet midrash,* along with the rest of the public buildings belonging to the now extinct Jewish community.

In the file from the bishop's archives was a work order for one Abu Namir to create a plaque. The plaque has written on it the name of the *bet midrash*, the name of the donor, and the date. They had attached it to the western wall of the building. The document was partially moth-eaten; only part of the benefactor's name was legible: 'Aharon.' Yoshua was positive it was the same Aharon ben Ephraim ben Eliezer of fabled Hoshiya. According to a letter found in the bishop's file, Aharon Dori wrote his memoirs there.

With the upcoming excavation, Yoshua's goal was to find additional clues to the mystery of the king mentioned on the cover page. His best hope was to find the *gniza*, the place in every *bet midrash* and synagogue, for the storage of old books and papers of holy status before they buried them.

When Yoshua reached the door, he noticed a slot carved into the stone doorpost at a slant, about shoulder height on the right side. He understood that after his long quest, he at last found the right building. The slot was the spot for the *mezuzah* (is a piece of parchment inscribed with specific Hebrew verses from the Deuteronomy 6:4–9 and 11:13–21). This had to be the *bet midrash* of Aharon of Hoshiya!

Yoshua stood there, contemplating the significance of the confirming the identity of the building. A most unusual feeling came over him, as if something had touched his soul. The intense impression caused his body to quiver. Yoshua sensed the building calling to him to expose her secrets.

Yoshua shook his head. "*Maybe I am dehydrated,*" he thought. He removed his backpack and took out a liter and a half bottle of water. He drank half. Next, he leaned forward. He removed his hat and pour the remaining half on his head. Despite the water, the sensation hadn't left him. Yoshua was a soldier and scientist, not a psychic or kabbalist. There was something hidden here calling to him.

For the first time in many years, he felt God had directed him to this place and time. He leaned against the doorframe for support. As was his custom at the beginning of every dig, he prayed. Ruth taught him to begin each new project with the words.

"Holy One Blessed be Your Name, King of the Universe, help me reveal the hidden here for the glory of your Name."

The first unusual thing he noticed about the small chapel-classroom was that one had to step up upon entering, rather than down. He squatted to be close to the floor. He examined the strange phenomenon. They installed the present floor on top of the previous one. Once inside the chapel, he found it lit by a single shaft of light, shining into the center of the room, from a single window in the western wall. Two more arched apertures had once existed high on the walls, but they had been closed up with bricks in the past. The structure was plain and unimpressive, with walls thick for the style of building. There were only five double rows of benches. Every one of benches was of rough, old, worn wood. The lectern for the teacher (layperson or priest) had a faded blue cloth covering which was unraveling at the edges.

Two curious neighbors, Santiago Alvarez and Carlos Velasquez, wandered over to check out the stranger. After Yoshua's short, but impressive introduction in fluent Spanish, relieved the neighbors' fears.

"Why are you there?" they asked.

"I am an archaeologist and we hope to excavate this building."

The neighbors took turns telling him the history of the building.

"The community hadn't used the chapel as a church for many years. When we built the new church fifty years ago, the Church used the building as a school," said Mr. Alverez.

"Until fifteen years ago, they used the building as a religious classroom. However, since they never installed gas and electricity. They used it only during the days of the warm months. Do you know the legend of this church?" asked Velasquez.

"Legends are my primary field of research, so he I am eager to hear anything you know about the place," Yoshua replied.

"It's haunted," Mr. Alverez stated with a straight face.

"On dark, windy nights one can still hear the cries of those murdered in this place." Yoshua's eyes opened wide. He knew from the decoded file that the local Commission of Inquisition murdered every member of the Jewish community. Maybe this was the source of the strange tale.

Yoshua shook hands with the neighbors.

"Thank you very much for your helpful information. I appreciate your help."

*****

Next, Yoshua went to the church to see the local parish priest.

"Are you Padre Emanuel Jorge Garcia?

"Yes."

"I have a letter of of introduction from the Bishop of Granada," Yoshua informed him.

The priest read the bishop's letter.

"Please extend a warm welcome, Prof. Yoshua Rosenberg, to Nido de Aguila. Do everything in your power to assist him."

The padre extended his hand to Yoshua.

"I was born and raised in Nido de Aguila. I still remember studying in the little room on warm summer days, when the temperature inside was rarely more than a few degrees cooler than outside. There is a traditional in my family. They believed the little chapel haunted, because of the people who died there. The neighbors swear they sometimes hear the screams of the murdered."

"Murdered?"

"Yes, murdered."

"Padre, thank you for your gracious welcome and for sharing your story. I'll be in touch."

Yoshua learned long ago, when dealing with legends, there was always some grain of truth to them. He thought, *"It might not be precisely as told, but there's a good chance people died here, and not naturally. Churches are normally not the site of murders. Either it happened before the building became a church, which means the chapel was the bet midrash, or there might have been some local feud. Europeans considered Churches as being holy and places of sanctuary. Killing people in a church was a heinous crime. Both theories fit the story. If the building turns out to be Bet Midrash Ohel Rivka, the logical conclusion is the Inquisition probably tortured and murdered the Jews of the village there. What am I getting myself into?"*

\*\*\*\*\*

For his last stop before siesta, Yoshua went to find Juan Ophosi, the only member of the Ophosi family who could sign the property over to him. The padre had given him directions, and it was only a short walk to Ophosi's home.

"Senor Ophosi, is an elderly gentleman. At this time of day, he will be at his small winery next to his home, more than likely 'tasting' his own Mantilla wines," the padre said with concern. Anxious about the negotiations to buy the building, Yoshua did several breathing exercises to calm himself. Knowing Mr. Ophosi liked to drink would help him with his negotiations.

# JUAN MARTIN

At midday, Juan sat in his favorite spot in the winery's courtyard, in the shade of a large gnarled cork oak. There were no secrets in Nido de Aguila. Long before Yoshua reached the winery; Juan knew who he was, where he came from, and what he wanted. The Ophosi clan had fallen on hard times in the past twenty-five years. As the family expanded, the farm and winery weren't profitable enough to sustain them. Many left their beloved soil and went off to the large cities to seek jobs in hot, stuffy factories. They wrote to Juan about how they missed the quiet, fresh air and open spaces. Juan made a silent prayer.

*"Please, let it be true that this stranger from the Holy Land wants to buy that stupid piece of property."*

Juan considered his ancestor from 1580 as insane. Who in their right mind would will the rights to the property of the church? To make it worse, he volunteered to pay the property taxes. The building laid between the Alverezs on the north and the Velasquezs on the west. On the east was an unpaved parking lot. Adjacent to the parking lot and stood a three-story school belonging to the church. The old chapel had been nothing but a headache for the family. It siphoned off much needed cash into village tax coffers.

*"How did this foreigner obtained permission from the church to buy the property? How did he know that after hundreds of years, the building had reverted to the ownership Ophosi family only five years ago?"* Juan thought.

Juan could see Yoshua making his way between the whitewashed walls along the cobbled lanes of the village. The Israeli walked with a straight back toward the little plaza near Juan's home. The air was thick with the smells of lunch. The aromatic smell of onions and garlic frying in olive oil wafted from the windows overlooking the little alleys. Yoshua arrived at the winery as Juan finished reading the newspaper.

Waves of heat rose from the hot stones of the cobbled plaza. Juan watched as Yoshua removed his hat and wiped perspiration from his face with his sleeve.

Yoshua entered the courtyard of the winery through its arched stone gate. He spotted Juan at once, approached the small table where he was sitting, and introduced himself in perfect Spanish.

"Are you Senor Juan Martin Ophosi?"

"Yes."

"I am Professor Yoshua Rosenberg from Israel. I wrote to you I was coming to discuss with you the sale of your property that used to be a chapel."

"Please take a seat Professor."

Juan found himself unprepared for the appearance of such an esteemed professor or his fluent command of the language. Surprised by Yoshua's complete control of the scenario, Juan realized this would not be the simple affair that he and his family had planned.

Upon completing the pleasantries, the dance of the negotiations began. For the next hour, the men dueled verbally. Juan enjoyed himself. He summarized their agreement.

"I'm willing to sell, and you're willing to buy, the old chapel!"

Yoshua nodded, but added a condition.

"I'd like to see the official deed of ownership before we continue."

"Okay, tomorrow we'll go together by car to Cordova. The deed is in the Land Registry Office. We'll get the official copy of the ownership papers for my attorney, so he can write up a contract transferring ownership."

# BOMBING IN CORDOBA

The next morning, Juan parked in front of the hotel at 6:45 sharp. Yoshua waited for him on the bench in front of the hotel.

"Good morning! It's warm for so early in the day."

"Good morning! No problem, it's a dry heat." Juan's old Seat sedan had no air conditioning, and Yoshua expected they would suffer from the heat and dust before long. Taking advantage of Yoshua's captive ear, Juan talked as soon as he got behind the wheel. "The village of Nido de Aguila is one of the few places in Spain where the local population can trace their history back to Roman times. Close to the village are interesting Roman ruins of an extensive farm complex from 250 to 450 A.D. The village even escaped the incursion of the German tribes after the collapse of the Roman Empire."

"How do you know these things?" Yoshua asked.

"We have maintained the history of our village by an oral tradition passed from one generation to the next." Juan Martin answered.

"After the Moorish invasion, the local emir allowed Jews to settle in the town. Two communities of Jews and Moors lived in harmony for two generations. It was only after the surrender of the Emir of Granada to King Ferdinand, that Torquemada brought the Inquisition to the town. The Inquisition murdered every the Jew and Moor or expelled them from the country." Next, Juan threw in his blockbuster.

"Did you know that our family name goes back to 1482?"

"That's interesting, tell me about it." By this time, they had entered the southern district of Cordova and stuck in morning traffic.

"The maternal side of the family were simple farmers by the name of Fernandez. The Fernandez family converted from Judaism to Catholicism when Seville fell to the Christians. They fled from Seville and came to Nido de Aguila. Their youngest daughter, Rosa Maria, fell in love with Yosef Alphasi, and they married. By the time the Inquisition reached our village, they had four children. Yosef agreed not to convert Rosa or the children back to Judaism and had obtained the protection of the local priest. However, with the imminent arrival of members of the Commission of Inquisition from Cordova, the local priest changed the registry to save the family. A minor change, small, and hard to recognize. The priest changed the name Alphasi to Ophosi. So, Professor, I have Jewish ancestors and am interested in helping you," Juan told him.

Yoshua was processing Juan's revelation when Juan swerved the car into a miniscule parking space. Miraculously, he found a space next to the government building housing the *Colegio de Registradores* (Land Registry) office. It took Yoshua a few seconds to recover from the heart-stopping maneuver. In the meantime, Juan was already out of the car, waiting for him on the sidewalk.

"Ahh, after that hot trip, what a pleasure to come into an air-conditioned building," Yoshua said.

Juan Martin removed his handkerchief and mopped his forehead and smiled.

"This building is a beautiful example of the Baroque style. You're right, the air conditioning is more important at the moment!" While Yoshua enjoyed the architectural beauty of the government office, while Juan asked at the information desk for the location of the Land Registry office.

"The office we need is right around the corner here on the ground floor," Juan Martin told Yoshua. They came around the corner.

"Ugh, there must be a line of thirty people waiting and only two overworked bureaucrats behind the counter, shielded by plate glass. Professor, grab a number from that red dispenser next to the wall," Juan Martin suggested.

Besides the crowd in the line, other people made the congestion worse as they walked up and down the corridor to other offices. After taking a number, they were lucky to get two seats when a young couple got up to leave.

They sat on the hard wooden bench. After a few minutes of holding his briefcase, Yoshua put it on the floor near his feet. To his surprise, another briefcase was there. "Quickly." he asked in a loud voice so everyone could hear.

"Excuse me, to whom does this briefcase belong?" No one answered.

"Whose briefcase is this?"

Again, no one answered. Concerned there was a bomb in the briefcase, Yoshua thought fast about how he could save the greatest number of people. Jumping up onto the bench, he took everyone by surprise as he yelled at the top of his lungs in his most "take command" tone.

"To whom does this briefcase belong?" Now people paid attention. The man sitting opposite Yoshua said,

"The couple who sat there before you; the man came in with a briefcase."

"My name is Professor Yoshua Rosenberg. I'm an officer in an anti-terrorist unit in the Israeli army. This is a suspicious object." He pointed to a woman with a cell phone in her hand who had stopped talking to listen to him.

"Please, call the police and tell them we have found a suspicious briefcase, left by someone." Yoshua prayed the scared civilians would carry out his next command.

"Now, as calmly as possible, will the people closest to the door leave the building and tell anyone they see outside to get away from the building." Twenty seconds later, Yoshua added.

"Now, everyone around me, please leave. Stay calm and orderly." But before that could happen, a few people further along the corridor panicked and ran toward the door, pushing, shoving, and screaming. Pandemonium broke out within seconds. Employees poured out of their offices, adding to the confusion and difficulty to escape. Still standing on the bench, Yoshua looked at the mass of hysterical people, untrained in emergencies. Faced with an immediate life-threatening scenario, their survival instinct kicked in, and they would do anything to live.

Seeing there was no way to get to the door, Yoshua jumped off the bench, grabbed Juan's arm, and hugged the wall, heading against the flow of the crowd. They went only a few meters before Yoshua opened the closest door, and they ran toward the far end of the room.

"This must be Divine intervention," Juan Martin said.

"Why?"

"This is the archives room of the Registry office. See, the room is full of long rows of metal shelves with thousands of files."

"Great, but let's get as far away from the explosion as possible. As they ran through the large room, they gathered two state employees along with them. As they reached the back wall and ducked, a massive explosion tore through the building, sending shock waves throughout the structure. The walls shook—metal shelves and cardboard files tumbled on them from every direction. It was raining documents, folders, and binders.

The files buried Yoshua, but still on his feet in a squatting position. His ears were ringing, and he felt something wet on his face.

"Juan Martin, are you Okay?" Yoshua called out.

"I think so, but we smothered in files and this metal shelf has fallen on us."

"I will try to get us out of this mess," Yoshua said.

Using his powerful thigh muscles, Yoshua thrust his weight against a metal shelf. Keeping his back straight to avoid injury, he lifted the mass little by little, centimeter by centimeter. He gave one last shove, fueled by adrenaline, and the shelf toppled over in the opposite direction, freeing them from their prison of metal, cardboard, and paper.

"Oy!" Yoshua said.

"What's wrong?" Juan Martin asked.

"Unfortunately, a falling metal box struck the man next to me. It's now embedded deep in his skull. I am covered in his blood, tissue, and bone fragments."

Yoshua's body went into shock. He felt transported back in time, and he sat on a destroyed bus in Jerusalem with his friend's blood and body parts splattered all over his torso.

"Yoshua, why are you so silent?" When Juan received no answer, he called repeatedly to Yoshua. After the tenth time, Yoshua heard him.

"Juan, I'll be okay. Give me two minutes to do my breathing exercises. They help calm me," Yoshua replied.

Everything around Juan was in total shambles, but he felt good fortune was with him. He waited for the professor to gather his wits.

"Professor, I am happy for three reasons," Juan called out.

"What three reasons?"

"God brought you from the Holy Land to help my family. You saved me from being torn apart by a Basque separatist's bomb, and the aisle in which we have found ourselves, holds the file they were looking.

Yoshua tried to assist Juan to his feet. He pushed the helping hand away and commanded, "My dear professor, we aren't going anywhere, because right in front of our noses is the file we need. With this mess, it'll be weeks before the government will have time to find it for us. Sit now, and I'll find the file for the old chapel."

Amid the chaos, Juan's pragmatism take-charge attitude amazed Yoshua. The man had spunk. "Give me a second, and I'll help you. I have to do something first." Yoshua turned to the other state employee, checked his status, and reset his dislocated shoulder.

For the next twenty minutes, while the entire building crawled with police, firefighters, medical teams, and reporters, the two dust-covered and bloodied men searched in the aisle. Juan led the way and appeared to have some mysterious force guiding him. Juan stopped. Yoshua, who was scanning files to his left, right and on the floor, smacked into Juan's back. He backed away, looked up to his right, and spotted what they were looking for. The file, dated 1895, had the word "Update" written across the cover. Without a word, he put his left hand on Juan's shoulder to steady himself, reached up, and grabbed the file. It didn't take Juan more than a few seconds to understand what Yoshua was doing and for them to make their way to the photocopy machine on the opposite wall.

"Look, the photocopier is still on. Let's clean off the dust and rubble," Yoshua said.

"The explosion hasn't knocked out the building's electricity," Juan Martin added.

They cleared away the mess and copied the file. Yoshua noticed a page with a file number of the Catholic Church Archives in Granada. His total recall kicked in, and he realized it was the number of the file that contained the coded pages Gefen had deciphered.

When they finished, the state employee who witnessed the entire escapade called to them.

"Please help me over to my desk." With Juan at his left and Yoshua on his right, the employee shuffled over to his desk. He pulled open his drawer and took out three rubber stamps. The first was the official stamp of the archives, the second stated that a copy was true to the original, and the third was his stamp of notary.

"Please photocopy another copy of the file while I prepared some forms." With both copies ready and the forms filled out by Juan, the employee certified the copies with both rubber stamps and his stamp of notary. Juan and Yoshua couldn't believe their eyes. The employee handed them the notarized copies, kissed both men.

"Thank you for saving my life. God bless both of you."

Yoshua put his copy in his briefcase and guided Juan and the state employee toward the door of the destroyed archive room.

"If we work together, we can remove enough debris from in front of the door so we can get out," Yoshua said.

After three minutes of working, Yoshua and Juan pulled the door open enough for the three to squeeze out. The scene in the corridor was devastating. There was a gaping hole in the outside wall where the bomb had detonated. The ceiling had collapsed. Everywhere laid dead and wounded, still unattended. They met three emergency workers who took the wounded state employee off their hands. Another medic checked them both. It took the medic three minutes to clean the blood off Yoshua. When he found no wounds, he commented.

"How did the person next to you die?" Yoshua explained what happened. The medic used his radio to contact the police and tell them the story.

Yoshua and Juan made their way out of the damaged building. Forewarned by the medic, the police waited for them.

"We heard from eyewitnesses about the foreigner who spoke fluent Spanish. He warned everyone about the possibility that the briefcase being a bomb. Are you that man?" the police officer asked Yoshua.

A woman ran up to Yoshua and hugged him.

"Thank you for saving my life. This man is a hero," the woman told the police officer.

Yoshua turned to the officer.

"Yes, I warned everyone to be calm and leave orderly. However, the order broke down and a stampede to the door occurred."

The police officer turned on his radio and reported, "Chief, I have found the man who warned everyone."

"I'll be there as fast as possible," the chief of police answered. Ten minutes later, the chief of police showed up with his entourage. The chief and the commander of the local Guardia Civil interrogated Yoshua and Juan for forty minutes.

\*\*\*\*\*

The police finally released Yoshua and Juan. They returned to the car. The blast went in the other direction and they found the car undamaged. They got in and were grateful to drive back to Nido de Aguila, alive in one piece. Neither man paid attention to their surroundings. On the way back to Nido, Juan missed their turnoff. Both men were lost in their private thoughts until they saw the sign "Welcome to Granada." Juan pulled over to the side of the road and tried to gather his wits.

"I'm sorry, I missed the turnoff and now I've added an extra hour to our trip."

"My friend, this is the hand of God directing us."

Juan thought to himself, *"This Jew is a strange man."*

"Juan, please take me to the bishop's residence."

"Why would you want to see the Bishop?"

"Mr. Ophosi, I'm serious. The bishop will help us."

When they arrived at the bishop's residence, the guard at the gate called the house to announce them. The bishop answered the phone.

"Professor Rosenberg, let him inside." Juan pulled up to the front of the house. The bishop, followed by an entourage of ten men, came out to meet them. In the confusion, Yoshua forgot they wore the same clothes from the bombing. Plaster dust and blood covered his shirt.

"My God, Yoshua, are you okay? You have blood all over you." the bishop said, shocked to see them in such a state.

Juan stood in awe until the bishop stepped forward. He went to his knee and took the bishop's hand and kissed his ring. The bishop put his hands on Jaun's shoulders and lifted him.

"There will be time for formality later. Show my friends where they can take a shower. Please find them clean clothes." Everyone had heard the news of the explosion and of the foreigner who saved so many lives.

"This is the hero from the registry office," one of the staff members said. Every one applauded. Yoshua bowed his head.

"Thank you," Yoshua said as he bowed his head toward them.

"Bishop, I will leave the file with you to peruse while I take a shower and change clothes."

When he returned, Yoshua made a request.

"May I use a phone to call home to let everyone know I'm safe?"

"Use the phone as long as you need," the bishop replied.

After Juan showered and changed. They asked him to join Yoshua and the bishop. Juan walked into the bishop's ornate office. Once again, he went up to the bishop, fell to his knees, and kissed the ring on the bishop's hand. The bishop helped the elderly man to his feet. He smiled at him.

"This is the first time you've met a bishop?" Tongue-tied, Juan couldn't get even a single sound out of his throat. He was in awe of how Yoshua moved so freely with the bishop and his assistant, the monsignor.

After reading the file and discussing the project for fifteen minutes, the bishop turned to Juan.

"I believe after the hundreds of years that the Ophosi family helped the Church, it's time we return the favor." The bishop removed a piece of official stationery from his desk. On it he wrote:

> The Roman Catholic Church thanks Juan Martin Alphonso Ophosi and the Ophosi family for generations of faithful service to the church and the selfless donation of their building for use as the local church for hundreds of years. May the Lord bless him and his family with a life of health, wealth, and happiness.

The bishop turned to Yoshua to bless him.

"Yoshua, may your negotiations be straightforward and honest," he said, eyeing Juan, who understood the implication.

"Shuki, please keep me informed about everything you find during the excavation." With the blessings and warnings completed, the three men finished drinking their coffee and said their goodbyes.

The car trip back to the village was quiet and contemplative. Juan thought, *I had such an excellent plan for fleecing this foreigner, but now that the bishop has his eye on me, I must re-evaluate my entire approach to the deal."*

\*\*\*\*\*

Yoshua also had time to reflect on what happened, and while his mind wandered, he thought of his *biological father.*

*"Why am I thinking about my father after so many years? My father's an enigma. Mom told me he came out of war-torn Europe to the Holy Land. He had a great love for the Jewish people and the Land of Israel. Twenty years ago, when I wanted to learn about my family roots, I came up with nothing. Would I still hit a dead end today? My father entered Eretz Yisrael illegally. The only record of him existed when the British army arrested him as a Palestinian terrorist."*

*"That's a laugh. During the 1940s, the British Mandate called Jews 'Palestinians'. I should have asked my mom to let me have another look at my father's British Mandate ID card. It must be twenty years since I have seen the ID card. I was so excited to see the name 'David' written on the line that identified the document owner's father, that I didn't pay enough attention to the other information on the document. Well, at least we named David after his great-grandfather. I wish I had known him."*

Yoshua put his thoughts aside.

"Juan, please stop at the next place I can buy a new cell phone."

In the next shopping area they came to, they found a cell phone store. Ten minutes later, Yoshua came out with a new phone.

When they arrived at the hotel in Nido de Aguila, the two men who were strangers only two days before embraced each other as friends.

"Professor, remember to be on time for the meeting with the attorney," Juan Martin said.

Back in his room, Yoshua sat at the desk. He was meticulous and kept an up-to-date backup of his cell phone on his laptop. He plugged in the USB cable and downloaded the information he lost when the explosion destroyed his phone.

Even though he showered at the bishop's residence, Yoshua felt the need for another. He got in the shower and stood under the hot running water for almost twenty minutes. As the hot water did its work, Yoshua eased out of command-and-control mode for the first time since the bombing. The scene at the registry office penetrated his consciousness—flashing red and blue lights, the blare of sirens, and the screams of the injured and frightened.

Yoshua had experienced a similar scenario. Now he couldn't keep out the horrible memories of what happened in Israel thirty years earlier when he was a passenger on a city bus blown up by a bomb placed by Palestinian terrorists. In that case, his best friend from the army, Yaniv Harel, saved his life. Yaniv sat in the seat in front of Yoshua, took most of the blast. Yaniv's entire torso ended up splattered over his entire face and shirt.

When the medical teams evacuated the bus, they found Yoshua in shock, not moving, barely breathing. His mind was trying to come to grips with a new horrifying reality. What the medics found him in shock, covered in blood, tissue, and bone fragments. At the hospital, he remembered understanding everything that was being said, but couldn't speak. He wanted to tell the doctors he was fine. He wanted to tell the nurses removing his friend's remains from his face that they should do the job with more dignity and not wipe with gauze pads and throw them away as if it was nothing. It would be another two days before he could communicate with the world that had so desecrated and humiliated human life.

The flashback caused goose bumps over his arms, and a cold sweat broke out on his forehead and back. He waited a few minutes, dried off, and put on his pajamas. He tapped his cell phone and opened the photo gallery app. Yoshua swiped back and forth between a vintage photo of his father and a recent photo of his son, David. It was uncanny how much the two looked alike. He wondered what traits he inherited from his long-dead father.

# BLUEPRINTS

Yoshua sat at the desk in the hotel room and attempted to write an email when he noticed his hands shaking. *"I'll do my mental exercises to calm myself,"* *he thought.* But, after five minutes, he still had a hard time keeping his fingers on the keyboard. "This is it. Here comes a full-blown attack!" As much as he tried to control his body with his mind, it seemed to have a mind of its own—like a severe case of Parkinson's disease. Yoshua grabbed his phone and tried to select the number for home, but his shaking fingers kept touching the wrong name. It took six tries to tap the correct number.

"Hello, who is this, please?" said David.

By this time, Yoshua's teeth chattered so violently he could barely speak. He clenched his jaw as hard as he could and spoke with his mouth closed, "Beni (my son) get your mother quickly."

*"Ima* (Mom) come quick, *Aba* (Dad) is having a seizure." Tears poured along his face. This wasn't the first time David had been around Yoshua when he had an attack. He understood this was the price his father paid for working in the anti-terrorist unit. You can't kill close up and have friends die in his arms without consequences.

*"Aba,* you know we love you, and we'll help make this pass quickly and—"

"—Shuki *ahuvati* (my love), I'm here," Ruth said as she grabbed the phone from David.

"I should've known that if there was trouble somewhere in the world, you'd be in the middle of it." Hearing Ruth's voice caused the shaking to subside. The army therapist had trained Ruth on how to treat Yoshua. These were tested procedures she had used many times.

She understood the importance of using specific words and tone of voice to help him get the seizure under control. There was a silver lining to his attacks; it brought them closer together. While they talked, Yoshua laid his soul bare and shared his innermost feelings with Ruth. It was the best therapy possible. The more they did sessions together, the faster his recovery. When she held him, she got the best results. The therapy had worked over the phone several times before.

While Ruth talked with Yoshua, David picked up his cell phone and called his uncle, Ysrael, Yoshua's younger brother. He was an officer in the police's famous anti-terrorist unit. It was standard procedure when Yoshua had a seizure; first Ruth would treat him and afterwards Ysrael would talk to him.

The brothers shared many of the same experiences.

"Uncle Ysrael, its David. *Aba* is having an attack. *Aba* was the foreigner who saved those people in the Cordoba bombing." In moments like this, Ysrael wished there wasn't a conspiracy of silence around his brother. Yoshua thought the two of them were the entire family they had. Quite the opposite. They had a vast family, and everyone waited for the day when they could welcome Yoshua into their lives.

Their family helped Ysrael get through troublesome times after facing death and dying around him. Ysrael's job brought him to so many bombed-out buses he lost count of the number of dead bodies he dealt with over the years. More than once, Ysrael hunted terrorists with his brother's reserve unit. Together, they spoke for the dead; bringing balance to the world; justice for those murdered by acts of barbarism.

Ysrael waited for a text message from David to let him know that Ruth had finished talking to Yoshua.

"Yael, will you sit with me while I talk with my brother?" Ysrael asked his wife. They went into their bedroom, and Yael wrapped her arms around Ysrael to support him while he helped Yoshua. When the text message arrived, it included Yoshua's new phone number.

Ysrael and Yoshua talked for twenty minutes. By the end of the conversation, Yoshua's jaw unclenched. His hands stopped shaking, and he smiled.

"Thanks for the help. I love you, and I'll do anything for you. You only have to do is ask."

"No problem: Now, get out of that hotel room, find something to eat, take a walk around town, buy presents for your kids, and something nice for Ruth. Love you, we'll talk later." After the call ended, Ysrael thought, *"Yoshua wasn't spouting idle words; he saved my life three times and once took a bullet intended for me. How do people go through life without this kind of relationship? We're brothers, genetically, spiritually, and comrades-in-arms. It's our relationship that gives purpose to everything we've done in our lives."*

*****

After the momentous day in Cordova, Yoshua wanted nothing more than to take Ysrael's advice. He wanted to relax and have a quiet meal. He headed downstairs to the hotel's quaint, rustic dining room, with its rectangular solid oak tables and sturdy chairs.

The room had four tables set with white tablecloths. Each one had a vase of colorful flowers.

When he sat, the waiter came over.

"What can I get you this evening, professor?"

"Fresh salad, orange juice and fresh fruit for dessert," Yoshua requested.

As he got up to leave, Padre Emanuel walked up to his table. "*Buenos noches*, senior Professor."

"*Buenos noches, padre*, good to see you."

"I'd like to you about the little chapel."

"Please join me for a cup of your wonderful local coffee," Yoshua offered.

"Thank you for the offer, but I recently finished dinner, and I can't be late for the catechism class I teach this evening; I shouldn't linger too long." He sat opposite Yoshua and got down to business.

"Since this entire business began with the old chapel, I also became interested in its history. I wrote a history of the church in our fair village, and I dug around in the old files in the parish archives. As you know, the land bordering on the west and east of the chapel belongs to the Church. I found the architect's blueprints showing the entire area when the church added two classrooms to the adjacent school about seventy-five years ago. I made a copy because I thought they would be of some use to you."

"Well, this is a pleasant surprise, Padre. Thank you very much for your help."

"I read your second book after they translated it into Spanish last year. I was late for Mass for the first time in twelve years. It was hard to put it down."

"So now, I thank you on two accounts—first, for the blueprints, and second, for the compliment. I never intended for anyone to get into trouble for reading my books."

"It was well worth it, Professor. I would very much like to discuss with you about your theory on the evolution of legends. Your command of the subject is inspiring."

Padre Emanuel and Yoshua rose from their chairs, shook hands, and said goodbye. Yoshua paid the bill, headed back to his room, and thought about his visitor.

*"The Vatican hammer will fall; the question is when. The padre's too concerned about a little or nothing of a place. Everything connected to the chapel is suspicious. This scenario calls for one of my favorite English idioms: I'm going to 'play my cards close to my chest.' Intelligence is power and knowing when to reveal information is an art. Until the time is right, I'll play along and be gracious, open, and cooperative."*

\*\*\*\*\*

*Yoshua* cleared off the desk and turned on the reading lamp. He unrolled ten centimeters of the blueprint, placed his Bible in the upper left corner, his electric razor on the lower left corner, and the heavy glass ashtray on the right side. At first glance, he couldn't find the chapel, but he saw the parking lot and, to the east, a three-story building. He found the houses of the neighbors to the north and west. He worked backward from the three-story building and came to a structure larger than the chapel. The shape of the structure wasn't right. It was only by identifying the school next door to the chapel that he could identify the building.

Since the first day in Nido de Aguila, he'd been back to the chapel several times. It showed no internal signs of being more than one room, and he assumed that the rest of the structure had another purpose. According to the blueprints, on the northeastern end of the primary room, there was another room of the same size that didn't appear to have an external door.

The significance of the additional room struck Yoshua, and he let out a low-pitched, "Wow!" He thought, "The church must've bricked up the room. People *don't block off rooms. Building costs are too expensive to close off space arbitrarily without a good reason. Maybe, there exists something intrinsically offensive to Catholic belief that caused them to seal it. What offensively secrets does this room hold which would cause the Church to seal it? Is this what I'm looking for? Maybe I'll find the gniza there? Will there be clues to where they buried their old holy papers?"*

In the excitement, Yoshua forgot the time.

"My God, I'm five minutes late for my meeting to buy the chapel." As Yoshua gathered his things together, he thought, *"I'll keep the sealed room a secret."*

# NEGOTIATIONS

Out the door he went. Leaping down the stairs three at a time, Yoshua rushed out the door of the hotel and into the cool mountain night air of southern Spain. The great fireball of the sun was in its last stages of setting and the last orange-yellow rays of the day were penetrating through a few wispy clouds outlining the hills behind the village, creating a multicolored halo. The cool, westerly breeze caressed his face like the hand of a lover as he trotted along the dusty lane, kicking up tiny clouds of dust with each step. Arriving at Attorney Rodriguez's law office, he found the place stuffed with a large assortment of people.

The entire Ophosi family had gathered there, along with the mayor of the town, Hector Martinez. Juan took Yoshua by the hand and introduced him to every family member.

"Now we will toast our guest," Juan Martin said.

"Do you have any beer?" Yoshua asked.

"What kind of civilized man doesn't drink wine?" Juan gave him a strange look. Shrugged his shoulders and gave him a bottle of local Spanish beer. Yoshua wasn't about to explain why he couldn't drink their wine. First, everyone toasted Yoshua for saving Juan's life in Cordoba. They toasted Juan, the mayor, the king, the government, and on and on, until everyone was more than a little inebriated.

After Juan toasted everyone, he felt the effect of the alcohol. He grabbed Yoshua by the cuff of his shirt with his left hand and Rodriguez with his right hand. Juan dragged them over to the table and sat them down.

"Well, my friends, let's get down to business."

"From the plans the parish priest provided me, the total area of the building, along with the front and back court, is two hundred twenty square meters. My client appreciates your saving his life the other day. He has instructed me to inform you can have the property for twenty-five hundred euros a square meter, for five hundred fifty thousand euros," said Rodriguez, clearing his throat with a small cough.

Stunned, Yoshua sat there with his mouth open. "The going price of the buildings in town is five hundred fifty euros a square meter. I can buy an empty five hundred square meter plot for thirteen thousand euros," Yoshua said.

The picture of Avraham, the patriarch, negotiating with Efron, the Hittite, came to his mind. Avraham sought to buy the cave of Machpelah as a sepulcher to bury his wife, Sarah. Efron first praised Avraham as a grand prince of the land.

"My lord, listen to me: a piece of land worth four hundred shekels of silver. What is that between me and you?" Efron knew Avraham needed a place to bury his wife and would not haggle over the price too much, so he demanded a king's ransom. It looked like Yoshua was in the same trap. They knew he would give anything to buy the little chapel.

Yoshua smiled back at them and thought for a few seconds. "Please inform my illustrious friend that I appreciate his regard for me and that he does me great honor to sell me this diminished little hovel, whose garden is a bed of beautiful native thorns, brier, and stones. It appears we're not talking about the same building. Dear friends, what's this sum between honorable men? My offer is one hundred twenty-five thousand euros."

Juan's face darkened, and his eyes narrowed; abruptly, the entire room became quiet. No one breathed for the next five seconds. A big smile broke out on Juan's face. This was a man after his own heart. He liked nothing better than bargaining over an item.

"Don't forget the historical value of the building. Since you saved my life, we will be large and offer the building to you for four hundred fifty thousand euros." Yoshua rolled up his sleeves, pulled out a pad and pencil, and doodled a few figures. He folded the paper and handed it to Rodriguez without looking at Juan. Before Rodriguez could open it, Juan grabbed the note from his hand. It read one hundred thirty-five thousand euros.

Juan turned red as he thought of his loss of face before the entire family. He had told them he would fleece the rich foreigner and make everyone a small fortune. His hands were sweaty and his head itched. He countered Yoshua's offer with his own, "Three hundred fifty thousand euros." This brought a gasp from every one of his relatives as they realized they had lost almost thirty-six percent of their promised riches.

"How fortunate that our mutual friend, the Bishop of Granada, has blessed this transaction," Yoshua said calmly, looking up at the crowd of Spanish faces in front of him. This brought more gasps from the Ophosi clan. Juan had failed to tell the family that the bishop knew about the sale. He remembered the warning the bishop gave him, and a look of concern came over his face. His dilemma was a profit or the damnation of his soul. His conscience was bothering him, but not as much as his need to restore the family fortune.

"My friends, you have three minutes to decide on my final offer of..." Yoshua paused for a good ten seconds to be sure he had everyone's attention. "One hundred forty thousand euros paid in cash tomorrow." Before they could answer, he added, "After three minutes, I lower my offer by five thousand euros a minute."

*"What guts this fellow has. Faced with adversity, he launches an attack,"* thought Juan. Considering the scenario, he came up with his own offensive. "My dear friend, Professor Rosenberg, I'll give it to you for three hundred thousand euros and you have two minutes to decide or the place won't be for sale. There are more fish in the sea."

"You want the price for a whale, but you're selling is a sardine. For five years, you've failed to sell the building. There are government restrictions on the uses of historical buildings, makes this tough sell."

Juan's eyes opened wide as he thought, *"How did the Israeli find out about our property and the conditions surrounding it? He must have learned of them when he and the bishop met with the cardinal."*

Yoshua smirked and simply sat there, looking at his watch as the seconds ticked away. After forty seconds, the Ophosi tribe got a little uncomfortable. After a minute passed, and still Yoshua didn't look up or make a sound. With only forty-five seconds left to the ultimatum, everyone yelled at once. Bickering back and forth, the seconds ticked away. It was now a matter of honor. If Yoshua didn't answer within the two minutes, they could not sell the building—the family's only nest egg. They needed the money so badly that with fifteen seconds to go, everyone was screaming at Juan to sell. Finally, with three seconds left, Juan, very frustrated, leaped from his chair, knocking it over. Looking at the calm man opposite him, he gave in to the demands.

The entire time, Yoshua was thinking, *"How unfair this entire story had become! Here's a descendant of a converted Jew whose ancestors had made money off the troubles of his fellow Jews. Now, here I am arguing with him over the price of the building that had originally been Jewish. Here I am seconds from paying them blood money."* On the outside, Yoshua was as cool as a cucumber, but inside he erupted like a volcano.

"Okay, one hundred fifty thousand euros, but the entire sum in cash and the deed will only list fifty thousand euros, so we have to pay fewer taxes," said Juan.

To the second, at the end of the two minutes, Yoshua looked up with a smile.

"My dear and honorable friend, you've done me a great honor to sell your ancestral holdings to me. For myself, and on behalf of the university and my Israeli government, I thank everyone you. Tomorrow, I'll go to the bank in Granada and wire the money."

Rodriguez pulled out the prepared contract and land deed transfer.

"Friends, please sit here with me and I will show you where to sign on the contract," the attorney said.

"Congratulations to the two of you," Rodriguez said, smiling. The lawyer handed each man a copy of the contract after two witnesses signed it.

"Professor Rosenberg, here are your keys," the attorney said as he handed them over.

After signing the contract, Yoshua wandered over to the chapel with his new keys in his trembling hands. He sensed this place would change his life. There would start a grand adventure. There was something mysterious and mystic about the structure. He felt this little building held treasures and answers too many of his questions. This fateful summer evening marked the beginning of the next phase of his journey to find the Light of Justice and so much more.

*****

Back at the hotel, Yoshua found his cell phone battery had run out of electricity. "I must use a local landline to call home and tell them the good news," Yoshua thought.

He fought with the local phone system for twelve minutes before he got a call through to Ruth. "*Mazal tov*, babe, the building is ours!"

"Oh, Shuki, that's wonderful news!"

"Babe, my new cell phone is dead at the moment, and the phone service here is terrible. Please call Gavriel and let him know."

"Sure, no problem; I'll see you soon, darling."

"Ruthie, how are the kids?"

"Everyone is fine and missing you. David has asked to come and work on the dig and I told him OK. My father will move in and take care of the kids while we're gone." Ruth smiled to herself.

"Shuki, I am so proud of what you accomplished."

"Please send my regards to your father. Give the kids big kisses for me. See you soon, my love. Bye."

Now, after the strain of the negotiations, Yoshua eased his guard. His mind wandered, and he reminisced about his friendship with Elisha.

"We grew up together and went to the same schools until we were fourteen. Afterwards, he went to Yeshiva

Neve Choron, and I went to the humanities specialty school. Even though we went to different schools, we continued to connect through our mutual love of archery. In the army, I went into the General Staff's rangers unit and I accepted him into the pilots' course—and he was a superstar. It surprised everyone when he chose helicopters over fighters. He became an attack helicopter pilot and studied for the army *rabbinut* (to become a rabbi). He was an extraordinary pilot and prevented many a dangerous scenario with his skillful flying and accurate firing from his Apache Longbow.

"Elisha, an ardent Zionist, instilled in me the love of my people and country. He taught me everything I know concerning the Inquisition. Now, what's he going to think about my buying something back that originally belonged to our people?"

Death and destruction had filled Yoshua's military service. After outstanding service during the first two years in his unit, they sent him to Officer Training School. During his four years as an officer, he lost sixteen men from his unit. None of their exploits ever became public knowledge. He kept the memory of those unsung heroes close to his heart. The files of his unit's operations existed somewhere buried deep within the archives of the army. He never left one of his men's bodies behind. He brought every one of them home for burial—from twelve different countries.

After the army, Elisha became a rabbi and a teacher in a *yeshiva* high school. Yoshua went on to university, where his brilliance became apparent. His eidetic memory forged his meteoric rise within academia. Often, in times of reflection, he thought of his childhood friend. Even though they went their separate ways, they still stayed close friends. Little did Yoshua know that besides being his friend, Elisha's assignment was to stay close to him.

After entering the army, Yoshua gave up his archery. Instead, Elisha encouraged him to study together. Often, they would talk about their experiences in the army. Another thing Yoshua didn't know was that, because of him, Elisha didn't become a fighter pilot. Elisha understood he had a better chance of helping Yoshua as an attack helicopter pilot than as a fighter pilot. Twice, Elisha assisted in the withdrawal of Yoshua's unit by providing cover fire from the air.

*"One thing that still bothers me,"* Yoshua thought, *"is that Elisha isn't only smart, but brilliant, yet he stays out of the limelight. He could've been a professor if he'd chosen to do so, yet, he worked with teenagers instead. He could've been a world-class archer. Yet, despite the time he invested in the sport, he enjoyed going out to the range and shooting. His answers to every one of my questions are always the same. 'Yoshua, they're mundane things with no deeper meaning. Now, working with our young and shaping their minds and souls, that's rewarding.' Well, it's still nice to know I have a friend out there from the days when we were in diapers together."* Yoshua opened his laptop and sent Elisha an email about his day and how he'd bought the little chapel that Jews once owned, stolen, given to the church, and now back in Jewish hands.

Early the next morning, Yoshua was on the phone contacting his team members about flights to Spain. As he spoke with each one, he thought about what an impressive team he'd assembled. Ruth was a well-known anthropologist and archaeologist; Aviva, a specialist in restoration; Sasha an expert photographer and molecular biologist; and David, post-high school, pre-army, full of enthusiasm.

***** 

Gefen's fast advancement in her studies of restoration amazed Aviva. Her art work moved forward on a parallel track. Aviva also noticed that Gefen often asked, "How is the search for *Bet Midrash Ohel Rivka* progressing?"

Aviva felt sad going off now while Gefen was advancing so well with her studies. It was awful she couldn't bring her with them.

"Gefen, *chamuda* (cutie), Yoshua called to tell me the good news and how much he appreciated your help in identifying the location of *Ohel Rivka*."

"Aviva, I would like to come with you to Spain. I think it would be a magnificent experience to restore a five hundred-year-old building to its previous glory."

Aviva stared at Gefen, not sure what to say. She thought, *"God, I wish this kid was mine."*

"Aviva, I've checked out what's involved—the tickets, health insurance, food, lodging, and security. I talked with my parents and they agree this would be an excellent opportunity for me to see if I like art restoration before investing in three years of university study. My father said he will pay for the entire expenses."

"Listen, *chamuda*, I'm only one peon. Yoshua is the effendi. He has the ultimate word. If you want to get his approval, you first have to get Ruth's. Whatever Ruth wants, is what will happen!"

"Will you talk to her about me?"

"Sure, there's nothing in the world I'd like more than to have you with me in Spain." Aviva thought about it for a few moments and realized what the real problem.

"Gefen, you need to understand the problem is not the dig itself, but that David will be there. Putting two healthy teenagers of the opposite sex, of the same age and in such close quarters, is not something a mother of a religious boy would find acceptable." Aviva replied. She remembered every crazy thing she did in her last year of high school—things that would shock Ruth, her best friend, had she known.

*****

Ruth called Dr. Arieli to tell him the good news. She didn't know how well informed he was about anything involving Yoshua. "Are you going to be taking Aviva's brilliant apprentice, Gefen Nimrodi?" Dr. Arieli asked.

"You need to understand. I'm only going for three weeks because David has to enter the army soon. I know Yoshua would not be crazy about David and Gefen living under the same roof. You know I would fulfill almost any request you would make of me, but I'm also concerned about David and Gefen being in such proximity for three weeks."

"I considered this point and weighed the pros and cons. Besides the fact that Gefen wants this so much, it would be beneficial. After the help she has provided, you owe her something for deciphering the coded documents from the Bishop of Granada's archives."

"Yes, I am aware of it, sir," Ruth replied.

"She has sunk her teeth into her work and she could learn so much from Aviva. It would be like on-the-job training. If you run into any other codes, she could solve them for you. Besides, they are only two teenagers and you are four adults. She could sleep with Aviva, and David with Sasha," Dr. Arieli said.

"Having Sasha watch after the morals of my son would be like asking a cat to guard the cream. However, I'll consider what you've said and speak to Yoshua. I'll call you as soon as we decide." Ruth laughed at the thought of Sasha as her son's moral counselor.

She was still smiling when the phone rang.

"Ruth, Dr. Arieli called me to ask if we would consider taking Gefen with us on the expedition," Aviva said.

"He called me, also, asking that we reward Gefen for her contribution."

"Ruth, he said she will cover her expenses."

"She's very serious about this, but I'm concerned with David and Gefen being in such proximity for three weeks?"

"Despite that problem, we owe her. Gefen would benefit from the experience. We need to let her know we appreciate her contributions," Aviva commented.

"I'll call Yoshua and ask his opinion."

"Thank you, I'll talk with you later."

Ruth called Yoshua in Spain.

"Hi, babe, what's on your mind?" Yoshua asked.

"Yoshua, please consider what I'm about to ask you before you answer me."

"Yes, what is it?"

"I received a phone call from Aviva asking that we invite Gefen to join our team in Spain, in appreciation of her help. She said she would cover her own costs."

"Listen, babe, I appreciate the help Gefen gave us, but it's also a matter of insurance, her total lack of experience, and that David will be there."

"Shuki, honey, she will cover her own expenses, including insurance. As far as David goes, we are four adults. I hope that between the four of us, we'll be able to keep a lid on the juvenile hormones."

"Aren't you concerned about her total inexperience in the field?"

"Gefen has done us an enormous favor by breaking those codes. We should show her our appreciation by inviting her to Spain with us. She's keen to learn. I think the positive aspects offsets her lack of experience." Ruth had run into the brick wall of the conspiracy of silence around Yoshua. She wished she could tell him the Dr. Arieli had already decided the issue.

"Babe, I'll think about it and get back to you."

*****

Yoshua relaxed on the bed, watched the slow movement of the blades of the ceiling fan. He considered his team. *"Ruthie received her PhD in taphonomy, making her an expert in knowing how objects decay and degrade over time. Her bachelor's degree in physics and chemistry is crucial to interpreting data from both organic and inorganic sources to differentiate between the work of ancient people and that from artifacts of living creatures and elemental forces.*

*"Sasha brings a brilliant mind and a BSc in molecular biology. I remember the first time I laid eyes on him in my introductory archaeology class in the spring of 2009. Smart aleck flashed me a wicked smile,*

*blue-eyed and blond-haired. Yeah, okay, I was jealous because he looked like he worked out three times a week at a gym and had a body most people only had in their dreams. But, I have to give it to him, he's been fiercely loyal from day one and no one could ask for a better friend. And, he gave up two weeks of his summer to volunteer at the excavation in Jerusalem."*

*Sasha showed up every day and during his breaks, he photographed the site and the people working there— granted, he got an up-close look at a Jebusite home from the 12<sup>th</sup> century BCE. I have to give it to him; those photos were breathtaking. He is a good Russian boy, three years as a soldier in the Golani infantry brigade, a PhD student, now on the hunt for a serious girlfriend. I enjoy having him as my* ben beit *("adopted" son).*

*"Aviva and Ruthie—both forty-eight years old, exact opposites, and best friends. Go figure."*

*Images of Aviva and Ruth flashed inside Yoshua's head—coming in and out of focus in quick succession— Ruthie on the university lawn, at her mother's funeral, standing under the* chupah *as a beautiful bride, Aviva running on the track, and in her stunning navy dress at the wedding. The images kept coming, alternating with flashbacks from Yoshua's youth, and brief moments of sleep.*

\*\*\*\*\*

Ruth and Aviva's families lived next to each other for over forty years in Jerusalem's Rahavia neighborhood on Ibn Ezra Street. Their fathers served in active military service together. They were fellow officers in reserve duty in the same battalion. Ruth and Aviva went to preschool together from the age of fourteen months and were inseparable.

Ruth was two centimeters shorter than Aviva, a little heavier, with curly brunette hair, and deep, bright, smiling brown eyes. She was not a stunning beauty like her friend, but she had a pleasant disposition and a cute, round face. It was her magnificent smile that was the heartbreaker. When she turned that smile on someone, they simply melted. Ruth was very gregarious, which always seemed to attract the boys. On the surface, the two girls were complete opposites, and maybe that's what attracted them to each other when they first met. As they grew up, their interests remained similar until high school, where Ruth majored in humanities and Aviva in natural science.

In the army, the girls had their first major separation. Ruth went to the artillery, where she became a staff sergeant teaching new recruits about munitions and weapon systems. Aviva ended up in the communications corps, where she advanced to officer's training school and ended up in charge of communications for an infantry brigade. The girls called each other the entire time and tried to arrange their vacations from the army at the same time so they could be together. Few of their new friends could understand this almost obsession to be with each other.

University followed her army service, and that's where Ruth met Yoshua. The tall, handsome scholar turned many girls' heads. People talked about him as one of the most brilliant minds on campus. He often missed classes, as he was an officer in one of the army's most elite secret units. Since both of them were in the same anthropology and archaeology classes, their paths crossed often. It was only in the second year that Yoshua got up enough courage to ask Ruth out on a date. They saw each other and study for exams together.

\*\*\*\*\*

That summer, a terrorist left a bomb at a bus stop in downtown. Ruth's mother, Miriam, had sat on a bench above the bomb. The bomb killed four and wounded fifteen people. Yoshua was there helping Ruth and her family from the first minute he heard the tragic news. Unfortunately, Yoshua was too familiar with funerals. His father had died when he was only two years old. A terrorist roadside bomb killed his stepfather during reserve duty. As a soldier and officer in an elite army unit, Yoshua had laid to rest many comrades-in-arms during his military service.

During the *shiva* (the seven days of mourning), Yoshua was always there to get things done. He arrived at 5:45 am for morning services held in the mourner's home and left only after he knew Ruth was asleep at night.

Two weeks after the attack, an intelligence officer called Yoshua.

"I've received information on the terrorist cell that carried out the attack on the bus in Jerusalem. I was told to keep you informed," the officer said.

A close friend of his was the current officer in command of the special anti-terrorist unit.

Yoshua called his friend.

"Shlomi, I want to join you on your raid. They killed my girlfriend's mother."

"I'll get permission from the administration and get back to you," Yoshua's friend told him.

Yoshua joined the small unit for their foray. The terrorists were hiding in the NPK neighborhood of Rafiah, a hotbed of terrorist activity. The action was as precise as a surgical procedure.

"Yoshua, you will act as the leader of the backup unit, while my specialists go over the rooftops and enter the target house silent as a mist rolling in from the sea," Shlomi told him. Yoshua's unit surrounded the house, ready to take out anyone who tried to escape. They didn't fire a single shot. The guard had fallen asleep and the first wave of rangers garotted him. Quiet as cats, the four-man team crept along the half-finished concrete staircase. They had to be extra careful because there were ends of rebar sticking out everywhere. In the ground floor room was the bomb factory. The factory had every chemical and electronic gear for making detonators and bombs. There were at least four bags of ammonium nitrate, each twenty-five kilos, leaning against the back wall. In a side room lay the other three terrorists, sleeping with their weapons nearby. Within thirty seconds, every one of them breathed their last breaths. Silencers at close range hadn't disturbed the neighbors.

The next evening, Yoshua showed up at the Adler's apartment, still in uniform.

"I'm sorry, Yoshua, Ruth isn't home," Elimelech said.

"She's supposed to meet me in twenty minutes at the library to study. I came by to give you something. These are the men who made and placed the bomb that killed your wife." Yoshua handed him an envelope containing photos of the slain terrorists. With that, he turned around and left to meet Ruth at the library.

Yoshua didn't see Elimelech cry. He cried not only for his murdered wife, but for how emotional he felt. The prince of his tribe (Asher) had brought him justice. Elimelech pondered the puzzle of Yoshua. *He found it difficult to comprehend Yoshua's leadership abilities. He hadn't learned it from his father, who died when he was a toddler. While his step-father was a wonderful man, he wasn't a leader.*

After the first thirty days of mourning and the placing of the stone on Miriam's grave, that Elimelech caught Yoshua alone as they left the cemetery. Elimelech had seen too much death, and time wasted frivolously, to beat about the bush. He stopped Yoshua, looked him straight in the eye.

"Yoshua, what are your intentions for the long term with my daughter?" Elimelech inquired.

Caught a little off guard by the brash frankness of the question, Yoshua gave serious thought to a subject he had not yet thought through.

"Well, sir, I love your daughter."

"She loves you."

Yoshua stared at Mr. Adler.

"Ruth has never said those words, but I am aware of it because of what she does."

"I see what is in your heart. What bothers me is what you do on reserve duty. She will sit at home waiting to see if you come home alive," Elimelech told him.

"I am aware of the problem, and that is why I haven't asked Ruth to marry me. Do I have the right to ask her to make such a sacrifice? I wish I could say that I would retire from my anti-terrorist unit, but I have lost too many friends and family members to walk away. If I don't do it, someone else will have to fill in for me," Yoshua explained to Elimelech.

"I will support her through the troublesome times. You need to have a frank discussion with her. I have no doubt that no one will love my daughter as much as you will," Elimelech stated.

"Sir, I am humbled by your character analysis of me. I'll talk to her." To Yoshua's surprise, Elimelech wrapped his arms around him and kissed him on both cheeks.

Yoshua and Ruth's discussion wasn't easy for either. At the end, Yoshua stated his opinion.

"Ruthie, I'm far from perfect, but I will love you with all my heart and soul."

Tears rolled down her cheeks. She felt like a fraud. Dr. Arieli had encouraged the union. She had accepted the challenge because of the importance of fulfilling the prophecy. In her generation, that laid on the broad shoulders of Yoshua (Aluz) Rosenberg. The Holy One Blessed be He brought Yoshua to her, because he was her soul mate.

The seconds ticked by and Ruth stared at Yoshua, and fear crept into his heart. *"Maybe she doesn't feel the same way as I do."*

"According to Jewish law, one may get engaged and married during the `year mourning period for a parent. You know, the end of the school year, after final exams, would be a good time to get married—either before the seventeenth of *Tamuz* or after the ninth of *Av*. Your father spoke to me and gave his permission and blessing for us to marry."

"Yes," came out before she could even think of its ramifications.

Yoshua stood there with his mouth open.

"Close your mouth, Yoshua, or you'll catch some flies."

"Since I spoke with your father, I wake up every morning thinking what a glorious thing it would be to see your face."

A conflict raged in her heart: duty versus reality. Rebbetzin Rivka and spoken to her many times over the past six months about Yoshua.

"My husband and I worry about him every time he goes to reserve duty. We are lucky that our son, Elisha, is his best friend. He always calls Elisha and his brother Ysrael after he has finished taking out a target. I understand we are asking you to make enormous sacrifices. I won't do it if the situation wasn't so important." the Rebbetzin had told her.

*****

That's how things worked out. At the end of the school year, they married in Jerusalem at the *HaKotel HaMa'aravi* (the Kotel or Western Wall), ten days after *Shavuot*. The plan was to have an open buffet reception before the *chupah* (marriage canopy) followed by dancing. Afterward, they would invite only close family and friends to a *seudat mitzvah* (a required joyous meal). Ruthie and he were both students and had little money for a wedding.

After Yoshua told Ysrael of his intention to marry Ruth, he contacted Dr. Arieli.

"Mazal Tov Ysrael. Please contact your family and I will contact the rest of the community," Dr. Arieli told him.

"Sir, I will do everything in my power to help Ruth."

"I never doubted you would make the offer," Dr. Arieli replied.

"Ysrael, contact all your uncles, aunts, and cousins. They contacted the rest of the Aluzians."

"Yes, sir."

They invited their friends, family, colleagues, people from work, and from the army. The both of them estimated one hundred eighty guests. Ruth convinced Yoshua that if they held the ceremony at the Kotel, they might as well invite anyone to the *chupah* and dancing. The morning of the wedding, Ruth's brothers, Gavriel and Shlomo, put up posters around the plaza adjacent to the Kotel.

From the plaza, the two brothers joined Ysrael and went to escort Yoshua back to the Kotel from his apartment at married student housing near the university. It's customary that in the days before a wedding, for someone to accompany the groom to watch after him. Elimelech was at Yoshua's place, helping him get dressed for the wedding. The boys came in, and Elimelech greeted his sons with hugs and kisses.

"Ysrael, this is my future father-in-law, Elimelech Adler."

Ysrael and Elimelech greeted each other as if they had never met. Yoshua had no idea that the two had known each other for over two years. Ysrael put out his hand to greet his brother's future father-in-law. "I am amazed at how much you two boys look alike; you could be twins!"

The witnesses at the wedding were Elisha and Tzion. The couple asked Dr. Arieli to marry them. The *chupah* was ten meters in front of the Kotel. The couple's brothers held three of the chupah's poles, and the fourth held by Gavriel's second son, Akiva.

People arrived in droves. By the time of the reception, there were already seven hundred people! When it was time for the *chupah*, thirty minutes later, there were over a thousand people.

The crowd parted, and Elimelech on right side and Gavriel on the left side, led Yoshua to his bride. He was wondering, *"Who are these people?"* Tens of men danced in front of Yoshua, leading him to his bride, to cover her with the veil. However, when they came close enough to see Ruth, Yoshua stopped walking and stared. She was in the most stunning wedding dress he had ever seen. The only thing that came to his mind was, *"I'm marrying royalty."*

She sat there smiling at him, and his knees got weak. She was spectacular. Elimelech and Gavriel urged Yoshua forward. There's a folk saying that every bride is beautiful. At that moment, Yoshua felt how good everything was. It was not a saying it to be nice. Ruth was a stunning bride. Standing next to her was Aviva, who normally got every man's attention. But not tonight.

Ysrael was standing next to Ruth's brothers. They were clapping their hands and singing. Tears came to Yoshua's eyes. He looked back to Ruth and next to her stood his mother. He nodded to her because he knew precisely what she was thinking, *"If only his father was here to see his son marry." Yoshua deeply believed that his father's soul was there to participate in his son's joy.* Yoshua walked up to Ruth, covered her face with the veil, and whispered, "Ruthie, you are gorgeous; you have taken away my breath." Dancing and singing started again, and they led Yoshua to the *chupah*.

The music changed and Zahava Rosenberg, on the right, and Esther Yaroni on the left, led Ruth toward the *chupah*. Between the breathtaking beauty of his bride and the vast crowd, Yoshua lost track of everything. He did what they asked of him, but he simply could not take his eyes off Ruth. When he smashed the glass with his foot, the whole place erupted in "*mazal tov!*" The bride and groom had little time to kiss their parents and siblings before swept away to the *cheder ichud* (a room for the couple to be alone for the first time). There were so many people waiting for them. They only spent fifteen minutes there before coming out to dance with everyone.

When they started dancing, there were already forty-five hundred people! Within minutes, people seated Yoshua and Ruth in chairs and lifted overhead. Yoshua looked at everyone gathered, bewildered. A sea of humanity filled the entire area up to the small fence. It was as if the city had emptied itself into the plaza of the Kotel. There must have been over ten thousand people celebrating their wedding!

A strange thing happened, as everyone was dancing in a clockwise direction, another group danced in a counterclockwise direction. Three minutes later, another group formed a circle around those going counterclockwise and danced in a clockwise direction. Yoshua couldn't believe his eyes; the men dancing in the inner circle wore white shirts. In the next circle they had worn beige shirts, and in the next circle everyone wore powder blue shirts.

For the next ten minutes, the hundreds of men danced with perfect precision. The only thing that came to Yoshua's mind was, *"It's like I'm watching a military maneuver."* The circles opened and ten girls, moving in unison, brought Ruth seated on a chair. They handed her chair off to four immense men who carried Ruth to her groom. The four of them moved with such precision that Yoshua thought, *"Wow, professional dancers!"*

As Ruth approached him, the music changed. Rav Carlebach stood there playing his guitar and singing.

*"Where did he come from?"* Yoshua thought. For the next twenty minutes, the famous songwriter and singer fulfilled the commandment of bringing joy to the bride and groom. When Rav Carlebach finished, he went over to Dr. Arieli and they exchanged warm greetings.

An even stranger performance followed. The ten young athletic women who had escorted Ruth came forward. Everyone stopped dancing and made a sizeable space for them. The girls were obviously athletes by the way they moved. They formed a circle, and each took out three throwing knives, which they juggled. After four or five times of juggling by themselves, they juggled one knife leftward to the next girl.

"My God, Ruthie, look at the skill with which those girls moved the knives from one to the other," Yoshua said.

"Now they're doing it faster," Ruthie said.

"The knives have become blurs as they move between the different girls," Yoshua said. Suddenly, without seeing where it came from, someone tossed a round piece of wood into the air in between the girls. Before Yoshua knew it, the girls had each thrown one knife they were juggling. With a loud thwack, the ten knives hit the target simultaneously. Twice more this occurred, and each time these amazing girls hit the target at one time. Yoshua looked at Ruth, who was clapping wildly along with everyone else. The only thing he could think of was, *"Who are these girls and why are they at our wedding?"*

The girls moved into a line opposite the young couple and placed their right hands open on their hearts and extended them out toward the couple. Little did Yoshua know Elisha stood behind them. Together, the girls blessed those present.

"Long life to those who serve their people." Yoshua didn't see Elisha salute the girls in return.

The dancing went on for forty minutes. The music stopped, and then people dispersed. Dr. Arieli and Gavriel smiled at each other, impressed by the turnout for the wedding.

"Don't you believe we may have gone overboard?" Gavriel asked.

"Maybe the girls went a little too far, but it's very traditional for us. Guardswomen always come to a royal weddings like this one. Besides, after serving their two years, they deserve a little exposure to find husbands. Twenty young men have already approached me concerning the availability of the guardswomen."

"I guess I should be happy that you weren't there with your bow."

"Gavriel, have you ever known me to be more than thirty meters from my bow?" Gavriel shook his head and looked around to see which of Dr. Arieli's descendants was carrying his and his wife's bows. Dr. Arieli's youngest daughter stood a short distance away, a long cylinder strapped across her back. Gavriel stared at his friend.

For hundreds of years, our people prepared for any disaster. Being armed is a tradition, since the days of the Light of Justice. After the invasion of Hoshiya by the Malogoths, every Hoshiyan family has kept two bows and fifty arrows ready for use.

The American colonialists used the same concept with their Minutemen. Men who could respond to arms at one minute's notice. Dr. Arieli was a traditionalist and knew that a bow and arrow couldn't save them from gun-wheelding enemies, but he found it hard to break with tradition after so many generations.

The next morning, Yoshua bought every newspaper. When Yoshua returned to their room, he gave half of the newspapers to his new bride.

"Babe, there must be articles concerning the wedding last night. See if you can find an article regarding those girl jugglers."

After ten minutes, Yoshua looked at Ruthie. "Not a single article in any newspaper about our wedding or the knife throwing girls. How can that be?" Yoshua asked.

*****

With a big grin on his face, Yoshua sat up in bed. It was nice to reminisce about the old times. To this day, almost twenty-five years later, he never found out who those girls were. Thinking about it made him want to call his father-in-law. The two had become very close, and he had volunteered to take care of Yoshua and Ruth's four children whenever they were away on excavations. Picking up the phone, he dialed the number directly to Jerusalem. After ten rings, Yoshua realized no one was home, so he left a brief message after the beep, "*Aba*, its Yoshua. I hope everything is well. I'll call again soon."

*****

The next morning, Yoshua was up early, and when he finished exercising morning prayers and breakfast, he sat to consider what he would do about Gefen. His gut reaction was to reject the idea, but he had grown up with only one parent and understood the importance of being appreciated. He would have to decide and give Ruth a call soon.

He left the hotel and went looking for the local hardware store. At 7:15 am, the place was already busy. Yoshua gathered every item he needed to begin their project. When the owner noticed there was a pile of tools and supplies worth a significant sum of money, he left his customer to his assistant and took care of the foreigner. It surprised him to find he spoke fluent Spanish.

The large sale brought a big smile to the owner's face, and Yoshua had no trouble arranging for delivery of the tools in the afternoon. He paid the bill and headed to the small lumberyard, where he bought sturdy planks to build ramps, scaffolding, and framing for the floor.

"What're you building?" the lumberyard owner asked.

"A storage and tool shed."

"Yesterday, I dismantled a wood frame shed two by three and a half meters. The walls are still whole in four pieces and the roof is in six pieces. It wouldn't take you over two hours to put it up. It already has two windows and a sturdy door. I can sell it to you for cheap."

"Let's look at it," Yoshua replied. As the owner had said, the structure was in good shape, now the question was about the price. They bargained over the price for ten minutes until they were both satisfied.

"I'll call you about delivering the shed after I have the floor prepared."

After lunch, the other supplies arrived. Yoshua made the frame for the shed's concrete floor. Four curious high school students came by to watch. "Boys, would you like to make some money? I need some help to build a storage shed." Every youngster agreed on the spot.

"First, we need to attach a water line to the water meter and put a valve on the other end," Yoshua instructed them.

"Now that we have water, we can proceed." After three hours of hard work, they stopped to wipe the sweat from their faces.

"We accomplished everything I want. The ground preparation and pouring the concrete went smoothly. I congratulate every one of you on a job well done.

"Please give me your names and phone numbers. I will call you in the evening if I need you tomorrow," Yoshua told the boys. He paid each boy for the number of hours worked, which brought smiles to their faces.

"Professor, we will be happy to help you again," the boy named Pablo said.

"Thank you Pablo," Yoshua replied.

It was only after they'd finished working that Yoshua remembered he hadn't called Ruth back concerning Gefen. Yoshua remembered the look on Gefen's face when Sasha put that cup with the vodka in front of her. She beamed. It was within his power to make that girl happy again. He picked up the phone and called.

"Hello, Yoshua, aren't you calling from Spain?" Elisha asked.

"I need to talk to you regarding a question of conscience," Yoshua replied.

"How can I help you?"

"Gefen wants to come to Spain with us. She has already talked to Aviva and has recruited everyone possible to influence me to allow her to join the team as Aviva's assistant. I have genuine doubts about including a seventeen-year-old girl who isn't a family member."

"Yoshua, Ruth talked to me about this girl and I met her with Aviva. I have to tell you, she impressed me with her abilities and desire to be part of your team. Maybe a young apprentice would be a good way to start a new generation of archaeologists."

"Elisha, I can't tell you how much I appreciate discussing this with you. I have to tell you I'm not concerned about Gefen and David getting physically involved. Besides, a little bird told me you son is interested in another young woman," Elisha informed Yoshua.

"That's the first time I have heard about this. How come my son hasn't said anything to me?"

"Talk to him Yoshua."

"I talk to David every day.

"What I'm worried about is that he will have his mind on her during his training or on active duty, and that could cause him to make a mistake that could cost his life, or others, or both," Elisha expressed his worries.

"Who is he interested in?" Yoshua asked.

"My blind friend, doesn't anyone in your family tell you anything?" Yoshua didn't have the slightest idea what Elisha was talking about. The silence on the line told Elisha everything he needed to know.

"Yoshua, for such an intelligent man, sometimes you don't know what's going on around you."

"What're you trying to say, Elisha?"

"To inform you, we will soon be in-laws, *Basha'a Tova!*" Yoshua stood there far away in Spain and could not get a word out of his mouth.

"My daughter, Hadar, has had a 'thing' for David for years. Yoshua laughed so hard that Elisha was getting worried.

"Yoshua, what's so funny?"

"It's always been my dream that my son marry your daughter, since the day she was born. I couldn't think of a better family for my son to marry into than yours. Well, if that's the case, I have no problem with asking Gefen to join us in Spain."

"May the Lord watch over you, Yoshua Rosenberg, your team, and your endeavor. May the Holy One, Blessed be He, rain upon you his blessings and May all your dreams come true," Elisha finished the call.

Elisha's hand was shaking when put down his cell phone. He looked at his father and nodded his head. A huge smile spread across Dr. Arieli's face.

"*Aba*, while I was blessing Yoshua, I almost called him by his actual name and title."

"Know this, Elisha. Everything that is happening is God's plan, and your namesake understood it. Let's do everything possible to expedite this great escapade. It's the right man, at the right time, in the right place, with the right people around him. Your job, my son, is to love and guide your friend."

# RED TAPE

The Antiquities Authority still had not approved the request for a permit to excavate the chapel in Nido de Aguila. At 9:00 am, Yoshua called the office in Madrid. It was not until 10:15 that he reached the correct bureaucrat to verify they received the application.

"I would like an appointment for tomorrow with the person who gives final approvals," Yoshua said.

"That would be Dr. Jose Aton Garza. He only has one time free tomorrow, at 8:30. File number, please?"

"Yes, it's 2014-3-375-876-C."

"One moment please while I look up your file number." Yoshua waited on the line for three long minutes.

"Oh! This request is from a foreign national. And you are?"

"I'm Professor Yoshua Rosenberg."

"Be sure you're on time tomorrow morning."

Yoshua knew he had to obtain a permit, even though it was a private excavation on private land. If they found anything of interest, the government would confiscate the find under the law of national treasures. Therefore, to avoid any chance of running into trouble with the authorities in the future, he wanted to obtain permits for the excavation as quickly as possible. Yoshua called his friend the bishop and asked, "Hello, Bishop, how are you today?"

"Oh, Yoshua, thank you. I'm fine. What can I do for you?"

"Could you put in a good word for me with the Antiquities Authority about getting our permit to excavate the building?"

"After saving so many people in Cordoba, you're a hero. So, I don't think there will be any problem. I'm sure everyone would expedite your permits."

"Thank you very much, Bishop. As always, it was a pleasure talking with you."

"God Bless, Yoshua, and don't worry about a thing."

Yoshua sat and gathered his papers concerning the chapel. Before coming to Spain, he and Ruth had organized the required maps, references, goals, and details of how they would care and store every find. Since this was not a normal excavation, but more of a restoration, the plan was to remove the paint and plaster on the walls, see if there was anything under them, and tear up the floor tiles to see if they could find the original floor. Yoshua hoped that under the layers, they might find some clues about Aharon Dori and his connection to the Light of Justice. Now that he knew there was a sealed room, Yoshua had high hopes that whatever had caused the church to seal up that room would provide him with clues.

He had a full set of blueprints from the local priest, detailing the location of the site, the legal bill of sale, a letter of recommendation from the bishop, and every necessary document and reference required by the government.

Yoshua took the train to Granada, followed by another train to Madrid. He would stay the night in Madrid so he could be at Dr. Garza's office on time, with no problems. He packed an overnight bag and took a taxi to the train station on the outskirts of the town. The air conditioning in the car had made the trip comfortable, but, when he stepped out of the taxi into the thirty-seven degree Centigrade weather, it was like a hot slap in the face. He grabbed his overnight bag and hurried toward the station building, hoping it was air-conditioned.

The time passed and before he knew it, Yoshua was at the Granada train station. He had a forty-minute wait until his train to Madrid. Yoshua walked over to a fruit vendor's kiosk and bought some fruit and the local paper. He sat on a chair in the waiting room eating fruit and reading the paper. The train arrived on time and by the time he finished reading the paper from front to back, the conductor announced they would pull into Madrid's Atocha train station in five minutes.

That night, Yoshua got a good night's sleep in a very comfortable three-star hotel. In the morning, after an early breakfast, he took a taxi to the offices of the Antiquities Authority in time to be there when the doors opened. Once inside, he went to the information.

"Please direct me to Dr. Garza's office?" He got there at 8:27 and gave the secretary his name.

"Dr. Garza is in court giving testimony against grave robbers. He left word that you should see Mrs. Rosa Maria Colon, who can help you." Yoshua followed the secretary's directions and after ten minutes found Mrs. Colon's office. There, he had to wait ninety minutes and received more forms to fill out. Once he had finished filling out those forms, she stamped them and sent him to Mr. Morillo, the civil engineer who had to examine the maps of the site.

Mr. Morillo's office was below two floors and in a different wing. There, he had to wait forty minutes for his turn and when he produced the blueprints; the priest had given him; the engineer oohed and aahed. "Professor, these are very rare and in excellent condition. We must have a copy of these. There's a shop five blocks from here that makes copies of blueprints." Mr. Morillo wrote the name and address of the shop. So off Yoshua went. He grabbed the first taxi and when he got to the shop, fifteen architects already stood in line.

"It'll take at least two hours. Go have lunch and come back," the young man behind the counter.

Yoshua left the blueprints and went in search of a greengrocery. Two hundred meters along the street on the other side, he found one. He bought fruit, vegetables, and two cold cans of local beer. He found a small park and had a picnic. The beer made him tired, so he took a short siesta and when he woke up, he felt refreshed. He walked back to the copy shop and luck was with him this time—the copy was ready thirty minutes early.

Yoshua returned to Mr. Morillo's office.

"I am sorry, Professor, Mr. Morillo is out for lunch." He waited another hour.

"Ah, professor, good of you to be here. I need the copy of your blueprints. I can find the new zone and parcel numbers via the old ones written on this blueprint via my computer."

It took him twenty minutes before he found the information. "Professor, I need to go over with you to where you intend to excavate. I will show you on this map where it is permissible, and forbidden to conduct the excavation."

"Our modern maps provided by the county showed where they buried the water, sewage, electric, and phone lines. There is no bathroom on the plot. There is a water meter you can connect to. There is also a junction to the sewage system is on the southern border of the land."

"I understand Mr. Morillo," Yoshua replied.

"There are phone lines running underground to the school next to you which the phone company can tap into."

"The building is so old that its electric line is still above ground, so there were no restrictions. Mr. Morillo took out his stamp, stamped the copy. That will be eighty euros for the inspection."

The rest of the afternoon he ran from one office to the next, filling out forms, getting official stamps, paying registration fees and after another three hours he still didn't know to whom he should give the forms for approval, because Mrs. Colon had left for the day. At six o'clock, Yoshua went across the street to a fruit stand and bought some tangerines and a few apples that he munched on while he drank a tall frosty glass of freshly squeezed Valencia orange juice.

Yoshua had not come prepared to stay over more than one night, but at the rate he was progressing, he could be in Madrid for two days. He wandered back to the Antiquities Authority and found that the clerk he needed had gone home.

Friday, July 6, found him stuck in a loop. It was a repeat of the day before, but this time, he was under pressure to get to his train on time. Once again, he was running from one bureaucrat to the next, and at 1:00 pm, he realized the bureaucracy had defeated him. He picked up his phone and called the bishop on his private line.

"Hello Yoshua, how are you," the Bishop asked?

"Thank you, your excellence. I'm well, but am being challenged by the bureaucracy of the Antiquities Authority. Can you help me with a little protection?"

"Well, of course, I will be pleased to assist you. The head of the department is a friend of mine and I would be happy to call him. Let me know where you are and I will make sure someone takes care of you." Yoshua gave him the information, thanked him, and said goodbye.

Yoshua waited for the department of planning to evaluate the proposed excavation at Nido de Aguila. Every request had to include detailed plans, names of those who would conduct the dig, and maps prepared by a surveyor. Here, Yoshua had submitted the new surveyor's map when he applied for the permit on the Internet. Besides, he now had a recent map that the Ophosis had requested when they received their ancestral inheritance back from the church.

Fifteen minutes later, a young man came into the office and asked in English, "Excuse me, sir, are you Professor Rosenberg from Jerusalem?" Yoshua nodded. The young man turned to the clerk at the desk.

"May I have the professor's file," he requested. The secretary found it at the bottom of the pile. The young man turned back to Yoshua and said, "Please come with me. My boss, the head of the Authority, asked me to bring your request to him."

Yoshua followed the young bureaucrat to the elevator and followed him in when it arrived. They went to the fourth floor and straight into the office of the head of the Authority. Dr. Jorge Antonio Varga stood and greeted Yoshua.

"Professor Rosenberg, this is a great honor for me to have you here in my office and working in my country.

I've read every one of your books and most of your published scientific articles. I'm a big fan of your work." Dr. Varga took the file from his assistant and spent ten minutes going over every document.

"You have presented us with thorough application. My assistant will check the facts and if everything is in order, we'll issue your permits."

For the next hour, Yoshua explained to the head of the Authority how they had come to this little chapel and what he hoped to find. The assistant returned, whispered some observations in Dr. Varga's ear, and left. Dr. Varga opened his top drawer, removed the stamps, and signed and stamp the documents where necessary. When it was over, Dr. Varga said,

"I hope you find evidence of your elusive Light of Justice. I'm sure, like many of your projects, this one will make a worldwide impact." The two men shook hands and a thrilled Yoshua left with every permit he needed to start the dig.

When he got outside, he called home. "Ruthie, darling, I got the permits to excavate the chapel." He had forgotten to tell her about the slot on the right doorpost, which he did now. "That's almost exclusive evidence it had once been a Jewish owned building."

"Oh, Shuki, that's splendid news. You have regards from the entire Arieli clan. *Savta* Rivka worries you have nothing to eat there."

"Tell *Savta* Rivka thank you for worrying about me, but I'm fine, simply tiring of eating fruit. Please get the team assembled and come as fast as you can. Listen, honey, I'm going to a realtor when I get back to Nido de Aguila and find us a house to rent for the summer. I don't think I'll be able to find a house with enough rooms for everyone to have their own room, so David and Sasha may have to room together, as will Aviva and Gefen. I'll also get kitchen things, and we'll make our food at home. There's a fish store here that sells live freshwater fish." Yoshua's voice changed, and he lowered it an octave and said, "I miss you, babe."

Ruth's heart melted as she whispered back, "I miss you, too. Can't wait to be back in your arms!" Yoshua heard some coughing in the background and his daughters giggling.

"See you soon."

"What are you going to do for *Shabbat*, Shuki? It's too late to get back to Nido de Aguila."

"I'll call Chabad. Before I left the hotel this morning, I knew I might get stuck here, so I looked up the name and phone number of the Chabad rabbi and stayed for *Shabbat* here in Madrid."

"Honey, I have to light candles here in a few minutes. Send me a text message and I'll read it after *Shabbat*. Love you, babe, and miss you."

"*Shabbat shalom*, Ruthie. Give kisses to the kids for me."

Yoshua left the Antiquities Authority building humming a tune. The world looked brighter. Colors were more vibrant, smells stronger, and the small white puffy clouds that provided a little relief from the relentless sun seemed more wonderful than normal.

*****

After evening prayers, as everyone walked toward the dining area, the Chabad rabbi approached Yoshua.

"Professor, would you honor us with a *Dvar Torah* (talk) at dinner?"

"It would be my pleasure, Rabbi."

After being introduced by the Chabad rabbi, Yoshua looked over everyone those gathered from the four corners of the earth to spend *Shabbat* together as Jews. He began,

"Balak had brought Balaam to curse the children of Israel. Yet, despite his own personal desires, he followed God's command and blessed them. Balaam took up the words that God put into his mouth, 'For from their beginning, I see them from the mountain peaks, and I behold them from the hills; it is a nation that will dwell alone, and will not be reckoned among the nations' (Numbers 23:9). 'Dwell alone' appears to characterize the Jewish scenario: a people that stands outside history and the normal laws that govern the destiny of other peoples."

Yoshua knew that if he wanted to make people think, he would have to shake the tree. He continued with these thoughts.

"The pull of the glitter and empty materialism of Western culture is causing a spiritual suicide. This occurs when we fail to pass on to our children a true ethical code that is not relative or changes with time. Something that is true must stand the test of time. It needs to have been true four thousand years ago, true today, and true in another four thousand years. Only when we return to being the nation that dwells alone, following the path of life laid out in the Torah, will we as a people reach our true spiritual potential."

When Yoshua sat, there was total silence. No one expected such a lesson from an archaeologist and scientist. Yoshua closed his eyes and Elisha came to his mind. Elisha would be proud of him, knowing that in faraway Spain he was "shaking the tree," trying to wake people up.

After dinner, many of those gathered came up to Yoshua to shake his hand and exchange a few words. As he was chatting, he realized even though he and Elisha were both educators, he touched people's minds while Elisha touched people's minds and souls.

After *Shabbat*, Yoshua thanked his hosts and took a taxi to the train station.

"When is the next train to Granada?" Yoshua asked.

"I will leave in twelve minutes. You need to hurry," the ticket seller said. He had purchased round-trip tickets to the train station at Nido de Aguila. However, the train from Granada to Nido de Aguila stopped at 7:00 pm, so he would have to stay the night in Granada. He found a small hotel right near the train station. He wanted to catch the first train out at 9:00 am. On Sundays, the service to Nido de Aguila started later than on weekdays.

During the train ride back on Sunday morning, Yoshua went over every official document. Before he knew it, the conductor announced they were pulling into Nido de Aguila. Yoshua put his papers into his briefcase and got up to stand next to the exit doors. The train came to a stop. He exited and walked into the old stone train station. Even at this early morning hour, it was too hot for the flies to be swarming and buzzing.

# EXCAVATION BEGINS

From the train station, Yoshua took a taxi back to the hotel and changed clothes. Once ready for a day of physical labor, he called the boys on his construction crew and asked them to come to work the next morning. Yoshua was conscious of Spain being a Catholic country and Sunday was not a day for construction and making noise. He spent the day going over the inside and outside of the chapel and decided about how they would proceed with the excavation.

After dinner, he had time—for the first time in days— to pick up the book he began reading on the flight to Spain; *The Foundation Trilogy* by Isaac Asimov. He wasn't aware of when he fell asleep, but he woke up at 5:15 am, still in his work clothes.

***** 

Monday morning, he called the lumberyard.

"When can you bring the components of the storage shed?"

"I'm not busy this morning. I can be there in forty minutes," the owner said.

The owner showed up in his large pickup truck with the sections of the shed loaded in the back. Together, the with his construction team, the six boys unloaded them easily.

"Listen, professor, I'm not busy. It can stay and help you put up this shed," the lumberyard owner volunteered.

With his help, they finished building the shed in an hour.

Everyone was glad, and Yoshua gave money to one boy.

"Please go buy cold drinks for everyone." After he returned, Yoshua showed the boys how to measure the lumber and make the framing for the shelves. He plugged in the circular saw, lifted it, and tested to see if it worked. A quick press of the trigger responded with the whirling of the blade and a short vroom.

"Ahhhh," Yoshua loved the smell of fresh cut pine. The heat from the spinning blade on the pitch inside the wood caused the aromatic compounds to evaporate and the air to smell of pine oil. Yoshua breathed it in deeply, enjoying the aroma of the wood. It didn't take long for the electric saw to cut through the marked lumber. Now, armed with two cordless screwdrivers and Yoshua's explanation of what to do, and the boys assembled the framing for the shelves.

As he watched the boys work, Yoshua reminisced. He learned his carpentry skills from Ysrael, who studied in a trade school because he wasn't interested in academic studies. Ysrael became rather skilled and, by his last year in high school, he made his mother a new bed and six-drawer dresser. Ysrael loved using tools, and in the police academy he found the tool at which he excelled—a sniper rifle. Like he could work magic with his tools on a piece of wood, Ysrael was by far the most skilled sniper in the entire State of Israel. Ysrael's skill with a rifle was a natural extension of his skill with a bow which he picked up for the first time at of age of six. Yoshua smiled when he thought about his brother. In their years of fighting terrorism, he in the army and Ysrael in the police. They had fought next to each other many times.

One time, they cornered a terrorist in a house in a village northeast of Jerusalem. The only reason the terrorist could hole up in a house so long was that it took the police helicopter ninety minutes to bring Ysrael to the location. Using infrared imaging and armor piercing fifty caliber ammunition, Ysrael set up his rifle and fired two rounds that killed the terrorist within three minutes of his arrival on the scene. He didn't even go into the house to see what the fifty caliber rounds had done. Ysrael folded his rifle, replaced it in its case, walked over to his brother, hugged him, and kissed him on the cheek.

"We're coming to you for Friday night dinner. I'll meet you at Bet Arieli," he reminded his brother. With that, he turned around, got back in the helicopter, waved once, and disappeared into the sky.

They soon lined the walls with shelves on which the boys organized every tool and piece of equipment. Yoshua and his construction crew of teenagers finished a faster than anticipated. He paid them as agreed and also gave them a nice bonus. Having large amounts of money available for an excavation taught Yoshua, many are a great motivator to get jobs done in a better way—instead of scrimping on every expenditure and worrying about if there would be sufficient funds to finish a short excavation. He knew the next step would be to get a plumber and make a bathroom.

*****

That afternoon, Yoshua took the train to Cordova to wait for his team at the airport. The reunion was emotional and while Ruth watched Yoshua and David hug each other. It amazed her how much David had grown. He was as tall as Yoshua now and almost as broad. They both forgot to shave in the morning and with the two of them wearing sunglasses, they could have been brothers instead of father and son.

Yoshua welcomed Aviva, Gefen, and Sasha. "Professor, I want you to know how much I appreciate that you've let me join this project." Gefen said.

"Let's hope you don't get too bored."

Ruth called to them.

"Look up and smile," and she took a picture of Yoshua and David with the crowd at the airport behind them. She made a silent prayer.

"Holy One, Lord of Heaven and Earth, watch over my son, David ben Yoshua ben Yaacov. Protect him and let me live long enough to see his children and grandchildren born upon my knees." Tears came to her eyes against her will and Yoshua, seeing Ruth become emotional, released David and wrapped his arms around her.

"Babe, I know that David's decision to follow me into the General Staff Rangers upset you immensely."

"I've already lived too many days and nights not knowing if my husband would come home from reserve duty. You would disappear to places where you couldn't call or be in contact with me."

Yoshua hugged Ruthie. "You brought home too many body bags. My thoughts of what the future held for David and his friends interrupt my sleep at night."

Yoshua kissed Ruth, held her tight, and whispered in her ear.

"I know why you're upset, and I pray that I've sacrificed enough of my life to allow Heaven to watch over him. On one side, we've buried so many friends and family, and yet on the other side, we have to understand this is the price of freedom." Ruth kissed Yoshua and wondered how he would react if he knew his son's hidden agenda. The boy took his heritage seriously and intended to follow the path laid out by his namesake, the famous General David Aluz.

They needed two taxis to take the entire team and their luggage to the train station. The trip took longer than they anticipated. They almost missed the train south. The trip was uneventful except for the extraordinary scenery of the Sierra Nevada Mountains he watched through his window. The train pulled into the small old station at Nido de Aguila.

"I feel as if we have gone through a time warp. The station is old and dilapidated and built long before the Spanish Civil War," Sasha commented.

"I have rented a four bedroom furnished house," Yoshua told his team. He gave the address to the taxi drivers. They pulled up to the cute house on the southwest edge of town. Their backyard looked out into a local olive grove.

"Because we have a large budget, I reduced the amount of work at home and hired a housekeeper who will come three times a week. The realtor told me the lady next door wanted a part-time job. I spoke with her and she has agreed to clean, cook, and do the laundry. Her name is Juanita and you'll meet her tomorrow morning."

Yoshua divvied up the rooms; one for Aviva and Gefen, one for David and Sasha, and one for himself and Ruth. While everyone unpacked, Yoshua whipped up dinner. He had learned that the Spanish dinner (*cena*) was traditionally much smaller than the main midday meal called *comida*. So, he made a big vegetable salad, Israeli style, an assortment of small sandwiches, and a big

Spanish omelet filled with red onions, peppers, and tomatoes. The long journey had tired everyone, so after dinner, everyone went to sleep early.

Ruth never told Yoshua, but she hated it when he wasn't home. In the old days, when he served sixty to ninety days in reserve duty, she was always fearful something might happen to him. She snuggled into his muscular arms and laid her head on his chest. She hadn't realized how tired she was, but in two seconds she was out like a light. Yoshua stroked Ruth's hair, and before he knew it, he was asleep.

The next morning, Aviva and Gefen got up early. "Come on Gefen, let's go buy groceries for breakfast and lunch," Aviva suggested. By the time they returned, Yoshua and David had finished their exercises and morning prayers. Yoshua's mother raised her sons in a religious home, but during his regular army service, his unit suffered grievous losses in a terrible firefight with terrorists who had seized a bus full of civilians. The trauma left him with many questions of faith. As a result, he followed the rules of keeping kosher when in his mother's home and later his and Ruth's, but outside the home, Yoshua hadn't kept strictly kosher. In the past two years, he changed, mostly because of his children's influence on him, especially David. They would sit and talk about Jewish philosophy for hours on Friday nights and *Shabbat* afternoons.

With David next to him as they prayed that morning in southern Spain, Yoshua thought about the continuous line of men in his family who had kept their people's tradition. He wondered what his own father and grandfather would have been like if they had survived. He spoke to his father,

"*Aba*, you would have been so proud of your grandson. David's turning out to be such a fine person."

\*\*\*\*\*

"We made a big purchase. We now have a large assortment of food. Everyone make yourself a bag lunch to take along for later," Aviva said.

"We will need to buy a used refrigerator to keep at the chapel for food and drinks," Yoshua said.

"An espresso machine wouldn't hurt, boss," Sasha suggested. After breakfast, the team headed off to the chapel on foot.

Three hundred meters before the chapel, they came across an old van with a for sale sign in the window.

"Look, someone is selling a van," Yoshua said. Yoshua stopped and went to the nearest house to ask to whom the van belonged. A young woman dressed like a hippy answered the door. She wore torn jeans, a tie-dyed T-shirt, and a small scarf around her very curly hair—which made it look like it was exploding out the back of her head. "How much do you want for the van?"

"Even though it doesn't look so great on the outside, every one of its moving parts is in excellent condition," said the owner. They haggled over the price for a few minutes.

"Can I take it for a test drive?" Yoshua asked.

After the test drive, the owner inquired.

"Do you want to buy the vehicle?"

"Yes."

"I'll take you to our police station, which also serves as the Department of Motor Vehicles," the owner said.

At the police station, they transferred the ownership of the van with no problems. The vehicle registration clerk was the owner's uncle. Yoshua paid in cash.

"We now have transportation," Yoshua announces to everyone's applaud.

*****

Yoshua brought his team to the Chapel for the first time.

"It's L-shaped," Ruth commented.

"Yes, there are no openings on western wing," Yoshua replied.

"The building is unimpressive. I thought you said it was a church. Where is the cross?" Aviva asked.

"The local padre removed all the symbols of their faith," Yoshua informed them.

"I like it," Gefen announced.

"Why?" Aviva asked.

"The building is so plain. I bet it has lots of hidden secrets," Gefen answered.

"Well, code girl, from your lips to God's ears," David added.

"Wow, Dad, you did a serious amount of work here before we came," David said. Ten minutes later, Yoshua's young construction crew came.

"Do any of you know a plumber? Yoshua asked them in Spanish."

One boy, Pablo, raised his hand.

"My father is a qualified plumber."

"Pablo, please call your father."

Pablo's father came over fifteen minutes later.

"We need a bathroom with two toilets completely walled off so both a male or female can use it simultaneously," Yoshua said.

"I'm busy for the next two days, but in the meantime, I'll give instructions to my son on how to prepare the floor and what pipes to lay before pouring the concrete. I'll also put together a drawing you can give to the city hall to get a building permit."

*****

"The first order of business is to photograph the site before we peel back the walls to reveal the secrets beneath," Aviva said. Yoshua pointed at the western side of the building.

"See those three arches about two-and-a-half meters up the wall?" Yoshua asked.

"Someone filled those arches in with bricks in the past. We need more light. We'll knock out the bricks and put in glass," Ruthie said.

Everyone waited while Sasha photographed every aspect of the chapel, inside and out. Sasha and David went to the shed, got tools, and built a small scaffold that would allow them to work at the proper height to remove the bricks. Yoshua took measurements, photographed the arches with Sasha's camera, and with their new van, went off in search of a glazer.

Aviva and Ruth showed Gefen how to survey the building before initiating any work on it. "It's important to measure the depth of the doorframe as it tells you the thickness of the walls. Here, the original building had a double wall of fired clay bricks, for insulation, to reduce heating and cooling. It's important to look for cracks or breaks because they could reveal secrets that lay beneath," Aviva said.

"Similar to restoration work, it's important to be thoroughly familiar with the materials of your trade. It's possible to date objects by their composition. In every era, people used different materials for the construction of an object. Similar to the distinction between a bronze or iron based sword," Ruth added.

"For example, the composition of yellow paint made in the twelfth century will differ from yellow paint made in the eighteenth century," Aviva said.

Ruth pointed to the floor. "They make these inexpensive clay tiles from talc-like clay powder that they harden by fire in a kiln. Afterwards, tiles are glazed and fired again to create the finish. These tiles are probably from the end of the nineteenth century or early in the twentieth century."

Yoshua returned from giving his order to the glazier and caught the end of the explanations to Gefen. "*Chamuda*," he said, "one of the first things I noticed was that the floor is higher than the baseboard of the doorframe. To save money, the church cemented these tiles on top of the previous floor."

"Gefen, therefore, we survey the site before we attempt excavation or restoration," Yoshua said.

"Let's get started on taking paint samples before we remove the paint from the walls," Ruth said.

"We'll start on a spot fifty centimeters to the right of the door. Luckily, the people who painted had been misers. They used cheap white lime," Aviva pointed out to Gefen,

"We will use a handheld XRF analyzer. X-ray fluorescence (XRF) is an analytical technique which employs the interaction of x-rays with a target material to determine its elemental composition. The readings the XRF provides the range of elements present and their proportions. XRF is a non-destructive method to determine the elemental composition of the test material. The best thing about it is we can analyze delicate and fragile artifacts at normal atmospheric pressure without risk of damage. The micro-XRF is nondestructive, it provides for fast and easy analysis of objects as diverse as manuscripts and metallic artifacts. It is simple to use," Ruth explained.

"I use XRF technology regularly in my work at the Israel Museum. Not only curators and conservators use this technology, but anyone who needs an elemental analysis, like geologists," Aviva added.

"Archaeologists use the application of XRF technology to shed light on the specific materials and techniques used in manufacturing of an object. It helps to determine its likely origin, and authenticity. This technology can also identify corrosion products and their probable causes. XRF can assist in the initial conservation and subsequent day-to-day care of the many priceless historical objects we find in archaeological sites," Ruth said.

Aviva positioned one of the wooden benches next to the wall.

"The work we do demands everything is done precisely. We write data for analysis on standard forms with date, time, place, and names of those doing the analysis, the object, and a space to describe the analysis." Aviva removed the hand-held analyzer from its plastic carrying case.

"It looks like something straight out of a sci-fi movie. It's rather similar in appearance to the old ray guns in pulp science fiction novels from the 1950s. See this small screen on the back. I point at the object to be analyzed, press the trigger, and the machine displays the analysis on the screen."

Ruth placed a small, rectangular stainless steel tray on the floor directly below, where the analysis would be carried out. Aviva extended her hand with the XRF. She read the analysis to Ruth, who wrote it on a form. When the women finished the analysis, they worked on the walls. Ruth sanded the outside layer with extra fine sandpaper and cleared away the dust with a camelhair brush. After an additional thirty seconds of standing, Aviva stopped her, took a large round magnifying glass, and examined the spot.

"I am looking for subtle differences in color. As an indication, we have reached an older layer of paint," Aviva said. Once again, Aviva extended the XRF gun and made an analysis.

In the meantime, Ruth gathered the dust, placed it in a small manila envelope, and wrote the necessary identifying information along with the code number of the analysis form so they would know which sample went with which analysis. Aviva learned long ago how tedious this work could be. If the place to be analyzed was an uncomfortable place to work, it would take twice as long. Aviva and Ruth had used the XRF gun many times. Every ten minutes, they rotated their positions, which kept them alert and much more efficient.

"Gefen, come look. The first two layers are recent—cheap, plastic lime that crumbled away easily. The paint underneath is to some extent off white. That is the color a lime-wash would change to after thirty to fifty years," Aviva explained to Gefen.

"With every layer exposed, we collected the dust for chemical analysis and Sasha takes photographs. The next layer was even more off white. It's now easy to distinguish between the layers. The church didn't paint the chapel on a regular basis. The building had been around for hundreds of years, so there were probably many layers. Every so often, we have to stop the work to check our progress," Ruth told Gefen.

"We need to slow our pace. Please switch to a finer grade of sandpaper," Aviva said. Dust collected at their feet as they removed layer upon layer of plaster and paint. They drew closer and closer to the original walls.

Ruth and Aviva were so focused on their work, they hadn't paid attention to the background noise. David and Sasha had completed the scaffold and stood near the ceiling with the five-kilo hammer opposite the filled in arches. David swung the hammer, and it smashed through the bricks.

The noise startled the women. They turned around to see what was happening. David had removed his shirt because of the heat. Aviva watched Gefen observe David swinging the hammer again, his muscles rippling under his skin. She leaned over to Ruth, nodded toward Gefen and afterwards at David, and whispered to her friend.

"Your eldest son will be a lady-killer!" Shocked by her friend's comment, Ruth first glanced at how Gefen stared at David. Ruth took stock of the situation. She inspected her son for the first time in years. It shocked her how much he looked like his father at that age. It reminded her how much Yoshua had affected her on the rare occasion she had seen Yoshua without a shirt.

Ruth perspired like everyone else, but made her mind up. She got up from the bench and walked across the small chapel to the sound of five kilos of steel pulverizing the local red brick. The dust and particles of crushed brick flew everywhere, and by the time she got to the scaffolding, she was coated with dust from head to toe. As she was about to open her mouth, the sound of the hammer on brick changed and the head of the tool broke through. Immediately, cool air rushed inside. Ruth stood opposite the open door, savoring the cool feeling on her skin and the delicate scent of lavender from the neighbor's garden. She just stood there as if she was in front of a fan.

David handed the hammer to Sasha, who widened the hole. The hammer continued to crush the brick, and more gray mortar and red brick dust fell on everyone. But now there was a smile on their faces. David climbed down the ladder to get a drink of water. Ruth walked up to him while he upended a one and a half liter bottle of water and gulped half of it in one shot. He wiped his lips with his left arm and smiled at his mother. Her heart melted. "My God, Aviva's right, he will be a lady-killer!"

"*Beni* (my son), please put your T-shirt back on, it's not proper for you to be bare-chested anymore, especially with Gefen here. You're not a child, and it would be much more modest to at least leave your T-shirt on."

Slightly embarrassed, David's smile changed to a strained grin, and he apologized.

"It was so hot up there and I sweated so much, I acted without thinking. I'm sorry, it won't happen again."

"I know I can count on you." Ruth reached out, stroked his cheek, and smiled. As David walked away to get his shirt, Ruth turned to find Yoshua watching her. He smiled, and her knees felt wobbly.

"*After so many years of marriage, that man still can reduce me to jelly with a smile,*" she thought

Yoshua walked over, wrapped his arms around Ruth, and held her to his chest.

"Do you know how much I love you, Ruthie," he whispered.

"Seeing you there with our son made my heart sing. How could such a wonderful person as our son have descended from me if you hadn't been my partner? Thank God he takes after you and knows little of my past," Yoshua commented.

Ruth knew Yoshua had worked hard to change his rage against the murderers of his people. He had wracked terrible revenge on the enemies of Israel. There were horrible stories of exacting an eye for an eye against terrorists—stories she only knew about from his nightmares. Things he shouted out in his sleep. Yoshua had done things in the army that made her hair stand on end. Thank God, with help, the nightmares had stopped. But Major Yoshua Rosenberg still felt guilty about how he desecrated the concept of man being created in the image of God by taking lives without difficulty. There were many secrets in their family, and Ruth knew more than either her husband or son realized. She also knew the path her son was on in his upcoming military career, and she feared the consequences.

Leaders of the community had spoken to the young men in the army and those before the draft. The men wanted to serve together, but their parents pleaded with them not to concentrate on so many of them in one place. If, God forbid, any major disaster would occur, it would destroy their community in Israel and throughout the world. Many young Hoshiyan men made aliyah to become Israeli citizens. Hoshiyans wanted to serve with their fellow brethren. Tears of frustration rolled along Ruth's face, streaking through the red and gray dust.

"Shuki, he will go to the army in a few weeks. It will be very difficult for me. I lived through hundreds of sleepless nights worrying if I would ever see you again." She cried softly so only Yoshua could hear. He steered Ruth around and, holding her, led her outside. They stood in the shade cast by the storeroom.

"Ruthie, I know what dangers he'll be exposed to in the Rangers. I talked to him, but he still wants to serve there with his friends. I also know what drives him to do it. He wants to prove that he is every bit as good as his father." Little did he know it had nothing to do with his son's decision.

"I talked to Elisha about it since his son is also involved in that group. He told me Ahuva is distraught and worried, like you are. It's hard for me to tell David not to continue on this path since I did it myself and don't regret my decision."

"Shuki, I'm scared for David's life. I know deep inside you believe you're living on borrowed time and so not afraid to die. I think you're wrong. The Holy One, Blessed be He, kept you around in this world because you still have some aim to fulfill. The bullets that flew around you were never a threat because *Hakodosh Baruchu* (the Holy One) was watching over you. None of us knows what David's path will be in this world. God created mothers with a biological makeup to worry about our offspring. Shuki, I need your support." Yoshua wrapped his arms around Ruth and held her close. They stood like that for over a minute. Ruth looked up and kissed him on the right cheek. She cocked her head and said, "Let's get back to work."

Yoshua went to the small grocery store on the same street as the chapel. He bought the local paper.

"Do you know where we can get a used refrigerator?" The owner of the store thought for a second and his eyes opened wide.

"Professor, you're in luck. Old Mr. Durango died last week and his children are selling everything in the house." Seeing Yoshua smiling back at him, the owner broached another subject.

"Professor, how long will you and your team of archaeologists be in our fair town?"

"Our intention at the moment is to be here for three weeks."

"Oh, that's great! Maybe instead of paying cash the entire time, you could open an account with me. Then, before you leave, we'll make an accounting."

"Okay, that works for me. Here are two hundred fifty euros to open my account." Yoshua understood that the man wanted to tie their shopping to his store. He had been to the other three small grocery stores, and everyone had similar prices. The only cheaper grocery stores were in Granada, which made it not worthwhile unless they had an extensive shopping list. After the store owner opened the account, he called Mr. Durango's house. He and caught one of the deceased's children. They talked for two minutes. The store owner hung up and made an announcement.

"Mr. Durango's children are at his house right now. They want to sell you anything you need from the household."

"Thanks for your help." Yoshua said as he shock the man's hand.

*****

When Yoshua arrived back at the chapel, he called to Sasha and David on the scaffold.

"Come there. We're going to a garage sale to get some things we need. They have a refrigerator for sale." They piled into the van. They headed first for the ATM to get cash. Afterwards, it was a quick trip to Mr. Durango's house.

When they got to the house, they found the late owner's four children going through his belongings, putting the things they wanted in one pile and those they didn't in another. "This is a treasure trove for us," David observed. Yoshua bought the refrigerator, a table with six chairs, an espresso machine, and a new microwave was still in the box, a computer desk, a sink, faucet, two folding beds, sheets, pillows, blankets, three fans, and two lamps.

David noticed a folded easel leaning against the wall. "Dad, why don't we get the easel for Gefen? There is also an entire box of art supplies," David said.

"You have a member of your team that paints," the eldest daughter asked.

"Yes, two members are excellent painters," Yoshua answered.

"This would have made my father ecstatic that someone can use these art supplies. It would have made our father thrilled," the eldest daughter said. Yoshua dickered over the price with the eldest daughter and got an extra discount when he paid in cash. They loaded their new belongings into the van and headed back to the chapel. They unloaded everything from the van, and the last item out was the art supplies. While Sasha was unloading the box, he saw Gefen.

"Look what we found for you." Gefen took the box from Sasha, sat on the van's tailgate, and opened it. For her, it was Aladdin in the treasure cave. There were sketchpads, charcoals, watercolors, oil paints, canvases, a small hammer, tacks, and enough wood for two frames.

"Thank you for being so considerate," Gefen thanked them.

Sasha walked over to where David was lifting the five-kilo hammer to finish knocking out the remaining bricks.

"You did a good thing to put a smile on that girl's face. It's what your mother would call *chesed* (doing an act of kindness)."

At 2:55 in the afternoon, the chapel fell silent. Ruth and Aviva turned to see why the noise had stopped. Sasha and David were grinning from ear to ear. They looked like two ghosts. One could see was their eyes as dust covered them from head to toe. However, they removed every brick from the arches.

Every one felt the breeze created by opening the two archways.

Ruth stopped sanding; she had run out of paint. There was gray plaster exposed in the test area. Ruth looked at Aviva with a question mark on her face.

"Ruth, I have a feeling that here in the middle of Andalusia, the Jews who founded this community would have used the very talented local Moslem artisans. Would you ask Yoshua if we have a rubber mallet and if he could make us a simple wooden chisel? If there's something behind that plaster, I don't want to ruin it." Ruth left the chapel and returned a few minutes later with the tools.

Aviva held the chisel in her left hand and the rubber mallet in her right lined up the chisel, and struck the end with a serious blow. The chisel's nose flattened out a small amount, but the force of the blow caused a hunk of plaster to fall to the floor. The hole was a little less than a centimeter square. Aviva examined the spot with the magnifying glass. Satisfied that she had caused no damage, she made three more quick strikes. When Aviva stepped back, a green color greeted her efforts. Excited, Aviva picked up the magnifying glass and recognized the pattern at once. "This is green marble!"

"The closest source of green marble is Sweden. Someone invested a significant amount of money to build this place!" Yoshua said.

˙ David and Sasha followed Yoshua to where Aviva and Ruth were standing—and grinning like Cheshire cats. Without saying another word, Aviva pointed to the hole in the wall with the magnifying glass and handed it to Yoshua. His eyes opened wide—they had their first major find. Yoshua took the magnifying glass and examined the spot. After seeing the green marble, he examined the hole carefully. He saw where the paint ended and where the plaster started. Yoshua stepped back and handed the magnifying glass to Ruth. Everyone took a turn to see their first breakthrough and had the same thought.

"Why would the church plaster over such expensive green marble wall tiles?" Gefen asked.

"Boss, there's something wrong in this place. I have an uneasy feeling something not kosher happened here," Sasha said. He paused to consider the possible theories that would fit the information they had up to this point.

"No one would cover over expensive imported marble walls if the walls were in good shape. At the minimum, they would've stolen the tiles because of their beauty and value. The church, way back at the turn of the sixteenth century, must've felt something was so wrong with this place that they covered the walls with plaster and painted them, hiding the origins of this building."

"Elegantly put, Alexander. The only thing that comes to mind is that they wanted to erase the Jewish origins of this place. If they were in a hurry, the fastest way would be to plaster the walls and then paint over the plaster. It would be much faster than pulling off the tiles, making repairs, and then painting," theorized Ruth.

*****

The next day started earlier. The men rose at 5:00 am, did a series of stretching and power exercises led by Yoshua. They ran for twenty-minute in the fields to the south of the house. They returned, showered, and then David and Yoshua put on their *taphilin* (phylacteries) and said their morning prayers.

At 7:30, Juanita arrived to begin her duties as a housekeeper. Yoshua introduced her to the team.

"Juanita, every member of the team are vegetarians, but we eat only certain kinds of fish. Fish that have fins and scales. We will buy all the food and kitchen supplies," Yoshua explained to her in Spanish.

"Yoshua ask Juanita about herself?" Ruthie requested from her husband.

"I am forty-eight years old, unlike most Europeans I married young, and had four children, two boys and two girls. Now that my children are older and out of the house, I have lots of free time. It thrilled me when this job opportunity came along," Juanita explained.

"I have never been out of Spain and being able to work for foreigners sounded glamorous. I learned English three months ago." Juanita switched to English.

"I know a little English. You help if you talk to me in English," Juanita said.

"No problem, will help you with your English," David said.

"Gefen, how's your English?" David asked.

"Anyone serious about mathematics and cryptology has to know English," she said with a South African accent.

"Where did you get the accent?" David asked.

"My teacher in school was from South Africa.".

Yoshua went into the town and met the plumber who handed him the drawings and forms he needed to receive a building permit. It was a small town and everyone knew what was going on, especially the sale of a local building to foreign scientists. It took an hour to fill out the forms and pay the fees. The town's civil engineer, who doubled as the building inspector, came with Yoshua to examine the site. After talking to the electrician and the plumber, he signed the forms and stamped them approved.

While Yoshua dealt with administrative details, the rest of the team followed orders from Aviva. They prepared to strip the walls. Aviva lifted the mallet and chisel.

"I will show you how to hold the tools properly and control the amount of impact one exerted on the chisel with the hammer," Aviva said.

She demonstrated the importance of the angle of the chisel and the strike on the head of the chisel to avoid damage to the marble wall underneath.

They cataloged every paint sample and prepared to send for further independent analysis to an outside laboratory.

"I will send a second set of samples sent to my graduate students in Jerusalem for analysis," Ruth said.

The layers of paint were thick as white wash was crude. There was an average of thirty-three point five millimeters of paint between the outer layers and the original marble walls. Aviva measured a square meter in the northeast corner as a test region. First, with the chisel and mallet, she sliced into the paint at a forty-five-degree angle to begin the removal of the layers.

"Aviva, aren't you concerned about mistakes by the team," Ruth asked.

"No, that layer of plaster will absorb every mistake and protect the marble underneath," Aviva replied. After a few minutes, Aviva stopped chiseling and Yoshua measured the depth of the hole with a caliper. She had removed twenty-seven millimeters of paint and had exposed the lime-based plaster.

"I brought with me stiff plastic brushes, but I don't have enough of them. Yoshua, please take one and go to town and see if you can get another six brushes like it." The bristles of the brush were stiff enough to remove wet plaster without scratching the marble. The team worked hard to remove the paint. They hauled in buckets of water from the new faucet that the plumber had installed. The team attacked the walls with the water and brushes. The test area grew wider and wider as the paint and plaster disappeared. When Yoshua returned with more buckets and brushes, everyone joined in widening the hole. They progressed downward along the wall, avoiding scratching the marble.

Aviva exposed the last section adjacent to the original marble wall. Slowly, the small hole expanded, and they were exposing the junction of four different marble tiles. The top two were green with white marbling. Below them were pure white tiles inlaid with beautiful black marble geometric designs running along the entire length of the tile.

"Aviva, look at the design we have uncovered," Ruth said.

"Wow, it's a flat double helix that weaves through a line of rhombuses that are end to end," Aviva said. She measured the various parts of the design.

"Both the rhombus and the double helix are four centimeters wide. This part of the design was eight centimeters wide. Two centimeters above and below the rhombus is a solid black line one centimeter wide," Aviva said. She made more measurements.

"The entire geometric design is twenty centimeters wide. The lower right tile was again green with white marbling and the lower left was pure white, with a hint of gray marbling. The art work is exquisite," Aviva said.

Everyone came over and lent a hand to expose that section of the wall. After two hours of painstakingly delicate work, they had exposed enough of the wall to see its true design. They had exposed a large area on the wall shaped like a plus sign. The cleaned section ran fifty centimeters wide, from thirty centimeters above the floor up to a height of two meters. At seventy-five centimeters above the floor, the arms of the plus to the right and left were a meter wide. Each tile was twenty-five centimeters tall and forty centimeters wide. The wall was white marble up to seventy-five centimeters. Next came a twenty-five-centimeter tall green marble tile, followed by another white one that had the geometric design running the length of the wall. Above the white tile, with the design, was another green tile. Above, the green tile was white until the ceiling.

Aviva showed Gefen how to clean and polish the exposed section of marble wall to restore it to its former glory.

"First, you go over the stone with a soft damp cloth. Next, with a clean dry rag, you applied hydrogen peroxide. The hydrogen peroxide cleans away the leftover specks of paint and dirt particles. You finish the cleaning with a chamois cloth."

"That's the entire process?" Gefen asked.

"No." Aviva removed a bottle of marble polish from her bag, applied the polish with another dry cloth. "You finish the process by buffing with a dry chamois cloth," Aviva explained. Aviva handed Gefen the cleaning materials and cloths and set her to work.

The results were magnificent. Sasha set up lights and took photos of Aviva polishing the tiles with the geometric design. When she realized she was being photographed, she threw the chamois cloth over his camera. Aviva was angry when Sasha took the photo. However, when he developed it in black and white and submitted it to an international photography contest, he took third place. When a major photojournalism magazine ran an article on the chapel six months later, that photo of Aviva was the most prominent photo in the piece.

Gefen's patience displayed in the restoration work fascinated Sasha. He photographed her from various angles as she concentrated on her work. Everyone had to get used to Sasha photographing them as he did it during the entire process. Sasha had many photos of what the wall looked like before and what it looked like now. It was amazing beyond their dreams. The team looked at the results of their work and wondered what had made someone cover something so beautiful. The inlay work was so exact; it was difficult to distinguish the joints between the two marbles with the naked eye.

That afternoon, Yoshua got a call from the glazier.

"Professor, your windows will be ready tomorrow. We can come at 11:00 to install the windows."

\*\*\*\*\*

In the evening, an hour after dinner, Yoshua called everyone into the living room to discuss ideas about what they had discovered in the chapel.

"Considering the quality of the workmanship and the materials used, this was an expensive undertaking. The imported green marble alone made it expensive. We haven't exposed the ceiling and floor. We don't have the slightest idea of the extent the builders invested in the artistic portion of the building. I'm sure that even uneducated soldiers fighting in Ferdinand's army would've recognized the building as something of great value. Thorough history cultures robbed building materials from the conquered to make their new homes and public buildings. Here, they covered it over," Yoshua said.

"My question is: if there was something so offensive there that they could not strip the edifice of everything of value, why wasn't the structure destroyed?" said Aviva.

"What we know for sure is that it was once a Jewish owned structure and most likely the *Bet Midrash Ohel Rivka* mentioned on the cover page that Tzion and Yoshua found in the binding of the *Mishne Torah*. We can understand that the new Spanish rulers of Granada wanted to recoup their losses from conducting a war. Therefore, I have to agree with Aviva, why they didn't strip the building materials from the structure?" said Ruth.

"Gefen, what do you think?" Yoshua asked. People didn't ask her opinion about anything. She opened her mouth to say something, but none of what she had to say made much sense. She shock her head.

"I have an alternative theory," Sasha said.

"Let's hear it," Yoshua encouraged his student.

"What if the Jewish community itself feared the Catholics would pilfer their stunning bet midrash. If the Christians knew there were valuable materials in the building? Maybe it was the Jewish community that plastered over the walls to hide its beauty. That way, when the town fell to Ferdinand and Isabella, the Spanish would think it was a poor community and not strip or destroy the structure."

The team looked at Sasha with wide-open eyes.

"This alternative theory explains much better what we have found," Aviva said. Yoshua smirked, nodded his head, and congratulated his student.

"Very elegant theory, Mr. Chrominsky. Your idea would answer the obvious questions we've brought up in the discussion."

That night, Yoshua called Gavriel to give him a progress report. He had uploaded photos for Gavriel to look at while he described what they had done. "My God, Yoshua, the walls and the design are beautiful."

"Yes, aren't they? If nothing else, this is a significant discovery for the art world. The workmanship is exquisite."

"Yoshua, we will have troubles with the authorities. Once they see the walls, they'll declare the site a national treasure."

"I fear you're correct. In cases like this, when archaeologists discover something beautiful, the discovery can become your worst nightmare. The authorities stick their noses into your business."

"Yoshua, no one expected such a find. From what I see of your work there, you'll get a few more papers out of this excavation. If you can find another clue to who the Light of Justice is, we can take it from there. We must wait and see."

"Let's hope. It's late in Israel, so I'll let you go to sleep. Please send our regards to your lovely wife. *Lila tov*."

"*Lila tov*, Yoshua, and *mazal tov* on your find."

# REVEALING THE WALLS

The next morning didn't start like the previous ones. Sasha showed up in his running shorts at 5:20 and asked, "Do you mind if I join you in your exercises and run?"

"It would be our pleasures to have you join us," said Yoshua. The three men fell into pace with one another, and by the time they returned from their run, they were telling jokes and laughing. Sasha was an amiable person to be around as long as you maintained your loyalty to him. He would give you the shirt off his back. However, if you crossed him, he was a formidable foe.

There was a rhythm to their work. Everyone was flexible and tolerant of the others' likes and dislikes. At the chapel, everyone had the right to listen to the music of their choosing. The variety ranged from Chasidic to reggae, to classical, to *Mizrachi*, and to heavy metal. Food was the same—everyone took turns making their favorite meal—according to the supplies they had available. One person made breakfast, another lunch, and a third dinner. To live and work successfully in such proximity, everyone needed a large degree of flexibility and tolerance. Gefen didn't even know how to make a hard-boiled egg, so Aviva took it upon herself to teach her a few simple recipes.

For the next two days, the team worked on removing the paint and plaster from the walls. Aviva had Gefen work at her side so she could supervise her. She didn't want to take any chances with the care of the geometric design area. It was amazing to watch Aviva and Gefen work hour after hour, with what seemed to be an almost endless amount of energy and patience. For Gefen, this work was like meditating. It amazed Gefen at how she got caught up in the discovery's excitement.

Piece by piece, they exposed the original wall to the light of the world once again after five hundred twenty-five years. At the junction of the eastern and northern walls, they found their first big discovery. While Yoshua was chiseling away on the layers of paint, he heard the chisel striking metal. The sound was so distinct that everyone stopped what they were doing and came to see what he found.

"Gefen, please hand me the metal tack hammer. I want to map out the size of this metal plate," Aviva said.

"Do you remember I mentioned we found a receipt for a memorial plaque? Maybe this is that plaque ordered by the man named Aharon?" Yoshua suggested.

Everyone waited impatiently while Aviva worked out the dimensions of the plate. The excitement caused the team to work on the area with great enthusiasm, but with a little too much force. Aviva saw what was happening.

"Stop, you'll damage the wall if you continue with such force." She stepped up to the wall and pushed everyone away. With patience that drove everyone else crazy, Aviva worked methodically and delicately to uncover the plaque that was approximately thirty centimeters wide and forty centimeters long. In such a place of worship or study, a plaque signified either a memorial to a deceased loved one, or someone who made a donation to the structure or organization. Every few minutes Aviva stopped to examine the progress of the work and gauge how much more she would have to remove to expose the plaque.

Aviva's phone rang, interrupting her concentration. She looked at her phone to see who it was calling.

"It's the independent lab with the analysis of the paint samples."

"Please read me the results and send them to my email account," Aviva requested.

When she finished talking with the lab, she reported to the rest of the team. "The results are what we expected; they matched the team's analysis with the XRF gun by ninety-three point four percent. Except for the last two layers of paint, the rest were simple water based whitewash. The last two layers were expensive linseed oil-based paints."

Aviva returned to a spot next to Gefen and continued the removal. When she concentrated on a project, it was as if the rest of the world didn't exist. The minutes ticked away and the rest of the team became more and more agitated, standing around, forced to do nothing but watch Aviva work. Aviva turned to the rest of the team and shooed them away.

"Go back to work on the other wall in the meantime. As soon as I expose something, I'll call everyone over to see it." They took up positions along the opposite wall and, unenthusiastically, removed the layers of paint that camouflaged the original marble walls. Every few minutes, someone looked over his or her shoulder to check on Aviva's progress.

Three hours later, Aviva finished exposing the outline of the plaque. Her heart pounded when she observed engraving on the plaque. It was still impossible to read because the paint filled in the grooves. Aviva walked over to her supplies. She selected a bottle of 70% ethanol and a chemical stripper based on methyl chloride. In the chemical hood, she mixed one-to-one ratio of ethanol and methyl chloride to dissolve the paint. She took a brush with hard plastic bristles and, ever so gently, brushed in a circular pattern to remove the last layers of paint on the plaque. The first area exposed was the upper left corner of the plaque.

"Look everyone, the plaque is bronze," Aviva said excitedly. Now, the team gathered around to watch the progress. Slowly, Aviva's work exposed the letters under the paint.

"Look," Gefen, "called out. They are Hebrew letters." "Congratulations, Dad. Your research has proven correct. We've found the *bet midrash* from the right time. The next task is to find evidence that this is *Ohel Rivka,*" David said.

Sasha laid his tools on the ground and went to get his camera. He set up the lights and tripod while Aviva continued to bring to light. After over five hundred years, the words engraved on the plaque. Aviva moved away from the wall. She had removed sufficient amounts of paint to expose the letters. Ruth read what was written aloud.

"These marble walls were donated to Ohel Rivka by Aharon ben Ephraim Dori (servant of the king) in memory of his loving wife, Orit." A joyful group hug formed immediately, followed by back slaps, high-fives, and a funky version of the happy dance by Sasha and Gefen."

Yoshua smiled from ear to ear.

"Bull's-eye. It's the same man from the title page."

Ruth came over and kissed him.

"Well, how does it feel to have done the research that has proven that this is the correct place? Right?"

Yoshua turned to Gefen and bowed from the waist. "Gefen, we wouldn't be here today if you hadn't deciphered those pages we found in the bishop's archives.

It's a great feeling to know my hypothesis was correct."
Yet he had a nagging feeling about the plaque.

"What does 'servant of the king' mean?" Yoshua asked.
Everyone shrugged their shoulders.

"During the Islamic period, there was an emir, not a
king. When the Christians took over, they expelled the
Jews from Spain in 1492. So how could this Aharon Dori
be 'a servant of the king' in a Christian land? Did this
patron of the Jewish community believe he was a servant
of the Light of Justice?"

David looked at his mother for guidance.

"Love, how have you jumped from 'servant of the king'
to that king being the Light of Justice?" Ruth asked.

"What other king is there?" Yoshua asked in return.

Aviva showed Gefen how to use specific tools for
cleaning the commemorative inscription. The rest of the
team continued their work, removing paint from the walls.
Sasha and David worked together little by little, moving
downward, exposing the entire inlaid black marble.

When they finished that area and moved on to the floor
tiles, they noticed a cracked tile. They removed the broken
tile and saw that the white marble wall continued
downward. David removed the cement from underneath
the tile, revealing yet another tile below.

"Aviva, can you come over here and look at this? How
should we proceed?"

She inspected the tiles for two minutes. She next went
to the main entrance. Aviva examined the relationship
between the floor, walls, and the entrance.

"The threshold of the door is lower than the floor—
Yoshua commented on this the first time we examined the
chapel. It is obvious there are several layers of flooring,"
Aviva observed.

"If the chapel needed a new floor, why hadn't the old tiles been removed and replaced with new ones?"

*****

Ruth returned to the house to cook food for *Shabbat*. Not long after, Yoshua called a halt to the work and everyone headed back to the house to prepare for *Shabbat*. For the first time, the team would be together outside of Israel for a *Shabbat*—this would not be a typical experience for any of them. Twenty minutes before sundown, everyone was on their cell phones calling their families and loved ones to find out how they were and wish them *Shabbat shalom*. Ruth cried as she spoke to her other three children and her father.

After the phone call, David hugged her and reassured her.

"*Ima*, the kids are OK, and *Saba* knows how to take care of everything."

"Thank you, David. It's time you got into the shower." Ruth hugged him and kissed him on the cheek.

Everyone was in a good mood after what they had discovered in *Ohel Rivka*. When the time came to light *Shabbat* candles, Ruth and Aviva turned to Gefen.

"Please join us to light Shabbat candles," they invited.

"I've never lite candles before."

"Please join us," Ruth encouraged her, setting out two candles for Gefen. After candle lighting, Yoshua and David went outside to the back porch and recited the prayers for receiving the *Shabbat*. Later, they sang the psalms of the service of receiving the *Shabbat,* the evening prayers. They had pleasant voices. Afterwards, Sasha turned to Gefen and whispered to her.

"I am moved by their intent (*kavana*) of their prayers.

Yoshua felt content as he watched David pray with great kavana; he believed in what in his mission. Yoshua lost his place in the prayer book as his thoughts turned to his other children at home with his father-in-law. He made a silent personal prayer.

*"Creator of the heavens and earth, King of the Universe, watch over my children. Help me raise them to be good people. Give them an open, giving hand; an eye that sees the good in man; and ears that do not run after gossip. Help me teach them the most difficult of lessons— watching what we say. Guard their tongues from sin and let their mouths only be opened to say positive things."*

Ruthie glanced at Yoshua and recognized that far-off look in his eyes. She wondered,

*"Where is his mind?"* She smiled when she looked at David and thought, *"It's time to cut the apron strings— he's eighteen; I need to treat him like an adult. He's an excellent student, hardworking, caring, easy to be with, and committed."*

Ruth had invested so much into her eldest. If anything would happen to her husband, she had to have David ready to step in and take up the reins of leadership of the Aluzian people. Ruth made a silent prayer, *"Our Father, Our King (Avinu Malkanu) watch over my husband and son and guide them to the fulfillment of your prophet's words."*

After prayers, everyone gathered around the table. Ruth had brought with her a handmade cover for the *challot* (bread) that her grandmother made, and a silver wine goblet they received as a wedding gift. The two items felt like home, among the paper plates and plastic cutlery. They sang *"Shalom Aleichem"* ("Peace Be Upon You"), Ruth and Yoshua blessed David, and asked Gefen, "Do you want to be blessed also?

Gefen looked, instead, at Aviva. That one look melted Aviva's heart; she had never blessed a child. She placed her shaking hands on Gefen's head and said the parental blessing. Aviva gathered Gefen in her arms and kissed her on the cheeks. It was very emotional for everyone, and it took a few seconds to recover. Together, they sang "*Eishet Chayel*" ("Who Can Find a Virtuous Woman"). It must have been the meditation Yoshua had done while watching David, because he sang with *kavana* (intent) he hadn't felt in a long time. Ruth felt it immediately and intended, after dinner, to find out what was happening.

*****

Dinner was relaxing, and they had a decent meal from the limited supply of kosher food available. The discussion at the table was light. Sasha showed his humorous side and entertained the group poking fun at Israeli politicians. Ruth asked David to say for a few minutes about the weekly Torah portion, Pinchas.

David thought for a few seconds. He understood knew what subject he would talk about.

"Pinchas, was the son of *Elazar* and the grandson of *Aharon* the Cohen. He wasn't an accepted figure in Jewish life and especially among his own generation. *Zimri,* head of the tribe of Shimon, blatantly desecrated God's will, causing Pinchas to take action on his own. The killing of Zimri, without proper judicial process, upset the people of Israel."

"David, what did he do?" Sasha asked.

David looked at his father, who nodded to him.

David's face turned red as he spoke.

"Zimri, the prince of the house of Shimon, openly had sex with the daughter of the Midian king."

Sasha roared with laughter. When he stopped laughing, David continued.

"It was the people's opposition to Pinchas's actions that caused the Holy One, Blessed be He, to intervene on his behalf. The Creator blessed Pinchas and granted him the gift of eternal priesthood and peace. The people challenged Pinchas's motives, but God vindicated him."

"Yes, it took God's direct intervention to calm the objections to Pinchas's actions. It's important to emphasize that there are no other acts of holy zealotry mentioned in the Torah. Nor is there any other approved holy zealotry by Jewish tradition. Pinchas is the exception and not the rule in Jewish life and tradition. It's difficult to measure the characteristic of zealotry. It's tricky to distinguish between personal quirks and true zealous behavior is for the sake of sanctifying the name of God. Jewish history is littered with the victims of other peoples' religious zealotry perpetrated upon us—zealots whose real motives were false piety, bigotry, and financial gain," said David.

"I think that's the real reason we're here. I'm sure we will find some of that false piety and bigotry on the other side of the wall in the chapel," said Aviva.

"Often, we see that the would-be zealot covers his own inadequacies and misgivings by attacking others in the name of something holy," said Sasha.

"This is the reason the people of Israel questioned Pinchas's motives in killing *Zimri*. The Talmud tells us that Pinchas should have been accused of murder. Only God's direct intervention in the affair saved Pinchas from unwarranted criticism and public disapproval. By getting directly involved, God gave a twofold message: to protect Pinchas and to warn us of the dangers of zealotry. God won't step in again to rescue the zealot from public and historical disapproval," said David.

After dinner, they sang *Shabbat* songs—even Gefen. "How do you know these songs, Gefen?" Ruth asked.

"I am familiar with *Shabbat* rituals from visiting with my grandparents when I was young."

Ruth shared an anecdote from *Perkie Avot*. They drank coffee and nibbled on a variety of nuts and seeds. It was near midnight when they rose from the table. They went out to the veranda to enjoy the cool breeze and fragrance of the hyacinths growing in the garden. Everyone enjoyed the evening and felt they had created communal experience, which helped to unify the team.

After a few moments of stargazing, Aviva brought up the subject of the flooring. Ideas flew around on the distinct possibilities; to where everyone had expressed their opinion except Yoshua. He sat in a corner, silent, thinking, trying to tie together the data they had about *Ohel Rivka*. *"Something is missing, but for the life of me, I can't remember what."* Aloud, he vocalized his thoughts.

"What's bothering me is why they left the plaque in place if it was offensive to the church; why wasn't it removed? The section of the original wall we've exposed so far is of unusually high quality marble and appeared in good shape. Why would the church order such beauty covered up?"

"Maybe the community started their cover-up too late. Perhaps they didn't finish the work by the time the Christians conquered the surrounding area. What about the sealed wing of the building?" David said. Hearing David's ideas, everything came together for Yoshua in a flash, and he put together his disaster theory.

"The analysis of the number of layers of paint and plaster on the walls showed that the depth of the plaster and paint was the same for the three outer walls. However, the wall that forms the separation between the room we're working in and the closed off wing is different. That wall lacks the two layers of linseed oil based paint and the plaster is much thinner, which means they applied the first layer of paint after the other wing was sealed. This would seem to support Sasha's theory of what happened," said Aviva.

"We know from Padre Emanuel's records that the local Commission of Inquisition ordered the other half of the chapel sealed. They ordered never to open the sealed room. The question is, what's in there that the church and/or the Spanish monarchy never want to see the light of day?" said Yoshua.

Ruth suggested a different, insightful approach to the subject.

"I think we need to believe in the Holy One and His path. Sealing a room means something needs to stay hidden. Ordering the closure of the room means there's something inside they don't want the world to see. Have any of you considered that despite the desires of the church and Ferdinand and Isabella, while they thought they were hiding evidence of their crimes, God actually caused them to preserve the evidence of their crimes," Ruth explained her theory.

"A case point is the death sentences on the ten great sages of Israel by the Romans during the second revolt. When they investigated the reason for the decree from heaven, a *bat kol* (a voice from heaven) came and told them this was justice for the crime of Yosef's ten brothers, who sold him into slavery. The Holy One Blessed be He waited over a thousand years before serving justice. It's not for us to decide when God meters out justice. We must have faith that God always provides justice. I predict that whatever is on the other side of that wall will be a tool of justice," Ruth said.

"Well said, Mom," David said as he wrapped his arms around Ruth and kissed her on the cheek.

"Now, I understand why the Vatican is so interested in what we're doing here. I need to contact the Israeli Ambassador. We need to warn him about the Vatican's interest in the excavation and the potential trouble we could get into. We're in a country that still supports the Catholic Church," Yoshua said.

"Every Jewish artifact which existed at the time the Catholics took over control of Granada, they destroyed. The conquerors would have melted any Jewish artifacts of valuable metals. Afterwards they would have burned any made of flammable materials. Historical records show they destroyed any stone or pottery items considered Jewish artifacts. They could have erased any symbol of Judaism in the place. What made the room intrinsically repulsive to the Inquisition?"

"Historical documents reveal that in many other places, Jews who didn't convert were tortured and burned at the stake. The Inquisition destroyed numerous synagogues and institutes of learning," said Aviva.

"On Sunday, we should concentrate on the wall of the closed off wing, but we must be careful. It's well known that caves or rooms that have been closed off for hundreds of years contain potentially dangerous fungal spores. You know the so-called curse of the pharaohs! We must get special protective suits and breathing apparatuses before we can attempt to open the sealed wing," said Ruth.

*****

*Shabbat* was a relaxing day. Sasha and the girls slept late. They gathered to eat at 1:00. Afterwards, everyone took a nap. *Shabbat* afternoon was extensive in Spain during the summer. They ate their third meal at 6:30 and at 9:00, after evening prayers, they made the *Havdalah* service, separating the *Shabbat* from the rest of the week.

*****

Refreshed from *Shabbat*, the team headed back to the chapel on Saturday night. They continued exposing the marble walls. At 9:30, Yoshua called Gavriel in Jerusalem, "*Shavua tov* (A good week), Gavriel."

"Shavua tov to you."

"Gavriel, I want to give you an update about what we're doing."

After four minutes of listening to the news, Gavriel said, "You've been fortunate so far to have found so much in such a short time."

"We want to start on the wall that separates the two halves of the structure. We're concerned about how the Vatican will react to whatever we find there. You remember I told you about the conversation I had with Cardinal Rossini, the President of the Pontifical Commission. The survey of the outside of the building, including the roof, revealed there were no openings leading to the sealed off portion. If the church sealed it up, it was for a good reason. Opening it might be like opening

Pandora's Box. We're in a Catholic country that barely tolerates us."

*"Tomorrow morning, I'll call the Ministry of Foreign Affairs and express your security fears."* Yoshua thought, *"I need to institute changes to increase the security of the team and the chapel."*

"Listen Yoshua, I'll get on the phone to a friend of mine in England. He's a heart surgeon in London, an amateur archaeologist, and a big fan of your work. He has access to fiber optic equipment that could assist your project. I'll see how fast he can get the equipment to you.

"We're proud of your progress so far. Take care," Gavriel added.

"Thanks, bye." Yoshua opened his laptop, looked up the email address of the Israeli Embassy in Madrid, and composed an email outlining what they were doing and the conversation he had with Cardinal Rossini. He didn't want to sound like an alarmist, but he had concerns that the Vatican can put serious pressure on the Spanish government to halt the revelation of the secrets of the *bet midrash* or even have them arrested. He also sent a copy of the message to Gavriel and Ysrael. To be on the safe side.

*****

When he got off the phone with Yoshua, Gavriel called his contact in England. He was lucky to catch Dr. Simon Jamerson, as he was a very busy surgeon. Simon listened to what Gavriel told him.

"I've waited my entire life to serve. You know I'll do everything in my power to make this project go forward. I can raise at least four hundred thousand euros in an hour.

It would honor my entire family to assist. I have family members in the international food industry who know how to prepare a shipment and get it to anywhere in the world as fast as possible," Dr. Simon Jamerson replied.

"Is it too big of an imposition to ask you to go to Spain?"

"Sir, I would give up a few days of surgical profits to make sure this project succeeds."

"On the personal side, how are you holding up," Gavriel asked.

"Uncle, I am busy all the time with the children, grandchild, and my surgical practice," Simon replied.

"Simon, Esther told me many times she was so happy with you. You are a good man. I am sure you will find love once more," Gavriel encourage him.

"Thank you, sir. Your words are a great comfort."

*****

Sunday started for the men of the team at 5:20 am with their workout. They took some extra time and ran for thirty minutes, after deciding they should run in a different direction each day to get to know the town and the surrounding area better.

After breakfast, they began work at the chapel at 8:00. The town was quiet—most of the people were still practicing Catholics and on Sundays they went to Mass. After Mass, they returned home for a traditional family meal.

"Let's try to keep the noise level lower. We need to consider our neighbors," said Yoshua.

"I suggest we try to finish removing the paint and plaster on the northern and southern walls," said Aviva. The team, working in pairs, finished the removal by noon.

"These white and green marble walls are beautiful. The original *bet midrash* must have been stunning. The room was a remarkable work of art. Its stonework was impressive, especially considering the tools available in those days," Aviva remarked.

Sasha used a wide-angle lens to photograph the walls. Ruth sat with her laptop to work on an article. A smiling Yoshua winked at David, "Why don't you and I haul out the rubble."

So far, Gefen's dedication and patience surprised Aviva. "Gefen, why don't you and I finish the restoration work on the plaque?"

They returned to the house at 4:00 pm. Ruth and Yoshua wrote and submitted one article to an archaeological journal and a second to a photojournalism magazine.

"If we have free time, I'll set up my new easel outside and start on a few ideas I have running around in my head about combining the local landscape with some of my codes," Gefen said.

"Call me when you have something for us to see. I'm very interested in your ideas," Aviva said.

"Maybe you'll join me?"

"Thank you, honey, but I stopped doing original work a long time ago," Aviva replied.

At 4:30, Yoshua's cell phone rang. David was standing next to the coffee table where Yoshua had laid the phone. He leaned over, saw it was a call from Israel, and tapped the speaker. He motioned for his father to come. David yelled in the phone's direction.

"David Rosenberg speaking."

"Oh, David, how are you? Is your father there?"

"I've called him and he's coming now, Professor Yaroni."

"Tell your father that Dr. Simon Jamerson, a financial backer of the project, will come on Monday with the equipment need to open the sealed room."

Yoshua came into the room, heard the conversation, and said, "Gavriel, its Yoshua."

"Yoshua, Dr. Simon Jamerson, is taking off time from his practice to bring you the gear and supplies. He has equipment to open the sealed room according to health department protocols. As I told David, he's an important financial backer of the project."

"That's very nice, but why is he coming here?"

"The equipment is expensive and he can't leave it unattended, so he volunteered to bring it to Spain, set it up, and operate it—to save time. While we're talking, he's having everything packed. His family has a freight company and they'll fly the equipment to Granada. He'll meet the freight customs agent at the airport, and they promised to get the equipment out of customs by 5:00 pm on Monday. One of Dr. Jamerson's cousins works with the Spanish authorities on a regular basis. They have a way of not paying customs," Gavriel told him.

"How?"

"If you declare the equipment for scientific use, and file an affidavit to ship the equipment back to England when the research finishes, there will be no customs charges. Please meet Dr. Jamerson at 1:30 at the Granada-Jaen Airport on Monday afternoon. Assist him in every way to get the equipment cleared through customs. I understand the project is developing faster than anyone thought. Let's thank God that Dr. Jamerson has the free time and equipment to help us out. *Shavua tov* to everyone. I have a good feeling about this. Be well Yoshua, *shalom*."

"*Shavua tov*, Gavriel."

\*\*\*\*\*

Early Monday morning, the plumber showed up with his son and Yoshua's teenage construction crew. With Sasha and David helping, they had the bathroom's outer walls up by 10:45. While the construction was going on, the plumber and two of the boys connected the water and sewage lines. At noon, they cemented the first toilet in place.

"We'll have everything finished by the end of the day," the plumber assured Yoshua.

\*\*\*\*\*

At 12:30 pm, Ruth drove Yoshua, David, and Sasha to the train station for the trip to the airport. The trip to Granada passed quickly and when they got off the train, they headed for the air terminal. David carried a cardboard sign with Dr. Jamerson's name on it. They made it to the arrival gate as people came off the plane from Madrid. David held up his sign, and the trio waited for the English doctor. The fourth to the last person to leave the plane walked up to them and introduced himself with a big smile.

"Hi, I'm Simon Jamerson. You must be Professor Rosenberg." He held out his hand to Yoshua.

"A pleasure to meet you, sir," Yoshua replied in his best English.

"The supplies and equipment I sent are being unloaded from the plane and transported to customs right now. I have custom's declaration already filled out. We can claim the supplies after the Spanish authorities examine everything." For the next two hours, they battled with the same windmills that Don Quixote must have fought hundreds of years ago. Finally, frustrated with the lack of progress, Yoshua decided they needed to do something.

Once again, Yoshua felt the hairs on the back of his neck standing up and he thought, *"If I mention anything to Jamerson, he'll think I'm paranoid. I'm convinced the delay is being caused by the iron hand of the Vatican closing upon us. What could be so damaging to the church that so many forces are working to assure that what's hidden remains that way?"*

Little did Yoshua know he wasn't being paranoid enough. The Jesuits, who he thought he had defeated at the cardinal's residence, were still busy trying to stop the Israelis. They had pressured Padre Emanuel to provide reports on the Israelis' whereabouts, progress, and discoveries.

Dr. Jamerson called his cousin in England, who was a friend of the director of the freight company. It took forty-five minutes for the *protekzia* to kick in, but when it did, things moved. The inspection finished only when the inspectors had to go home. The custom inspectors taped closed the boxes. Scientific equipment is exempt from customs fees.

Joshua leaned close to Simon.

"The inspectors are making this more difficult that necessary."

"Yes, but if we complain they can delay the release of the equipment for days."

The work day was coming to a close. The Spanish glanced at the clock on the wall. With a scowl on his face, the inspector lifted his stamp. His hand hovered above the permits. Simon and Yoshua smiled at the inspector. His hand came down. He stamped every import permit, releasing everything Simon had shipped. Yoshua didn't realize how much Jamerson had brought with him. There were twenty-four large boxes of equipment and supplies. He thought, *"The involvement in this project is disproportional in funding, labor, and political intrigue for a normal archaeological expedition."*

Jamerson appeared to have endless funds at his disposal. He rented a truck and a car for transport. The four men loaded the truck. Later, with Yoshua behind the wheel of the car and Sasha in the truck, they drove out of the airport. At last, they headed off for Nido de Aguila. The tiny convoy arrived back at the house at 11:30 pm. Only Ruth was still awake. She knew she couldn't sleep until Yoshua and David were home safely.

Dr. Jamerson stood at the front door waiting for Yoshua to introduce him to Ruth. When Yoshua got the message and began the introduction, Simon gave Ruth a big smile, and she smiled back at the handsome physician. "It's a great pleasure to meet you, Dr. Rosenberg. I've read several papers you co-authored with your husband."

Yoshua thought, "Simon and Ruth are far too relaxed for a first meeting. There's no of the tension I'd expected when first meeting someone. I never know what the other might be, so I'm always somewhat guarded at a first meeting, but not these two." He said, "Have the two of you met before?"

Taken aback by the question, Simon and Ruth answered simultaneously, shaking their heads.

"No, we've never met before." Strange as it was, Yoshua let it go because he trusted Ruth one hundred percent.

*****

The next morning, Yoshua, David, and Sasha got up at 5:00 am, got dressed, and started their workout. They did calisthenics for fifteen minutes, worked out with light weights they had jerry-rigged, and went for a twenty-minute run. To stay in shape, Yoshua did this workout every morning since he left active duty in the army. It amazed him at how easy it was for David. For the past three years, Yoshua and David had been working out together—a basic joint activity that helped cement the bond between father and son. Yoshua taught David how to shoot a pistol. They went to the firing range twice a month to fire fifty rounds each. Over the years, David honed his skills. He was as good a marksman as Yoshua, at ten to twenty-five meters.

When they got home from their run, they showered and went into the living room, where they found Simon putting on *taphilin*. Yoshua stopped in his tracks.

"Why the shocked look? Don't Jews put on *taphilin* everywhere in the world?"

"Why, yes they do, however, I had no idea you were Jewish."

"My parents changed their name when they came to England in 1938. Our family name was Yavetz. My Hebrew name is *Shimon ben* (the son of) *Avihu*."

"Do you have any children, Dr. Jamerson?" David asked.

"I have four children. My eldest son is Ori, twenty-six, who recently finished medical school. He wants to specialize in trauma. Next is my sweet Nava. She married a man who owns the finest archery shop in Great Britain and makes handcrafted bows. My younger daughter, is Michal, who is the spitting image of her late mother."

"I'm sorry to hear that your wife died," said Yoshua.

"She didn't die, someone murdered her."

"My God, how dreadful. I'm sorry to hear that. When did this happen?"

"Four years ago, last month. The police say it was a robbery gone wrong, but there was no evidence of that being true. The Holy One, Blessed be He, gives, and he takes away, blessed be His name."

Yoshua stared at Simon for a few seconds, and thought, *"This man is serious about his faith in God."*

*"When the terrorist bomb blew my best friend apart on a bus. His body took most of the blast and, saving me, I hadn't been able to show his faith in God. I cursed Him, instead. My anger burned in me like a great incinerator. Why had my friend died simply to satisfy the hatred of a creature in the form of a human being? My unit extracted a fearsome retribution on those responsible for the bombing—"* Yoshua didn't realize Simon continued to speak while relived that moment in his memories.

"—Michal is engaged to a nice man who's finishing his studies to be an electrical engineer and my youngest also named like you, David, but he's twenty and he's studying at a *yeshiva* in Jerusalem."

David looked away so his father wouldn't see him. He had met David Yavetz at the *shiur* (class) that *Rebbetzin* Rivka gave on Musar (ethics) every Thursday night at 8:00. David Yavetz never used his English name. David did something he shouldn't have, but he hoped it would make his father think. "Ori, isn't an English name. Why did you pick that name?" David asked.

Simon had to think fast about what he would say. Concerned, he looked straight into David's eyes, and David moved his eyes up and down. Simon understood and went along.

"We have a tradition in our family to give the name, Ori, to at least one child every generation, because one of our ancestors, Ori Yavetz. He was a unique man who not only successfully cut across ethnic boundaries; he was also a judge, general, and spy. My Ori was born the same day my great-grandfather, named Ori, died."

"David, is there something going on here that I should know about?"

"I was told by Professor Yaroni that you lost not only your father, but also your stepfather. I guess we have many things in common." Simon said.

Yoshua thought, *"Now, I'm totally confused. There've been far too many surprises."* Meanwhile, David and Yoshua got out their *taphilin*. Yoshua explained to Simon.

"These were my father's *taphilin*. I used to put them on every day until I joined the army. I only started again two years ago, after a serious conversation with my son and my friend, Elisha Arieli."

"May I see?" Yoshua watched his every move. Simon handled the *taphilin* as if they were some sacred artifact. He examined them carefully, shaking his head up and down. When he saw the small emblem on the bottom, a gigantic smile broke out on his face.

"Do you know what that emblem is? It's also embroidered on my father's *tallit* bag. My mother told me she thought it probably had to do with the factory or *sofer* (scribe) who made them."

Yoshua watched Simon's eyes as he formulated his answer. It took him almost a minute to decide what to say.

"Blessed is a son who carries on his father's heritage." The answer took Yoshua and David by surprise.

"These are valuable items; real Judaica. The emblem isn't the mark of the producer or *sofer*. The insignia represents an organization to which your father belonged. My *taphilin* are embossed with the crest of the jaguar, the symbol of a sister organization. Was your father a military man?"

Yoshua thought, "*The questions are getting stranger by the minute. There's something going on here, but for the life of me, I can't figure out what.*"

"In fact, he was. Mother used to tell me stories about how he fought with the partisans against the Nazis. Afterwards, my father fought the British between 1945 and 1949 to achieve independence. Once again, he battled with the Arabs from 1947 until 1950, when he left the army with the rank of colonel. He died in 1966, when I was two years old. He died of a massive coronary attack only a few weeks after my brother, Ysrael, was born," Yoshua explained.

"Your father's fame was well known among many people in many lands. People who fought with him tell endless stories of his heroism and selfless sacrifice. My uncle, may he rest in peace, fought with your father in the Polish forests between 1941 and 43."

David saw his father shocked beyond the ability to speak.

"You know stories of my grandfather?" he inquired.

"Yes. Besides being a famous man, but humble. He let no one praise him in public. That's why you won't find his name in any books. He saved many Jews during World War Two and played a crucial part in helping Colonel Mickey Marcus organize the Israel Defense Force in 1948. The two of you have much to be proud of. Your father and grandfather sacrificed much to protect the Jewish people, may his soul rest in peace. My uncle was a great admirer of your work, Yoshua. On his death, two years ago, he bequeathed two hundred thousand pounds sterling for your work."

David and Yoshua stared in disbelief at Dr. Jamerson. "Unfortunately, the will was in probate court because my aunt challenged the will. She died two months ago, and the money only became available five days ago. That's why I never contacted you before. I didn't want to give you any false hopes. However, when Gavriel called me for help, I told him it wouldn't be a problem because the money left by my uncle to you, in honor of your father, was now available." Simon lied to Yoshua with a straight face.

Yoshua thought, "*I have to sit. Not only is there information out in the world about my father; there are people who knew and loved him. I will* absolutely dedicate *my spare time to finding out more about the mystery that is my father. I'll have to start with Dr. Arieli—he once told my mother that he had known my father. This project, in faraway Spain, is revealing not only ancient history, but the history of my family.*"

*****

For the first time in his life, David had the veil of his grandfather's existence lifted in the public. So many times, it had been on the tip of his tongue to tell his father about his grandfather. David felt sad for his father. Despite the great love he had for his father, he swore to remain silence. The price of breaking that silence was far too great. David had asked Rav Elisha Arieli about this conflict between the conspiracy of silence around his father and honoring one's parents. Rav Elisha told him.

"Under normal circumstances, honoring one's parents comes first. Here, involved with the safety of so many hundreds of thousands, the *bet din* (court) gave approval for you and your siblings to maintain your silence. Remember, if you ever have any problem with dealing with your father, you are to call your uncle Ysrael, or me."

David could recount the family history by memory for four hundred years. In Dr. Arieli's library, there was a book about their family that covered over eight hundred years of its glorious history. Sometimes he wanted to scream about the injustice to his father. David felt the pressure that had been building over the past five years. If he revealed to his father what he knew, he, as the eldest and heir to the house of Aluz, would have to keep his own son in the dark about his heritage. So they had invested many years in his father; it would be a waste to throw it away, especially if it was only a matter of a short time before he fulfilled the prophecy.

*****

Simon walked into the dining room/saloon from outside after finishing praying. Everyone sat at the table. Ruth stood up.

"Simon, I want you to meet my best friend. Simon came to the head of the table, where he could see everyone.

"Dr. Simon Jamerson, I would like to introduce to you Dr. Aviva Berger," Ruth said. They stared at each other.

Neither could say a word. Simon's heart pounded. He thought, *"What's happening to me? I haven't felt like this in four years. WOWWWW!"* Unknown to him, Aviva was feeling the same thing. Ruth stepped in after a few seconds.

"Simon, Dr. Berger is our expert on restoration." Aviva feared to give Simon her hand, for fear he would feel her rapid pulse. All the two of them could do was nod at each other.

Gefen picked up on the sexual tension between them. She identified Simon as a threat to her relationship with Aviva, who was the first person who she had opened up to. Now, if Aviva would fall in love with the handsome, rich English doctor, he could sweep her off her feet and take her back to England. When Ruth introduced Simon to Gefen, she gave him the cold shoulder.

Sasha watched Simon and Aviva as he sipped his coffee. He wanted to defuse the uncomfortable scenario. "Would you like something hot to drink, doctor?"

Simon shifted his gaze from Aviva, looked at Sasha, and had to blink twice before his brain re-engaged. "Black tea with a drop of milk, please." Sasha handed Simon a plate of cut vegetables and, with his free hand, gave him a friendly slap on the back. Laughing, he said, "Doc, roll your tongue back in to your mouth. Your eyes are so dilated, if they got any bigger, they'll pop out of your head."

Simon turned beet red. "Please forgive my poor manners, Dr. Berger." Aviva nodded, afraid that if she spoke, it would betray what she was feeling.

"Doctor, you're not the first man to respond in this manner to my aunt. You will have problems because she's much nicer than she is beautiful," said David.

"David, in fact, it's none of our business."

"Sorry, *Ima*, I don't agree. We have to live together here for the next two weeks; anything that affects Aunt Aviva, affects us, because she's family." David winked at his "Aunt." Overcome with emotion, Aviva hugged David. At that moment, she understood how much she had lost by following her career and not marrying and having children.

"David, I'm so proud of you—about how you feel about Aunt Aviva. I cannot agree with you more. She is family—as if she was *Ima's* biological sister," said Yoshua. He smiled at Aviva.

*****

Simon had received brief biographies of every member of the team. He thought, *"I knew the beautiful artist was single. Now, I know how much the Rosenberg's respect and love her. She must be an incredibly impressive person. I think Gefen perceives me as a threat, which makes little sense. There was danger in her eyes. What's her relationship with Aviva?"*

Sasha tapped his watch, reminding everyone they had work to do.

*****

After breakfast, Gefen went into the kitchen to talk to David. "Do you believe in love at first sight?"

"I didn't, until I saw Dr. Jamerson and Aviva, now."

"Do you know what love is?"

"I can only tell you about the people in my life. Take, for example, Dr. Arieli and his wife. Every breath that he takes around his righteous wife is an act of love. It's the way he looks at her, speaks to her, respects, and protects her. Hadar's parents are the same way. Rabbi Elisha is unbelievable to be around. He dedicates every moment of his life to love. When I say he's in love with his wife, it's an understatement."

"I see how your parents speak to each other, and my opinion is that they love each other profoundly."

"It's true, my parents are still in love, and it seems to grow from day to day, yet they still don't reach the level of the Arielis. If I can dedicate myself to that kind of marriage, I know I will have accomplished something in this world."

"David, how is it the two of us grew up in the same city less than a kilometer from each other, and yet we grew up as if in two different worlds?"

"Gefen, Don't measure our worlds by a physical, linear measurement. We come from different spiritual worlds where we don't measure the distance in meters. It's measured in the development of one's soul. We could have been living next door to each other, yet there still could have been a significant difference in our ways of life. One can't measure their level of morality and ethics in a linear fashion. For example, patterns of behavior acceptable in your circle are completely unacceptable among the people with whom I live. Gefen, do your friends have tattoos on their bodies?

"You are forbidden from even the smallest tattoo?" Gefen asked.

"Yes, what your friends will do is not what the people I live with will do."

"Now, you understand when I say it's not the distance that separates our lives, but the depth."

# CIRCLES EXPOSED

Tension in the chapel was almost a physical thing. Simon and Aviva avoided looking at each other or talking to one another. Yoshua and David appeared to be in deep reflection, moving like zombies, responding to orders, but little else. Ruth became concerned and took Yoshua aside during their coffee break. "What's bothering you and David? Did the two of you have a fight?"

"No, babe, the opposite. It turns out Simon is not only Jewish, but knew of my father. His uncle fought with my father when they were partisans in Poland. That's the reason we got all this equipment. His late uncle bequeathed two hundred thousand pounds sterling for my research, in honor of my father."

"My God, that's fantastic news. We should celebrate somehow." Ruth thought, "I hope Yoshua buys my enthusiasm because I have no idea what's going on, and I'm getting nervous."

"Ruthie, my love, don't you understand—all those years while Simon's uncle was alive, I could've learned about my biological father from him."

Ruth thought, "*I feel bad for him. His biological father is such an enigma.*" *Most of his Israeli military records don't exist. Someone erased them on purpose. Even the Mossad had next to nothing about their agent, Colonel Yaacov Rosenberg. Few people knew he was a spy, and if his records exist, someone buried them deep inside a classified safe. Yoshua's only piece of information was that his grandfather's name - David. His mother had told him his father lost all his family during the Holocaust. Yaacov worked for the Mossad after leaving the army in*

*1949. When he died, all his records went missing, without explanation. It appeared Yaacov's life would remain shrouded in mystery."*

\*\*\*\*\*

The next two days, they devoted to unpacking, setting up and calibrating equipment. On Thursday, Sasha and David helped Simon set up their first experimental drilling.

Aviva concentrated on the tile floor. With a small chisel and hammer, she chipped out a broken tile and its attached cement. Underneath was a bed of fine river sand. The Lord must have been directing Aviva's hand because she found another broken tile underneath the sand. That tile was three centimeters thick with another two centimeters of cement. There was five centimeters of sand under the tile. Aviva reached into the hole she'd created and lifted out the broken pieces. The pieces measured five centimeters. More sand lay underneath the second tile.

Aviva used a plastic cup to remove the sand. She had scooped a few times when a whitish-gray marble floor with darker gray marbling became exposed. Sand from the surrounding tiles drained into the hole, and the tiles tilted from the loss of support. Aviva grabbed hold of the tile to her right and pressed with all her weight. The tile snapped cleanly at the grout line between it and the next tile.

"Yoshua, Ruthie, come here quickly!"

Aviva's voice was so loud and shrill; the entire team came running. The second Yoshua saw the marble floor, he turned to his son.

"David, get the wheelbarrow and ten large boards." A flurry of "oohs" and "ahhs" came from the team, who all had their heads over the hole, like a football huddle. David set up a ramp leading from the door to the small courtyard. He brought the wheelbarrow over to where Aviva had exposed the marble floor donated by Aharon Dori. Yoshua went to get hammers, and within minutes, everyone was knocking out tiles and removing sand. The male machismo took over as David, Sasha, and Yoshua competed against one another to see who could remove the most tiles and sand. After a while, Simon joined them, and soon the two elder men found themselves pitted against the two younger men.

The hole expanded at a rapid pace. All the men took turns hauling debris outside.

"We will exceed our capacity to store with all of this debris," Yoshua said.

"I'll call the building supply store and find out where we can rent an open container for the tiles and sand," Yoshua said.

After numerous phone calls Yoshua announced, "I found a contractor who will bring us container in two hours."

After the break, Yoshua changed tactics. "We'll finish removing both layers of tile and cement, but we'll leave the bottom layer of sand in place to protect the marble from any potential damage."

The container arrived on time, and they placed it next to the bathroom and shed. Once again, the hammers rose and fell, pulverizing the tiles covering their ancient heritage. The sweat flowed like salty rivers from every pore of their bodies. A madness had fallen on Yoshua. He did everything wrong. They had lost any historical information that could come to light by the proper removal of the tiles and their careful examination. He turned into the type of archaeologist he hated most—a grave robber.

By 7:30 pm, they had filled three quarters of their rented container.

"We need to leave an area for Simon to set up his equipment and the area next to the door where they can set up the clean room. Because of the late hour, we'll leave the exposure of the floor till tomorrow morning," said Yoshua.

*****

At 5:20 am, Yoshua, David, Simon, and a sleepy Sasha met in the house's backyard. David explained their workout plan to Simon, and everyone followed Yoshua's lead.

The run went well, and when they returned, startled them.

"We're not done yet for today. I have a surprise." He went into the house and returned with a box.

"I bought throwing knives, and we'll practice with them because it's against the law for tourists to have firearms," Yoshua informed them.

While Yoshua set up the target, Simon went into the house. He came back with a long cylinder from which he removed a compound bow. The three Israelis stared at him as he strung the bow and removed some target arrows with simple points. Yoshua thought, *"It's obvious from the quality of that bow—it was expensive. If Simon invested so much money in a bow, and brought it with him from England, he must take the sport seriously."*

"Simon, how long have you been doing archery?" Yoshua inquired.

"Since I the age of five. I had a small bow given to me by my grandfather."

"Do you have a family tradition to participate in archery?" David asked.

Simon looked at David before answering. This was the second time he had asked him a provocative question in front of his father.

"You could call it that. Archery goes way back in our family history. We have all kept the tradition over the years. My father's two bows are over six hundred years old, handed down through our family from father to son."

Yoshua thought, *"I simply don't understand. There're too many surprises that make little sense." He knew Jewish history, so he set his exceptional memory to the task. Where in the world in the 1400s would there have been Jews using bows? The answer came to him in an instant, "Plain and simple, there wasn't any place in the world where Jews used weapons like bows for the past six hundred years."*

"Would you teach us your technique of archery?" David asked.

"My pleasure, it would be an honor to teach the three of you how to use a bow."

Yoshua caught David after breakfast, threw an arm around his shoulder, and steered him into his bedroom.

"What was all that malarkey about learning archery from Simon? Why didn't you tell him you've been training with *Savta* Rivka and the other boys since you were six?"

"Well, Dad, it'll be hilarious to have him teach us and watch his face when we hit the bull's-eye every time."

"Good Lord. Since when are you a practical joker? I'm not happy about this. It's *gnevat dat* (theft of one's opinion). I didn't raise you to do such things. Please, we'll go together and explain the truth to Simon."

As the team was leaving the house to drive to the chapel, Yoshua nudged David. "Dr. Jamerson."

"Yes, how can I help you?"

"I gave you the wrong impression this morning."

"On what subject?"

"Archery. I've been doing archery since I was six. My teacher is *Rebbetzin* Rivka Arieli. She also taught my father when he was young."

"Wow, I've heard through the grapevine that *Rebbetzin* Rivka Arieli has been an outstanding teacher of archery in Jerusalem for past sixty years. Yoshua, do you still do archery?"

"Similar to David, I started at a young age, but when I joined the army and used firearms, archery didn't fit in with what I was doing. I've rarely picked up a bow these past thirty years. However, my brother, Ysrael, still practices. Ysrael is exceptional with a bow, but doesn't enter competitions because the police want him to stay anonymous. He's an officer in the police anti-terrorist unit." Yoshua smiled, remembering the good times with his friends and *Rebbetzin* Arieli.

"David, I'm impressed by your integrity that you told the truth and didn't play a practical joke," said Gefen.

"It wasn't me; my father set me straight."

*****

When they arrived at the chapel in the morning, a surprise greeted the team. A small crowd of curious neighbors came to investigate the noise and rubble the foreigners created the previous afternoon. Among them was Padre Emanuel. Yoshua welcomed him.

"Good morning Padre. Let me introduce you to my team," Yoshua said with a smile. Once he completed the introductions, he signaled to the Padre to follow him.

"Come, Padre, there's so much for you to see. We've exposed the original walls and floor of the Jewish community that existed here before 1492. We have exposed both parts of the walls and floor. The original structure had marble tiles on the floors and walls. They are stunning pieces of art," Yoshua told the shocked priest.

Ruth unlocked the door, and the men moved the portable clean room to the side. They laid down thick, wide boards from the edge of the upper level near the door to the marble floor below. The Padre had used the small chapel for years and was intimately familiar with it, yet the second he stepped inside, he thought, "*I've walked into the twilight zone. New windows—with screens— there's so much light. This room was always dark and dingy, and now it's warm and airy. I can't believe how far down they've removed the old flooring. And the gorgeous marble walls they exposed; it's astounding. It's like taking a plain-looking woman and turning her into a supermodel. I feel guilty. I'm acting like a friend, when I'm supposed to spy on them on behalf of the church. The place is definitely impressive, but why was I ordered by the Superior General to spy on the Israelis?*"

David opened the storage shed. Sasha and Simon took the tools they needed. David and Yoshua took wide street brooms, threw them over their shoulders, and headed to the chapel.

Ruth explained to the Padre, in English, what they had found. Aviva and Gefen continued polishing the marble.

Aviva and Gefen stood at the ready with the large brooms while David and Sasha used broad, flat shovels to remove the sand. After observing them for a few minutes, the Padre said, "I have something that can help you, Professor."

"What would that be, Padre?"

"A few years ago, we had a terrible winter and there were awful floods. We used a wet and dry pump to suck up the water. We could hook it up to your generator and you could pump this sand straight into the container outside."

It took them three hours to set up the pump. Once everything was in place, David and Sasha took hold of the six-inch flexible plastic pipe. Sasha nodded, and Yoshua hit the switch. The ten-horsepower engine kicked in and started sucking up the sand. It took the combined strength of both men to control the intake pipe, which had a life of its own; swaying from side to side.

The noise was almost unbearable, but it was like magic. Before their eyes, as the sand disappeared, it revealed an exquisite floor. It was obvious from the materials, designs, and combination of colors that the Alhambra in Granada had a major influence on the person who designed the floor and base tiles. The base tiles of white marble carved had the same complex weave of inlaid geometric designs as higher on the wall. The creator had employed inlaid stone of various colors for his central designs. The various colors made the floor even more vibrant. There was what looked like a fancy black border similar to the base tiles.

As the sand disappeared down the hungry, gaping mouth of the suction pipe, a spectacular central design appeared. There were three adjacent circles, each done in black marble. Within each circle was a single large word in bold Hebrew letters. Only the circle on the right had more words. The words were golden colored marble inlaid into the top central portion of the circles. The artistic Hebrew letters were the same font as the book title page they had found. They were easy to read: *emuna, tzedek, tzadikut* (faith justice, and righteousness). The design placed the circles in a triangle. The top circle had *emuna* written inside. The circle with *tzedek* below and to the right, and *tzadikut* to its left.

The upper circle was filled with white, puffy clouds and two small, chubby, winged cherubs—the word in the circle was 'faith.' This circle represented heaven. The circle on the right held a crude map of the Mediterranean area, with the Iberian Peninsula being the most prominent geographic feature. In rich, brown marble with white veining was the landmass of the Mediterranean basin. Surrounding the land, in blue marble with white veining, was the Mediterranean Sea. The word in that circle was 'righteousness,' evidently representing this world.

However, the left-hand circle held a map of something not even close to resembling anything known land mass in this world. The land mass and sea were in the same color marble as the map of the Mediterranean basin. In the center was written the word *Hoshiya* and on the eastern side of what looked like a coastal area was written, in smaller letters, the name *Ramat Tzion*. The word in gold marble was *tzedek* (justice).

Yoshua turned off the pump, and the silence was unnerving. The three words on the maps were the absolute evidence they found the right place. Written on the cover page they found in the binding was the name of a nation, Hoshiya, and the name of one city, Ramat Zion.

"If one of these circles represents heaven, and another represents this world, so Hoshiya must be another world," said Aviva.

Padre Emanuel turned to Yoshua and confessed. "Professor, it's hard for me to accept many things that go on in this world. Many of them suggest we allow these ideas and concepts to fall into the realm of science fiction, which makes it easier for us to accept them. If you want to know why, there was a double set of tiles on this floor; it was because I'm sure the church couldn't deal with the concepts are before us. Science fiction didn't exist then. Professor, please keep me informed about what you find. It appears the people who lived here before had a different outlook on the world than all their neighbors. Please excuse me, I need to meditate on what you found here," the padre informed them and then left in a hurry.

Emanuel thought as he left the old chapel.

*"The shock of the discoveries was too much for a simple parish priest. I have no idea what to do, but at least I understand now why I was asked to spy on the Israelis."*

David laughed to break the tension. "Padre Emanuel looked pretty shaken up when he left. Hey, *Aba*, maybe we've found evidence of aliens or some kind of alternative dimension."

"David, don't be silly. In those days, people still thought the world was flat. Are you going to tell me there were people living here five hundred years ago who were more advanced than everyone else?" Ruth moved behind David, and when no one was looking, she tapped his ankle with her toes. When David turned around, he got a steely eyed look from his mother.

He looked at her, tilted his head, and opened his eyes like "What?"

"David, stay out of this and keep your opinions to yourself. I don't need to tell you how careful you need to be around your father," Ruth whispered.

It felt like an eternity passed, while everyone was lost in their thoughts about the significance of what was before them. But only Ruth noticed how 'green' Simon had become when he saw the word Hoshiya exposed. David broke the silence.

"We better finish this job, take photos, and discuss what we've found." No one moved, so he changed the tone of his voice and ordered them.

"Okay people, let's get moving." Everyone moved like zombies; they did their jobs, but the atmosphere was subdued. As the last of the sand was being vacuumed into the container, other things became apparent.

While everyone else contemplated what they had revealed. Gefen looked at it differently. She observed the colors, spaces, designs, and sizes of the tiles—she realized she was seeing some kind of pattern.

"*If I look at it correctly, maybe I could see repeated patterns. Maybe the walls and the floor have a hidden message? I need to take detailed measurements and notes about the interior of the bet midrash and see if it is a giant code,*" she thought.

Yoshua still stood stone like while everyone else came to life. His mind flooded with questions.

"*Why does the circle of tzedek have the name Hoshiya in it? Why was only one city or town inscribed? What was so special about Hoshiya that the man who donated*

*the floor had this inlay designed and placed here? Did
the existence of Hoshiya create a threat to the Catholic
Church? Was this why they covered the floor over?
Padre Emanuel's reaction clarified that he'll be calling
his superiors as soon as he's out of hearing range. The
pope will know about this soon."*

Aloud, he said, "If design on this floor upset the church,
how come they didn't destroy it?"

"Sasha's theory makes more sense now. The church
never saw the floor. The people of this community had put
a new floor down before the final Spanish victory. That
still leaves the mystery of what is on the other side of the
wall that divides the chapel."

*"Was the word tzedk written in the circle of Hoshiya
because that was the home of the Light of Justice?"* he
thought.

He removed a small pad from his shirt pocket and
began scribbling notes. *"One thing to consider is the size
of the circles—if there were chairs, benches, and lecterns
spread out here, then one wouldn't see the entire floor.
Wouldn't the design have been more appropriate in the
foyer where everyone could see it? Yet, here it lies, smack
in the middle of the floor of what was once an active bet
midrash,"* he contemplated.

"Professor, what if the floor is more of a message for
future generations?" Gefen asked.

"One thing is clear, the person who commissioned the
floor equated Hoshiya with justice, and it wasn't part of
the Mediterranean because otherwise it would've appeared
in the circle of righteousness. The other thing that stands
out is there're no names written in the circles of faith and
righteousness, thus emphasizing even more the names
written in the justice circle. This floor has got to be

relaying some message. Babe, what do you think?" inquired Yoshua.

Ruth thought, *"I'm standing here looking up into his very confused eyes and my heart is pounding at an insane rate. I could stop all the doubt right this minute and stop the fulfillment of the prophecy. The community would have to wait at least another two generations because my children know all about their heritage. I have to pull it together and get myself under control. It's time for my old friend, the compartmentalization trick. I'm going there now—to the place where my two dead grandmothers are lying on their reclining beach chairs—and now I'm taking three deep, cleansing breaths. My mind will become clear, and my heartbeat will slow down. Ahhhh, better. Now, I need a good argument that'll open a window of opportunity to get Yoshua to believe in the existence of Hoshiya on his own."*

Ruth answered her husband.

"Rashi teaches us concerning the first words of the Torah, 'In the beginning He created….' This passage calls for a midrashic interpretation, as our rabbis have interpreted it: The Holy One, Blessed be He, created the world for the sake of Torah."

"Babe, I'm sorry, but I don't follow."

Ruth thought, *"I need a few seconds to remember the proper arguments. Here comes the big dilemma: to bring up the arguments now or wait until some future time. Creator of the Universe, guide my tongue so I don't make things worse. Help Yoshua understand and accept. Okay, I'm all in, here goes."*

"In the Midrash, Bereshit Rabbah, we find the first reference to *Hakodosh Baruchu* creating multiple worlds before forming this world: 'And there was evening.' One can read the Hebrew to suggest 'evening' was a reality before the creation. Hence, we know a time order existed before this one. Rabbi Abbahu said, 'This proves the Blessed Holy One went on creating worlds and destroying them until He created this one.' Abbahu reasoned, 'And God saw everything that He made and behold, it was very good.' Good is a comparative term. We can understand in the following manner, 'This pleases me, but those [worlds] did not please me.' In chapters 3:7 and 9:2, we see that the same verse is used in a slightly different way. Other sources also use Genesis 2:4: 'Now these are the generations of the heaven and earth when 'they' [rather than 'it'] were created; and Isaiah 65:17, 'For behold, I create new heavens and a new earth, and the first ones shall not be remembered, neither shall they come into mind.'"

"Ruthie, what're you talking about?"

"Our sages deal with this universe as not the first or only universe. We find this idea which repeated in various ways throughout Jewish tradition by our sages: Zohar I 24a-b, and the Or ha-Hayyim 1:12. Hasidic tradition explains the existence of prior worlds because the description of this creation begins with the second letter of the Hebrew alphabet, bet, Genesis 1:1."

Ruth thought, "*I can see he doesn't understand—give me strength—I have to charge forward.*"

"There are two traditions of multiple worlds or universes in Jewish tradition. There are diachronic universes that exist separated in time, the term diachronic meaning something happening over time. There is the notion of synchronic multiple worlds. Synchronic worlds are a well-known theory represented by the 'Four Worlds' and 'Seven Heavens' models, and the not so well-known 'Seven Dimensions of Earth' model, Leviticus Rabbah 29:11; Seder Gan Eden; LOTJ p. 15."

"What!! What is going on here? I know you're a good Bible scholar, but babe, these are some real esoteric sources. Besides, why in the world would you have thought about this?" The second Yoshua saw Ruth's face change; he knew he made a mistake.

"Yoshua Rosenberg, didn't you pay any attention to the discussion with Chaim at the dinner table on Friday night, three weeks ago?"

"I got nothing," Yoshua admitted.

"Pay more attention to the fact that our younger son is a science fiction fan. At the table, he asked about parallel universes and multiple universes. The children and I spent a half hour discussing the subject. God works in mysterious ways. We were talking about what we thought was an esoteric question, and now, we found it might not be at all esoteric."

"Are we also going to debate how many angels can dance on the point of a needle?"

"Shuki, for a scientist, you can sometimes have a closed mind. All I'm saying is I'm trying to find a theory to fit the evidence."

"Ruthie, I'm lost." He lifted his arms to the "I surrender" position.

Ruth gave Yoshua the same glare she gave her students, who asked dumb questions.

"Shuki, think of the evidence we have so far. We have the cover page of a book that states Hoshiya existed. We have evidence that the man who wrote the book existed, and we have a map on the floor showing us that Hoshiya was or is another world. You're always preaching basic scientific thought. Aren't you always saying make the theory fit the data and not the data to fit the theory?"

"Babe, did you stop to think maybe this man, Aharon Dori, might've been delusional?"

"Yoshua Rosenberg, that's an awful thing to say about someone when you have no evidence to support such a wild accusation. I'm surprised by you. You're trying to make the data we have at hand fit your preconceived ideas."

"Okay, I'll take it back. You're right, I have no evidence to support the theory that Aharon Dori was off his rocker. However, besides evidence regarding this one man, we have no supporting verification that any of this is true. Babe, it's like the Internet. Because I get emails stating some information, doesn't make it true. There were, are, and will be endless con artists in this world. Let's find some supporting evidence in either direction. Afterwards, we can rehash all of this in the future."

# HEART ATTACK

"The next problem is how to work without damaging the marble floor," said Yoshua.

"I think the only way we'll be able to work with all this equipment in the room is to cover the floor with bulletproof, shatterproof sheets of see through acrylic," said Simon.

"Where would we get enough money to buy such flooring?" Aviva asked.

"Don't worry about money, Aviva. There's still plenty left in the fund my uncle left for Yoshua's research."

"To cover the floor with acrylic tiles, we have to remove everything from inside the chapel. We need to remove the last two sections of the upper floor. The two outside steps removed, and adjust the doorway to be the same level as the marble floor," said Yoshua.

"David, go with Simon to Granada and buy sheets of acrylic," Ruth said.

Ruth turned to her husband.

"Yoshua, call the local hardware store and find out where you can purchase transparent acrylic tiles."

\*\*\*\*\*

That evening, Ruth got a call from David.

"*Ima*, we got to Granada fast. Simon and I are staying at the Alhambra Hotel, located in front of the *Juderia* on Torrijos Street. We received *Aba's* text message with the location of the company that makes acrylic sheets. We plan to go there first thing tomorrow morning."

"David, you can trust Simon. I love you, bye."

"Love you, too. Bye, *Ima*."

"What did you mean by 'David, you can trust Simon?' That's a strange thing to say, we hardly know anything about the man—except that he came out of nowhere with everything we need, like Santa Claus bringing gifts," said Yoshua.

"I was suspicious at first, but I watched his eyes. Eyes never lie, Shuki. He's a man who cares about what we're doing and understands its significance. David, who I know you taught to take care of himself, has no reason to doubt Simon is a good man. We're lucky to have him with us. Besides, the other night I put on my Sherlock Holmes deerstalker hat and checked him out on the Internet. According to my search, everything he told us is true." Ruth winked at Yoshua. "Remember, he came recommended by Gavriel."

Yoshua thought, "Married *over twenty years, and she still surprises me from time to time."*

"Dr. Rosenberg, did I ever tell you I love you? Did I ever tell you the greatest thing that ever happened to me was that you became my wife and bore us four absolutely fantastic children?" he said as he wrapped his arms around her.

Ruth's heart melted, and she slipped into his arms. *She ached to share with him her greatest secret, but she knew in her heart the day would come, and as with everything else they shared, they would share that too. With love and understanding, she prayed.*

The two slipped away to their bedroom, and Yoshua locked the door. Maturity brought patience and understanding. That night was one of those rare times when the body and soul of two lovers united in unending tenderness. They finished and lay in each other's arms.

Yoshua felt sad when he thought of all the time he had been away from his family.

"Why did you let me work so hard all these years? Now, when I look back, we should've had a big family. I should've spent more time with you and the kids instead of chasing ancient ghosts and terrorists."

Ruth touched his lips with her index finger and shushed him.

"The Holy One, Blessed be He, works in mysterious ways. Look how fortunate we are that we can work together and spend time together. My love for you continues to grow. I feel I'm the luckiest person in the world to have found and married you. Hold me tight and let's savor this special moment together." She laid her head on Yoshua's right shoulder and hugged him as she prayed: *"Master of the Universe let my husband understand when the time comes I did nothing to hurt him, but only to encourage him to fulfill his destiny."*

*****

The next morning, the reduced team headed for the chapel in their banged up van. Officials of the Spanish Antiquities Authority and Health Department scheduled this morning inspect their preparations. If satisfied, they would give them the okay to proceed with opening the sealed room. As they approached the chapel, they saw four men standing next to the chapel's door, waiting for them. One, Yoshua recognized as Gavriel; the others were Yossie Tzubari, the minister in charge of the Israel Archaeological Authority, and his two bodyguards. Gavriel turned to see the team pile out of the van. Yoshua and Ruth ran over to hug him. Yoshua welcomed the minister warmly and introduced the team to the minister. Out of the corner of his eye, Yoshua noticed Ruth and Gavriel standing at the far end of the courtyard, talking excitedly in soft voices.

Aviva opened the door with fanfare to show off the magnificent chapel. Minister Tzubari and Gavriel stopped on the threshold of the door and gasped at the beauty of their work had revealed. Yoshua ushered them in while explaining the procedures they had employed to expose the marble interior. When Gavriel saw the three circles and maps on the floor, shock registered on his face. With his right hand, he grabbed his chest and slid to the floor.

Everyone rushed to him, and Aviva started CPR while Yoshua ran to the neighbors to find out if there was an ambulance in town. Yoshua ran around for ten minutes, trying to find some assistance.

"The only ambulance is in a village fifteen kilometers to the south," a neighbor down the street told him.

"It will take twenty to thirty minutes for the ambulance to arrive. The town's clinic is closed because the doctor was on vacation in Majorca," the neighbor added.

Yoshua arranged for the ambulance and returned to the chapel. One of Minister Tzubari's bodyguards served as a medic in the army. He examined Gavriel and gave him a dose of the heart medicine he always carried with him. After thirty minutes, the bodyguard assured Yoshua that Gavriel wasn't in any danger and volunteered to go with him in the ambulance. Gavriel sat up as the ambulance pulled up—at the same time as the inspectors from the Spanish Antiquities Authority.

"Listen Shuki, if I go with Gavriel now. There's only a slight chance they will release him in time to come back to the house before *Shabbat*. If not, it'll give me time to buy fruit and vegetables and whatever I can find that's kosher."

"Ruthie, there's a little food here—some crackers, instant soups, and noodles. Take them with you. It's better than nothing. Babe, maybe you want me to go with Gavriel instead?"

Ruth smiled at Yoshua, and thought, "*I need a quick excuse. I'm afraid Gavriel, in his weakened state, might make a mistake and say something we'll all regret.*" She said, "Shuki, you stay with the minister and make us some good PR. Tell him about the Vatican's interest and our fear of being put out of business."

"Call me when you get there, and call again at 4:00 pm to let me know the status," Yoshua said as he threw her a kiss. Ruth and the bodyguard rode in the ambulance with Gavriel to the hospital in Granada, leaving Yoshua to deal with the Spanish bureaucrats.

For the next five hours, the Spanish authorities checked every nook and cranny and fired off a nonstop stream of questions. It was obvious from the beginning that they were not happy with the excavation, and if they could, they would have stopped the Israelis' activities. The inspectors had received a phone call from Cardinal Rossini in Rome. He passed on to them a blessing from the pope. He made it evident, they should do everything possible to stop the Israelis.

\*\*\*\*\*

Since Gefen had nothing to do, she took out her sketch pad and charcoals. Her mind wandered to what she had observed at the house the previous night. Her hands seemed to work on their own, and before she knew it, she had drawn the Rosenbergs embracing—enclosing the couple in parentheses of simple code. She smiled as she drew in the code that translated, "As one, their heart soars in the heaven on the wings of angels."

Shock registered on Gefen's face when she realized what she had drawn. She thought, "*Am I jealous of them? I never saw a couple of that age in love. I don't remember my parents' interactions being anything but proper and correct, but with no fire or passion in them. There's something about the warmth those two create.*" She crumpled the sheet and dropped it next to her chair. She turned to the two inspectors and drew them, taking greedy bites out of a miniature chapel that they were both holding in their hands—like a sandwich. David wandered over, saw what she was drawing, laughed, and put his hand over his mouth. "Gefen, don't let anyone see that."

*****

"Its obvious official harassment will be the standard here," Minister Tzubari grumbled to Yoshua in Hebrew. "My Spanish counterpart will get an official complaint. I know its noise, but maybe it'll keep them off your backs for a while."

"Thank you, Mr. Minister."

The Bishop of Granada still had no idea the pope was working against the Israelis. How could he have known it was the pope who allowed the excavation to begin in the first place? The pope feared information being leaked, so it was only on a "need to know" basis. He informed only people directly involved.

Because the bishop supported the Israelis, and there was a diplomatic mission from Israel, the Spanish inspectors had no choice but to give Yoshua the stamped forms, which allowed him to continue to excavate the site.

Minister Tzubari noticed Gefen looking at the walls and floor, and walked over to her.

"What do you see that the rest of us don't?"

"Mr. Minister, I see patterns in the color, design, and sizes of the tiles that aren't natural. I think they designed the structure as a code for future generations, but it's a code I've never seen before, and I don't understand it."

"Are you a cryptographer?"

"Unofficially, Mr. Minister. This is a unique code and probably needs a key. Until we discover the key, it will be a mystery."

"You have me intrigued. I have to leave now to catch a plane back to Madrid, where I'll be spending *Shabbat* with the ambassador. You'll be in my thoughts; I'll be praying for you to find the key."

"Thank you, Mr. Minister."

Before the minister could leave the chapel, things took a turn for the worse. Four carloads of reporters showed up, requesting to take pictures and interview the Spanish Antiquity officials. Minister Tzubari fumed.

"The Spanish authorities leaked the find to the local press," the minister complained. Yoshua stood in the doorway with his arms open to stop all the journalists. "I am sorry you may not come in here for fear of causing damage to the floor."

"You, sir, the photographer. You may come in and take pictures. Afterwards, you share them with your colleagues." The rest of the day was a loss, as the Spanish officials gave interview after interview and took credit for everything happening at the site. Yoshua was only included when questioned about interpreting the circles.

"We will study the unusual map with its unusual names and lettering. Not only do we not have any substantiated references about any of the names in that circle, the actual calligraphy is also unusual. The Hebrew letters written here match the same font as used in the title page of the Hoshiyan Chronicles. The style is artistic, yet distinct and easy to read. Because of the rarity of this font, it adds more credibility to linking the floor and the title page," Yoshua explained.

"We sent photos of the floor to our department in Jerusalem. My assistant, Tzion Vardi, is working with Professor Nachemia Stern at Bar-Ilan University to find matches to the same font. We will soon be able to shed some light on the historical origin of the finds."

*****

At 3 pm, a huge black truck with silver racing stripes pulled up in front of the chapel. The passenger side door opened, and David and Simon jumped out, joking and laughing. Aviva thought, *"They've become friendly in three days. I can't believe how much I've missed Simon. He's smiling at me—there goes my heart pounding again. What's happening to me?"*

Simon thought, *"For the past hour, I've thought only about Aviva. Now, I'm smiling at her like an idiot—I can't wipe this grin off my face. All I want to do is run over to her and wrap her in my arms. What is the Holy One, Blessed be He trying to tell me?"*

The truck driver climbed down from the cab. Yoshua introduced himself, shook hands, and directed him to a nearby cantina where he could wait until they finished unloading. Simon and David opened the latches on the back of the truck, rolled up the tarp, and let down the guardrail. Inside was a pile of metal framing and stacks of cardboard boxes with meter squared acrylic tiles.

Yoshua greeted Simon, shook hands, and told him about Gavriel's medical problems. Simon was more upset than Yoshua would have expected. On purpose, no one had told Yoshua that Simon's murdered wife was Gavriel's niece.

"I must go to the hospital and see Gavriel. Perhaps there's something I can do to help him. I am a thoracic surgeon."

"I called the hospital fifteen minutes ago—the doctor treating him said he was all right and there's nothing to worry about. Ruth will stay at the hospital with him over *Shabbat*."

"Listen, Yoshua, I would better if I examined him myself. It's not a long drive to Granada, and I can get there well before *Shabbat*."

"We're all going to see him after *Shabbat*. If you want to wait, we could all go together."

"Thank you for the offer, but I'd prefer to go now."

"Okay, but before you rush off, we need to discuss how to install the acrylic." Simon spent the next five minutes explaining the installation procedure. When he finished, Yoshua gave him a brief update on what they had accomplished in the past three days.

"Sasha and I conducted a thorough survey of the outside of the chapel, especially the area around the sealed room. There were no openings of any kind anywhere in the outer walls or on the roof. We took soundings with a hammer and it's obvious the walls and ceiling are both thick."

\*\*\*\*\*

Simon went back to the house. "Oh, hi, I'm finishing packing the camping cooler with food for *Shabbat* for you and Ruth and Gavriel," said Aviva.

"I will pack a bag."

"Good idea. Here, I packed a suitcase for Ruth. Thank you for going to look after Gavriel."

"Thanks for the food."

Simon returned to the kitchen a few minutes later with his overnight bag and two bunches of flowers he had picked from their garden.

"Nice," said Aviva.

"Yes, for Gavriel and these are for you. *Shabbat shalom.*"

"They're lovely. Thank you. *Shabbat shalom.*" Simon smiled, waved goodbye, and bumped into the door on his way out... because he couldn't take his eyes off Aviva. He got in the rental car, drove off, and waved to her again as he turned onto the road leading out of town.

Aviva didn't know why, but when Simon was out of view, she started crying. She went back inside and into her room, where Juanita found her crying.

"Oh, Aviva, doctor," Juanita had to think of the word for a few moments, "steal," and she touched her chest over her heart.

Aviva looked at Juanita and shook her head up and down.

"The English doctor has stolen my heart."

Juanita didn't know the words in English, "*Él es un hombre muy guapo.*" Aviva stared at her. With her hands, Juanita tried to explain, "*Hombre, hombre.*"

After a few moments, Aviva understood.

"Man."

"*Si*, man *muy guapo*."

"Oh, Juanita, I got it, 'Dr. Jamerson is a very handsome man.'" Juanita smiled and nodded. Aviva thought, "*Not to belittle him. He is handsome, but I've gone out with even more handsome men. That isn't what's drawing me to him. It plain makes little sense.*"

*****

With Ruth and Simon gone, and everyone concerned about Gavriel's health, Shabbat suffered from a lack of enthusiasm. Aviva moped around, and David escorted her out to the veranda for a talk.

"Aunt Aviva, what do you know about Simon?"

"I'm a little embarrassed to say, but I searched him on the Internet and found personal information about him. He has four children; a boy, twenty-six, two girls, twenty-four and twenty-two, and his youngest is a boy, twenty. He's a well-respected Harley Street thoracic surgeon. He has many testimonies from his patients about how he saved their lives. Four years ago, an intruder murdered his wife. The police say was a robbery gone wrong. But, they found no evidence to support that theory. The evidence available made it look similar to a professional hit. The murder devastated him, and he stopped working for four months. He runs a mobile free clinic every Thursday. He performs operations for elderly Jewish people, gratis, and he visits them at old age homes."

"The man sounds almost too good to be true. I see there's a definite attraction between the two of you."

"Do you think he likes me?"

"Aunt Aviva, you could twist that one around your little finger. He's crazy about you!"

"Stop it, you're making me blush."

*****

Twenty minutes after *Shabbat* ended, Ruth called. "*Shavua tov*, love. Gavriel is much better, and the doctor is releasing him into Simon's care. We should be back in Nido de Aguila in two to three hours."

"*Shavua tov*, babe. That is marvelous news."

David and Sasha agreed Gavriel would use their room. After Gavriel arrived, and they got him comfortable, Simon said, "Gavriel, I don't want you flying home for another five days. On Thursday, Ruth, David, and Gefen are planning to fly home. David has to enter the army and Ruth wants to spend time with their other children. You will fly home with them. I don't want you to exert yourself. David will take care of your luggage."

"You needn't make such a fuss over me, but I appreciate all you're doing, and I will follow the 'doctor's orders.' Now, you can all relax and get back to your lives. I'm okay."

With everyone settled down and Gavriel tucked in for the night, Simon said, "Aviva, would you care to take a short walk with me?"

"Yes, Simon, I would love to take a walk with you." She seemed so calm to him, while he was a bundle of nerves.

Gefen watched the two of them walk out the door. And she wanted to hate Simon for taking Aviva away from her. She dreamed of someone looking at her the way Simon looked at Aviva.

Simon and Aviva walked westward toward the edge of town. They didn't speak at first. After a couple of minutes, Aviva broke the silence.

"We're all so appreciative of how you've taken care of Gavriel. He's a dear friend and longtime colleague."

"From the little time I spent with him, I found him to be a warm, caring, considerate, and gentle soul," Simon lied, not wanting to reveal that they were related. For the next ten minutes, they spoke about everything except what was on both of their minds. Where was this whirlwind of a relationship going? They were both too scared to broach any serious subjects, so they talked about the excavation, and when that petered out, they walked home in silence, smiling at each other.

*****

On Saturday night, David and Sasha finished excavating the two remaining sections of the floor. On Sunday morning, the men fell into their exercise routine, but after not working out on *Shabbat*, they needed to limber up more than usual. The camaraderie they had established benefited the four of them.

Yoshua and Gavriel dedicated the day to building the acrylic floor covering. With the entire team assembled and Gavriel observing, they tackled the construction of the lightweight, but sturdy, metal framing. The framing was like a puzzle. One piece snapped into the next. It could be any length or width. Once the frame was in place and anchored, they could lay the acrylic tiles within each square frame.

"Dad, we got half of the framework completed. Sasha and I can bring in boxes of tiles and you and Dr. Jamerson can continue with the frame. Mom, Gefen and Aunt Aviva can put the titles in place," David suggested.

"I wanted to rent a forklift, but it being Sunday, no one will work," Yoshua said.

"Your neighbors wouldn't appreciate the noise of a forklift during their Sunday family dinner," Gavriel reminded him. Everyone pitched in and within two hours, they finished the job.

Yoshua emailed the Spanish health authorities to arrange an inspection of the health precautions they installed. He hoped that if they opened his email the first thing Monday morning, he would get a quick response.

On Monday at 10:00 am, Yoshua got a phone call from the Spanish health officials.

"Professor Rosenberg, we appreciate you applying for an inspection," the official said. He grilled Yoshua on their proposed procedures for examining the sealed room. "We won't give approval until we discuss the matter at length with Dr. Jamerson, and he will have to register with the Ministry of Health in Madrid."

"Okay, thanks for your prompt reply. I'll get back to you on this," said Yoshua.

"Gavriel, do you have Minister Tzubari's personal phone number? We need to call on our power players now or the red tape will be endless—they're trying to delay us on purpose."

"You're right."

The minister answered after three rings.

"*Shalom*, Gavriel. How are you feeling?"

"Thank you for asking. I'm much better. I need your help with a bureaucratic problem here." Gavriel told him about Yoshua's conversation with the Spanish heath official.

"Gavriel, I'll take care of the problem right away," Minister Tzabari replied. The minister called the prime minister in Jerusalem. He called the foreign minister, who called the Israeli ambassador in Spain. The ambassador called the Spanish Minister of Health and lodged a formal complaint. The minister begrudgingly called his people at their branch in Granada. Against their will, they allowed Dr. Jamerson to submit the necessary forms required to recognize him as a physician by email. They designated him as the consulting physician to supervise the opening of the sealed room.

The decision caused a horrible backlash when the Spanish minister of health called his prime minister, who called the Israeli prime minister, to ask, "What is so important about some tiny chapel in a flea-bitten little town in the Sierra Nevada Mountains?"

"Mr. Prime Minister, I can ask you the same question. Why is your Dept. of Health and the Antiquities Authority making our people so much trouble?"

"One moment, my personal secretary has something to tell me about this subject. Unknown to Israeli Prime Minister Naveh, his secretary was a Hoshiyan, and was in daily contact with General Har Zahav. He briefed the prime minister on the importance of the site.

Prime Minister Naveh returned to the phone to speak with his counterpart in Spain.

"Mr. Prime Minister, I want you to know Professors Rosenberg and Yaroni have the full backing of not only Hebrew University but also this government, and the entire nation. We will appreciate your help to make their official problems disappear speedily. They have informed me this site has a high potential for yielding artifacts and data concerning an important Jewish community that flourished in the Emirate of Granada over five hundred years ago."

The Spanish prime minister had no choice but to follow the diplomatic norm and ignore the pleading of his advisers and ministers.

"I will take care of this."

"Thank you for your concern and send my warmest regards to your lovely wife and children. I'm looking forward to meeting you at the EC discussions on industrial development next month in Brussels," the Israeli prime minister said.

After the phone calls between Spain and Israel, Prime Minister Naveh's secretary called Dr. Arieli. He explained what had happened. Rivka heard part of the conversation.

"Micki, were you able to help Gavriel and Yaacov's boy?"

"Yes, the excavation in Spain is progressing better than expected." Micki told Rivka what they had discussed. He headed for his study, sat down in his recliner, and contemplated.

*Every time he thought about Yaacov, Rosenberg, his heart and soul cried. He thought, "The same old debate has been gnawing at me for sixty years—what if Yaakov's approach had been the correct one? Yet, I knew the people of Israel were not ready, at that time, for such knowledge. I wasn't sure that supporting Gavriel was the correct action, either. Well, I stuck to the path laid out by the prophet Elisha. Time will tell. Meanwhile, there's much to learn and even more to teach. Now, I need to focus on the task at hand—preparing for my lecture tonight on ethics in medicine."*

# SEALED ROOM

The next morning, after their run, while they walked to cool down, Yoshua threw his arm around David's sweaty shoulder. "I can't tell you how proud I am of all your achievements and how you've been a big help here. Please do nothing foolish in the army and also don't allow others to do foolish things."

"*Aba*, you shouldn't worry so much."

"You will learn the hard way like every recruit before you." Yoshua said.

"Aba, I will have friends to depend upon," David replied.

"You're about to enter a training program that will change your life forever. Little mistakes can cost a person a limb or their life, God forbid. I've no doubt you'll be an outstanding soldier and you'll have no problem becoming an officer. I've never pressured you to follow my example and never expected you to follow my path in the army. Be strong, have a brave heart, keep your friends close—there's nothing like a comrade-in-arms for whom you're willing to lie down your life and vice versa." Yoshua couldn't go on; he stopped walking and thought, *"He'll be in danger soon and there's nothing more I can do to protect him. That's the price for being a Jew; free in our own homeland. David's sons and his son's sons will need to serve in the army."*

He gave David a powerful hug.

David had tears in his eyes as he hugged back. Any harder, he could've cracked a rib, but David's worries were different. He prayed, *"Holy One, Creator of heaven and earth, guide my father on the right path. Open his heart to his heritage and people.*" They walked back to the house, arm in arm.

Ruth saw them coming down the road. She thought, "*Was last night my last good night's sleep for the next six years? Am I going to have that empty feeling in the pit of my stomach again, unending worry, and always being on the edge of feeling overwhelmed?*"

After breakfast, Yoshua helped Ruth and David finish packing for their trip home with Gavriel. Aviva helped Gefen and reassured her.

"The latest I'll be coming home is Tuesday. Yoshua has us booked on a Monday evening flight." They bid each other a tearful goodbye, and Gefen took her luggage out to the van. When Yoshua pulled away, Aviva stood in the street and waved as long as she could see the van. Ruth wrapped her arms around Gefen.

"*Chamuda*, Aviva is coming home in a few days." She's safe; there're three strong men to protect her.

During the trip to Granada, Gavriel and Yoshua went over the detailed plans for the rest of the excavation. While chatting about the past week's events.

I've had several nights of little sleep. I've had strange dreams about my father," Yoshua mentioned.

"That's disturbing. I don't understand why this place—this town, this chapel—would cause you to dream about your father who passed away so long ago," said Gavriel.

*****

At the airport, before going through security inspection, Gavriel pulled Yoshua aside. He smiled his warm, fatherly smile.

"Your father would be so proud of you today; if only he had lived to see how far you've come. Yoshua, you've already done some splendid work here, but I believe this place has more mysteries to expose. Keep me informed of your progress. If there's anything you need, there's still some money left in the Jamerson Fund," Gavriel informed him.

Gavriel did something out of the ordinary. Instead of shaking Yoshua's hand; he reached out and hugged him.

Gavriel's out of character behavior astonished Yoshua. *Why would he act so because of the mention of his father's name, "Why is it that every time we speak about this project, you bring up how proud my father would be if he could see me no*w?"

Yoshua looked at Gavriel's eyes to see if he would tell the truth.

"Yoshua, I'd love to discuss this subject with you, but I have a plane to catch. If I miss my connection in Madrid, I'll have to wait nine hours for the next flight home. I'll send you an email. Your father was a dear friend, and even after all these years, one doesn't forget one's good friends. He was a prince among men." He turned toward the security checkpoint and put his hand luggage on the conveyor. The boarding call for his flight came over the airport's public address system.

Yoshua was so emotional when he took David into his arms, he could barely speak.

"David, always understand how much I love you. I'll always be there for you." They separated, and Yoshua took Ruth into his arms, and against his normal behavior, he kissed her with a passion that took both of their breath away.

"Give my love to your father and kisses to the kids for me."

"Don't worry about David; he can take care of himself." Ruth walked away, still looking back at Yoshua over her shoulder. Her heartbeat accelerated, but she sensed something bad would happen.

*****

While driving back to the chapel, Yoshua thought about what transpired at the airport. "*Who was my father? It was so strange, that time I looked up his military records. They were water damaged, and the ink blurred in strategic places—no date of birth, city or country of birth. I don't even know how old he was when he died. Mom refused to talk about his background, always saying 'it didn't make any difference.' Yaacov Rosenberg was a total mystery. He appeared out of nowhere at the end of World War Two and died when I was a young boy.*" Yoshua's attention returned to the road when he entered the town. He went straight to the chapel to join the team for lunch.

During the morning, Aviva and Simon searched, but found no evidence of the ark that would have held the Torah scrolls. There was no border on the floor along the eastern wall, next to the sealed off room, which seemed to indicate that the space on the other side of the dividing wall was once an integral part of the *bet midrash*. They also surveyed the ceiling. If the ceiling had frescoes, the Church destroyed them long ago on their side of the wall.

They chatted while they worked, and Aviva told Simon her entire life story. After an hour, he told her about his life.

"I married my childhood sweetheart, and we lived a fairy tale life. We had four exceptional children, job, house and still in love with each other. All that ended the day someone murdered my Esther."

"It must have been very difficult," Aviva said.

"The police reported it as a robbery gone wrong. However, it had all the signs of a professional hit. The authorities' failure to find a reason for the murder," Simon told her.

"In the years since my wife's murder, I've met hundreds of women, but you're the first person to cause my heart to pound in anticipation."

Aviva's eyes grew wide at the personal revelation. She thought, "*Simon is serious about his intentions.*"

# ESCAPE WITH THE EVIDENCE

Cardinal Rossini called the deputy minister for the interior, Ernesto Palmerio.

"You must stop the Israelis from continuing the excavation."

"I'll make every effort to follow your desires." Palmerio called his counterpart at the Ministry of Health.

"Tell your inspectors to be very strict with the Israelis." The Spanish health inspectors showed up at 2:30 pm with an axe to grind.

What the health inspectors found amazed them. When they completed the inspection, they spoke quietly to each other.

"We have found nothing to complain about." The inspectors grilled Simon, hoping to trip him up while Yoshua translated. Everything was in order, and the inspectors could find no fault with Simon's precautions and explanations. The inspector filled out the forms and stamped them, much to their displeasure.

After leaving the chapel, the inspector called Cardinal Rossini on his private phone.

"We couldn't find any reason to delay the Israelis. They prepared for every eventuality we questioned them."

"How am I going to stop these Israelis if I can't get help from the Spanish government? I'll have to take more dramatic measures," said the cardinal.

"We will return early tomorrow morning to be present when they drill through the separating wall," said the inspector.

After the inspectors left, Simon sat everyone down to discuss conduct the next phase of drilling and search with the endoscope. He went over the procedures.

"Once we take an air sample via a syringe, we inject the sample into a compressor with a fifty-micron mesh filter. No pathogen can pass through a filter with pores that small. They will examine the filter under a powerful microscope at 20x100 power. We will stain the filter with florescein diacetate. All living cells absorb florescein diacetate. Under UV light, the stained living cells will florescence. I will cut the filter into quarters and place them into Petri dishes with various nutrient agars to see if it's possible to grow anything on them. We will seal the Petri dishes and place in a biohazard bag. The Spanish health authorities will take the samples to their laboratory."

*****

The Spanish health inspectors arrived at 8:00 am, this time in a friendly mood. The glove box impressed them. The inspectors went over the preparations one more time and were even more satisfied by the precautions taken by the team than they had been the previous day. Everyone suited up in biohazard suits.

It was not until 2:30 pm that they got the go-ahead to drill. Yoshua fitted his hands into the glove box, lifted the spray bottle filled with isopropanol, and sprayed the entire inside and tools. As he lifted the drill, he closed his eyes for a second and said, "Holy One Blessed be Your Name, guide us in your wisdom, and let whatever we find in this room be a glorification of your Name." Yoshua stopped again, before pressing the trigger of the drill. He thought, *"What a strange circumstance. I'm not as religious as I was as a youngster; more traditional since the army. However, I have never said a prayer in the middle of an archaeological excavation. I have a gut feeling there's something serious on the other side of this wall. Something about this project is testing my faith."*

Yoshua pressed the trigger, and the drill spun and dug into the reddish-orange fired brick. Red-orange dust fell in a small pile at the bottom of the glove box. He applied continuous pressure on the drill and it continued to cut into the brick. Abruptly, the pitch of the drill changed, the resistance to the drill bit increased, and out came gray dust. He had hit the cement behind the brick.

"If you've hit cement, that means there's at least another layer of bricks before you'll get into the airspace of the sealed room," said Aviva.

Yoshua pulled the drill out and measured the depth he had drilled against the length of the drill bit.

"If a second layer of brick is as deep as the first, the drill bit wouldn't make it all the way through the second layer of brick."

Yoshua turned to the inspectors, "If you don't mind, we need to change the drill bit."

"Professor, please move and allow me to sit in your place." The inspector lifted the drill, placed the bit in the hole, and pushed it to the end. Everyone heard the soft thud as it hit the second layer of brick. The inspector nodded, satisfied they hadn't cut into the air space on the other side.

"Sasha, is there a longer drill bit?"

Sasha sifted through the tools in the toolbox and came up with an eight-millimeter bit, forty centimeters long. Yoshua exchanged the two bits, sprayed the inside of the glove box with isopropanol, and drilled again. After forty seconds, he reversed the direction of the drill. He pulled the drill out of the hole slowly, while the drill was still spinning. Gray dust fell from the hole as the whirling bit came out. He repeated the process and the second time, the dust turned to red again.

Yoshua stopped drilling.

"I would like to remove the two piles of brick dust to compare them."

"No problem, professor," the first inspector said. Yoshua transferred the dust to Petri dishes, lifted the glove box, and removed the samples of red dust which he passed to Aviva. She examined both samples under the microscope.

"Yoshua, the two samples are identical. They closed the room with a double layer of bricks."

Aviva rechecked to see if the syringe was in place on the glove box so they could take an air sample. Meanwhile, Simon and the health inspector reexamined all the gaskets of the glove box to make sure there were no leaks. When satisfied, the inspector gave the okay to continue.

Yoshua continued, and the drill spewed red dust onto the floor of the glove box. With the drill resting in his left hand, he applied pressure with his stronger right arm. The pile of dust grew larger and larger. Abruptly, the anticipation was over—Yoshua jerked forward and the drill broke into space. There was a slight swishing noise, barely audible. Yoshua had trouble withdrawing his hands from the glove box; it felt as if there was a vacuum in the box. Aviva moved to the syringe and lifted the plunger. The plunger fought her the entire way up. To everyone's surprise, the plunger leaped right back down. Three times, Aviva tried to take an air sample. Seeing that she was not succeeding, Simon tried his hand—once again. The plunger jumped back into its place. Simon turned to the inspector, who looked on very confused.

"There's no air in the room. It's evident there's been a vacuum in there all these years."

Next, both inspectors tried their hand at extracting an air sample. Time after time, the younger inspector tried to pull out the plunger, only to have the vacuum suck it back to its original position at the zero line. With increasing frustration, he tried to accomplish a simple task. After ten tries, the elder inspector pushed his colleague aside and attempted to wrest a simple air sample from the glove box. After the eighth try, with his face flushed red from frustration, he gave in to the inevitable.

"It's obvious; there was no air in the room. There's no possibility of any aerobic pathogens growing in a vacuum," Simon vocalized what everyone thought.

"Inspector, we have all seen the obvious evidence no health risks will come from the sealed room," Dr. Jamerson said.

"There is no reason to delay us from opening the wall," Yoshua added. They couldn't delay any more for health reasons.

One inspector spoke to Yoshua in Spanish, even though both inspectors spoke English.

"You're free to proceed any way you would like. There's no biohazard here." He removed four forms from his briefcase, filled in the blanks, and stamped them with his official seal. He handed the forms to Yoshua and walked out. The team gathered in a huddle and laughed and joked for the next three minutes.

What caught Yoshua's attention was that it was obvious Simon understood every word they said in Hebrew, even though he refused to speak the language. Everyone moved back over to the drill hole to begin their investigation of the sealed room. Simon closed the valve under the syringe. Simon went out to the storage shed and brought back an air filter. With the filter in place, they opened the valve and heard the air rushing into the room for the first time in over five hundred years.

Next, Simon brought in an air compressor.

"We can pump air through a sterile filter until we create an equilibrium of air pressure between the inside and the outside." Every few minutes, Aviva recorded the air pressure in the inner room with an air pressure gauge. At last, she nodded to Yoshua that they could continue.

The drill hole was one point eight meters above the new acrylic floor. The custom-made endoscope fiber optics embedded in a cable attached to a video camera. Images appeared on a large LCD screen. They had attached the endoscope to a computer, which recorded all the images. Dr. Jamerson attached the flexible cable to a telescoping boom. The person holding the endoscope determined where the camera pointed. The boom could telescope from eighty centimeters to two point five meters. Yoshua and Sasha handled the boom, while Aviva and Simon manned the computer. The light and camera were tested first to see if everything was functioning. Together, Yoshua and Sasha fed the boom into the room.

Yoshua thought, *"That double layer of brick bothers me. No one wasted building materials, especially for an interior wall of a church. What's behind this wall that was so horrific that the church had sealed it with a double wall? Why didn't they destroy the entire building? Maybe the church wanted to show off how they had defeated the Jews and Moslems. They demonstrated their power by converting Jewish and Moslem places of worship into churches.*"

It took only a few seconds for the endoscope to pass through the hole and enter the room. From their calculations, they knew the sealed area was only five by seven meters. The first image that showed up on the screen was the *bima* (central lectern) from which they read the Torah.

Simon zoomed in on the back of the room. In the background, they could make out the *aron kodesh* (Holy Ark) of the *bet midrash*.

"Hey, the walls were plastered over, which gives credence to Sasha's theory that the Jewish community covered the walls and floor to hide them from the conquering Christian troops. They probably were also responsible for the first layer of floor tiles over the original marble floor," said Aviva.

The *aron kodesh* seemed about one meter wide and made of what looked like dark, stained walnut. The *paroket* (covering over the door) was missing, and the door was open, but they were too far away to see anything inside.

"Begin a one hundred eighty-degree sweep of the room at that height of the hole," Simon asked Yoshua. Sasha, not being proficient with the tool, accidentally turned it upward. What flashed on the screen amazed and astounded everyone. The entire ceiling had frescoes from all the different holidays. They were all breathtaking in detail and the use of color. Vibrant blues, reds, browns, and greens contrasted with soft yellows, beiges, sky blues, and chartreuse.

Everyone crowded around the screen to look at the beautiful fresco on the ceiling.

"The style the painter employed shows the influence of the school of art at the time. The structures, people, animals, and plants were not to scale. As in contemporary works among the Christians, most of the figures and objects lacked depth. Most of the paintings were somewhere between two and three-dimensional," Aviva critiqued the frescos.

"Could this be the reason the church sealed up this half of the *bet midrash*?" Sasha asked.

"Highly unlikely, there's nothing in these paintings that's intrinsically anti-church," Yoshua said.

With their computer program, Simon and Aviva created a three-dimensional search grid. They numbered the x-axis with integers, the y-axis with English letters, and the z-axis with Hebrew letters. Simon divided the space into five equal squares along each axis, which gave 5x5x5=125 cubes within the search grid.

For the next three hours, they explored the ceiling. When they scanned the area next to the brick wall, the paintings had extended into the chapel itself. There was a scene of a *succah* with a man holding the four species (palm branch, citron, willow, and myrtle). Another scene showed the people dancing with a Sefer Torah. The third scene was a family sitting at a table eating *matzot*. Next to the wall was a pair of uplifted, slender female hands opposite a table with two candles, two loaves of bread, and a chalice of wine.

Yoshua and Aviva set up two ladders next to the wall. On the second to the top rungs, they laid a thick wood plank. When satisfied it was safe, Aviva selected a number of tools and brushes and climbed the scaffold. With an art restorer's skill and patience that came from years of training, Aviva began the slow, painstaking job of trying to uncover the ceiling paintings in the primary room.

At 9:00 pm, they returned to the house for a late dinner. Everyone went to bed early. Yoshua couldn't sleep, so he reviewed the day's discoveries.

"The more we discover about the chapel, the less we know. The whole thing makes little sense. The parts of the puzzle don't fit. Why would the church go to such lengths to hide those ceiling paintings? There must be something else in that room that was so anti-church or embarrassing that they wanted it closed up forever."

Yoshua continued his analysis of the scenario.

"*If whatever is in there was so much against their way of life, why not destroy the building? Maybe, in the heat of the moment to wall up the room. When people aren't thinking with their heads, but with their emotions, it could be they wanted to punish someone by closing part of the building—perhaps causing someone financial harm. The wall itself expressed the power of the church. Ophosi said his family had once been Conversos. Maybe they suspected the Jews who converted here of secretly carrying on with Jewish religious practices. The wall would be a constant reminder to 'keep the faith,' so to speak. So, who was this Aharon Dori?*" When he fell asleep, Yoshua had troubled dreams with vague recollections of his biological father. He was trying to tell Yoshua something, but he couldn't understand what his father was saying because he was speaking a language Yoshua didn't understand.

\*\*\*\*\*

"Since we can safely enter the sealed room, we should start by removing our equipment next to the wall that isn't necessary," Simon suggested. Sasha and Simon removed the glove box, dismantled the table, and they were now ready to begin their survey of the sealed room. Yoshua arrived and saw the smile on Simon's face. He understood good news awaited him.

"Nu, what's the scenario?"

"The mission is a go—time to launch."

"We need to set our strategy. Let's go over the scenarios that could crop up."

Yoshua walked up to the hole in the wall, stuck his nose in, and took a deep whiff of air. There was only a musty smell like a room left uncleaned for years. There were no dead, rotting rats in there.

Since they had started with the ceiling, they continued the grid search. They photographed each cube via the optic fibers. The first grid was 1-A-*Hey* (the fifth Hebrew letter). Next came 2-A-*Hey*, 3-A-*Hey*, and so on. Then they moved on to the next lower level; 1-A-*Dalid*.

Many of the cubes were air space. The examination moved quickly. When what occupied the area of 1-A-*Bet* appeared on the endoscope screen, everyone screamed

"Oh, my God." There, staring back at them, was a mummified female. She sat on the floor with her back to the wall; a child lay in her arms, hugged to her chest. Her face angled toward the child. It appeared as if she kissed the top of the children's head. The child clung to its mother. One could still distinguish the utter fear on both of their faces. They had spent their last moments of pain and suffering in this world, together, bound one to another for the past five hundred twenty years.

After a few seconds of shock, Sasha felt the endoscope slipping out of his hands. As he grabbed the end of the endoscope, the lens at the end of the optic fiber did a quick scan of the floor. The light fell on body after body, all apparently killed by suffocating together in the sealed room. Simon froze.

"*Baruch dayan emet* (Blessed be the True Judge)," he intoned. The team repeated the phrase after him and, at once, realized what lay before them.

As Simon panned the lens, it fell on a figure with *pe'ot* (sidelocks) and a long, white beard.

"Look what that man is holding," Sasha said.

"He is holding an open Sefer Torah in his hands," Aviva added.

"His left hand is holding the left handle of the Torah, and his index finger on his right hand is pointing to a particular verse," Yoshua said. Simon zoomed in to where the fingers pointed. It was obvious after the first two words, "*Shema Ysrael, Hashem, Elokanu, Hashem Ichad!* (Hear O'Israel, the Lord our God the Lord is One)" to which phrase he was pointing.

The team crowded around the monitor to see the horrors of the Inquisition. Sasha continued panning the room.

"My God, so many children," Aviva whispered, wiping the tears from her eyes. The scene repeated itself time after time. Several children huddled around adults who hugged their offspring to their bodies. They sought to could protect them from the horrible fate inflicted upon them. Tears fell from their eyes as they realized the enormity of the travesty that had taken place in this small *bet midrash*.

Yoshua had witnessed the insane cruelty men inflicted upon one another many times. Despite his previous experiences with death, murder, and warfare, he wasn't immune to what he witnessed now. He had seen innocent men, women, and children torn to shreds by terrorists' bombs designed to inflict maximum pain and injury. Here, the peoples' deaths were slow; they knew there was nothing they could do to prevent it. He had spoken for many deaths; a messenger of retribution. He made a silent prayer, "*Hakodosh Baruchu*, please deliver those responsible for this act into my hands so they may know that justice exists in this world."

"It's obvious, they were Jews who refused to convert, or *Conversos*, caught practicing Jewish customs. The Inquisition sentenced them to die as a community; sealed up in this room forever," Sasha said.

"That makes this a Jewish cemetery. The Spanish should have no rights to it, especially since they're the ones who murdered these people," Aviva said.

Yoshua hung back while everyone vented. When the time felt right, he stood up, blocking the monitor.

"Okay, quiet down, everyone. Congratulations to everyone. This is a spectacular find. However, the second this gets out, the Spanish authorities will close this excavation."

"The NGO owns this building. The Spanish government has no authority on what we do inside the building," Sasha vented.

"I am convinced the Vatican is behind our troubles. They've sought a reason to shut us down, and now they have it. They'll confiscate everything we've found here. If we try to stall them, they'll also figure that out. We don't have over two or three hours before we'll have to notify the Antiquities Authority. Failure to report such a significant archaeological find would get us deported, and we'll never be able to find out what happened here. The church and the Spanish government will do everything in their power to conceal what we've revealed," Yoshua told them.

"Now we know why Cardinal Rossini was so interested in this project. He had preknowledge that if we would find in Ohel Rivka: A massacre perpetrated by the Inquisition. Thank God, half of the team is safely on its way home," Aviva said.

"We should inform the health authorities first. Until they arrive tomorrow and decide what to do, we can work throughout the night. Next, they'll call the department of antiquities, who will act fast to close this excavation. What we need is documentation of everything we do until tomorrow morning, and we need to get the copies out of the country," Simon said.

"Sasha, you and Simon take as many photos and video clips as you can. When you finish, come help me. I'll get the big grinding disc and cut my way into the sealed room. I want to disturb the room as little as possible. As soon as it's practical, we'll crawl inside and cut out the wall from the inside out. We don't want debris to fall into the room with the bodies. Now, let's get moving people! We only have a few hours before we must contact the authorities," Yoshua said. Everyone tore off to their chores as if being chased by a thousand screaming banshees. Aviva found a spare camera and began taking photos, as well.

Yoshua rushed to the storage shed and grabbed a roll of plastic film and a box cutter. He ran back to the chapel, covered Simon's equipment with the plastic, and placed a few tools on top so it wouldn't fall. He plugged in the disc grinder and attacked the wall with the twenty-centimeter revolving disc. The special tile cutting disc bit into the brick wall and chewed it up as if it made of butter, but they had a serious problem. As the disc worked its magic, friction reduced its width. It only took two minutes to reduce the width of the disc enough so it couldn't cut through the two layers of brick. Yoshua thought,

*"Oh, great. The building supply store is closed and I have only two more discs. One, I have to keep for the last cut, so I'll have to cut as deep as possible with the other two. If I can make a hole big enough to get my arm and the two-kilo hammer inside, I'm pretty sure the disc can cut deep enough for me to knock the wall out with the hammer by pounding on the inside."*

It took fifteen minutes to cut a hole thirty by thirty centimeters. Now it was a question of how much could they cut before the discs were at a point where they were useless. Sasha cut from the outside, and Yoshua swung the hammer against the inside of the wall. It took twenty minutes to open another thirty centimeters along the wall.

Aviva volunteered to squeeze through. Simon took a small stool, leaned into the hole, and dropped the stool on the other side so it would be easier for Aviva to climb back out of the hole. Yoshua cut another piece of plastic, folded it over a few times, and laid it on the bottom of the hole so Aviva could slide through and not get hurt on the rough ends of the bricks and mortar left by the hammer.

*****

Aviva wiggled her way through the hole. Holding a flashlight in her mouth, she raised her right leg and, struggling, got it through. She balanced herself on her right leg and pulled her left leg through the hole. Once on the other side, Sasha fed the floodlights to Aviva. In the meantime, Simon attached the floodlights to an extension cord and fed the line to her.

Unexpectedly, Simon called to Aviva.

"Aviva, don't turn on the lights. Best that you leave this room before it reveals its horrors." Aviva attempted to argue with him, but he cut her off.

"Aviva," he said, "how many times have you been with corpses?"

Now Yoshua realized what Simon was saying, "Aviva," Yoshua said softly, "come out of there. Let Simon or me be the first to turn on the lights in there—if vomit in there, there will be forensic evidence of our being in there. I want you out of here by tomorrow so the Spanish Authorities cannot come up with a reason to arrest you."

"Yoshua, you're being a male chauvinist," Aviva said.

"My dear," Simon said, trying a different tone of voice, "please let me deal with the dead. I've been doing it for years. There are many dead people in there. Please come out, you don't need that sight haunting your dreams for the rest of your life."

To their surprise, Aviva wiggled out without an argument. There were tears in her eyes. Simon took her into his arms and pulled her out. She shook badly. As they asked her to come out, she had turned around and her flashlight had fallen on a woman lying prone on the floor next to the wall. There were two dead children next to her. The ends of her fingers were worn off and covered in dry blood. The women had a frantic, crazed look on her face. There was a huge bloodstain on the wall above her head on scratched bricks. This mother had tried to scrape her way out with her fingers. She had died trying to save her children.

Simon had to hold Aviva because she couldn't stand on her own. Her dust-covered cheeks were streaked with lines where tears had run down her face. Sasha headed for the hole in the wall, but Yoshua stopped him. "Sasha, my friend, let me do this. I've been around bodies torn apart by bombs and missiles. I know what these images can do to you every night. I've fought my demons and have defeated them. Now I can take on any demon, and as the psalm states, 'even though I walk through the valley of the shadow of death, I will not fear.'" At that moment, they became not only professor and student, but comrades-in-arms.

"Together, we will face this specter of death," Yoshua said.

Simon sat in a chair next to Aviva and held her in his arms. She had her head on his shoulder. She sobbed quietly for the death of a woman and her children who had been dead over five hundred twenty years and whom she had not known. Simon whispered comforting words to her to calm her down. He could feel her beating heart through their shirts. He was counting the beats. They were lower in frequency. It would take a few more minutes and she would be calm.

With Sasha's help, Yoshua snaked his way into the sealed room. Once inside, he turned on one floodlight. He looked around and saw the dead lying all over the room. He vowed at that moment.

*"I swear on my life I'll do everything to learn your story and no one will forget you anymore. I, Yoshua the son of Yaacov, swear before that open Torah that I will use every ounce of my strength to see that this travesty does not go unresolved."* Tears fell from his eyes against his will.

"Sasha, please start up the disc again, and hand me the five-kilo hammer. Let's cut a doorway through this wall."

Yoshua accepted the large hammer from Sasha and selected a spot that would cause the least amount of disturbance to the scene. Sasha stood parallel to Yoshua on the opposite side of the wall. He put on safety goggles and a dust mask, hit the switch on the tool, and applied the mighty whirling disc to the red bricks with as much pressure as possible. A mixture of brick and mortar dust flew back at him.

After ten minutes, Sasha cut the power—the abrupt silence was eerie. He slapped the wall twice. Yoshua lifted the huge five-kilo hammer, and with an intensity bordering on insanity, smashed that five-kilo piece of steel into the brick wall. The steel head of the hammer impacted on the baked clay, crumpling it into tiny pieces, and dust that flew back at Yoshua. Repeatedly, he smashed the wall as if the strikes of the hammer were aimed at the sadists who perpetrated the crimes all around him.

Yoshua remembered seeing the tank and the artillery boys swinging those same hammers, fixing the sections of the great iron treads that their vehicles rode on. He soon found out why three men needed to do this job. Yoshua had always stayed in good physical shape. However, after swinging the hammer for fifteen minutes, every muscle and sinew in his arms and shoulders ached. Yoshua lowered the heavy head of the hammer to the floor and leaned on the handle to rest. He thought, "All of this would be much easier if David was here to help, but, thank God, he and Ruth are on a plane flying home to safety." Sasha handed Yoshua a bottle of water. He smiled weakly at Sasha and nodded his head in thanks. He was too tired to speak.

Aviva recovered enough to straighten up and wiped the tears from her face. "Simon, I hope you know how much I appreciate what you did for me. It was a harrowing experience to be there with all those dead people. I've not dealt with death on this level before." She leaned over and kissed Simon on the cheek. They walked to the dividing wall to check out the progress.

Great rivers of sweat poured down Yoshua's face and back. When Aviva looked through the hole and saw how exhausted Yoshua was, she ran to the refrigerator and brought back three bottles of water. The first, he poured over his head; the second, he drank in four gulps; and a third, he handed it to Sasha, whose face was covered in brick dust. When Sasha removed his safety glasses, his eyes stuck out like yolks on sunny-side up eggs.

It took Yoshua and Simon an hour and a half to remove a section of wall large enough to walk through. Sasha and Simon walked into the sealed room for the first time. Sasha turned on the floodlights, illuminating the immensity of the crime committed five hundred twenty years earlier.

Bodies littered the room; all in a pristine state of preservation. The vacuum had acted as a perfect preservative. Though dried up, their clothes were in perfect condition, and their hair and skin. Simon slumped to the floor and tore his shirt. With tears pouring down his face, he reached into the ancient brazier was in the room, took a handful of five hundred-year-old soot, and threw it over his head. He looked around and his eyes said everything. Everyone put down their tools and spent the next five minutes in silent prayer for the dead.

Now, after five hundred years, someone remembered them. Simon recited Psalm 130, "*Shir Hamalalot*, from the depths I call You, *HaShem*. My Lord, hear my voice, may Your ears be attentive to the sound of my pleas. If You preserve iniquities, O God, my Lord, who could survive? For with You is forgiveness, that You may be feared."

When Simon finished, everyone was silent. This small community had been cut off by the pinnacle of hatred. A hate fostered by an enemy that had not only murdered these people, but had erased their memory until this moment. Something happened to everyone during those few moments. They knew from this point on, their lives would never be the same. It forged a bond between them—not one of friendship or love—but similar to that which binds soldiers who have been under fire together. Now, each knew that no matter what it would happen, they had to reveal the story of these people to the world. Each swore to himself the suppression of this community's murder would no longer continue.

"From the grouping of the bodies, they had died as family members together. However, some groupings overlapped," Aviva observed.

"There must have been some intermarriage between the groups and that was what caused the overlapping," Sasha pointed out.

"The room isn't large and there are dead everywhere," Yoshua pointed out.

"Most of the parents sat with their backs to the wall and children clung to their parents in false hope of rescue," Aviva said.

Simon made a quick count. "There are forty-six dead."

"Look over there. I would approximate that woman to have been around thirty years old at her death. Her left hand is holding a man of similar age. With her right, she is holding the hand of an older woman," Yoshua said.

"The bodies are so well preserved. You can see that the two women are mother and daughter," Simon said.

Sasha and Yoshua struggled to find places to set up floodlights—they had to be careful not to disturb anything. Sasha took still photos while Yoshua used a small hand-held video camera.

The most striking figure was the older, white-haired, bearded man holding the open Torah scroll and pointing to the words *"Shema Ysrael."*

Aviva saw two men in the corner of the room. Each with their arms wrapped around several large volumes.

"Yoshua, come quickly. There's something of great potential value here." Yoshua made his way carefully between the dead. Each time his foot touched the ground, a thin layer of dust lifted off the floor in a small cloud surrounding his ankles. Simon moved to the corner with a floodlight and set it upright above the two dead men.

Yoshua noticed a piece of parchment on the ground next to one man. Yoshua removed his trusty camel hair brush and cleaned away the dust He reached into his left pants pocket, removed a long forceps, and lift the parchment by its left corner so he could read it. The words stood out as if written yesterday. He read aloud for all to hear.

"I, Matityahu the son of Shmuel, the son of Aharon Dori, greetings to whomever will find this." The team came to a stop and listened carefully to the words left behind over five hundred years previously.

"My father has thankfully died from his wounds and will not suffer anymore torture at the hands of the Inquisitors. I hope I will be as brave as he is when my time comes. I saved only one thing, hoping that one day someone will find this and know the story of my grandfather's people. If you can read this, you are Jewish. Please give us all a proper burial and say *kaddish* for us. May the Hand of the Lord guide you to us quickly. Blessed be God, the merciful."

They turned their attention to the men holding the books.

"These men felt these books were of greater importance to them than being with their families," Sasha said. Simon removed a small paintbrush from his shirt pocket and leaned over the two men. Slowly, with the incredible patience of a surgeon, he cleaned away the dust to see if there was a title on a binding.

Little by little, the dust fell from the books. What laid beneath caused Simon to lose his balance. Written in bold Hebrew letters was *Sefer Uzziel* (Book of Uzziel). Luckily, he twisted himself to fall at the two men's feet in an empty place on the floor, disturbing none of the archaeological evidence. He hit the floor hard on his right shoulder and instinctively rolled and came up on his feet. Sasha rushed over to him as fast as he could, sending up a cloud of dust. He found Simon shaking as if he had malaria.

"Are you all right?"

"I'm okay, it's not bad." He deliberated to himself.

*"I can't believe there's a copy of the Book of Uzziel here—like the copy my father has in his library at home. He read the stories of the personal side of the Light of Justice to us, as was customary in all Hoshiyan families. The King's son, Uzziel, wrote the book."*

"Yoshua, please come over here," he said. When he stood up, Simon noticed the hole in the wall. Yoshua made his way carefully to Simon, who whispered.

"Major Yoshua Rosenberg, we have hard decisions to make." Yoshua understood why Simon had addressed him by his military title. He had a duty to protect the people of Israel. When Yoshua didn't answer, Simon continued,

"How many men have died in your arms while sanctifying the name of the Lord and protecting the people of Israel? Would you spit on their graves or throw away their sacrifice or put people in danger for personal gain?"

Yoshua felt the same thing that Simon experienced— he also understood that these books were so important that these people had died to protect them.

"I feel it in the depths of my soul that these people died because of these books. Look at the secret compartment there in the wall. They must have hidden the books there and opened the compartment only after sealed in here. They took those books out of their hiding place, so whoever came and discovered this travesty of justice would also find the hidden books. Look at these dead. We need to take those books and escape. I have family in Gibraltar. I can get there."

"You can't do it, Simon. It's too obvious, and the authorities will know. We might save the books, but we won't be able to save the dead themselves. We need to take some calculated risks to save both the dead and all the artifacts. If we steal the books, we'll never see these bodies again. They'll destroy them for sure."

"Yoshua, you told me the Vatican had an abnormal interest in this project. Cardinal Rossini called you after you published the title page of the *Hoshiyan Chronicles*. There's a good possibility the *Chronicles* are among these books."

The thought the *Hoshiyan Chronicles* existed and could be a few centimeters from where he stood drove Yoshua crazy. He fought with his evil inclination to take the books and run. He considered the moral and religious weight between the bodies and the books.

"The dead are more important than any book or artifact."

"The Catholic Church is interested in these books because there's something in them that threatens the church. If they get their hands on these books and bodies, they'll disappear forever," said Sasha.

"We should smuggle all this photographic evidence out of the country. Next, we've can remove the books from their arms. Afterwards, rearrange the bodies to make them appear natural, and not cause any suspicions," Simon suggested. Yoshua noticed a change in the tone of Simon's voice—he was informing, not asking—but before Yoshua could say another word, Simon said, "You're able to do this work here today because of the money I'm providing. If you oppose me, I'll withdraw my support and close this excavation within the hour."

"Simon, what could be so important that you're willing to risk so much?"

"I will risk nothing. I'm taking the books and leaving for Gibraltar."

Everyone stopped working and gathered around. Aviva said, "Yoshua, I've always supported you, but, in this case, I can't agree with you. They murdered these people for one reason only—because they were Jews. There's a good chance that what Simon is saying is also true. I think the potential for embarrassing the Spanish government and the church is far too great to think they will ever allow this information to get out. The question is whether you're a Jew first or an archaeologist."

"I don't think you have a chance of getting away with these books without destroying them. If they're ruined while trying to smuggle them out of the country, we'll have done all of this for nothing. If you try to provide the books with the care they need, you'll attract attention to yourself. I would rather fight with the Spanish over the rights to research whole volumes and not half destroyed ones. I understand what our chances are to succeed. What I will agree to is that Simon takes all the photographic evidence that we gather in the next two hours, transfer it to an USB drive, and head for Gibraltar. That way, Gavriel will have all the evidence and be able to get it to the press. We must preserve the books as best as possible, so even if it isn't in our lifetimes, the information they hold will come to light in the future," Yoshua said.

"What of the mass murder of these people?" Simon said.

"I agree you should smuggle photos of everything to Gibraltar," Yoshua said.

"We need to stop bickering and get to work. First, we need to contact the Spanish health authorities and have Simon tell them we suspect a health problem and we want the place quarantined. We'll tell them we have the proper equipment to allow us to continue to work. All we need is for the police to seal off the area. That should give us twenty-four to forty-eight hours," Aviva said.

"If we lie to them and they find out, we'll see none of this again," Sasha said.

"I realized my idea was not only impractical, it would give the authorities a way to slam this place shut— suspicion of a biohazard. In fact, there's a good chance that's the reason they'll use. Simon's question is not only to Yoshua, but to all of us. With the evidence before us, it's time not to be scientists, but to worry about the effects this will have throughout the world. We must stop a cover-up by the church and the Spanish government by any means. Time to step up and be counted," Aviva said. She looked at each of them. She stuck her hand out in the middle of the group. Hands shot out and everyone had their hands together, forming a pact except Yoshua. All eyes turned to him to see what he would do.

Yoshua put out his hand, going against all that they had trained him to do. He never had so much as a parking ticket in his life. *He understood that by taking this path, they would cause an international incident. Its consequences would ruin relations between his country and Spain on one side and the Catholic Church on the other, yet the grotesquely twisted figures lying at his feet screamed at him for justice. If there was one thing his late mother had drilled into him, it was to seek justice at all times. Yoshua thought of his mother as he put his hand out and knew that it was the right thing to do. He could feel her looking down on him and smiling, knowing that he will risk everything, personally and professionally, for these dead who deserved justice.*

Yoshua prayed as he looked at his co-conspirators.

"Thank you *Hakodosh Baruchu* that Gefen, Ruth and David are safely away from here. We all go to prison without trials!" Immediately, Yoshua changed gears and thought like an army officer; what could they do to maximize the amount of data they could get out and how to slow down the enemy?

# STAY OR RUN

It was now Wednesday, 25 July.

"I believe the chances of the authorities arriving soon are slim. Let's go back to the house, shower, *daven*, and eat. I want everyone to prepare a small backpack with absolute necessities, so it will be ready when the police show up to detain us," said Yoshua.

When the team returned to the chapel, they documented its contents in the proper archaeological manner. They took measurements, and Sasha used graphic modeling software to create a 3D model of the layout of the dead of *Ohel Rivka*.

It was difficult for Yoshua to resist grabbing a book to find out what had cost these people their lives. There were so many questions about what happened in this place—Yoshua's head spun with the possibilities. He thought,

"Now that I've measured the books and the size of the cubbyhole, it's evident they had hidden the books there, but why? Why take them out of their hiding place if they were about to die? Why had the note stated that if someone was reading the note that most likely they were Jewish? How could the dying man know that? Why hadn't the Inquisition burned them at the stake like so many others who they caught maintaining their Jewish traditions? Very little of this made any sense. Maybe it's an issue of viewpoint; I need to stop thinking like a modern scientist and start thinking like a medieval Jew who the Inquisition will murder for being Jewish. As much as their lives were similar to mine, they still differed in critical areas. I'm a warrior while they were noncombatants. I walk upright, afraid of no man; they walked bent over, afraid for their lives and livelihood at every step."

\*\*\*\*\*

It took eighteen hours from the original notification for the antiquities inspectors to arrive at the *bet midrash*. As with the previous Spanish bureaucrats, they arrived with chips on their shoulders. Yoshua met them outside.

"Take us immediately to the discoveries reported to the ministry," the inspector demanded. They assumed the foreigners wouldn't cooperate. They had no idea what awaited them, so when they entered the sealed room, they were shocked into silence.

After fifteen seconds, one of them took a few photos with his cell phone and sent them to his supervisor. He called his supervisor, who astounded by what the photos revealed. His reaction was to shout at them, "Close down the site immediately. I'll call the director of the authority and inform him of what's transpiring there in Nido de Aguila."

The inspectors shouted and demanded all materials be handed over. Calmly, Yoshua got out his permits and showed them to the inspectors.

"You can see we've followed every condition written in the permit granted by your office. We have broken none of these conditions or any laws."

The inspectors huddled and discussed what they would do until they got instructions from their superiors. One went to the police, while the other would make sure the Israelis destroyed nothing. Fifteen minutes later, the local constable, Juan Hernandez, showed up with the antiquities inspector.

"*Hola*, Professor." Hernandez and Yoshua greeted each other, to the chagrin of the inspectors. The senior of the inspectors interrupted the questions about family.

"Officer, please arrest this man for destroying a national treasure."

Hernandez gave him the evil eye.

"I don't know where you learned your manners, but here when people are asking about each other's families, you do not interrupt with demands. Let me make this clear for you, gentlemen. They have kept me up-to-date from the beginning of this excavation. I sat with Professor Rosenberg and went over all the details of his permit. They have broken no laws, regulations or conditions of their permit. What you're asking me to do is falsely arrest these people and confiscate their property with no legal basis."

The frustrated inspectors sputtered at the police officer, who laughed at them. Hernandez added, "We might be a small backwater town, but we know the law and you can't come here trying to get us involved in some illicit action. If you think you can close them down and steal all the artifacts for yourself, you're wrong." With that, Hernandez took out his handcuffs, and before the inspectors realized what was happening, he cuffed the two together.

"You're under arrest for instigating false charges against innocent law-abiding people, on suspicion of using your position as inspectors to steal antiquities, and so, breaching the public trust act."

The inspectors shouted at Hernandez until he removed his gun from its holster.

"Are you two adding resisting arrest to your charges?" That shut them up quickly, and Hernandez hauled them out of the *bet midrash*.

Yoshua knew it was a temporary victory.

"Aviva, please call the Israeli embassy in Madrid again. Tell them what happened, and what we expect to happen. We need a diplomat here to protect us."

Aviva called the embassy and talked with the head of security.

"The antiquities authority's inspectors tried to have us arrested, but the local constable refused to arrest us on false charges."

"Dr. Berger, the ambassador, has requested from the minister for the interior an explanation of why the government is harassing Israeli citizens. Especially since, they're following, the conditions of their permit to excavate. So far, doctor, we haven't received an explanation in return."

Yoshua and the team weren't idle. "Sasha, round up all of our laptops, remove the hard drives, smash them with the five-kilo hammer, and burn the pieces.

"I hope that helps your frustration. Sasha make sure we don't leave evidence for the police," Yoshua said. He gave each person a shopping list of items to buy—the purpose of which they didn't understand—and sent them each in a different direction on an "outing to shop." He thought, "*If we actively oppose the authorities, we'll end up in a jail and we might never again see the light of day, or a hit squad could show up. I better be careful not to scare Aviva about the potential dangers that lay ahead. This might be our last night of freedom for some time. So, the moral dilemma is it would be easier for us to escape from Spain. Afterwards, fight with the authorities from a distance. If we run, it's likely we'll never again see the bodies or the books. If this small community had died sanctifying God's name, so we should do as much as possible to see they didn't die in vain. In five hundred years, the world has changed. Now, the State of Israel stands as their savior. Interesting how things work out. General Dori wrote the Hoshiyan Chronicles. The Hebrew word Hoshiya means to save or rescue. In the days of the expulsion from Spain, the Jews had no one to rescue them. So, in keeping with Jewish culture and values, if they named a country Hoshiya, it must have been some kind of refuge. Hoshiyianu HaShem, (God rescue us)."*

"Yoshua, we can't let the Spanish authorities or the Vatican get hold of the bodies or the books. After what these people sacrificed hallowing the name of God, we can't sit back and turn that into a defiling of His name," said Aviva.

"We can't hide what we found from the authorities. We can't remove the bodies without destroying endless amounts of evidence. Listen, we're scientists, not grave robbers. Truth and justice will not be factors in play here. Even though we own this chapel and the permits allow us to expose and investigate, its paper, and the government can make all the paperwork disappear as if it never existed. We need to find leverage against them so we can trade for the bodies and the books."

"They have no legal rights here. We bought this plot and building. This is private property. Let's fight them until the Israeli government can come to our aid," said Sasha.

Yoshua smiled at Sasha. How easy youthful solutions seemed to them.

"Sasha, fighting the authorities will only get us killed. Rights, legal purchase, mean nothing now. This is a major embarrassment to the Spanish government and the Vatican. It doesn't matter if it's over five hundred years old."

"Sasha, they can declare martial law, or say the area is being quarantined because of the outbreak of a major disease. The Health Ministry can say the area is infected with hoof-and-mouth disease. Once they seal the surrounding area, they can do whatever they want and no one is the wiser," said Aviva.

"Fear and embarrassment are the last two things you want to cause a government. They'll strike back and strike back hard. I know in my heart it's a mistake to hand over everything we found to the Spanish government, but to anger them on their own soil is a death wish," said Yoshua.

"To our great misfortune, Yoshua is correct. We need to stop a cover-up by getting the data out of the country. We need an advantage we can use to barter with the authorities. Without changing their attitude, we are in trouble," Simon commented.

"Simon isn't an official member of the archaeology team. He's in Spain as a tourist and can go wherever he wants with his European Economic Area passport. He's the only one who can legitimately leave without official repercussions," said Yoshua.

"Copy all the data to my laptop, and I'll head for Gibraltar. I have relatives there who can help me. If I can make it across the border, I can direct the rescue mission to get the rest of you out of jail," said Simon.

"Why are you so sure we'll be arrested?" Aviva asked.

"My grandfather told me, in Russia, always keep your nose out of anything to do with the government. The second you anger them, your life won't be worth living. All governments are the same: they want to save their own tails before all other things. Don't poke sleeping dogs," Sasha told them.

Aviva finished copying all the files to Simon's laptop. He made his goodbyes, shaking everyone's hands, until he came to Aviva. He took the offered laptop from her hands and for a second, both of them held the computer. They looked each other in the eye and both felt the tug. Aviva whispered, "Come back for us, Simon."

"I'll move heaven and earth to make sure you're safe." Embarrassed by the depth of the emotion with which he had spoken to Aviva, he blushed. Simon turned to leave, then turned back. "It's been my privilege and honor to have been part of this historical event. May the Holy One Blessed be He watch over all of you and may we meet here once again as free people in possession of all that we've found."

*****

Simon didn't head directly for the border, where he suspected the Spanish police would wait for someone from the team attempting to escape. He took the A-92 west to Antequera. There, he refueled at a petrol station, paid in cash, and headed south on the A-45. At Los Pradillos he switched to the AP-46. He bypassed Malaga and took A-7 to Fuengirola. In town, he asked for directions to the marina of Puerto Deportivo de Fuengirola. At the marina, he went searching for where he could rent a small sailboat that he could handle by himself.

After searching for fourteen minutes, Simon still hadn't found a boat to rent. With every passing minute, he got more nervous about being caught by the police. The bag on his back with the laptop seemed to grow heavier by the second. As the fifteenth minute passed, he found a boating shop that rented sailboats for day-trips. He engaged the owner in Spanish, which got the man to relax and put him in the mood to bargain. Though Simon felt the tension to complete the transaction quickly and get safely to sea, he didn't want to attract any unnecessary attention. He acted calm, smiled, and shot the breeze with the owner.

"*Senor*, there are only a few hours of light left to sail."

"It's such a beautiful day, and the water looks so inviting that even if it's only for a few hours, it will be worthwhile on such a glorious day."

Among the owner's sailboats was a Contender class dinghy, which is a single-handed, high performance sailing vessel. Simon pointed to the boat.

"I'll take the Contender class dinghy."

Seeing that the tourist even knew what the type of boat he wanted, demonstrated to the owner he understood sailing. "*Senor*, when was the last time you sailed a Contender?"

"Two months ago. I was in Gibraltar visiting my cousins and we raced three of them."

"You must leave a deposit. You can use your credit card."

Simon bargained with the owner for the next ten minutes until they came to a price on which they could both agree. He needed to remain calm enough to finish bargaining with the shop owner, not to appear suspicious.

Simon figured it would be about an eight-hour trip to Gibraltar. He reasoned that by leaving at 2:00 pm, by the time the owner got worried about him, it would be dark and much harder for the Spanish coast guard to find him out in the water. He selected a small enough sailboat that would not have a radio.

Simon used his cell phone for the last time. He called his cousins in Gibraltar and explained the scenario. One of them owned a small yacht.

"George, do you think you can meet me along the way and pick me up? We'll switch places—you can return the sailboat and I'll be safe from the Spanish authorities."

"We can set out to meet you within the hour. If you're in a Contender and have a good wind, we should be able to meet you somewhere around Estepona." With the phone call over, Simon held his arm over the side of the boat and let the phone slip out of his fingers into the salty water. It short-circuited and became untraceable. Now Simon had to concentrate on his sailing.

He hugged the coast as much as possible, never wandering more than six to eight hundred meters from shore. A calm sea helped. An easterly wind pushing him along at twenty knots. With a few hours to go until he met his cousins, Simon had time to think.

*"Why didn't I insist Aviva come with me? Yoshua's probably right about them being arrested. Oh my God, the thought of Aviva in an overcrowded prison in constant danger."*

*There's no denying the attraction. It's mind-boggling that the chemistry between us is so strong. I need to get a grip and slow down. I don't know enough about her to be thinking long term—which was precisely what I'm thinking about. She's an outsider; how would she able to join the community? Even if they accept into the community and, God forbid, the marriage failed, would she keep the secrets and not interfere with the last prophecy? Maybe Ruth can help me; she understands the scenario and didn't discourage a relationship between us.*

Simon sailed automatically, not paying attention to details. Evey five minutes he would glance at the sail to check its status. Salty mist whipped across his face from the bow. Cutting through the water at high speed didn't even register. Every so often, Simon would wipe the excess moisture from his face.

*"I have to admit she's a striking beauty, but that's not what's most attractive about her. She's intelligent, articulate, worldly, committed, has a great sense of humor, and loyal. It's strange to watch her look at Ruth and Yoshua. For Aviva, Yoshua is just an extension of Ruth. Yet, I saw Aviva smile when Yoshua spoke or looked at Ruth. She appreciated how much Yoshua loved her. Aviva devoted herself to Yoshua and his search for the Light of Justice, because he treated Ruth with such affection. It's amazing to watch the deep friendship between the two women."*

*Simon missed the special spiritual connection he had with his late wife. They held hands whenever possible; a slight squeeze was enough to signal their love for each other. The memory of those special moments was enough to warm his soul. He had grown to think lightening didn't strike twice. Unexpectedly, in an unlikely place, he found someone special again. Simon thought of the great love stories of his people. Special people love* in a special way. *He smiled as he thought about the great love affairs of the Arieli family. Growing up in an atmosphere of genuine love encouraged the children to follow the same patterns of behavior, and each following generation to keep that special love alive. He thought, "Even today, people who know Micki and Rivka Arieli understood the level of devotion that can exist between two people. After sixty years, they love each other more with each passing day."*

Before Simon knew it, he saw the blinking lights of his cousin's yacht. As arranged, his cousins were waiting for him at Estepona. Simon switched places with his cousin, Ian, who would take the sailboat back to its owners. He also gave him the keys to his rental car, which he would drive to Gibraltar after he arrived in Fuengirola. Together with his other cousin, George, Simon sailed to the safety of Gibraltar.

*****

When Simon didn't return on time, the owner of the boating shop contacted the coast guard.

"Senor, if your client doesn't return in another hour, we will start a search."

*****

Meanwhile, Deputy Minister for the Interior Palmerio issued an all-points bulletin for the arrest of Yoshua, Sasha, and Aviva. He sent their descriptions to every police station in the country. When Hernandez received the notice, he called Yoshua to warn him. Sasha and Aviva were at the house, making preparations according to Yoshua's instructions. He called them, "Sasha, take Aviva and go to Juanita's house for a while. Don't come back until after you see the police leave our house.

*****

When Simon and George got into port, they headed straight for George's office. "The first order of business is to arrange for the data to get to Jerusalem, but not electronically—no Internet, no cell phones, too much risk of surveillance," Simon said.

"What do you have in mind?" George asked.

"A duel approach—two couples, two different airlines, two different times," Simon suggested.

"We can use our cousins, Max and Freeda, as the first messengers," George recommended.

"Max and Freeda, both in their seventies, are dumpy looking on the outside, but sharp as tacks inside," George said.

"For the second couple," George said, "could be my niece, Yael, with her husband and their fussy two-year-old."

They took it for granted that every party would accept their request, no questions asked. On behalf of *Clal Ysrael* and their community, George booked first-class tickets from Gibraltar to Tel Aviv.

"I chose two different airlines, one with a stopover in London and one in Madrid. The first flight left at 10 am the next morning, the second at three in the afternoon," George informed Simon.

He also booked two nights at a hotel in Jerusalem as a thank you treat.

Simon and George went to both family's homes without calling ahead. They explained in the briefest of terms what they needed done. Both couples response was, "We are honored to serve. It will give us an opportunity to visit with the king," they answered. Simon gave an USB drive to each couple.

"Please, take only your laptop case and a carry-on bag. A young man holding a sign with your name will meet you at Ben Gurion Airport. He'll take the USB drive and take you to Jerusalem," Simon explained.

When they returned to George's office, Simon asked George to call Ruth in Jerusalem. "Ruth, its George, Simon's cousin. I hope everything is well with you. I have family coming to visit in Jerusalem tomorrow, and I would appreciate it if your assistant, Tzion, would meet them at the airport."

"Hello, George. Nice to meet a cousin of Simon's. Yes, whatever you need." George gave Ruth the flight numbers and names, and they exchanged parting greetings. Ruth put the phone down and thought, *"That call was so off-the-wall, I had to agree. I can't wait until Yoshua gets home so I can find out what in the world is going on."*

*****

The two couples executed Simon's plan flawlessly. Within twelve hours, Tzion brought both USB drives to Ruth's apartment. They flipped through the photos—there were no words.

"Tzion, please take me over to Bet Arieli. I have to get these photos over there immediately. Ruth grabbed her laptop, the other USB drive, and rushed out of the house with Tzion.

When she walked into his office, their eyes met. They needed no greetings. She handed the USB drive to him. When the first picture went up on the big screen in the communications center, everyone stopped working.

"I thought I had seen everything bad this world has to offer, but I was wrong," Seth Har Zahav said.

"It's a horrendous thing. However, those responsible are long dead and the only reason we'll use this material is to get the release of our people and rights to the bodies and artifacts. Under no circumstances will we employ any of this material anyone personally," Dr. Arieli ordered his administrative staff.

"Yes, the whole thing is unbelievable."

"I assume Simon got the photos out of Spain. I should call and thank him."

*****

The phone rang, and George answered it. "George Yavetz speaking."

"Thank you and Simon for getting the information out of the bet midrash in Nido de Aguila." George's body went stiff when he realized that Dr. Arieli was calling. He and Simon had hung out together in case Yoshua needed them. George turned on the speaker. Dr. Arieli's soft, grandfatherly voice came over the phone.

"Blessed is a nation that has sons like the two of you."

"Thank you, sir," the two answered in unison.

"Simon, my son, how is Yoshua holding up?"

"He's very resourceful, sir. I'm convinced he no concept of the significance of what he found."

There was total silence on the line for about fifteen seconds while Dr. Arieli thought about what he would say next. "Simon, as always, be very careful with your words. This is a delicate scenario."

"Sir, the entire community will assist Simon, said George."

"Boys, it's late here and I must go back to my wife. She wakes up every time I get out of bed. I don't want her to lose sleep because of me. I would like to stay on the line chatting, but she's waiting.

"Regards to your righteous wife, may she live to one hundred and twenty. Goodnight, sir."

"Goodnight, boys."

George was wide-eyed after the conversation. "Simon, he blessed us."

"Yes, George, we're very fortunate. Today is a date we must write on our calendars, to remember for eternity."

\*\*\*\*\*

The next morning, Simon called Aviva first thing. His heart pound in anticipation. When she didn't answer after four rings, he worried the Spanish had already arrested them. On the sixth ring, Aviva answered.

"Simon, is that you?"

"Yes, it's me. I'm so happy to hear your voice. I've been apprehensive. Aviva, I'm concerned about your safety."

"Simon, I understand you're worried, but sometimes in one's life, when one has to stand up for justice. This is one of those deciding moments in my life. I wanted, so very much, to go with you to Gibraltar, and not be in danger of being arrested and thrown in prison. However, I agree with Yoshua. We need to secure the rights to bury those people and investigate every artifact from the chapel. To do this, we cannot create a scenario that will guarantee the Spanish authorities will never give us what we seek."

"Aviva, nothing in the world will keep me away from you."

Aviva thought, "*There goes my resistance. I need to face reality. We'll pay dearly for our actions, and God forbid, something should happen. I want him to know.*"

"Simon, the Spanish act swift and hard. I can't get that image of the mother and child. She tried to claw her way out, with her fingers rubbed down to the bone. If I am to look myself in the mirror, I have to stand up for those dead," Aviva told him with tears.

"If anything should happen, know one thing. I'm sure our souls are meant for each other. I love you. It makes little sense, but that's how I feel."

"Aviva, I also love you. I know it's been a short time, but I've not felt this way for a long time. Promise me you won't do anything stupid."

"Right, I'll try. If it comes to it, bury the three of us together." Simon wiped his tears away.

"Aviva, I'll turn the world upside down to get you back," Simon promised. Between her tears she whispered, "I love you Simon."

Despite everything, Aviva smiled to herself; she felt warm all over, and she thought, "*Someone loves me for who I am, not because of my looks or position in life. I see now how similar Simon is to Yoshua. Simon talks to me the same way Yoshua talks to Ruth. That makes sense considering that Yoshua grew up in the Arieli's home as much as with his own mother. The way Simon and Yoshua speak to others reminds me of how Dr. Arieli talks to Rebbetzin Rivka. I dreamed of the day I would meet a man like Dr. Arieli—kind, loyal, soft-spoken, always a kind word for everyone, and a smile on his face. The Arielis are an exemplar of how two became one. They're so in tune with each other that just the slightest smile or squeeze of their hands, a soft kiss, a caress, or that look in their eyes is enough to understand how much they love each other."*

\*\*\*\*\*

Simon prayed, "May it be your will, Lord my God and God of my fathers, grant that Aviva will lie down in peace and rise in peace. Please watch over her thoughts that they should not upset her, nor that she should have evil dreams. May all her actions be perfect in Your sight. Grant her light, and not the sleep of death, for You give light to the eyes. Blessed are You, Lord, whose majesty gives light to the entire world."

\*\*\*\*\*

In the morning, Simon visited the websites of the local Spanish news agencies and searched for a story about the Israelis in Nido de Aguila. He thought, "*Baruch Hashem*, they haven't been arrested yet. His next move was to look for the best criminal defense attorney in Spain. He found via the Internet the attorney he sought in Madrid. Dr. Mateo Diego Montoya-Robles was not only a well-respected criminal attorney, but he was also on the advisory board of the European Criminal Bar Association (ECBA).

Simon picked up the phone and called the law firm.

"I am sorry, sir, Dr. Montoya-Robles is out of the country. I will direct your call to one of the other partners, Alfonso-Jorge Delgado-Mendoza."

"Please."

"Dr. Jamerson, tell me your story," Alfonso encouraged. Simon told him about the archaeological excavation, about what they found, and the failed attempt to arrest his fellow team members. After twenty minutes, Delgado-Mendoza stopped Simon.

"This will not be cheap. I will charge you for research hours and if necessary, appearance in court is more."

"Money is not the problem. Time is of the essence," Simon told him.

Delgado-Mendoza called in an associate and told him to prepare for the case by calling the police in Nido de Aguila. Meanwhile, he did an Internet search on "Yoshua Rosenberg"

"I am impressed by what we found about your professor. Not only is the man an internationally acclaimed archaeologist, educator, and author, he had for years been an officer in the IDF. If they had arrested him on charges of terrorism, it's preposterous," Delgado-Mendoza told Simon.

# VAULT UNDER THE VATICAN

When the pope hung up with the king of Spain, he ordered his personal secretary.

"Please cancel every one of my appointments for the rest of the day." He proceeded via the back staircase to the headquarters of the Swiss Guard. There, he took four men to accompany him to the special vault. At the door to the vault, the commander of the guard punched in a code to which only he and the pope had access. Once the door opened, the four Swiss guards stood outside while the pope went to safe-deposit box number 2312. He stood in front of the box for a few seconds and pondered.

"I never thought I'd have to use this key, but here I am with a potential disaster on my hands and I need to know what my predecessors buried away."

The pope inserted the key. Following the instructions, he turned it first clockwise and afterwards counterclockwise, releasing the alarm mechanism. The actioned freed the box from its lock. Now he could remove the safe-deposit box. He pulled on the cold metal handle and the long, narrow safe-deposit box slid out on its well-oiled track. With great trepidation, the pope took the box, walked the one meter distance to the table on his right, placed the metal box on the table, and lifted its lid. Inside was a key and a piece of laminated paper with an eight-digit code. He replaced the safe-deposit box, used his key in the reverse, and left the vault.

The pope stood outside the vault, thinking.

*"What could be so dangerous to the church that it's locked away in such a manner? How many popes stood at this same spot preparing to defend the Mother*

*Church? As the shepherd of the Catholic faith, like any shepherd, I have to keep the wolves away from my flock."*

With his Swiss guards in tow, he headed for the nearest elevator that would take them to the lowest level of the vast underground city that existed below the surface of St. Peter's Square. When the elevator door opened at the bottom-most level, the pope turned to his left and headed one hundred meters to where another guard stood on duty. The guard hadn't had a single visitor to this part of the compound in the twenty years he had been on duty. Seeing the pope, he stood at attention and saluted him and his commander. He punched in a code known only to him and his commander, which opened the massive oak door to a small stairway.

Opening the door caused the lights to turn on in the stairwell. The pope thanked his guard. The guard informed the pope.

"We installed an intercom fifteen years ago. When you get in the vault, please check to see if intercom is working. That way, if you need anything, you only need to call me on the intercom," the Swiss Guard explained.

The guard also reminded the pope.

"Your holiness, you need to enter your personal code into the computer."

The pope headed down the stairs alone. The temperature there was much cooler. Centuries before they had cut the stairs out of the living rock. Huge dehumidifiers ran 24/7 to remove the moisture seeping through the rock. After thirty-four steps, he came to a small alcove of two by three meters. Before the pope stood a massive titanium door with a keypad to the left. He extended his finger to punch in the code for the massive door, but it hovered millimeters from the keypad.

*"I've been a loyal Catholic my entire life. What might be behind this massive door? My biggest worry is I might find documents dangerous to the church and conflicts with my ethics. The instructions from previous popes were precise. 'The church came before everything else, and the means justified the end—which was the preservation of the church. There was nothing more important."*

After convincing himself, he followed in the footsteps of the many righteous men who had served before him. The pope punched in the code. This door led to the most secret storage facility in all of Christendom. The huge, reinforced steel door opened on its hydraulic hinges and there now stood before the pope, an ancient iron door. He removed the key from his pocket and inserted it into the door. The mechanism was well-oiled, and the tumblers turned with ease. The door opened and there in front of him were the best-kept secrets of history.

He sat at a small desk and turned on the computer. Every year when they cleaned the room, they placed a new computer on the desk. The information in this computer existed nowhere else in the entire world. A large battery powered the computer. There wasn't an electric outlet in the entire vast room. There were three gasoline driven generators to provide electricity for lights, cleaning or maintenance.

When the computer came up, the pope entered his password and waited while the logistics program that cataloged every item stored in the vault loaded. The pope entered "Aharon Dori" and waited for the results. Within seconds, the monitor flashed again for the pope to enter his second password. After entering the second password, the location of the information appeared, "Row 34, position 455, 5 stars." The system expressed the level of danger of any item in the vault by the number of stars that came after the item's location. The system ranged from no stars, meaning no danger to the church, to five stars, which meant an immediate and serious threat to the survival of the church. No item in the vault had less than three stars after its location.

The pope repeated the procedure and typed 'The Hoshiyan Chronicles.' The result was the same. Trepidation seeped into the pope's bones like the chilly dampness from the river that soaked into the walls of the vault so far underground.

*"What had this Aharon Dori done? It must have been terrible if Alexander VI erased him from history and only exists here in this hidden vault. What could be in that chapel that could be so dangerous to the church?"* He looked up at the map of the storage facility and headed down the long corridor until he found row thirty-four. He turned left and walked for another forty meters until he came to a sign that showed the number four hundred fifty-five.

There were four large boxes. Close by was a table and an intercom. The pope realized he would be there a long time and called the guard. "Testing, one two three."

"Yes, Holy Father, what can we do for you?"

"Please send a guard to help me move boxes. I'll be here for a while, so please send plenty of coffee and have the chef make food for at least enough for two meals."

The pope took two latex gloves from the box at the head of the aisle and put them on. The treated gloves left no residue when one touched an item. He opened the first box and searched inside. The third item he saw was a leather-bound book with the emblem of the Grand Inquisition of Spain. The reading table was a laminar flow hood to protection rare and old books and documents. He looked at the instructions on the side, took the plastic squeeze bottle of alcohol and a large piece of cotton wool, and washed the stainless steel surface of the table. The pope waited for thirty seconds and replaced the plastic squeeze bottle in the far left corner and threw the used cotton wool in the garbage pail next to the hood. He turned on the overhead light and adjusted the intensity. The pope pushed his glasses up on the bridge of his nose, removed the tome from the storage box, placed it on the cleaned surface, and opened it.

The Tribunal of the Holy Office of the Inquisition (Spanish: *Tribunal del Santo Oficio de la Inquisición*), commonly known as the Spanish Inquisition (*Inquisición española*), was a tribunal established in 1480 by Ferdinand, the king of Spain. The mission of the Inquisition was, in theory, to maintain Catholic orthodoxy in their kingdoms. In actuality, they replaced the commission was under papal control. Ferdinand and Isabella used the commission to rob and murder Jews and Moors. It became the most substantive of the three different manifestations of the Inquisition and lasted much longer than the Roman and Portuguese versions. Ferdinand and Isabella used their religious zeal to both fill the coffers of the state and satisfy their sadistic tendencies.

Ferdinand and Isabela created the Inquisition to ensure the orthodoxy of those who converted from Judaism and Islam to Christianity. This regulation of the faith of the new converts intensified after the royal decrees issued in 1492 against the Jews, and 1501 against the Muslims, which ordered them to convert or expelled from Spain. These new decrees violated the religious freedom guaranteed in the 1492 peace treaty between Ferdinand and the emir of Granada.

The Spanish monarch's decision to fund the Inquisition increased their political authority, weakened opposition, suppressed minorities, and profited from confiscation of the property of convicted heretics. It reduced social tensions between the three religions by eradicating two of them. Ferdinand used the reasoning that the kingdom needed protection from the danger of an imaginary enemy to justify these Draconian measures.

After five minutes of reading the material that had lain there for over five centuries, the pope realized the church was in more trouble than he had suspected. In today's world of instant information, connections, and emails, the pope realized how difficult it would be to defend against the horrors that the Inquisition carried out in the church's name. They understood the world press would condemn them. The Church needed to ready itself for the coming combat with the world press. The more he read, the more sweat broke out on his forehead. The pope removed his linen monogrammed handkerchief and wiped away the sweat that was dripping into his eyes. Ten minutes later, the guard buzzed at the door. The pope got up and walked down the long corridors of shelves to the door, worrying the entire time about what possible actions he should take to prevent damage to the mother church.

The guard had a wheeled cart loaded with drink, food, and snacks. Together, they returned to the table where the pope directed the guard to remove the boxes, place one in the reading hood, and the others on the adjacent table. The pope stayed in the vault for thirty-six hours. When he finished reading what he felt was a representative amount of material, he knew the horrors of the past were coming back to haunt them.

The Pope concluded that the Grand Inquisitor had tortured those people for the pure sadistic joy of inflicting pain. The Grand Inquisitor's objective was to find and destroy every copy of the *Hoshiyan Chronicles*. He was sure the community of Nido de Aguila, where the book had originated, must have at least one copy, yet the torture and death of four of its members didn't break these people. The local commissioner of the Inquisition ordered his torturers to herd the remnants of the small Jewish community into their place of worship. Guards forced them, at sword point, into the eastern corner. Masons came. The Jews were forced to watch as the double brick wall was built that would seal their fate forever. No amount of weeping or pleading stopped the sadists from their work. The local commissioner believed what he fulfilled God's commands, when in reality he was a sick psychopath. Now the present pope could not go back on centuries of church policy of supporting the Inquisition.

The Pope knew the horrors of the Inquisition, but he had never read material about the actual procedures carried out. The torturers of the Inquisition were true sadists, depraved lunatics, and psychopaths. They poured molten lead down people's throats; they stretched them on racks until they pulled off their limbs. These men of the cloth had raped every woman for their own pleasure and afterwards inscribed it as if they had done something good because they had degraded the

Jewesses. They burned thousands of victims at the stake in front of jeering, vicious, anti-Semitic crowds of citizens screaming for blood.

After reading for ten minutes, the Pope ran for the wastebasket, leaned over and vomited everything he had eaten in the past twelve hours. The taste of half-digested food was on his tongue, and his throat felt raw and on fire. He wiped his face, weakly straightened up, went to the food cart. The pope poured himself a glass of water and walked back to the wastebasket with his mouth open and tongue out to avoid having to taste the vomit. He took three sips of water, swirled it around his mouth, and spit it out into the wastebasket. Afterwards, he turned and walked over to the intercom.

"Commander, I need your help. I've vomited. Please come and help me. I don't want people coming in here." The commander of the guards arrived quickly, analyzed the scenario, and demanded the pope come with him. The commander went to the wastebasket, grabbed the plastic liner, and tied a knot in the top to stop the spread of the awful smell.

"Your Holiness, please allow your personal physician to examine you before you return to the vault."

After a twenty minute examination, the doctor turned to the pope and commander.

"Your Holiness is in good health. The vomiting was a reaction to the stress caused by what you were reading. You are free to return to your work," the doctor said.

*****

A media storm would hit them with the power of a category five hurricane. The pope knew he had to prepare for the coming storm. What bothered him the most was what Pope Alexander VI had written.

I issued a papal order to destroy every copy of the books written by Aharon Dori, so there shall be no evidence it ever existed. The copy in this file must never leave this room. After reading it myself, I ordered every other copy within Christendom burned. The mere thought Hoshiya might have existed would undermine basic tenants of the church and our concept of creation. Any future pope reading this will mean the discovery of another unknown copy of the *Chronicles*.

Evidence from the *Hoshiyan Chronicles* showed the Jews of Hoshiya were much more technologically advanced. They had bows that had better range, were easier to shoot, and were more accurate. Their most feared weapon were naphtha throwers that could throw an arch of fire forty yards. They had advanced medicine, science, and weapons. I fear a Hoshiyan army bent on revenge for every awful act the Christians did to the Jews in the name of God—an army of eighty thousand Hoshiyan troops could have conquered every European country.

Sedition is by far the worst aspect of the *Hoshiyan Chronicles*. We saw how the ideas propagated by the son of Satan, Aharon

Dori, turned men's heads away from Mother
Church and our way of life. After reading a
section of these chronicles, I understood
their magic and how enticing the words were
to a man's heart—to make him turn against
the church and for everything it stands for.
That is the reason I ordered the Duke of
Magdeburg to destroy the rebel baron, his
people, towns, and fortresses, and make
them as if they never existed. I have erased
the rebel baron and his entire family from
every history book.

You might think the dead bodies are a
problem; they are nothing compared to what
seditious ideas are written in the *Chronicles*.
That is the reason I ordered every other copy
destroyed. Whatever you do, stop the
publication of the *Chronicles*!

"God save our souls," the pope thought, "if this ever
gets out to the public. What could be in the *Chronicles*
that's so dangerous that it's worse than the murder of
forty-six souls! So, Alexander VI made the only entry in
this file, which must mean no one has found a copy of
the *Hoshiyan Chronicles* in over five hundred twenty
years." The pope had his own intelligence unit, and it
was time to employ their services to find out precisely
what was going on in Spain.

The pope buzzed the intercom and asked the guard to
come and help him put everything back in its proper
place. While he waited, he wrote a note detailing his
plans to stop the *Chronicles* and slipped it into the first

box. After cleaning up and making sure nothing was out of place, the pope signed off the computer and returned to his apartment to shower and make a phone call. The call was to the tiny black ops unit of the Jesuits.

"Alberto, please come to my private office for an eight o'clock meeting," the pope ordered.

"In the meantime, send a representative to the police station in Granada to find out as much as possible," the pope added. The pope went to sleep after being up forty-eight hours straight. He was so tired that the second his head hit the pillow, he was out.

# BLACK OPS

While events were transpiring in Rome, the king of Spain called his prime minister and related the conversation he had with the pope.

"The pope told me, 'This will be a humiliating international incident. Please arrest the Englishman for smuggling out the data. Do we have a way to lose the evidence?'"

"Your Holiness, that is extreme measures to take against a few archaeologists," I replied to the Pope.

"Your majesty, if the pope called you directly, this incident must be of extreme importance to the Church," the prime minister commented.

"Yes, I agree with you. I don't want to impose a policy on you. Please see what you can do within the law," the king encouraged.

"I can send a team of my police SWAT unit to clean up the mess," the prime minister replied.

"I realize how damaging the entire story will be for our nation. Even though over five hundred years have passed, the last thing Spain needs right now is to bring up the questionable past of the Inquisition—with our economy in such trouble and unemployment so high," the king said.

"I'll be happy to give the order to arrest the Israeli team, confiscate their equipment and data, and seal up the chapel," said the prime minister. When the prime minister finished with the king, he called Deputy Minister Palmerio.

"The king and the pope are encouraging us to take action against a team of Israeli archaeologists and prevent what they found from reaching the international press. What can be done?" the prime minister inquired.

"Mr. Prime Minister, I received an update from the Antiquities Authority. If you remember, Prof. Rosenberg was a hero at the recent bombing in Cordova."

Palmerio saw a great opportunity for the orders he had received. He was a man who always thought on his feet and could react quickly to new scenarios. It was a member of his cell who placed the bomb at the land registry office in Cordoba. The news had concentrated on the heroic intervention of the Israeli scientist and how he saved so many lives. Now Palmerio did something about the meddling professor. He issued orders.

"I am not satisfied with the Israeli archaeologist's version of the events. He could have planted that bomb and tricked everyone by exposing it. If we charge the Israelis at Nido de Aguila acts of terrorism, we can do whatever we want. I can fulfill the pope's wishes. We can detain them, confiscate everything, and throw them in prison without a trial. Additional evidence will show that Yoshua Rosenberg planted the bomb in Cordova."

Palmerio and his anti-terrorist unit planned how to capture the cell of foreign terrorists. All those concerned met in the scenario room of the Ministry for the Interior in Madrid. Prepared maps covered the table. Various colored arrows showed the Deputy Minister's proposed strategy to capture the dangerous terrorists.

Palmerio explained to his officers, who would lead the operation.

"Since the town is in the Sierra Nevada Mountains, and escape would be easy, I want you to deploy troops to surround the town and seal it. Once every access to the town is secure, helicopters will transport the attack teams from the northwest. That will keep the hill dominating the town between them and the chapel until the last minute. There's a small square close to the northwest side of the hill." He pointed to the officer who would lead the assault.

"Repel down there. That way, the Israelis won't hear you coming. We'll contact the local police to close off the streets that are along your route to the target. Next, with a local constable as a guide, hike along the road parallel to the chapel and take control of the area. Get snipers on the roof of the building and surround the chapel. Once you have eyes on the chapel and the activity there, make your assault—that way the terrorists will not have time to respond."

When Palmerio finished the briefing, he went back to his office. There, he called his connection to the Vatican. He had met the director of security at the Vatican several times. They had cooperated on several projects over the years. When the director of security received the photos from Palmerio, he understood the gravity of the scenario and sent an urgent message to the pope.

*****

The phone rang, and Ruth called from the lab.

"Shuki, the photos have arrived, and I have taken them to the authorities." She didn't tell him she had gone to Dr. Arieli before she had contacted the Foreign Ministry.

"Ruthie, I love you and the children very much. Don't worry about me. I know how to handle myself." Ruth cried and the only could thought came to him was, *"Thank God she and the children are safe. I know she's worried because Aviva chose to remain and not escape with Simon.*

"Listen, babe, invite your father to stay over until I get home." Ruth burst out crying even louder and he could hear Tzion asking what was wrong.

"Babe, let me speak to Tzion for a minute."

Ten seconds later, Tzion came on the phone.

"Hey boss, I am sure they will drop you in the toilet."

"I know. Listen, Tzion, call my father-in-law and have him come over and take Ruth home. Call my brother and tell him I've run into trouble and not to do anything stupid."

"Boss, I don't agree with you. You're not fighting Arabs. These are Christians with a two thousand year history of hating and killing Jews. Don't be naïve. The Spanish could easily throw the three of you into the section of the *bet midrash* that you opened and seal it again with you inside."

"Tzion, don't get carried away. Too many people know we're here. We've contacted the embassy and asked for help."

\*\*\*\*\*

In the scenario room on the top floor of Bet Arieli, General Har Zahav received a report from Tzion about his conversation with Yoshua. On the other side of the room, Elisha argued with Ysrael.

"Elisha, you have the power to initiate a call to arms." Elisha stared at Ysrael as if he'd fallen on his head.

"Elisha, don't procrastinate about this. God forbid, something should happen to Yoshua. God knows when the next time will be when we'll have the proper conditions to fulfill the prophecy."

"It's been over one hundred years since the last organic unit of the army fought in combat," said Elisha.

"I'm not asking you to enlist people. I'm asking you to call for volunteers from the Royal Aluzian Guard. As a prince of Aluz, I have the right, in my brother's absence, to lead the Royal Aluzian Guard."

Ysrael turned and walked over to the far wall, where a battle-ax hung. It was an ancient weapon; over a thousand years old and was the symbol of power and authority among the Aluzians. He took it off the wall, which caused the noisy scenario room to become deadly silent. Every pair of eyes stared at Ysrael, who took two steps toward Elisha, and tossed the weapon at him. Elisha knew this day would come; he thought he'd be better prepared. He sidestepped, caught the handle of the ax, and raised it above his head with the handle parallel to the ground and the blade above him.

Through this action, Ysrael passed his authority over Aluzian military decisions to the royal house of Arieli. Everyone understood the significance of the act. Though Ysrael had the right to make a call to arms among Aluzians, his concern was the unity of the Hoshiyan people. Thus, he passed his authority to Elisha, the heir apparent.

Dr. Arieli sat in his office and thanked the Holy One, blessed be He that they tested Elisha and not him. Everyone understood what it meant. The time for him to step down as the head of the community was near at hand. He needed to hand the position over to the capable hands of his son. Dr. Arieli knew he couldn't allow a general call to arms to save Yoshua—that would give away too much.

Dr. Arieli walked into the scenario room and called for order.

"Listen to me about what you're proposing. If you have a call to arms, Yoshua will learn about it and that will interfere with fulfilling the prophecy. Ysrael, put together a team of ten Aluzians with the proper skills. I received a phone call from the attaché for cultural affairs at the Israeli embassy in Madrid. The ambassador has sent him to Yoshua, Aviva, and Sasha with diplomatic passports, but the Spanish police turned them away from the area, because of a 'biological hazard.' The Spanish government is telling the public that the Israelis released a deadly disease when they opened the sealed room. They've also issued an arrest warrant for Simon, being the physician responsible for the leak. It's a matter of a short time before they arrest Yoshua and his team. We're so close that we cannot let the Spanish government and the Vatican get in our way. I'm ordering you to save the three of them. Whatever it takes and no matter the cost, get the job done. I'll cover the entire costs myself." Everyone saluted Dr. Arieli in the Hoshiyan fashion.

"Servant of our people, your word is our command," said Ysrael.Dr. Arieli feared this day his entire life. He was a physician his entire professional career and for the first time he was ordering men to into a deadly scenario. It was also the first time he had officially acted as king.

*****

Two police helicopters hovered over Nido de Aguila's central plaza. The black uniformed anti-terrorist assault team rappelled down. Their gloved hands slipped along ten meters of nylon ropes. The anti-terrorist officers carried automatic rifles with a bullet in the chamber. They wore bulletproof vests, thick gloves, and helmets. Each officer hit the ground, ready to fire.

They crouched and awaited for the full team to assemble.

"Men, Deputy-Minister Palmerio told us we are up against terrorists with years of military training. These are dangerous people." Juan Hernandez met the officer, shaking his head.

"Lead us as close as possible to the chapel without us being seen," the commander ordered Juan.

"They are unarmed and will not resist," Juan told the counter-terrorist officer.

"How do you know?"

"I know Professor Rosenberg well, and he told me there would be no resistance," Juan replied.

The officer in charge had doubts. Every piece of intelligence he received indicated there were only three scientists.

"Listen Juan, we have files from the ministry about all three Israelis. All of them were in combat units. They are a serious potential threat. The professor is a trained killer and his brother is a sniper," the officer told Juan.

"You've gotten it all wrong. Professor Rosenberg is in an antiterrorism unit like you. You're correct, he has killed many, but terrorists, not innocent civilians," Juan argued.

"Be careful of Yoshua Rosenberg. He is an Israeli combat officer with decades of training," the officer warned his troops.

He issued his attack orders.

"Advance with utmost caution. I want two snipers to cover us. Work your way to the top of the building nearest the chapel. Set up a vantage point for covering the rest of our team during the assault."

"Safeties off. May sure you have a bullet in the chamber," the officer added.

They advanced in single file, rifles on their shoulders, and eyes glued to their advanced military scopes. The officers moved in tandem, swinging their rifles back and forth, searching for enemy combatants waiting in ambush for them. They stayed close to the walls of the building for maximum cover. Before turning the corner to the chapel, the officer took out a mirror on a expanding rod and surveyed the area near the chapel.

Yoshua knew all their tactics and sat himself in a place where the sun was behind his back. When the officer rotated the mirror, he saw a leg, followed by a flash of light in his eyes. He had caught the reflection of the sun directly in his eyes. He had to rest for forty seconds before he could see again.

"Sniper one what is happening outside the chapel?" the officer inquired.

"There is a man sitting on a chair drinking a cold beer. There are multi-colored wires attached to his leg going into the ground next to him," the sniper informed him.

The officer opened his phone and called the deputy minister.

"Yes, what is your status?"

"We have eyes on one of the Israelis."

"What is he doing?" Palmario asked.

"You didn't say anything about explosives. We don't have an explosives expert with us."

"What do you mean?" Palmario demanded.

"From his age, it must be Prof. Rosenberg. He is sitting in the open with a multi-colored wire attached to his leg going into the ground in front of him," the officer reported.

"What else is he doing?" the deputy minister shouted over the phone.

"He has a cold beer in his hand and a cooler next to him."

"Contact the local farm supply company and find out if he bought any fertilizer."

"Yes, sir."

"Juan, where is the nearest farm supply company?" the officer asked.

"There isn't one in Nido de Aguila. There are at least three within twenty minutes of here," Juan replied.

"Well, call them all and find out if the professor or one of the Israelis bought fertilizer."

"This will take time. I'll go back to the station and look up their phone numbers."

"Make it quick. I am sending one of my men with you," the officer ordered.

Juan jogged off with an anti-terrorist officer with him.

"Sniper two do you have eyes on the target?"

"Yes, sir. He has opened a parasol covered in aluminum foil. The reflection of the sun is in my scope. I can only look at his feet," the sniper reported.

Minutes ticked by and the heat increased. The anti-terrorist unit had uniforms that covered their entire bodies but their eyes. Standing in the sun, the sweat poured off them.

After ten minutes, Juan called.

"Two of the stores have had no foreigners in to buy anything. The third is looking through his records. As soon as he calls, I'll let you know."

The officer now poked his head around the corner. Yoshua finished his first beer and took another and slowly rubbed the cold beer over his face and forehead while smiling. He twisted off the top and took a swig.

"Ah," he said loudly.

Instinctively, the officer licked his lips. Yoshua raised the bottle to him in a toast and took another sip.

"Lieutenant, sniper one here. We are getting roasted up here fully exposed to the sun on the roof."

"Maintain your position to cover the assault," the lieutenant reminded him. The lieutenant looked at his men. They were all sweating.

"Okay, move to the other side of the street, where you can find shade," he ordered. Five minutes later, Juan called.

"Well?"

"They didn't sell any fertilizer to a foreigner," Juan replied.

The lieutenant peaked around the corner again. Yoshua smiled and waved to him.

The commanding officer raised his fist, which brought his men back to their feet and to the sunny side of the street. He kept his rifle aimed at Yoshua.

"I'll call Madrid for instructions," he told his men.

Deputy-Minister Palmario listened to the intelligence gathered by Juan.

"Okay, if you have no fear of a bomb, arrest him," Palmario ordered.

"What are those wires?" the lieutenant asked.

"Hold on lieutenant. I'll get back to you."

Three minutes later, Palmario called back.

"Send someone out there immediately.

The six-man attack team followed their officer into the open. When Yoshua saw how the police officers arrived. He broke out laughing uncontrollably. Seeing the officers perspiring profusely, he called out to them.

"Perhaps you would like something cold to drink?" Yoshua opened the cooler next to him and removed a can of ice cold beer. He raised it into the air, offering to them.

"This is sniper two. He's offering the men cold beers. Lieutenant, are you sure we are in the right place?" The lieutenant didn't know what to do, but after two minutes, he moved forward. He surveyed the area right and left. With his gun aimed at Yoshua, he closed the last three meters. Seeing nothing happening, the other officers joined him. Now all had their guns aimed at Yoshua.

Yoshua opened the cooler for them to inspect. He handed cold beer to the officers. They looked at each other, then at the cold beers in their hands. They wiped the sweat from their foreheads. Indecision gripped them. They shrugged their shoulders, and before their commanding officer could say a word, they guzzled the cold beer. This broke the spell, and the rest of the team strapped their rifles to their backs and rushed forward to get a cold beer. The snipers abandoned their nests to join everyone for a cold beer. The commanding officer called Palmerio.

"We have captured the dangerous Israeli scientist with no loss of life." He didn't wait for a response, but went to join his men and his captive for a beer.

Yoshua called to Aviva and Sasha to join him outside the chapel. "Where are the others?" asked the commanding officer.

"My wife, Dr. Ruth Rosenberg, took my son home because he enters the army in less than two weeks. The teenager, Gefen Nimrodi, also returned with my wife to Israel. The three of them left before we opened the sealed room. You can check with passport control at the Madrid-Barajas Airport."

Yoshua handed the commanding officer their permits, and it became obvious within minutes that the Israelis had broken no laws. The commanding officer didn't tell Yoshua they were being arrested for terrorism. He knew the charges were false, but that wasn't his problem; it was a political decision. Aviva slipped away to the bathroom and called the Israeli embassy.

"The police have arrived. They are arresting us and the helicopter will take us to Madrid."

It was a three-hour flight to a military airport outside the city. From the moment they arrived, everything changed—they handcuffed and put them in leg irons. Then the agents hustled into an armored car and transported to the central police station in Madrid. They were neither photographed nor fingerprinted and left sitting on wooden benches for two hours.

*****

Responding to Aviva's frantic phone call, the Israeli embassy dispatched a diplomat to Nido de Aguila. His

car had Israeli diplomatic plates. The police roadblock
ten kilometers before the town prevented them from
continuing.

"I insist you allow me to extract three Israeli nationals
in Nido de Aguila. They have diplomatic immunity. Here
are their passports," the diplomat stated.

"Sir, we respect your diplomatic credentials, but
there's a health hazard in the town of Nido de Aguila.
The place is under quarantine by order of the Ministry of
Health," the police officer replied.

Once Attorney Delgado-Mendoza received the news
of the arrest, he tried calling the police station at Nido de
Aguila. It took an hour, but he got through to Hernandez,
who listened to his story and informed him.

"Two antiquities inspectors tried to get me to arrest
the professor on false charges. I'm worried about the
professor and his team because the men who came to
arrest them weren't regular police. They were an anti-
terrorist unit. The professor is a good man and everyone
in town has high regard for him."

*****

Waiting for Yoshua and the team at central booking
was the Israeli ambassador. "I demand to see the three
Israelis arrested on false charges. You have no rights to
hold foreign nationals with diplomatic immunity. I am
here with a team of attorneys and journalists," the Israeli
ambassador threatened.

The police commander of Madrid kept the diplomats
and attorneys busy, stalling them while the police slipped
the Israelis out the back door. The police took them to a
different police station. Little did anyone know that the

team members were being charged with espionage, obstruction of justice, theft of archaeological artifacts, fraud, money laundering, and tax evasion.

The police commander had no sympathy for terrorists. He did everything possible to prevent the Israeli ambassador from seeing his fellow citizens. Representatives of the Spanish foreign ministry showed up to deal with the Israeli diplomats. A shouting match erupted and things got out of hand quickly. Each side, after ten minutes, stepped back and called their respective bosses. To everyone's surprise, eight other ambassadors from countries across the world arrived

"Why are archaeologists with diplomatic immunity being treated like terrorists? Didn't one of them had recently saved tens of lives in a terrorist bomb attack in Cordova?" the ambassadors demanded. The ministry employees had no training to deal with such a scenario or senior enough to confront nine different ambassadors. Within minutes, it was on news station across the world as local and international TV and radio networks discovered the story.

Among those wandering the police station was a representative of the black ops unit with papal diplomatic papers. He interviewed the arresting officers. Every police officer cooperated with him. He reviewed the photos the police photographer had taken. The agent copied the material and scanned the photos into his laptop. He sent the files to Alberto, who forwarded them to the pope. The papal agent blessed the police officers and their families, got up, and left. He walked straight out of the building as if he belonged there, passing the diplomatic confrontation, smiling to himself.

Alberto, at once, sent the information to the Jesuit's Superior General and the pope. He called his superior, discussed the scenario, and debriefed him. Ten minutes later, the pope himself called to talk with Alberto and discuss the options available.

*****

The Spanish government fell on the little chapel with a force far beyond a normal person's comprehension. Roadblocks closed every entrance to the town, and only residents could enter or leave. They declared the area adjacent to the chapel off limits to anyone not approved by the minister for the interior. Barbed wire fences sprang up, and the entire area looked like a military camp.

The deputy minister for the interior called the Granada medical examiner, Dr. Rodriquez.

"I am ordering you and your team to bag up the bodies and oversee their transport to a secure military site for storage."

The forensic lab in Granada sent its entire team to Nido de Aguila to remove the bodies.

When the Medical Examiner walked into the opened sealed room, he stopped, shocked at what he saw.

"I feel like I walked into a time warp going back five hundred years," Medical Examiner said to his assistant.

"These people died in pain and agony," his assistant replied.

No matter how anti-Semitic these men might have been, few could see what they found in the unsealed room without it stirring up powerful emotions. Many had tears in their eyes as they photographed and lifted the bodies into body bags.

On Monday 30 July, two military forensics experts showed up at the military site.

"We have orders to photograph, take tissue samples for DNA analysis and fingerprint each of the bodies.

In Granada, the medical examiner's staff, supplemented by four doctors from the university, attempted to fulfill the demands of the Deputy Minister of the Interior. The opportunity to examine so many five hundred-year-old bodies was too good to pass by. The chief medical examiner, Dr. Rodriguez, told two military forensics experts.

"I have a portable x-ray machine. Get me clearance and I will x-ray the bodies."

The military forensic experts took samples of the clothing back to the lab.

The pope was in direct contact with the minister and deputy minister of the interior. The minister reassured the pope.

"We have confiscated all the data about the bodies, and transferred them to a long-deserted underground bunker from the days of the civil war—that few people know about. Since Dr. Jamerson released the photos of the sealed off room, they showed it constantly in the international media. The destruction of the bodies and artifacts is out of the question. A very healthy dose of bureaucracy is the only thing that will help slow down the inevitable."

"Excellent, if you don't store the bodies and books properly, they might rot, and hopefully, much of the information will be unusable," the pope said hopefully.

\*\*\*\*\*

For Alberto to destroy the books and bodies, he needed access to them. The military site where they were being kept was too well-guarded. He had much better connections with the police than did the army, but he needed a reason to bring the bodies and books back under police protection. He reviewed once again the material his agent sent him and saw one sentence that was his savior. The medical examiner's office in Granada was running forensic tests. The medical examiner could move the bodies and books to the medical examiner's office for testing. Afterwards, he could easily arrange an "accident." His current thinking was a fire, because if the fire didn't do the trick, the water to extinguish it would destroy most of the evidence.

Alberto needed an ally with enough political power to order the move. He reread the report. Alberto saw Deputy Minister Palmerio was his most likely candidate. Alberto outlined his concept and sent it to the pope for approval.

"Your Holiness, I need you to pull strings to get the bodies back to Granada so the Medical Examiner can take more samples. I will get easy access to destroy the evidence."

"Alberto, I'll take of it right away. You can make arrangements in another hour," the pope told him. Alberto picked up the phone and called the papal representative in Madrid a few hours later.

"Father Vasquez, Alberto speaking. Has the pope contacted you concerning me?"

"Yes, Alberto, you have my full cooperation in any matter."

"Good, Father. I want you to contact Deputy Minister Palmerio clandestinely. You'll be negotiating with him in the pope's name. You're to make him understand that by helping Mother Church in her time of need, we will assist him with his political career."

"Yes, Alberto, I'll ensure the meeting stays secret and Palmerio will know the pope helps those who help protect the church."

The way Deputy Minister Palmerio agreed readily surprised Father Vasquez.

"I am happy to help the pope in this matter," Palmerio agreed. Palmerio smiled, overjoyed that the papal representative had contacted him secretly. This would give him an advantage over the church on an occasion when he needed help.

"Have no fear, Father Vasquez. I'll contact the general in charge of the base to transport the bodies to the medical examiner in Granada, where we can examine them under proper conditions."

"Thank you, Deputy Minister."

"May the Lord bless all your endeavors." Palmerio smirked at Vasquez's words. With the church at his beck and call, he could push his program of terror at an accelerated rate.

*****

The Spanish foreign ministry became inundated with requests for information about the discoveries. Many governments wanted explanations about what was being done about it. It now became obvious that Simon had escaped the country. International pressure built by the minute. Within an hour, the major international news agencies ran features on the discoveries and asked poignant questions backed up by the photographic evidence.

The avalanche of diplomatic activity that fell on the Spanish caused their entire foreign ministry to collapse under the strain. For the next thirty-six hours, stories of the Israeli archaeologists held front-page news throughout the world. Pictures of the dead community, and especially how the Spanish government reacted to the criticism, aroused the anger of many nations. The scenario got even out of hand at the United Nations.

"The General Assembly would like an explanation about what has transpired in Nido de Aguila," the secretary-general demanded of the Spanish ambassador and the papal observer.

The United Nations dealt with the problem of the Inquisition, false arrest, and the disappearance of the Israeli scientists. In the meantime, the pope and his operatives worked on plans for stealing the books were among the artifacts. There was no lack of allies for their objective. Among the police officers were many loyal to the Catholic Church. They were more than willing to do anything if it had the blessing of the pope.

Alberto moved his team of five experienced operatives to Granada. Their base was a Jesuit monastery. They set up a scale model of the medical examiner's offices and the laboratory where the bodies and artifacts were now being held. Alberto's team was constantly on their phones, talking with cooperative police officers. They gathered intelligence about the whereabouts of the artifacts, who guarded them, and what safeguards were in place.

The Vatican and the Spanish government were livid over the release of the photos. One thing the Spanish could not stop for long was diplomatic visitations to the captives, but the response to every request was that the prisoners were "lost" in the system.

\*\*\*\*\*

Simon spent *Shabbat* in Gibraltar. After *Shabbat,* he called Gavriel to get the personal number for the Israeli ambassador to Spain.

"There's no need to worry. *Rebbetzin* Arieli already called the ambassador. After she explained the scenario to him. After he saw Sasha's photos, he understood the ramifications of what they found at Nido de Aguila. She said she feared the Spanish will destroy any evidence that portrays them in a poor light. Especially the volumes discovered in the hands of the dead members of the community," Gavriel explained.

"We must do everything possible to stop them," Simon replied.

"Rivka said no one knows the identity of the books. Fear of embarrassment to authorities throughout history has caused the destruction of many irreplaceable books. She reminded the ambassador that Ferdinand of Aragon had burned over ten thousand Arabic manuscripts while he purged the Moslems from Spain. Rivka requested the ambassador demand a list of the artifacts, clothes, personal items, books, the Torah, and other holy books found lying next to the dead. She said the ambassador already had the photos from Yoshua's team, so he would know if they lied to him and left something off the list."

Gavriel opened the next subject with kid gloves.

"Simon, we haven't talked in several years. How are you doing?"

Simon thought, "Gavriel was Esther's uncle. The two were very close since her father died when she was fifteen. Should I tell him I feel guilty because I found someone to replace Esther? There's hope in my heart and what makes this more difficult is that Gavriel and Aviva know each other well." "Thank you, Uncle, I'm much better now. What do you think of Aviva Berger?"

"I've known Aviva for a long time. My option is you should consider her. I know Esther would want you to get on with your life."

"Uncle, what is loyalty to a loved one who has passed on?"

"Simon, loyalty to Esther's memory is not forgetting her, and moving on with your life. This world is for the living. It's not good for a man to be alone. It's incumbent upon a man to find a wife. You shouldn't make your home into a shrine to Esther. If you keep a small picture near your computer, where you see it. Don't make it obvious. It will look like a shrine. Have a memorial for her every year with the family. That will be enough. You should also make a schedule for you and the children to care for the gravesite three or four times a year—but individually, not as a group."

"I won't be coy with you, Gavriel, especially since Ruth has told you about what's been going on between the two of us. It's almost embarrassing to think how fast this happened, but Uncle, we've fallen in love and now they have arrested her. I don't know what to do with myself."

"It's true. Ruth told me what has been transpiring between the two of you in Spain. This is the reason I called. I know you're probably beside yourself with guilt that you didn't take her out of Spain. Aviva is an adult and decided on a path for her own reasons. Do everything to save her, but also rejoice in her decision to stand and be heard. She's a serious woman, one I'm proud to call a friend."

"Thank you, Uncle, for your words of encouragement. I'll take them to heart."

"Be strong and brave, Simon. You need to move heaven and earth to save the three of them. Nothing must happen to Yoshua. I'm sorry to say this, but he has to be your priority even though you love Aviva."

"I understand, Uncle. Thank you for calling; you've helped me."

*****

In Madrid, the Israeli ambassador called the commander of the Granada city police force.

"Commander, I am sending you an official diplomatic request to hand over the bodies of the dead Jews for proper burial," the ambassador requested politely.

"You have the wrong address, sir. Contact the Ministry of Foreign Affairs," he replied and hung up. He contacted his friend, the US ambassador, and asked for help. The US ambassador called the president.

"Mr. President, there's been a travesty of justice here in Spain and a clear-cut denial of basic human rights." He explained to the president what happened—how the human rights of the Israeli scientists were being denied and that the dead were victims of the Spanish Inquisition.

While the president spoke to his ambassador to Spain, his aide showed him the horrific photos of the mummified dead that Dr. Jamerson had released to the press. His hatred of imperialism burned in him.

"Mr. Ambassador, I will show the world that I am decisive in foreign policy. This is an excellent opportunity to strike out against the evils of imperialism," the president said.

"Mr. Ambassador, I knew the Spanish expelled their Jewish citizens who refused to convert. In school, we learned perhaps two sentences on the Spanish Inquisition. I had no idea the level of brutality. I'm sure there are few people who know about the Inquisition in such detail. These bodies bring to life this horrid period history."

"Mr. President, understand for historical information, a few people know anything. We've done a small survey here and what we found was that the Inquisition in Spain is glorified as something that purified Catholic Spain of potential enemies and non-Catholics. Few people know the truth behind Isabella and Ferdinand's policies, which, today, we call 'ethnic cleansing. They employed their fanatics as legal means of robbing part of a population and fulfilling sadistic natures."

The ambassador waited to hear the president's response. After ten long seconds, the president added, "I see that the Spanish Inquisition lasted from 1478 to 1834. The cruelty is hard to comprehend. What do the Israelis want?"

"First, the Israeli ambassador wants the release of his citizens, who the Spanish arrested on false charges. Second, they want the bodies of those murdered Jews released for burial in Israel, and last, he wants the Israelis the rights to study the Jewish artifacts found at Nido de Aguila."

"I see no trouble with these humble demands. It's too late to call the Spanish prime minister, but I'll do it first thing in the morning."

"The Israeli ambassador asked me to let you know that his people and government appreciate your action on this matter."

*****

Meanwhile, the Israeli ambassador had "Yossi," the station chief of the Spanish branch of the Mossad, come to his office. He explained what had happened.

"Yossi, I feared many of the artifacts will be 'lost' and something dreadful could happen to the falsely arrested scientists. Make this your priority," the ambassador told the station chief.

Yossi looked at the names of the captured scientists. "Nothing happens by chance, sir. I see that one prisoner is Dr. Aviva Berger."

"Do you know her?"

"My sister-in-law is an artist who had worked with her for several years. My sister-in-law praised her friend's talent and mourned the day that Aviva stopped doing original art. It appears God has made things come full circle. I am more than happy to help," Yossi said.

Yossi was not your typical spy. He had been a fine arts student and hired to be a forger. He worked his way up within the system and now, with years of field experience, headed for the Mossad station in Madrid. Yossi sat at his desk, contemplative of the problems he faced. *Who would benefit the most from the destruction of the bodies and artifacts? The answer was the Spanish government and the Catholic Church. He had a mole in the police anti-terrorist unit who told him about the arrest of the scientists, but nothing more. There was no other "chatter" from government sources about further actions. That left the church.*

He put a tail on every papal representative in Madrid and Granada. Yossi called headquarters in Jerusalem and talked to his boss.

"I will need special backup in the form of more agents to tail papal representatives. I will also need an emergency response team. I feared the 'loss' of the artifacts could be imminent," Yossi told his boss.

Two hours later, twenty-five men and women took off from an air force base in central Israel in a private jet headed for Granada. Among them were six men from a special intelligence unit that didn't even have a name. These men rarely wore a uniform and had signed up for a seven-year stint. Their files were hidden deep in the general staff headquarters, with access available to only three men. If James Bond had been real, these men could have been in his unit.

\*\*\*\*\*

The next morning, the president of the United States called the Spanish prime minister. Their conversation started cordially. Each asked after the other's family, but things fell apart quickly.

"Mr. Prime Minister, I would appreciate if you would release the falsely arrested scientists and the bodies for burial," said the president.

"Mr. President, since when does a foreign power have the right to request something involved in an internal Spanish affair? Did my government make demands about the terrorists who destroyed the World Trade Center? I refuse in no uncertain terms! I repeat, because this matter is a local Spanish matter, and no foreign power has any rights to interfere with terrorist activity in our country. You're overstepping your position. This is an internal Spanish matter that took place on Spanish soil with Spanish subjects and has nothing to do with the United States or any other country." With that said, the prime minister slammed down the phone.

The conversation between the two heads of state had been on speaker. The entire US cabinet was sitting in the conference room and heard what transpired. Outraged, the cabinet members shouted angrily about the Spanish. The secretary of state turned to the attorney general and asked his opinion of what could be done. The president was trying to cool down tempers, but the direct snub infuriated the cabinet.

"This is a serious breach in international etiquette and an insult to the United States and its president," the secretary of Defense shouted.

Seeing the political implications of what happened, the president picked up the phone, called the leader of the opposition. He informed him of what had transpired and asked him if he thought a bipartisan statement could be issued. His response flabbergasted the president.

"Mr. President, our party has already met. We discussed the disturbing events in Spain. I was about to call you to discuss the serious matter of the desecration of individual rights. Especially since that was the platform on which you ran for the president."

Two hours later, when the Secretary of State held a special press conference with the leader of the opposition party. They shocked the world with their joint statement.

"The illegal arrest and incarceration of the Israeli scientists is a shocking development. They received legal permits to excavate the site at Nido de Aguila. They had broken no laws and had discovered important finds that demonstrated horrendous violations of human rights by a previous imperialist Spanish government."

"The world has complained about the weak responses of the US president on foreign policy. Let me state emphatically, you are wrong about his position in this case. The president is a student of history. He is knowledgeable about the Inquisition and how it was used to rob innocent people through false accusations of religious impropriety. The expansionist regime of Ferdinand and Isabella fueled their expansion by preying on the weak and defenseless, stripping them of their basic human rights and property. The actions of the current Spanish government appalls the United States government."

"The response of the US government to the Spanish abuse it to declare the entire Spanish diplomatic contingent is now persona non grata. We have frozen every Spanish asset in the United States," the Secretary of State stated.

Ten minutes later, the longshoremen's union on the east coast of the United States made a declaration.

"We won't load or unload any cargo originating in, or destined for, Spain until they release the archaeologists from illegal incarceration."

The shock waves from this announcement cause an upheaval in the financial world. Spain, already in serious economic trouble, found itself on the verge of financial collapse. In retaliation, Spain expelled every US diplomat and froze US assets in Spain.

The photos Simon had smuggled out were over the entire news media. Tens of experts inspected the photos and reported that the photos authentic and untampered. The ghastly photos reawakened the world to the long forgotten horrors of the Inquisition. This led to grassroots movements to boycott Spanish made goods and the Catholic Church in many places in the world.

The liberal press in the US followed the trail the president had blazed—violation of human rights. Ratings shot up for every news channel that covered the story. There are many ways to cover a story: give the bland facts, give a slight bias, be biased, or as with many protests throughout the world, journalists pay people to "make the protest more interesting." Not merely reporting the news, but create it themselves. That's what the program the liberal press implemented. They would show the world just who was boss, and who controls what happened.

The Spanish tourist industry was the first to feel the weight of world opinion, egged on by the press. The press reported that people were canceling reservations at Spanish resorts. This resulted in thousands of tourists canceling their scheduled vacations in Spain. Visitors already in Spain cut their vacations short and went home.

*****

Masked policed officers hustled Yoshua, Aviva, and Sasha out of the police station into an armored car. They whisked them away to Valdemoro prison in southern Madrid. Valdemoro, known as "Madrid III," shares the problem of overcrowding like most Spanish prisons. They separated Aviva from the men. Again, they entered the prison with no processing. They received only prison overalls, a towel, soap, one roll of toilet paper, and a blanket. The guards dumped the men into an overcrowded cell with four Basque terror cell members.

"Let's hope tomorrow morning we can bury those two," one guard told the other, neither comprehending that Yoshua spoke Spanish.

One terrorist recognized Yoshua.

"Hey, that is the Israeli that warned everyone about the bombing in Cordoba. Not knowing Yoshua spoke Spanish, the terrorists spoke freely.

"When the lights go out, we will kill these two Israelis," the leader informed them. Yoshua informed Sasha of their cell mates' intentions. Yoshua took the two bars of soap and wrapped them in a towel. It wasn't much of a weight, but if swung hard enough, it would deliver a bigger wallop than a fist. Yoshua and Sasha picked a spot on the floor and waited for lights out. As soon as the guard passed by, they stood up casually. Before anyone realized, Sasha and Yoshua attacked the nearest terrorist. Yoshua bent his leg toward himself and shot it out like a catapult. Yoshua's boot foot connected with the man's jaw. The blow knocked him unconscious before the other three could react.

The other three jumped from their beds. Sasha and Yoshua picked up the unconscious prisoner. They threw him on their attackers. While the three untangled themselves, Yoshua searched under the unconscious terrorist's mattress.

"Pay dirt," he whispered to Sasha as his hand closed around the shank. All three terrorists were armed. One slashed at Yoshua. He barely dodged the blade. Yoshua swung out with his armed right hand, and sliced into the terrorist's forearm, opening up his brachioradialis muscle. The terrorist's shank fell to the floor and Yoshua kicked it over to Sasha—now it was two against two. The two well trained Israelis overcame their would-be attackers in forty-five seconds. Yoshua bandaged the attackers, gagged them, and tied them up with their sheets. He took the top left bunk and Sasha took the top right bunk.

In the morning, when the guards found the wounded terrorists, they hauled Yoshua and Sasha off to solitary confinement.

"You planned all of this, boss, didn't you?" Sasha asked.

"At least in solitary, it's safe from being murdered in the middle of the night," Yoshua answered him. For the first thirty-six hours in solitary confinement, they suffered under severe conditions—with no food or water. They survived by drinking water from the toilet—flushing it and catching the running water in their cupped hands.

What worried Yoshua the most was how Aviva was being treated. He smiled; Being single and having lots of free time, Aviva had dedicated a significant amount of her time to sports. She was athletic and had been studying martial arts for over fifteen years. Yoshua thought, *"Holy One Blessed be Your Name, watch over Aviva, the daughter of Yehudit and Alexander (Sasha), the son of Leah: Grant, that they should lie down in peace and rise in peace. Let not my sins and especially my arrogance bring evil tidings to them. Spread your wings over them, shelter them in peace in your bosom. Guard them from the evil that stalks the night and the wickedness that haunts us in the light of day. Guard their going out and their coming in. Blessed is God who hears the prayers of his people."*

*****

While Yoshua was praying for her welfare, Aviva fended off attacks from her cellmates. The four hardened criminals thought they had new, fresh meat.

"This new girl will be our 'bitch'. The four of them never had a chance. Aviva didn't wait for nighttime like Yoshua and Sasha had. She walked into the cell, quickly figured out who was running things there, walked up to her, and smashed her in the nose with the palm of her right hand. Crunch went the cartilage of her nose and blood spurted out all over the girl next to her. The second girl, covered in blood, jumped up, throwing her hands up in a knee jerk reaction—as Aviva had hoped. Exposed, Aviva leaned to the right and kicked her in the right side of her torso, which broke three of her ribs. That made two criminals down and two to go. The other two idiots went for the shanks, hidden under their mattresses. Meanwhile, other inmates in the vicinity screamed 'fight, fight'. Everyone came running, including the guards equipped with stun guns. They saw the two girls with shanks threatening the new girl. Zap, zap, and the two armed attackers fell to the floor, struck by one hundred thousand volts.

Within minutes, Aviva was on her way to solitary confinement—precisely what she wanted. The overcrowded prison was filthy. Garbage laid everywhere, and the prisoners made the scenario worse on purpose. Even solitary was not solitary. At first, they put Aviva in a cell with a woman who murdered her husband in his sleep, stabbing him thirty times. While the guards were locking the door behind her, Aviva attacked the psychopath. Before the two female guards could get back inside, the Spanish woman was out cold. They had to drag the prisoner out and call for a medic and a stretcher.

*****

Once the news broke about what the US president had done, the Israeli prisoners bore the brunt of the Spanish prison guards' anger. The world press echoed the war cry of "human rights" following the president's lead, while the Spanish press supported the prime minister one hundred percent. The rest of Europe tried to stay neutral, not giving opinions, and avoided anything that might show favoritism to one side over the other.

*****

Back in Jerusalem, the Rosenberg family worried about Sasha, Yoshua and 'Aunt' Aviva. "I can't believe so much has happened after we left," Ruth said to the children.

Simon had emailed Ruth the contact information of Attorney Delgado-Mendoza. She called him.

"Dr. Rosenberg, a total blackout about the prisoners has been imposed by the Spanish government. The earth has opened its mouth and swallowed them whole. All inquiries through formal and informal channels have come up with nothing. I will contact you the second I know something, Dr. Rosenberg," the attorney told Ruth.

Even Attorney Delgado-Mendoza, with all his connections, couldn't shake out any information about the prisoners.

Gefen was beside herself when she learned the Spanish had arrested Aviva. She disappeared into the Spanish penal system. Her parents tried to console her, but to little effect.

"Honey, let's look for Dr. Jamerson's phone number and you can be in direct contact with him," Gefen's father suggested. She called every thirty minutes to no avail until 1:30 am Sunday night when someone answered the phone.

"Hello?"

"Dis deh house of Dr. Simon?" asked Gefen in her poor English.

"Yes, I'm Michal Jamerson, Dr. Jamerson's daughter. My father isn't here."

"Dis Gefen Nimrodi from Yerushalim." Michal switched to Hebrew.

"How can I help? My father has spoken about you."

"I need to talk to your father about our mutual friend, Dr. Berger, in prison in Spain." Gefen began to cry and Michal realized there was more to the story than she had been told.

"Gefen, my father will be back in England tomorrow around 11:00 am. I'm picking him up at the airport. I'll pass along your message and he'll call you. How will my father get in touch with you?"

"I'll give you my phone number at home and my cell number." Gefen continued to sob. Michal realized the girl was in distress.

"Okay, well, the second I hear from my father, I'll give him your message."

"Your father is a lucky man to have Aviva Berger; she's a special person." Gefen felt penitent that she hadn't treated Simon better. Now Michal was awake. Her father hadn't told her about a relationship with Dr. Berger. Gefen realized at that moment how much all of them meant to her—Aviva, Ruth, Yoshua, and Sasha. Between the tears, she thanked Michal and hung up.

*****

Protests occurred in front of fifty-six Spanish embassies and consulates around the world. The more the Spanish tried to explain the clear-cut violations of their laws, the more the press ridiculed them and made a laughingstock out of them. Rabbinical leaders all over the world made the same announcement.

"We call on all the Jewish communities around the world to come and join our protests. There is conclusive evidence from sources inside Spain that the Medical Examiner's office is conducting autopsies on the Jewish corpses!" By the third day, the press estimated the number of protesters taking part in demonstrations was over four million people worldwide. At each protest, the organizers set up giant video screens. Broadcasts direct from Washington, DC enabled the protesters to feel connected to one another worldwide.

*****

In Israel, two and a half million people gathered in ten major cities in a show of empathy and support for their fellow citizens. Simon appeared on every major worldwide television channel—interviewed time after time. The press loved the suave, debonair English surgeon. He was articulate, persuasive, eloquent, and it didn't hurt that he was handsome.

News agencies also interviewed Simon's father, Andrew (Avihu) Jamerson. "I would like to thank the citizens of the world for their outpouring of support for the three Israeli scientists with whom his son had worked."

*****

Simon called the attorney's office.

"I am sorry. Attorney Delgado-Mendoza isn't in the office. He left a message. My staff works diligently with the Spanish authorities. We expect he will see Yoshua Rosenberg and his colleagues soon," the secretary explained.

Two hours later, the Spanish announced.

"We have issued an arrest warrant for the criminal, Dr. Simon Jamerson. We have sent a European Union extradition order to Whitehall. The charges included theft of artifacts and endangering the public, as Nido de Aguila is quarantined because of the outbreak of endemic diseases. Dr. Jamerson and his band of criminals released the diseases from the unsealed room. Dr. Jamerson was the physician on site and had signed that their procedures followed safe protocols. He is being sought as a danger to the public and a possible bioterrorist."

When Sergeant Juan Hernández heard the news, he went outside and videoed everyone walking around freely, without biohazard suits. He posted it on Youtube and it went viral in hours.

*****

After four days of worldwide protests, Cardinal Rossini ordered the papal black ops unit to act.

"What is your plan?" Cardinal Rossini asked.

"I have inside help. We will enter the city morgue and burn all the evidence. This will solve all our problems at one time. We will encourage the police guards at the morgue to go across the street for a cup of coffee." Little did he know that Yossi and his Mossad team had been following the black ops unit for the past three days and had discovered Alberto and his team in Granada. In fact, Yossi had once worked with the famous papal spy on a case of mutual interest and easily identified him.

Yossi followed Alberto to the Carthusian monastery; the Charterhouse of Granada. Yossi loved architecture, and he enjoyed staking out the place, as it's one of the finest examples of Spanish architecture. Yossi did research on the internet. In 1506, they built the first portion of the Charterhouse. Construction continued for the next three hundred years. He put on a disguise and went inside, hoping to spot one of the papal spies. What he found was that the building's plain exterior was nothing compared to the flamboyant interior of the monastery. Its complex, echoing, geometric surfaces made it one of the masterpieces of Spanish Baroque. Dressed as an aspiring artist, Yossi spent four hours sketching the interior with its numerous striking features. Finally, he caught sight of a member of the papal black ops unit. He had worked with the man once, and despite his disguise as a tour guide, Yossi recognized him.

Mossad agents found vantage points from where they could observe all traffic in and out of the monastery. They brought in an electronic eavesdropping truck. They parked, out of sight, two hundred meters down the street. Within an hour, the Mossad was listening in on all the papal black ops unit's phone conversations and Internet communications.

"Sir, it has become apparent that the papal black ops unit will destroy the artifacts," Yossi's communication officer told him.

Yossi contacted his superiors. He received from the Israeli Prime Minister Naveh the okay to stop the papal agents. Yossi gathered his team together.

"Our orders are precise: protect the artifacts. We must stop the papists from destroying the artifacts and bodies at all costs. Orders are to avoid bloodshed if possible."

"We have worked with the papal agents before when Israeli and church interests had coincided. The prime minister is looking at the long-term, overall scenario and doesn't want to burn any bridges, if possible," Yossi informed his team.

Yossi's team moved out two hours before the planned attack. At 10:00 pm, they came roaring up to the city morgue in three ambulances.

"There has been a terrible traffic accident and there were already six dead and maybe more to come," the driver shouted as he jumped out of the ambulance.

"With all the pressure to take care of the mummies, we have little place to put the new corpses," the duty ME explained.

"Leave the new corpses on their gurneys in the examining area. The morning shift will dealt with them," the Medical Examiner told the ambulance drivers. When the pathologist on call turned on the radio, the first thing he heard was news about the terrible traffic accident. He didn't know that the Israelis had staged it.

When the black ops team arrived, Alberto brought with him a letter from the pope thanking each one of the police officers for their help. Alberto suggested to the police guards, "Why don't you take a coffee break and we'll watch over the morgue in the meantime." They all agreed to step out for a "minute."

Once the police officers and pathologists left, Alberto ordered his team.

"Quick, let's get into the examination room where all the bodies and artifacts are." One picked the lock in ten seconds and the four papal agents entered. Each man carried a flashlight and a four-liter tin of chlorine triflouride, one of the most dangerous and flammable chemicals in the world. Once the team was in the morgue storage room, Alberto called his dispatcher/

"We are inside and will finish the job in a matter of a few minutes."

When he signed off, he felt cold steel at the base of his neck.

The six 'dead' bodies from the accident were an IDF special intelligence unit tactical team led by Yossi. Once moved to the morgue and the lights turned off, the Israelis unzipped themselves from the body bags. They prepared an ambush for the papal agents.

Yossie fired off orders. "First blow up dolls and placed them in the body bags. Now rearrange the gurneys and other furniture in the morgue to create hiding places that would make capturing the intruders easy."

Alberto looked to his right and left and saw all his men had their hands up.

"Oops, Alberto, it appears I've caught you with your hand in the cookie jar," Yossi said. The agent behind Alberto patted him down and removed all his weapons and the equipment he had brought with him. Alberto turned around and recognized the man he knew as Yossi.

"Well, old friend, a very inconvenient place for us to meet," Alberto said, shocked the Israelis knew about his operation.

"Alberto, we were once comrades, and I'm sure we will be again. So we will conduct ourselves as professionals. No is no needs for pain or embarrassed. You and your men will be our guests in Israel until this affair is clarified. On top of this, you'll inform the pope he'll call the Spanish prime minister, who will agree that a private security company will take over guarding the mummies and artifacts. I'll recommend which company. If not, we videoed everything that happened. We'll release the footage to the world press." Yossi smiled at Alberto.

"A very gracious offer. I see you want to preserve a good working relationship for future cooperation," Alberto said. Therefore, Alberto stuck out his hand, palm up.

"Please hand me my cell phone." He called the dispatcher.

"I need to call the pope and explain what has happened." The dispatcher patched Alberto to the Vatican. It took a few minutes, but with the proper codes,

Alberto conveyed it was an emergency. At last, the pope came on the line.

"Holy Father, we've run into major problems in the middle of our operation."

"What has happened?" Alberto told him—mortified. Once the pope heard the facts, he took the telephone number Yossi had passed to Alberto. Understanding he had no choice, the pope called the head of the Mossad. "Mr. Cohen (Eitan Yardeni's alias), I understand I need to thank you for not embarrassing my team of agents or the Catholic Church."

"Holy Father, I don't know your reasons for your actions, but I know we've worked on joint projects in the past, and most of our mutual interests will bring us together in the future. Therefore, for the sake of future cooperation, we'll put this down as a minor blip in our relations. Let's agree that you can use this phone number whenever you feel we have mutual interests in a subject. We can discuss it like civilized men and come to an agreement."

"Mr. Cohen, you're correct. I'll institute this procedure in the future."

*****

The two teams of agents left in the ambulances, and the police guards returned to their posts. Two hours later, the chief of staff of the prime minister of Spain called the Lion Security firm based in Switzerland and contracted them to guard the artifacts found in Nido de Aguila. The Israelis had by this time contacted Lion Security. The company had agents waiting outside the morgue in

Granada. Five minutes after the chief of staff got off the phone, the security team was in place.

# THE PRESS

After Deputy Minister Palmerio closed down the excavation, a flood of opposition confronted the Spanish government. The world, encouraged by the liberal press, became anti-Spanish. In America and Europe, protests sprouted outside Spanish embassies and consulates. This was a joint effort between ultra-religious Jews protesting against autopsies and Jews and non-Jews protesting against the denial of basic human rights of wrongful arrest of the Israeli scientists. There were also protesters demanding the Spanish government's responsibility to make amends for the horrors of the Spanish Inquisition. Photos of the horrible tortures—by burning, whippings, racking, breaking of bones, and amputation—that the commission of the Inquisition had inflicted upon their helpless victims were now in every international and important national newspaper and TV channel.

Most broadcasts showed the photos of the double wall the Inquisition had used sealed up the room. Many photos showed the wall in foreground and focused on the people who die of suffocation. The expressions on the faces of the dead, mummified children were enough to make even the most hardhearted people cry. The history correspondent for a major newsmagazine wrote an article detailing hundreds of years of exploitation in every Spanish colony under the Spanish imperial heel. The press was a school of sharks that smelled blood. Now, ganging together, they were going in for the kill.

A boycott of Spanish goods ensued. Ports over the world refused to unload ships carrying Spanish goods. Within seven days, the economic pressure brought the

Spanish government to its knees. Property and stock values plummeted throughout Spain.

In Jerusalem, Ruth worried about Yoshua and the team in prison. When at home, the children watched the news on TV. Ruth gravitated toward the TV and watched in amazement.

"I can't remember ever hearing such support for Israel by the liberal press. I wonder what their real agenda is. It's hard for me to believe they're supporting us only because of a historical event!" Yasmine, her eldest daughter, retorted.

"Honey, there is a difference between being against the present and historical governments of Spain and being an Israeli supporter," Ruth clarified for her daughter.

"I learned something pertinent in my American history class. The newspapers run by William Randolph Hearst and journalists like Joseph Pulitzer pushed the United States into war with Spain in 1898. Maybe the liberal press is trying to flex its muscles for something bigger to come. Maybe they are using Spain as a laboratory rat to see if they can shape not only public opinion but the foreign policy of various nations for their own financial agendas and for the ratings," said Chaim.

"That's an unusual theory. I hope we're not the ones at the end of the liberal press's power play," said Ruth.

*****

Giant conglomerates own the large media companies. In closed rooms throughout the capitals of the world, executives connected by videoconferencing. Together, they planned how they would make immense fortunes while looking like saviors.

"With depressed prices for property and stocks," the CEO of one megacorporation explained, "the Spanish will need foreign investment to pull them out of their troubles."

"However," another CEO added with a big smile on his face, "we'll be buying at reduced values. We'll be able to pick up endless deals that are, in reality, underpriced."

"All we need," a third CEO said, "is to keep the public's face shoved into the human rights 'violations' as a distraction."

"Afterwards, we'll come out," a fourth CEO said, laughing, "smelling like roses. We'll be able to make massive fortunes on the misfortune of Spain—for which we caused." This caused the CEOs a hearty laugh.

"Let's send journalists to Nido de Aguila to keep the public distracted from what we are doing behind the scenes. We need to keep our investments quiet by executing every financial transaction through shell corporations," the most powerful CEO declared.

# THE ARROW THAT DIDN'T FLY STRAIGHT

Yoshua's cell measured three by two meters. He had room for a simple steel-framed bed, a tiny sink, and a toilet. The prison service had constructed the solitary confinement cells from cement cinder block, which filled in the spaces between thirty-centimeter steel reinforced concrete girders. The outside wall was solid concrete, with paint chipping and flaking off in many places. Rust spots, from lack of maintenance, covered the steel door. There were two windows in the door—a small one at eye level, and one at floor level used for food trays.

Yoshua had to make his own schedule. He got up in the morning, washed his hands, said *mo'deh ani* (I thank), and the *birkat haboker* (morning blessings). He worked out for an hour and washed up as best as he could. At 7:00 am, breakfast should to show up. In theory, they had twenty minutes to eat before the guard came back for the tray. If one didn't have the tray back in place by the time he came by, there would be no food for two meals. The bored guards looked for action. For laughs, the guards would demand the trays back in less time, sometimes in a matter of minutes. This caused everyone to sit next to the door at mealtimes. That way, they had to eat as fast as possible— with their hands—the guards refused to give any cutlery, even spoons.

The guards made the prisoners' lives more difficult. They would use a microwave to heat the soup to boiling. Afterwards, they gave the inmates only a few minutes to eat. It caused them either to go without food or burn their mouths. Yoshua figured out a useful trick. He watered down the boiling food and eat it, even though it tasted worse than the original slop.

The guards woke everyone up at 5:00 am by running their nightsticks across the bars on the window in the door of the cells. Breakfast was at 7:00-7:20, lunch, which came rarely, was between 13:00-13:20 and dinner was between 19:00-19:20. Once a day, prisoners were to receive a piece of fruit, but the guards took it for themselves. On Sunday mornings, prisoners from solitary went outside one at a time. No matter the weather, the guards would spray the inmate with a fire hose, cover him with soap, and hose him down again.

Like the rest of the prison, solitary was overflowing with prisoners. Many of the tiny cells had two or even three prisoners in them. The guards would place deadly enemies together, knowing that one of them would end up dead. The guards had received instructions from the governor.

"Kept the two Israeli men in isolation. These instructions come straight from Deputy Minister Palmerio."

Between meals and in the evening, they had plenty of time to consider their scenario. Sasha was not a religious person. He was down-to-earth, and his upbringing taught him the importance of loyalty. In Sasha's mind, the opposite of loyalty was revenge. Sasha spent his time pondering ways to take revenge on his jailers. He also thought about the other members of the team. *Now I realize every one of us is family, as if they were blood relatives. I can't stand the fact that Aviva is in a stinking hole in this prison. She was always nice to me—even from the beginning, she welcomed me warmly. Damn! I'm so worried about her—she might be molested and abused in the prison—I'd like to get my hands on those sadistic guards. Aviva is a good-looking woman—both the prisoners and guards could take advantage of her."* These thoughts caused him to scream and curse at the guards in Russian. *"Maybe if I shout loud enough, Yoshua might hear me and know I'm okay."* The guards didn't understand what he was saying, but the tone of his voice told them everything they needed to know.

One guard knew a little English. He banged on Sasha's door with his baton and shouted at him.

"Dog, you shut mouth, or I hit face."

"You piece of putrid rotting maggot covered dog meat. I'm not afraid of you. Come on in here, and fight me like a man," Sasha shouted back in English. He and the guards took to screaming curses at each other, each in his own language. Sasha remembered a curse in Spanish, *"Usted tiene una cara como el culo de un mono* (you have a face like a monkey's ass)." During his years of active service in the army, he learned the curse from a fellow soldier born in Argentina. Now, he got the guards' attention, and they cursed him, his parents, his ancestry, and even his dog.

*****

Yoshua had plenty of time to meditate and think about his scenario. He, unlike Sasha, knew not to anger one's captors. During the first day of solitary confinement, he remembered how on *Shabbat* afternoons, as children, they had learned the psalms by heart. It was easy for him because he had total recall. He could quote every word he had ever read in his entire life. He now understood why the Holy One Blessed be He gave him this unique ability. Now, when he needed it, he could remember the words of comfort of King David. Psalm 143 came to his mind.

"A song by David. O Lord, hear my prayer, and consider my supplications; with Your faith, answer me with Your righteousness. And do not come judging Your servant, for no living being can be righteous (innocent) before You." Yoshua remembered how Elisha had explained, "King David felt afraid that he would appear unworthy, even compared to the wicked, for no man is perfect before the Lord."

Yoshua continued to repeat the psalm, "For the enemy pursued my soul, he ground my life into the dirt, he sat me in utter darkness, like the eternally dead." Yoshua felt, at that moment, as if King David, the prophet, had seen what would happen to him and had written these words for him. This was what the Spanish were doing to him.

*Rebbetzin* Rivka taught him to seek the comfort of the words of the great king, for his words were eternal and were for every man at all times. Yoshua repeated the words of the king of Israel.

"I spread my hands to You. My soul longs for You like the thirsty land, Selah. Hasten to answer me, Hashem, my spirit is spent." Yoshua stopped for a second and thought,

"*It's precisely the opposite. The words of King David strengthen me and gave me resolve.*" He continued, "Conceal, not Your face from me, lest I be like those who descend into the pit."

He had once learned with Elisha.

"Man, many times, thinks God doesn't answer his prayers, but its man who often prays for the wrong thing and doesn't listen to the words of his living God."

The last words of the psalm came to him.

"For Your Name's sake, *Hashem*, revive me, with Your righteousness, remove my soul from distress. And with Your kindness cut off my enemies, and destroy all who torment my soul, for I'm Your servant." Yoshua recalled the commentary.

"The goal of my life is to serve You, but how can I accomplish this if my enemies interfere? Destroy all those who oppose my efforts to obey You and to dedicate myself completely to my role as Your servant." A feeling of relief and calm came over Yoshua. He thought, "*I understand for the first time what drives Elisha; why he always strives to be 'a servant of the Lord.' I'm not sure where this path is taking me, but I know I need to return to my roots and rebuild, for as it says in Yermiahu 17:7-8, 'Blessed is the man who trusts in the Lord; the Lord shall be his trust. For he shall be like a tree planted by the water, and by a rivulet spreads its roots, and will not see when heat comes, and its leaves shall be green, and in the year of drought will not be anxious, neither shall it cease from bearing fruit.'*"

*****

On the second day of solitary confinement, Yoshua thought, "Now is a good time to remember how Elisha taught me to approach every 'challenge' that comes into my life. I need to start at the beginning. How did I ever get onto the subject of the Light of Justice? Who got me interested in the fabled 'superhero of justice'?"

Yoshua replayed the events in his head.

*It was during an incursion by my unit to gather intelligence on the comings and goings of terrorists deep in northern Lebanon. Our job was to set up an automatic system with audio and visual surveillance. We came ashore in rubber dinghies twelve hundred meters north of Al Minie at 1:00 am, with the help of the naval commandos. We had seventy-two hours to fulfill our mission before the commandos would come back and pick us up. My squad had four men—me, Tzion, Amram Giloni, and Erez Canaan.*

*Once ashore, we hiked into the foothills and headed due east toward Berqayl. West of Berqayl, we turned southeast into a narrow valley with a steep incline on both sides. I worried about going via that route, because if spotted there, we would have nowhere to take cover. Once through the valley, we headed south by southwest up a ridge to a height of about six hundred fifty meters.* Below us, the terrain dropped off steeply in two steps. One ledge was about fifty meters below, but it was the second one, two hundred fifty meters below us. Its enormous cliff was our target.

*At the base of the cliff stood a Hezbollah training camp. Once we were above the terrorists' camp, we moved west by southwest to the crest of the ridge, and we had a view of the entire camp below. We found an excellent spot among large boulders where they wouldn't spot from below, and we made camp. We only worked under cover of darkness, so during the day we had little to do but talk with one another. That's when I learned Tzion was a storyteller. During our last day, Tzion told his story of the Light of Justice.*

*I wasn't paying close enough attention to remember everything, but I remember the story of the red arrow. Since I grew up with archery from a young age, it was a story that interested me.*

*Tzion was a talented storyteller, and soon the three of us were anxiously waiting for every word he spoke. He told us regarding a country based on faith, righteousness, and justice; where their king ruled his people based on these principles. Tzion explained that the Light of Justice was a spiritual giant, and those close to him were outstanding teachers of spirituality. The story went that the Light of Justice and his three friends would meditate for a long time before any battle. The result was these four men's accuracy with a bow was renowned throughout the world. If he concentrated hard enough, the king could hit any target. We found many fully armored enemy troops after a battle with arrows that hit them in the eye or neck, where there was a tiny area not covered by their armor, or even at a joint in their armor. The Light of Justice even had a prayer that he said at the onset of any combat.*

*"Creator of the Heavens and Earth, Master of the universe, guide my hands that my arrows strike only those who deserve punishment and protect the innocent from me." Everyone knew the arrows he fired because their shafts were bright red.*

*Even at ninety, the Light of Justice's ability with a bow didn't diminish. During the war of the Malogoth occupation, the two armies were arrayed opposite each other. At a distance of three hundred yards. Tzion demonstrated how the Light of Justice lifted his enormous bow and drew back on it until the string reached his right ear. Everyone knew that when he fired his first arrow, it would be the signal to start the battle.. He closed his eyes and made as if he was praying and continued his story.*

*"The Light of Justice said his prayer and released the shaft. Both sides saw the arrow slice through the morning air. At least three thousand men on both sides could see that red arrow flying toward its target." Tzion paused to make it more dramatic and stared at each one.*

*"The arrow headed straight for the regimental commander opposite the Light of Justice." Tzion made a face of fear, as the man knew the arrow would kill him. Tzion leaped to his feet. He used his finger as if it was the arrow and showed us its path. "Four meters in front of the mounted Malogoth, the arrow veered somewhat to the right passing within a half an inch of the man's jugular vein it cut the strap of his helmet and buried itself in the left eye of the man five meters behind him." Tzion* put his fist *up to his head as if he had closed his hand around an arrow protruding from his eye.*

*Everyone laughed at his antics and the crazy story of the arrow that didn't fly straight, but Tzion didn't smile. He continued his story.*

*"The Malogoth soldier was on the verge of dying. He remembered the words his mother taught him tens of years earlier. Everyone was familiar with the Light of Justice's uncanny ability with a bow. He understood his fate was certain death. So he whispered, 'Shema Ysrael'. Abruptly, the arrow veered off around him. The arrow ended up embedded in the left eye of the standard-bearer of his unit, who was directly behind him. So shocked, the Malogoth officer fell off his horse. The Malogoth army had seen the miracle. They turned around and left the field of combat. The superstitious Malogoth's culture didn't allow them to fight such a powerful witchcraft."*

*The commander of the Malogoth regiment was one of the many kidnapped Hoshiyan children raised among those barbarians. He remembered only one thing about his previous life, and when he told the Light of Justice what happened, it revealed Light of Justice's greatness. He lifted the commander up from his knees, kissed, and hugged him. The Light of Justice proclaimed to everyone:*

*"Come and see the greatness of the Holy One Blessed be He, who hears the prayers of man. I prayed my arrows would not take the righteous with the evil, and he called out Shema Ysrael. Hakodosh Baruchu heard our prayers and instead of a dead enemy, we have welcomed home a long-lost brother. Thanks to this man, we have been able to sanctify the name of God before our enemies."*

It was only seven years later, while working on his PhD, that Yoshua ran into a story about the Light of Justice once again.

\*\*\*\*\*

In Jerusalem, Gefen ate or slept little. She talked to Simon at least five times a day, hoping for news. Simon told her of all the different routes he attempted to arrange a visit to Aviva and get her released from prison.

"Yasmine, I was wrong about the Englishman."

"In which way Gefen?"

"I was jealous of the time he spent with Aviva, but the more we talk, the more I like him." Gefen said.

"Do you think Simon loves my Aunt Aviva?" Yasmine asked.

"He is trying to move heaven and earth to get her released. Yes, I am positive he loves her," Gefen answered Yasmine.

When Simon told her their Spanish attorney could visit Aviva and had found her in good spirits, Gefen couldn't stop thanking him.

These days had also caused a major change in Gefen. Though her parents tried to help, they didn't understand what Gefen had gone through in Spain. She went over to the Rosenbergs more and more. They understood and gave her the moral support she needed. Gefen was at the Rosenbergs when word came that Aviva was okay in prison; she cried with relief.

*****

Stuck in solitary confinement, Yoshua didn't know the Lord heard his prayer, or that Ysrael and ten other Aluzians were in Madrid planning his escape. Their first idea was to kidnap the prison doctor's family and force the doctor to inject the three Israelis with something that would fake their deaths. We could send the bodies back to Israel. On the plane, we would give them a second injection to take them out of their chemically induced state of near death.

*****

The media's next step was to find out where the Spanish had taken the Israelis. Every media agency clambered for interviews with them while in captivity. They inundated the Ministry of the Interior with requests. The media research teams told their bosses.

"Interviews with the Israelis in prison would give our ratings a huge push. If we could get an interview with Dr. Berger even better. We could push the beautiful damsel in distress scenario that would make their ratings skyrocket," the head of research told the CEO.

Journalists, armed with vast amounts of cash, sought anyone to bribe who had information on the location of the Israeli prisoners. It didn't take over fifteen hours to find three separate sources who knew where the prisoners were, but they refused to speak with the media. Another hour of research on the Internet and they found leverage on one of the three. He was a middle-level prison authority administrator with a large gambling debt. It took another three hours to arrange pay for his debt. Once payment was confirmed, he gave them the name of the prison that held the Israelis.

The research teams of five different news bureaus investigated every employee of the prison. They came up with five people who they could bribed. One worked in the kitchen and he could provide information that the Israelis were all in solitary confinement. Thirteen guards worked in solitary—seven with the men and six with the women. They passed money, along with a miniature recorder, via a kitchen worker to a female guard. The female guard slipped the recorder into Aviva's cell by placing it under the bread on her food tray.

Aviva discovered the recorder as soon as she picked up the bread. At first, she thought, "*I can get my story out to the public.*"

Aviva spent an hour recording everything she could remember. After she finished, she had doubts. Aviva remembered something Yoshua once said. He had learned it from Elisha.

"If it sounds too good, there are strings attached." Deep in her heart, Aviva knew none of the major news agencies gave a damn what happened to them. So why would they smuggle a recorder into the prison? She thought about it a while before she eat the bread, which would be a sign she hadn't finished recording. That would give her time until the next meal.

Being in solitary confinement, Aviva had nothing but time to think. She ran many scenarios through her head, but none seemed plausible. She thought, *"What would an interview or my words do for the broadcasting station? Well, my words from prison would be a big sensation. The press would splash them all over the globe. More people would watch their news channel. That would give them better ratings. Better ratings would mean more advertising revenue—more money. What would I get out of it? They will catch my for sure. The other guards will blame me for the smuggler being fired and I'll suffer their wrath. In the eyes of the Spanish, I'm a terrorist. What can I say to change the public's opinion? Who will listen when I say* they falsely accused *me? If I say nothing, I'm safe, at the moment, in solitary and not being molested."* Aviva erased what she had recorded.

"Now, what to say that won't get me into trouble?" It hit her like a ton of bricks.

"Ha, I love Ruth's little pearls of wisdom. I can use all that faith she's been telling me about for years." She turned on the recorder.

Dearest Ruth,

You have been my best friend for as long as I can remember. But until this moment, locked away in a prison far from home, far from those I love the most, I realize not only have you been my true friend, but you also provided me with the tools to survive in this place— alone and forgotten to the world. I'm laughing aloud as I speak these words—how foolish those people are who believe I'm alone and this would break me and make me confess to a crime I didn't commit.

You taught me the Holy One Blessed be He is always with me. *Hakodosh Baruchu* only does good things for us. He is a kind, loving, and giving God; and He is always with us, even though it might not appear so to us at the moment. Therefore, it's incumbent upon me to find the silver lining in what's happening to me.

You also taught me everything that comes into our lives comes to teach us something. I remember you telling me God only tests those strong enough to overcome the challenge placed before them. He doesn't test the fragile who would break, but the strong who can create, out of a dangerous scenario, a *Kiddush HaShem* (a means of hallowing the Lord's name).

*Hakodosh Baruchu* always gives those challenged enough strength to overcome their challenge.

Aviva stopped the recording and screamed at the top of her lungs, "*Hakodosh Baruchu*, watch over me here. After all these years, you brought someone into my life. I don't know how, but I love that man so much. Please give me a chance for happiness. I don't regret my choice of not going with Simon, even though I love him. If we cannot protect our long dead brothers, who are we? What will we become if we turn our back on our past, on our heritage? A failure to bring them home will be a travesty of justice that I cannot live with." Aviva walked over to the small window that was a meter above her head. She screamed through the window, hoping Sasha and Yoshua would hear her.

"Yoshua, Sasha, be strong, we will prevail." Little did Aviva know she was in a different section of the prison, and there was no way they could hear her. Aviva returned to the recorder.

I will not fear, for I know God is always with me, even though I walk through the valley of the shadow of death. Ruth, I know you taught me to believe we all have the strength within ourselves. We have to dig deep within our souls and we find that strength and use it. Now, after all I've gone through, I realize everything you taught me was true. I stand here in a deep hole within the prison, not knowing where I am, but knowing the Lord is at my side and I have all I need to resolve this scenario. I feel invigorated as never in my life. My faith in the Holy One Blessed be He; and this experience will strengthen me and make me a better person.

I wish I had paid more attention when you and the children repeated psalms on *Shabbat* afternoons. I remember part of the 23rd psalm—besides its famous opening line.

"Also, when I will walk through the valley of the shadow of death, I will fear no evil, for You are with me." Ruth, please have the children pray for my soul.

Your loving friend, forever in your debt for teaching me the great secrets of life.

Aviva

P.S. Tell Simon I love him.

Aviva couldn't believe what she'd done, but she felt better and somehow lighter; more buoyant. She realized the words she recorded meant something important to her. She was sure the recording would never be broadcasted, but merely working it out in her head had helped.

Aviva remembered sitting with the Rosenberg children, learning the 22nd psalm. She tried to remember the words, "My God, my God, why have You forsaken me far from saving me, from the roar of my words. I call out by day and You do not answer; by night I find no respite." The children had taught her this was the prayer of Queen Esther when she fasted for three days before approaching her husband, the king of Persia, without being summoned.

Tears poured from Aviva's eyes; her throat constricted as she prayed with an intensity she had never known.

"I raise my eyes to the mountains; from where will my help come?" The words of the 121st psalm spoke to her and they pierced the innermost chambers of her heart. "My help comes from *HaShem*, Maker of heaven and earth. He will not allow your foot to falter; your Guardian will not slumber. Behold, the Guardian of Israel neither slumbers nor sleeps."

Then she had an epiphany. All these years, she missed all the spirituality Ruth was trying to teach her. It all came together; the sadness slipped away, and she knew, for the first time in her life, what she wanted to do with her life— not what job she would do, but what kind of person she wanted to become.

*****

"The Russian is a troublemaker and loudmouth; complaining all the time," the guards complained.

"Professor Rosenberg is a dangerous prisoner. He has injured three guards," the governor of the prison told the attorney.

What they didn't tell the attorney was that three guards had beaten up Sasha. Yoshua heard the entire episode from his cell and was ready for them when the guards came for him.

The door was in the center of the wall, so there was space to hide behind the door when it opened from the outside. As the first guard entered Yoshua's cell with his stun gun in his extended right hand, Yoshua threw his entire weight from behind the door. It swung back and smashed the first guard's arm between the doorpost and the steel door. He screamed in pain as the door crushed the bones in his forearm. The guards dropped the stun gun and Yoshua rolled on his shoulder, hitting the floor for a mere second. He scooped up the stun gun in his right hand, and as the other guards opened the door, he fired at the guard on the right, hitting him with the maximum—one hundred fifty thousand volts. The guard's body flopped about like a fish out of water.

The second guard holstered his stun gun so he could come to the aid of his injured friend. Yoshua continued his roll and momentum brought him back on his feet. While he was coming to his feet, his left hand was going into his pocket. He extended his left hand toward the guard and threw the dirt and paint on his face.

The guard reacted instinctively and threw his hands to his face to wipe away the dirt. Yoshua swung the hand with the stun gun toward the third guard and caught him in the chin, knocking him backward. He swung the stun gun in the other direction and hit the guard with the broken arm. With all three temporarily incapacitated, Yoshua grabbed additional stun gun cartridges from the injured guard. He quickly loaded a new cartridge and fired on the third guard with the maximum voltage. The guard was getting to his feet after being struck by the weapon. It knocked him off his feet, and he floundered about on the floor, convulsing from the electric shock. Angry about what they had done to Sasha, Yoshua relieved the guards of all their stun guns and cartridges, and fired on all three until they were unconscious.

Yoshua searched the guards for keys. Once he found them, he rushed to Sasha's cell, opened it, and stood there shocked to see how badly the guards had beaten Sasha. Sasha laid on the floor bleeding and covered in black and blue bruises. Yoshua lifted him off the floor and gently placed him on the steel framed bed.

"Sasha, you need medical attention immediately." Yoshua returned to the guards and gave each one another jolt. He opened the door to an empty cell, dragged the guards inside, tied them up with their belts and shoelaces, and gagged them. He took one of their radios and called for immediate medical assistance. "We have a badly injured inmate in the solitary block for men, room 2351." Yoshua didn't wait for an answer. He returned to his cell, locked it from the inside, and threw the keys, radio, and stun guns into the corridor through the small door near the floor.

Within three minutes, an officer, a guard, and two medics showed up in the corridor and found it littered with the guards' equipment. Sasha's cell was open. The medics rushed in and found Sasha had been abused from a beating and had been hit repeatedly by a stun gun. The two medics gave Sasha first aid.

"This man," the senior medic told the officer, "must be removed to the infirmary immediately." The officer and guard went from cell to cell checking all the prisoners and asked what they had heard. They all told the same story. "Three guards attacked a prisoner and when they finished with him, the guards attacked another prisoner." When the two new guards found their fellow guards hogtied and gagged, they asked who had done this to them. The hogtied guards cursed the Israeli professor.

"The professor is some kind of diablo (devil)."

"Your diablo locked in his cell, so it is impossible for him to have done this to you." the officer told them.

"I am suspending the three of you pending an investigation into your behavior concerning the abuse of an inmate," the officer told the guards.

\*\*\*\*\*

Once the news got out about where the Israelis were held, news crews inundated Valdemoro Prison and the town of Nido de Aguila. Every major newspaper, radio station, and television channel in the world had teams covering the excavation. Every one of them attempted to get interviews with the prisoners. There were between three hundred fifty and five hundred newscasters and their crews split between the town and the prison at any given time. When the news crews showed up at the prison, Deputy Minister Palmerio was furious.

"Get teams of investigators over to the prison. Lock down the staff and allowed no one to go home unless they have been strip-searched and interrogated," Palmario ordered.

Three hours later, Palmerio's phone rang.

"Boss, we found a female guard with the recorder. What do you want us to do with her?" the agent asked.

"Bring me the recorder and fire the guard, but don't bring charges against her. I want this kept quiet," Ernesto ordered them.

Ernesto Palmario listens to Aviva's translated words. "Now I know God loves me. If this had gotten out, it would've destroyed me. The last thing in the world I need is a female Israeli hostage spouting off about faith and ethical behavior. That would question the validity of the charges against her."

\*\*\*\*\*

Meanwhile, international and legal pressure succeeded to change the government's decision. The prison authorities allowed Attorney Delgado-Mendoza to visit Aviva in prison. What he found shocked him.

"When was the last time you could shower," Delgado-Mendoza asked.

"I've been here six days and haven't had a shower—even once—not a change of clothes or even a blanket to put on my mattress," Aviva told the lawyer. He turned to the commander of the watch.

"You provide this prisoner with the minimum conditions that every other prisoner receives. If not, I will bring lawsuits against you, the other guards, the officers, and the governor of the prison." This got the prison officials to move themselves. Aviva shower, given a change of clothes, and provided the first proper meal since she arrived. Delgado-Mendoza planned to stay for only fifteen minutes but ended up staying for three hours. He made sure Aviva received all the services and amenities allowed by the prison system, including being examined by a doctor.

"I would like to see my other clients now," Delgado-Mendoza demanded.

"I am sorry, under no circumstances will I allow you to see the professor or the Russian monster," the governor of the prison stated with a scowl on his face.

"After seeing the unbelievable conditions Dr. Berger suffered, I am sure you treated the two Israeli males much worse. I will go to court to get an order to allow me to see my clients. I will also be bring personal damage suits against you and the guards in solitary confinement," Delgado-Mendoza threatened.

"No one threatens me in my prison. Mr. Delgado-Mendoza, if you aren't out of here in ten minutes, I have

you thrown into solitary," the governor threaten in
return.

*****

To pass the time, Aviva picked up the paper and
pencil the guard had given her with orders to write her
confession. Instead, she filled her walls with original art.
She experienced a strong creative urge, as if creativity
poured from every pore of her body. Aviva's mind had a
hard time trying to cope with the sudden change. For
twenty-five years, she hadn't produced a single piece of
original art. For the first time in her life, she understood
the concept of freedom and spirituality. It didn't matter
how many chains they shackled her in or the depth of the
dungeon; they couldn't break her spirit. She felt free as a
bird—the high was unbelievable—she reveled in her
newfound freedom.

The first sketch was Simon kneeling over the dead
man, clutching the books, doing the autopsy report. Next,
she drew Gefen, patiently cleaning the wall tiles in the
*bet midrash*. She couldn't sharpen the pencil fast
enough; rubbing it on the wall every so often to make a
point. Aviva drew Yoshua and Ruth, walking hand in
hand. When she came to the children, she burst out
crying. She sketched, with tears pouring down her face.
Her lunch came, and she didn't even touch it. In rapid
succession, she drew David in his new IDF uniform,
Yasmine painting at her easel, Chaim reading from the
Torah, and Elana running in a field of wildflowers.

From the depths of her soul, she knew what she had
to draw—Yoshua and Ysrael. Aviva drew them as two
guardians of their people; the two brothers, shoulder to

shoulder. Between her tears, she drew the brothers with every ounce of love she could pour into them. She never got to finish the sketch. When the guard found that she'd desecrated the walls with graffiti, they forced her to wash the walls. Every morning she sketched anew, and every evening they forced her to wash the walls.

Sasha used his paper and pencil to write, in Russian, everything that had happened to him from the time he landed in Spain. His interrogators at first thought they had a confession, but were angry with him for writing in Russian. There was no one in the prison system who could translate what he had put down on the paper. The guards would have to send Sasha's confession for translation to Spanish. He wrote every detail of what occurred to them since finding the front page of the Hoshiyan Chronicles. After four days still had not gotten to the part about cutting into the sealed room.

# SPIRITUALITY IN PRISON

Yoshua got up every morning and repeated his morning prayers. He did a light set of stretching exercises. Different from Sasha, Yoshua used the paper to do origami, which the guards destroyed every day, often lighting them on fire in front of him. The rest of the time, they found him sitting on his bed, his legs crossed, his eyes closed as he meditated. By slowing down his heartbeat, he conserved energy, as they were giving him only one meal a day.

Yoshua was thankful his mind was still sharp, and it was easy for him to eat up lots of hours doing numerous jobs in his mind. On his second morning in prison, he spent his time reviewing the curriculum for his course on methods of dating artifacts. Lunch was horrid; it changed his mood, so he reviewed military operations he had participated in over the years. Dinner was boiling hot soup, which he watered down, only to find out they had already watered down the soup. The soup like drinking the water in which they washed the vegetables. It was, however, the first time he got a fresh piece of fruit, an apple, which he saved for the evening.

*****

Appreciative of the apple, Yoshua's mood improved. He sat down on the bed and wiggled his way into the corner so the walls of the cell would support his back. The cement wall was warm from exposure to the sun the entire afternoon. It was time for an accounting of what had happened.

*"Discovering the cover page of the Hoshiyan Chronicles led me to Nido de Aguila. There was the extensive amount of money for this project; raised so quickly by Gavriel. Since I arrived in Spain, there's been one adventure after another. First, the negotiations to buy the chapel. Next, the bombing at the registry office in Cordova. The priest showed up with the blueprints that showed a sealed off room."*

*Afterwards Simon arrived with tens of thousands of euros worth of equipment and fantastic stories of how Simon's uncle had known my father and left money for my research because to top it all off, discovering the remains of the Jewish community. Now I'm sitting in a Spanish prison, not knowing what will become of my life. Why had all of this come to me and not someone else, and why in this manner? Points to consider, One, no one knew what the binding hid. So it's impossible for this to have been arranged in order for me to find the cover page. Point two, the extraordinary interest the Vatican had in this project. If fate meant me to find that cover page and no one else, but why? Maybe the answer to the question exists further along in this bizarre drama. Point three, up to the time we found the chapel and confirmed it was the bet midrash mentioned on the cover page. Everything had been straightforward. We hunted down the information the same we researched projects many times before. Point four, the sale of the chapel led me to Cordoba and the bombing. Dealing with the bombing is the easiest part of the entire affair to deal with. The Spanish, though exposed to Basque terrorism for years now, don't have the same culture as we Israelis when it comes to suspicious objects. The Holy One Blessed be He placed me there to save lives of innocent people; God works in mysterious ways—this I can understand. This is easy and acceptable, but the story didn't stop there.*

Yoshua didn't pay attention to how much time had passed until the lights went out at 10:00 pm. He sat in the dark, still trying to figure out what was happening to his life, and since he didn't know if he would ever see the light of day again, he continued the accounting.

*"Point One: I've taken many lives during my career in the regular army and as a reservist fighting terrorists. I have no regrets about all that I've done. Those people were enemies of my people and had killed, maimed, blinded, and terrorized large numbers of Jews and Israelis."*

Tears came to his eyes when he thought about Ruth. *"Point Two: Here's another question I don't understand: how was it I found someone so wonderful to be my wife? Thank God I sent Ruth, David, and Gefen home. Not only are we partners in our private life, we're also partners in our academic life. We brought four wonderful children into this world—any couple would be proud of that. Point Three: I will not submit to incarceration for the rest of my life. The authorities can create scenarios where 'accidents' occur to their benefit. I'll have to act soon, while I still have the strength—before they starve me or beat me as the guards had beaten Sasha."*

Yoshua stretched out on the bed and continued to contemplate his life. He didn't realize he'd fallen asleep until the next morning when he woke up. He went through his exercises, prayers, and waited next to the door for his breakfast—that didn't come. The guards had no idea with whom they were dealing. On principle, Yoshua had reserved ten percent of each meal, in case the guards started adding drugs or poison to his food. What worried him was that they would drug his food, which he had no defense against. He ate a small amount of his reserve and sat to continue his soul searching.

*"I have no regrets concerning my academic career. Though I never found one of those objects that either confirmed an aspect of history or changed man's perception of his past, I did years of solid archaeological work that, as a whole, contributed to the science I've always loved. Now for the first time, I found something unusual; the floor in the bet midrash is a thing of magnificence. However, those three interconnecting circles bother me. The central circle represents heaven or Olam Haba, the world to come. The circle on the right appears to represent this world; with a crude map of the Iberian Peninsula. The circle on the left is the genuine mystery. There's a connection between the name, Hoshiya, on the cover page and the name of the map on the floor. Also, the name Ramat Tzion, the city where Aharon Dori had lived, showed up both on the map and the cover page. What are the possibilities?*

*First, according to the floor, there's heaven, earth, and Hoshiya. Since Aharon Dori claimed to be from this place, maybe it was another continent. That wasn't possible since they created the floor before Columbus sailed for the new world. Its possible Aharon Dori was an alien. Perhaps the third Hoshiyan circle represented another planet. That is too science fiction for me. Another possibility is what Ruth told me. Maybe Hoshiya is in another dimension with portals through which people went back and forth. That would make the poor man delusional. The most likely explanation is that Aharon Dori was Europe's first novelist. His book, wherever it was, had influenced him and his surroundings to where he made the floor to fit his book.*

*What also didn't fit were the three words in Hebrew translated to mean 'faith,' 'righteousness,' and 'justice'? These are serious words with serious connotations. Maybe the Hoshiyan Chronicles were stories Aharon Dori made up to teach people the lessons of these three words. Once again, what does that have to do with me? What in the world am I supposed to be learning from all of this?*

*"Edgar Rice Burroughs created hidden worlds in the dark jungles of Africa for his character to interact with. I remember reading the Adventures of Tarzan, but they weren't influential books of ethics. Those three words make everything different. Did Aharon Dori create a world in which he could teach morals and ethics? The problem is, most authors don't associate with their characters to the degree that they're delusional and think they come from those far-off lands. The problem with this line of thinking is that stories of the Light of Justice existed hundreds of years before Aharon Dori was alive. Since we don't have a copy of the Chronicles, there's no way to determine anything. If it was a novel, why was the Vatican so interested in it? Maybe Aharon Dori had been a mischievous troublemaker who wrote comments against the church or church doctrine?"*

Before he knew it, the window at the bottom of the door opened and there was a food tray. Yoshua jumped off his bed, rushed the short distance to the food, and eat. He didn't want to take the chance that the guards would play games with him. While he chewed the horrible tasting stew, he took the bread and put it aside, along with the pieces of sliced vegetables. He smelled everything before he ate it on the off chance they had added something to his food that he could detect. Sure enough, two minutes later the window opened, and the guard banged on the door, impatient to get the food tray back. Yoshua poured the last of the watery stew into his mouth and shoved the tray back through the hole.

Yoshua slowly chewed the food. When he finished, he sat back down to come to some conclusion. *"The floor in the bet midrash is haunting me. The word 'justice' now appears to tell me I'm suffering from the lack of it. 'Faith,' now that's something else. I'll need a lot of faith to see this through."* His subconscious kicked in, and he thought about the Passover seder. *"VHe sheamda lavotanu, this concept has stood by our fathers and us! For not one alone has risen against us to destroy us, but in every generation they rise against us to destroy us; and the Holy One, blessed be He, saves us from their hand!"* Yoshua felt his spirit uplifted. He understood now what Elisha had been trying to teach him his entire life.

*"If I have enough faith in HaKodosh Baruchu, everything that happens to me, helps me. I need to find the inner strength to see this challenge through to its conclusion."* The words of Psalm 102 came to his mind, *"A prayer of the distressed man: when he swoons, and pours forth his supplication before God."* Yoshua thought of this verse that Elisha had taught him, *"The word 'ahtaf' means to fold over or envelop. The word provides a vivid description of the starving man who is bent over (Rabak). That's precisely how I feel. The guards are starving us on purpose to weaken us."* Yoshua raised his arms in supplication and with tears rolling down his face, he repeated the words of the psalm, *"God, hear my prayer and let my cry reach You. Hide not Your face from me on*

*the day of my distress, incline Your ear to me on the day
that I call, answer me speedily."*

The words of King David bore deep into the inner
chambers of his heart. *Yoshua remembered what Elisha
had taught him so many years before.*

*"King David wrote Psalm 102 to articulate the feelings
of the poor man encased in misery. On a deeper level, the
psalm comes to teach us the catastrophic state of the
Jewish people in exile, when they were destitute and
demoralized. Though born into a free state of Israel, a free
man, in my land all my life, I now understand my fellow
Jews during the past two thousand years. How
appropriate that I should suffer in the same country that
murdered the forty-six Jews my team had found. There's
poetic justice to the whole thing. The Holy One Blessed be
He is giving me a practical lesson in how to empathize with
those dead families. The difference, today, is that I know
what true freedom is and now appreciate it even more. I
will not let the Spanish keep me locked up like a dog. It's
time to plan my escape."*

# THE END

If you have enjoyed

"Seeking the Light of Justice"

don't miss

the next book of

the Hoshiyan Chronicles,

# "Shielding the Light of Justice"

# PREPARTION FOR ESCAPE

# Preview of Chapter 1

Professor Yoshua Rosenberg knew it was time to stop being passive and use all his accumulated skills to prepare himself for the slightest opportunity that might arise to escape. Yoshua prepared his own opportunity. His total recall allowed him to remember every step he took in the prison. He remembered the location of every surveillance camera. He worked out in his head where the most likely blind spots were and how much time he would have to disarm his captors.

Yoshua considered his options. Confined to isolation, he had no one to talk to, so he would have to conduct conversations with himself aloud, to avoid mistakes he might miss by thinking about them. He said to himself, "I could fake a sickness to get my jailers into the cell. Once inside the cell, I could take them out. The simple guards don't stand a chance against me."

Yoshua held three black belts in three different martial arts. He started talking to himself again.

"I still have the pencil they gave me. With the proper speed, it could easily punch its way through a man's shirt and into his heart."

"Hey, shut up in there," one guard called out in Spanish. "Stop with all that foreign gibberish. If I hear you trying to communicate again, I'm coming in there to beat you black and blue."

Yoshua smiled. He now had a simple way of getting the guard into his cell. Suddenly, he had a thought; one that rarely came to him during combat.

"If they bring the guards up on charges, what would be their punishment? For sure, they would not get the death penalty, but there was another factor. If I leave them in a condition to contact their superiors, they would threaten my life. Then, they would fall under the law of *rodef* (pursuer) and it would become a question of *pekuach nefesh* (saving a life). Under those circumstances, I would have the right to kill them. My good friend, Elisha, would be proud of me, knowing I considered these questions before acting. I'll not only have to knock out the guards, but also make them incapable of communicating with their radios. The only answer, short of killing them, would be to break all the bones in their hands, so they couldn't handle their radios, weapons, or any other items that might impinge on my escape.

"Once I take out the guards, I'll have only a few minutes until reinforcements arrive, but in that time, I can release all the other prisoners in the solitary unit. There's a fire extinguisher on the other side of the door to my wing. If I could get to it, I could use the foam to keep the first wave of prison guards back.

"My goal will be to get to the control room located next to the solitary confinement wing. To do that, I'll have to exchange clothes with a guard and fake my way out of solitary, as if I'm the sole survivor of the guards. Thankfully, my Spanish is good enough to trick any guard."

"My chances are slim. Therefore, this will have to be a *scorched earth* operation—no prisoners left, no enemy left capable of attacking me from the rear. The more prisoners I can release, the better my chances, as they will increase the chaos factor."

Little did Yoshua know that while they confined him to the solitary wing, the Lord had heard his prayer and his brother, Ysrael, and ten other Aluzians were in Madrid planning his rescue and escape. Ysrael put his idea to the team for consideration. "The first thing we need to do is kidnap the prison doctor's family and force the doctor to inject our comrades with something that would fake their deaths. He'll write out death certificates. Then, they would send the bodies back to Israel. Once in the air, a second injection would be given to the prisoners to take them out of their chemically induced state of near-death."

"Ysrael," Itzhak Chorev asked, "are you willing to carry out the threat to kill the doctor's family, if he doesn't agree?" The expression on Ysrael's face made his answer self-explanatory. The other idea was to kidnap the prison governor's family and force the governor to transfer the Israelis to another facility. Along the route, however, they would ambush the convoy and rescue Yoshua and his team.

"There's a problem with each of these scenarios," Elad, the Panther, said. They called Elad the Panther because he could move in the dark, as if he had night fighting gear. He was silent, fast, and deadly. "First," Elad asked, "are we willing to carry out the threats against the families?" Everyone looked at each other and knew they couldn't shoot some child or innocent woman. "From the looks on your faces, it's obvious these scenarios are a waste of time."

"The other problem is that the Spanish government would destroy the bodies and the books," Ysrael said.

Ysrael decided he needed to think like his brother. "What would Yoshua do? He would do something devious." Ysrael and Yoshua were smiling at the same time because they both came up with the same idea simultaneously. The best way to escape would be to create a huge diversion and not have the search centered on him. Ysrael knew precisely what his brother would do to avoid blame. Ysrael and his team would not aim toward breaking out Yoshua, Aviva, and Sasha; they would cause a general prison break and let the authorities deal with eighteen hundred escaping prisoners and not three. By far, the simplest plans were always the best.

A plan crystallized quickly in Ysrael's mind.

"The first step will be to buy three uniforms matching the city's maintenance department. That team will make it look like they're doing repairs on the road to the prison, but, in fact, they will lay numerous roadside explosives, to keep reinforcements from getting to the prison."

Itzhak Chorev, the explosives expert, continued, "The next phase of the operation will be a silent night infiltration of the walls of the prison at three separate locations. We'll lay explosives and retreat."

Pinchas Aluz, Ysrael's second cousin, continued, "Ysrael, Yossi, Aviad, and I, the snipers, will each take a separate side of the prison and start the operation by taking out guards. Once the siren goes off warning of the attack, we'll detonate the explosives from a distance. They'll blow several holes in the prison walls. From that point on, our job will be to take out prison guards and search for Yoshua and his team. The men disguised as city workers will be our backup and will drive the getaway vehicles. We've selected off-road vehicles that will allow us to escape cross-country. Last, we'll cover the vehicles with thermal reflectors, so they can't detect us by the heat of the engines or our bodies."

# ABOUT THE AUTHOR

Dr. Barry Nadel was born in Texas (July 11, 1953), and grew up in San Jose, California (before it was Silicon Valley, in a traditional home that was shomer *Shabbat* and kashrut. He studied Archaeology and Anthropology and then switched to Enology and Viticulture, receiving his B. Sc. from UC Davis (1975) and then his M.Sc. in grape genetics in 1977. He was the first person to do grape tissue culture at UC Davis. In 1976 he won the Winkler Scholarship from the Dept. of Viticulture and Enology.

That same summer he made aliyah to Israel to do his PhD in plant genetics at the Faculty of Agriculture, Hebrew University in Rehovot, which he received in 1981.

Dr. Nadel worked as a researcher in plant biotechnology and physiology for six years at the Faculty of Agriculture. He then founded his own small vegetable seed company for twenty-two years, responsible for plant breeding stock seed maintenance and seed production.

He served in the Army reserves for 13 years in the artillery. Later, he was a full-time volunteer for the Border Police, responsible for the security of Moshav Kfar Pines for 10 years.

In 2002 he remarried to Hadassah, from Manchester, England, the love of his life. She died in his arms on July 20, 2004 of cancer. Hadassah was the catalyst for a total upheaval in his spiritual life.

Dr. Nadel served as chief scientist for a consortium medicinal Cannabis responsible for tissue culture, Agrotechnical research and plant breeding for two years.

Dr. Nadel has three daughters, one son and ten grandchildren (5 girls and 5 boys). He has been writing for over 40 years both scientific and non-fiction works. For the past 30 years, Dr. Nadel has been writing fiction. (www.drbnadel.com).

Dr. Nadel wrote an article about how to succeed at second marriages (https://sites.google.com/site/matrimonialadvise/) and two books about wine: Art of Kosher Winemaking and the Secrets of Home Winemaking.

In 2020, Dr. Nadel published three books on how to grow organically, vegetables, spices, and cannabis in greenhouses.

Thanks for reading my book. If you liked

the book, please leave a review on the site

where you bought it, or on Amazon or
Goodreads.

They don't need to be long and they don't

need to be 5 stars.

Below is a link to where to leave a review on

Amazon.

https://www.amazon.com/Seeking-Light
-Justice-Hoshiyan-Chronicles-ebook/product
-reviews/B00OLDW5PK/ref=cm_cr_dp_d_
show_all_btm?ie=UTF8&reviewerType=all_reviews

Made in the USA
Coppell, TX
20 August 2021